The Last Orange

*A mystery suspense; set in Hong Kong and London five years
before Hong Kong handed over the territory to China*

Margaret Alty

Published 2012 by arima publishing

www.arimapublishing.com

ISBN 978 1 84549 560 2

© Margaret Alty 2012

Printed and bound in the United Kingdom

Typeset in Garamond 11/14

In this work of fiction, the characters, places and events are either the product of the author's imagination or they are used entirely fictitiously. Any resemblance to actual persons, living or dead, is purely coincidental.

Swirl is an imprint of arima publishing.

arima publishing
ASK House, Northgate Avenue
Bury St Edmunds, Suffolk IP32 6BB
t: (+44) 01284 700321
www.arimapublishing.com

Chapter One
HONG KONG

He didn't think he would ever forget when he first saw her. It was in the same week Chris Patten, the new governor of Hong Kong, and his family arrived. Chris Patten was the man who had been appointed, somewhat surprisingly among certain circles, to take the colony smoothly up to the handover to the Chinese in nineteen-ninety-seven, in five years' time, but Roddie wasn't thinking about the future of Hong Kong where he had made his home for the past ten years, since arriving from England. In fact, later, when he tried to recall what had been on his mind that humid and sultry afternoon, he found it impossible to remember, but then, perhaps the truth was he didn't want to remember. All he did know, looking back to what had seemed in retrospect to be relatively trouble-free days before, for the second time his life fell around him like a pack of playing cards, was the sight of her, walking a few yards in front of him as he stepped off the Star Ferry and immediately becoming swamped by the usual mêlée of people waiting to board for the seven-minute journey back to Kowloon.

She was quite lovely; shoulder-length light brown hair with copper highlights and brushed smoothly back from her forehead; high cheek bones and deep blue eyes, the emerald green of her dress accentuating the paleness of her complexion. She wasn't tall; slim, but curvy at the same time, and there was a cool and tantalising aloofness about her in the way she held her head, looking directly in front and appearing to be oblivious to the hubbub around her. And then, impetuously, he did something he had never done before; he decided to follow her, quickening his step and pushing through the crowd. He had this crazy notion of not wanting to lose sight of her. It was unlikely he would ever see her again, but irrationally and, once again, entirely out of character, he wanted to hold on to the impression she had made.

She was still some distance away; any space rapidly being taken up by

3

late afternoon shoppers and office workers crossing and re-crossing diagonally in front of him along the covered walk-way above the main road outside the ferry piers, and she had reached the lights at Exchange Square, the traffic more dense here as the rush hour reached its daily crescendo, by the time he finally reached the pavement. He had missed the lights and watched as she crossed Des Voeux Road, reaching the other side several minutes before they had changed back to green. He saw her turn into Pedder Street and, although realising how ridiculous he was being, he continued to follow her. He was half-way along Pedder Street when commonsense began to kick in. You, Roddie Mortimer, he told himself, are one sad case! Momentarily distracted as a group of tourists, cameras slung around their necks, stopped abruptly in front of him and during what could only have been seconds, she had gone. He couldn't see any sign of her. Weaving in and out of the pedestrians further up the street and walking slower now, Roddie carried on, peering into each shop as he passed them, hoping to see her, but it was hopeless and with a sigh of resignation, he turned round to make his way back to Des Voeux Road where he knew he would be able to find a taxi to take him home. He didn't know why he stopped to look in the window of a shop selling pictures. It was an old, shabby building compared to its neighbours: a chic, freshly painted, bistro-style cafe; an herbalist with a fascinating display of a multitude of remedies promising to cure every possible ailment and an antique shop crammed with rosewood and lacquer furniture. He would have expected her to be in any of those, but she wasn't. The interior of the shop was dim, lit by a single lamp towards the rear next to a narrow wooden staircase, but he didn't miss a fleeting glimpse of emerald green at the top of the stairs. Without hesitating, he turned the rusty handle and went inside. Adjusting his eyes from the harshness of light in the street, he looked around. Nothing had been done to improve the years of grime: faded flock wallpaper which would at one time have been the traditional Chinese red; unvarnished and deeply scored wood-strip flooring and piled on two long trestle tables, oil paintings, unframed and, to him, not particularly appealing. They all looked as though they had been painted by the same artist; most of them views of the harbour and the skyline of Hong Kong with its skyscrapers and high-rise office and apartment blocks and, inevitably in the background, the darker outline of the Peak. The colours he had used were garish, harsh and unreal: crimson, orangey-gold, metallic blues, greens and yellows, literally setting his teeth on edge. Did people actually buy these, he wondered, walking further into the shop. Nobody had come forward out of the gloom to serve him; he appeared to be the only person in there and, not really understanding why, walked over to the stairs and from where he could hear voices, but too low for him to make out what they were saying. There was no woman's voice, but she must be up there. Intrigued now, wondering why she was here, he wanted to find out more and there was only one way to do that he decided, placing his foot on the bottom step.

'Good afternoon, sir. Can I help you?' the soft voice from the other side of the room startling him and causing him to stumble slightly as he swivelled round to see where it was coming from; he had been so sure he was on his own and hadn't noticed the table against the far wall, which presumably, acted as a makeshift cash desk: no cash register, or even an abacus which were still used by a great number of the older shopkeepers, but a square tin, rather like an old tea caddy, placed in the centre. The man now walking towards him and smiling, albeit somewhat ingratiatingly, was ageless. Why was it, Roddie thought for the umpteenth time, impossible to tell the age of a Chinaman.

'We have many beautiful pictures, sir.' he said quietly, looking up at him short-sightedly through rimless spectacles.

'Yes, I can see that.'

'Also,' he continued, 'we have many more on the next floor. Would you like to see them?'

'Well, yes,' Roddie agreed, instantly committing himself, 'I'm looking for something a little different; perhaps less touristy, if you understand?'

'I think you will find what you're looking for, sir.' he nodded, leading the way up the stairs.

Although there was more light, the room wasn't all that different from the one he had been in. More trestle tables and even more paintings, although up here, it looked as though this was where they carried out the framing as there was a work bench by the one and only window, fitted with a lathe and underneath, on the floor, a scattering of wood shavings. A number of framed pictures had been placed against the walls, but he wasn't interested, only too aware of feeling inordinately disappointed in not seeing the woman with the long hair and the bright green dress. There was a door at the top of the stairs, but it was closed and apart from the two of them, they were alone in the room.

He would have to buy one of course. He reckoned the man could be the owner and if that was the case, would not be pleased if he didn't. Roddie had been in too many small shops, not all that dissimilar to the one he was in now, not to realise this. He would not want to lose face and if he didn't make a sale he would consider he had failed. Serve me right Roddie thought for being so damned impulsive, walking over to the nearest table and desultorily flicking through what appeared to be hundreds of paintings all much of a muchness. A bit like pinning the tail on a donkey blindfold he thought, doing his best to make up his mind.

He had almost reached the bottom of the canvases when he found one which was totally different from all the others: simply called "The Clock Tower", but instantly recognisable as the only remaining evidence of the Kowloon-Canton Railway Station; the station having long since been demolished to make room for the Cultural Centre. The artist had captured the tall, slender structure reflected in the shallow water of two oblong pools, both of them edged by paths of mosaic tiling and shaded by uniform lines of palm trees. A tranquil scene among bustling Tsim Sha Tsui in Kowloon, the mellow peach and white stonework showing anyone interested in the history of the colony what earlier architecture had been like. In this one, a water colour and obviously painted by a different artist, the colours were far more subdued and bore a remarkable likeness to the old clock tower; a prominent feature on the waterfront of Kowloon, and he liked it. He hadn't seen any price tags, but not so surprising; he would be expected to haggle, although not too vigorously.

Fifteen minutes later he was out on the pavement again; the rolled up canvas under his arm and five hundred dollars lighter. During the time it had taken him to complete the transaction, nobody had come into the room and neither had he heard any movement downstairs. She must still be in the building, unless she had left by another door, but why would she have, he tried to work out, wondering how she could possibly fit into such an unlikely setting. He hadn't liked the atmosphere in there; also, there was something odd about all those paintings and what appeared to be a half-hearted attempt to frame some of them. The place could hardly be described as a gallery. Whoever owned the business wasn't exactly making an effort to entice prospective customers; it was as if they weren't all that interested in making sales he concluded. As he started to retrace his steps back towards Des Voeux Road he wondered how long the shopkeeper had been watching him, perhaps even noticing how he had tried to hear what was being said on the floor above. He was passing the cafe he had seen earlier and decided what he needed at that precise moment was a cold beer.

Ordering a San Miguel, Roddie sat down at one of the window tables, at the same time knowing full well why he was doing this; just in the unlikely event he would see her. The disappearing lady in green, he smiled to himself, as he waited for his beer, unable to get her out of his mind. He couldn't explain the strength of his immediate attraction towards her, something he had never experienced before. Not even years ago, when he had first met Clarissa. Theirs had been a whirlwind romance; passionate it was true, at least in the beginning, but their clash of personalities had made it impossible to sustain for long, although long enough for them to rush into an early marriage which, in hindsight, had ended the way everyone at the time had said it would. Not exactly in tears – Clarissa never cried, only in a peak of temper when she wasn't getting her own way, but nevertheless, with the assistance of her father's lawyer, she had managed to secure the larger part of their assets. He should have stopped thinking like this after all these years, but there were times when something totally disconnected with his disastrous marriage, triggered off the memories, memories which should by now have been well and truly buried. It could be, that seeing this woman reminded him of what he may have had, also of how singular and self-centred his life had become. It wasn't as though he was discontented, far from it, but on the rare occasions when he was being honest with himself, he had to admit there was some element missing, but so far, what this actually was, had continued to elude him. Living in Hong Kong suited him. His work as an industrial chemist for one of the world's largest research laboratories was stimulating and he had no shortage of friends. And, there was Louisa, of course. He'd met her a couple of years ago at a dinner party held by one of his colleagues and they had been quick to discover they had much in common. In many respects they were two of a kind, both recovering from broken relationships and doing their best to pull their lives back on to an even keel. Louisa, being editor of one of Kong Kong's magazines, worked a great deal harder than he did. He had been lucky in his career: deadlines with the accompanying stress played little part in his work, but for her it was different. He had learned a great deal about the cut-throat and competitive business she was in, but, blessed with an abundance of mental and physical energy, she appeared to thrive on each new challenge which, from what she had told him, occurred almost on a daily basis. But, passion? Love, even? Their relationship had never been founded on the former and he had always considered that to be a good thing, but as for love, well, again being honest with himself, he wasn't sure. It could be they didn't spend enough time together to really get to know each other. He could have asked her to move in with him, but he never had and Louisa seemed relatively happy with the situation.

Half-way through his beer and making up his mind to abandon such pointless reflections he decided to give her a call and find out if she was free for dinner that evening. Roddie was halfway through dialling her number when the door of the cafe opened and, there she was; the woman he'd been following, and not only had she come in, but was walking directly towards where he was sitting.

'I see you bought one of Charlie's paintings.' she said, as she made to pass his table, pointing to the rolled up canvas beside him.

'Charlie?'

'Charlie Wong,' she smiled, 'one of Hong Kong's much respected artists. I saw you looking at his paintings.' she added, continuing to smile at him.

'I didn't see you in the shop.' Roddie said; a half-truth, but he couldn't help thinking she was teasing him and he found this odd. The aloofness he had noticed when he had first seen her certainly wasn't in evidence now.

'Didn't you?' and he knew he hadn't fooled her.

'Why don't you sit down,' he suggested, pulling a chair out for her, 'and have a drink.'

'Thank you, I'd like that. By the way,' she went on, sitting down and placing her briefcase on the floor between them, 'I'm Juliet Warburton.'

'Roddie Mortimer.' he said, formally shaking hands with her, noticing the briefcase; she definitely hadn't had it with her earlier.

She said she would like a white wine and once the waiter had brought it to their table, along with another San Miguel for him, she surprised him by pulling off the elastic band securing the painting and, without saying anything, or asking if he minded, had un-rolled the canvas and was looking across the table at him with an unreadable expression on her face; the eyes, now the light was beginning to go and the waiter, appearing not to notice, hadn't switched on any of the table lamps, sparkled; their natural colour deepening, immediately reminding him of the Mona Lisa, a twenty-first century Mona Lisa, naturally. What was she thinking he wondered, taking a sip of his beer.

'This was a lucky find.' she said, rolling up the canvas again and placing it back on the table, 'Roddie,' she went on quietly, 'you were following me, weren't you?'

'What makes you think that?' there was no way he was going to admit he had been. He did have some pride.

'I saw you on the Star Ferry.'

'Did you,' he said, 'but I didn't see you, although I wish I had.' he added gallantly, intrigued and a little amused to find out what she was going to say next.

'You *were* on the ferry, weren't you?'

'Oh, yes, I was; along with what seemed a couple of hundred others.' he smiled.

'They do get pretty packed, don't they?' was all she said, raising her glass to him.

'How long have you lived in Hong Kong, Juliet?' hoping to sidetrack her; he was finding the way the conversation going embarrassing and he couldn't understand her; so very different from any other woman he had ever met. It wasn't only her forthrightness, but it was as though she had the ability to read his mind. He was sure she was aware of his discomfort but she wasn't making any attempt to make it easy for him.

'Practically all my life.' she answered. 'My father had a transfer here from Singapore; he worked for Standard Chartered and we moved here when I was seven. I did go to school in England, but spent every holiday in Hong Kong and then later, after university, I came back for good.'

'And your profession?' genuinely wanting to know and not even hazarding a guess what it could be.

'I'm an accountant.' she answered, 'I used to work for one of the 'big boys' in Hong Kong, but a year ago I decided to go freelance. I guess I just got tired of the strict regime of the profession; I found it all very stultifying.'

'A bold decision.'

'I didn't think so. And, quite frankly, I've had no regrets.'

'It must have taken a fair bit of courage though,' Roddie said, 'to break away from a guaranteed income and all that?'

'Not really. I'm lucky enough to own my own apartment and that's quite important where rents are astronomical, unless you choose to live on Lamma or Lantau and that's never appealed to me. I much prefer to be in the centre of everything.'

She fascinated him. So incredibly independent and with a confidence he envied. He wondered how old she was; a lot younger than he was, but it was impossible to even guess and he would never ask her.

'And, Roddie,' she said, taking another sip of her wine, 'what do you do? No,' she added, putting up a hand to prevent him saying anything, 'let me guess.'

'Go on, then.' amused, and leaned back in his chair waiting to hear what she would come up with.

'Something terribly serious?'

'To some, yes.'

'I think you work for a large company.'

'You're getting warmer.' enjoying the game.

'You're a lawyer?'

'No.'

'I didn't really think you were,' she smiled, 'lawyers don't usually go around following women!'

'Okay!' he laughed out loud, 'Interrogation over! I'm an industrial chemist and I've been working out here for ten years.'

'You must be clever.'

'Not all that clever.' he admitted.

'And modest!'

Light banter, inconsequential trivia; an exchange between two people who had only recently met, although he sensed an undercurrent, as if everything she was saying had another meaning, ambiguously mysterious. It was only an impression and it was possible this was the way she normally behaved when she met someone, especially a male. It could be a kind of barrier she had built up: one way of not becoming too close, too intimate, too soon, as if all the time she was talking to him she was actually sizing him up.

'Are you married, Roddie?' she asked, the question unexpected, although why it should have been, given she hadn't so far shown any reticence in what she'd said to him.

'I was.'

'I thought so; at least,' she quickly corrected herself, 'I didn't think you were married now.'

'Why do you say that?' unable to keep the smile from spreading across his face; she was incorrigible. In anyone else he would have taken offence, but for some inexplicable reason, his immediate reaction was amusement.

'Well,' she started to explain, 'you strike me as a fairly contented sort of guy and I didn't think you were married, because happily married men don't usually buy strange women a drink – or,' she added, the smile making another appearance, 'follow them either!'

'No comment!' he retaliated, 'Would you like another one, Juliet?'

'I would have loved another,' she said, 'but I'm afraid I have to leave; there are a number of places I need to go to before they close.'

'That's too bad.'

'Have you got anything planned for this evening?' she asked him, leaning down to pick up her brief case.

'Not really.'

'I wonder whether you would like to accompany me later on; you would be doing me a favour, actually.' she added, standing up and pushing her chair back.

'Yes?'

'Have you heard of "Annie's", the nightclub on Kowloon side?'

'Hasn't everyone?' he asked, looking up at her and waiting for enlightenment.

'Well,' she went on, 'I have a meeting there later on tonight with Annie Steed; she wants me to handle their accounts and, to be perfectly honest with you, I hadn't been looking forward to going in there on my own.'

'I'll come with you, of course, but it has the reputation of being a bit of a dive, but then, I guess you know that already?'

'I've never been to the club before,' she said, 'but when I met her a couple of weeks ago she seemed okay. Probably what you hear is greatly exaggerated.'

'Perhaps.' he said slowly and not in the least convinced she was right. He'd been to "Annie's" a few times and after each visit he vowed he would never go again. He'd been in enough nightclubs over the years to recognise a sleazy and dubious atmosphere and he hadn't liked the place one little bit. Also, he remembered the first time, not long after he came to Hong Kong, when Annie, a tall, skinny American, with a voice even louder than the high decibels emanating from the speakers encouraging people to dance on the microscopic dance floor, having introduced herself to him, had then proceeded to make something of an exhibition of herself at the bar, showing a great deal of leg and even more cleavage, all of which he'd found more than a little nauseous.

'So,' Juliet broke into his thoughts, 'you'll come with me?'

'I'll come with you.' he said, not exactly looking forward to the evening; he would have much preferred to spend it somewhere else with her, but it would seem this time he didn't have a great deal of choice.

Chapter Two
LONDON

'There's a call from Hong Kong for you, Mr Bailey.'

'Did they give their name, Tanya?'

'No, they wouldn't say, although I did ask.'

'Put them through.' Conrad Bailey told her, stifling a sigh, knowing in advance who it would be and that this could only mean one thing: bad news.

'Conrad; Denny here.'

'Hello, Denny, something wrong?'

'There could be,' Denny Yuan said in his perfectly modulated Cambridge-educated voice, 'but we're not taking any chances, which means, Conrad, the items will not be on tonight's flight as arranged.'

'Damn! You know what this will mean at the London end, don't you, Denny? It's going to be one hell of a job re-organising the next stage.'

'I do appreciate the inconvenience, Conrad. Of course I do, but as I've said, we're not taking any chances.'

'I trust you are going to enlighten me.' Conrad said, trying with difficulty, to suppress his frustration. He had known Denny for years, ever since their university days. Even back then he'd been cautious and many of them had often complained he'd been far too cautious. As students, most of them at one time or another, had done irresponsible things, which they used to dismiss lightly in their youthful arrogance as mere students' pranks. It was unlikely whether the word prank was even in Denny Yuan's vocabulary. The only son of a wealthy Chinese family, originally from Beijing, he had been strictly brought up and taught from an early age the full responsibility of carrying on the well-earned revered family name. And, if anything, he had become more wary, treating life like a game of chess; each move being well thought out in advance, and now, with a number of years experience working as he did, even more so. Conrad had never known him take any uncalculated risks and that he would have had a good reason for making these changes to their plans.

'Someone,' Denny explained, 'came into the shop earlier and seemed particularly interested in, not only the somewhat austere surroundings, but in what was being discussed upstairs.'

'Which was?' Conrad prompted, his heart sinking. He didn't like the sound of this; so far, since they started working together, they'd had a clear run, managing to avoid exposure. Their scheme, initially thought up by Denny more than six years ago, was a simple one: emeralds, mined in Colombia, were flown into Hong Kong on a regular basis by the same courier they had used from the beginning. From there, Denny, with a handful of trusted employees, prepared the emeralds for their onward journey to him in London. After that, it was up to him to re-distribute to four of Europe's capitals: Paris, Rome, Amsterdam and Brussels. No import or export duty came into the equation and by the time the emeralds reached their final destinations this was when their value soared and both he and Denny received their lucrative slice of the cake.

'We were discussing the final arrangements for tonight.' Denny was saying, 'It is possible he may not have heard, Conrad; I have no way of knowing, but there is one thing.'

'What?'

'He didn't come into the shop with the sole purpose of buying a painting, but what particularly concerns me is he could be police.'

'You don't think you might be jumping to conclusions?'

'I could be, but we have to be careful. There's a great deal at stake, but I don't need to remind you of that.'

'And who is he; have you been able to find out anything about him?'

'At this stage, only his surname. I can't give you a personal description because I didn't see him, but Freddie did; he'd been watching him from the moment he came in as a matter of fact.'

'And what is his name; not that it will mean anything to me, of course.'

'R. Mortimer.'

'English.'

'I would say so.'

'You don't think he could be a tourist?'

'I rather doubt it; you see, he did eventually buy one of our paintings and he used a Hong Kong credit card.'

'In that case, it shouldn't be all that difficult to find out more about him.'

'I wouldn't concern yourself, Conrad,' Denny said, 'we will do our utmost to discover exactly where he's coming from.'

'I'm sure you will, but meanwhile, I would like to know when I can now expect the delivery.'

'Conrad. Conrad.' he repeated, immediately taking him back to the time when he used to quite literally pull him back, remind him he was behaving irrationally, in other words, not thinking straight.

'Okay,' Conrad said, 'so, what is the next step?'

'The next step, my friend,' Denny said, 'is to make a few radical changes in the premises here, but they need not concern you. That will be my top priority, but to answer your question, it is going to be at least another week. I'm going to give our contact in Bogota a ring; ask if they can bring forward their next consignment, if they can, this will mean you will receive a double delivery. Two risks at this end, instead of one, if you understand what I mean; followed perhaps by a lull in future deliveries, but I'll get back to you. I don't want to press any panic buttons, Conrad. If Bogota gets the slightest inkling of anything amiss our source may dry up and that would be most unfortunate.'

It was not yet mid-day, but by the time they had brought the call to a close, Conrad felt he had already done a day's work, but as he reminded himself, talking to Denny always did have that effect on him. He buzzed Tanya to tell her he was taking an early lunch and not to make any appointments for the afternoon; he needed a few uninterrupted hours to sort out the various changes he would have to make.

Conrad was on his way out of the office when his mobile rang.

'Conrad, darling, it's me.'

'Clarissa. Where are you?'

'I'm at work, but I just wanted you to know I may be a bit late getting home this evening.'

'More overtime?'

'No, nothing like that. I had a call from Natasha earlier; she wants to meet me after work.'

'Nothing serious, I hope.' Conrad asked, frowning. It wasn't as if his step-daughter had ever caused them any concern, but, speaking to Denny and the potential seriousness of their conversation had unnerved him, making him fear the worse.

'No, I don't think so; in fact, she sounded quite excited.'

'Well, that's alright then. Perhaps she's had promotion.'

'Do you know, Conrad,' Clarissa laughed, 'that never occurred to me. I was jumping to conclusions as usual. I thought she may have got engaged to that young man she told us she'd met a few months ago, but you know, Natasha, she keeps her private life very much to herself.'

'No doubt she'll tell you all about it, darling. Will you be having a meal with her?'

'I don't think so; she only mentioned a drink, so I shouldn't be all that late.'

'Good, we'll eat out, then, shall we? I'd better make a reservation; where would you like to go?'

'How about that new Chinese restaurant in the Strand; I've heard it's very good.'

*

'Natasha! I don't believe what I'm hearing!'

'Come on, Mum, don't you think you're over-reacting?'

'I am not! You're talking about giving up a job with one of England's most prestigious newspapers and flying off to Hong Kong!'

'What's so wrong with that?' Natasha asked, 'Why shouldn't I want to further my career? I am only a club reporter after all. That isn't all that special; I'm just one of many, you know.'

'Natasha, for goodness sake,' Clarissa said, paying for their drinks and taking them over to one of the window seats. They were in the upstairs bar of the "Opera Room" in Trafalgar Square, Natasha having wasted no time in dropping what was to Clarissa, a bombshell. There were many times when she didn't feel comfortable in her daughter's company. Of course she loved her; there was no question of that, but this early evening, sitting across the low table from her, she realised how inept she was at trying to understand her. At times, like now, Natasha was so incredibly like her father: utterly single-minded and, once she had made up her mind, as it would appear she had this time, nothing would change it, no matter how tactfully the suggestion was made, and knowing from past experience, she was ill-equipped and the last person to even try.

'You sound extremely confident about going to a country you've never been to before, Natasha, and to finding work which, as you say, will further your career.'

'I'll have no problem there, Mum,' she said quickly, her green eyes sparkling as she raised her glass, reminding Clarissa for a fleeting moment of Roddie; of how he had looked when they had first met: ridiculously young, only twenty-two, the same age as Natasha was now, and full of enthusiasm for the future; a future which, sadly as it turned out, hadn't included her. 'Nicholas has told me all about the life out there,' Natasha was going on excitedly, 'and he says I'm bound to find a job quickly. There are simply loads of opportunities he said, especially in journalism.'

'But you scarcely know him, Natasha. Also, you haven't even introduced him to us.' Clarissa managed to put in and succeeding in interrupting what sounded very much to her like besotted admiration for the man.

'I should have, I know,' she said, showing the merest glimmer of contrition although it didn't last for long, 'Anyway,' she went on breathlessly, 'I know you'll like him. He's terribly sophisticated, not at all like the other boys I know. I would have brought him along to meet you, but he flew back to Hong Kong this morning.'

'I see,' Clarissa couldn't help smiling, 'so, it's Nicholas who is the real attraction, then?'

'Only partly,' Natasha admitted, 'but honestly, Mum, he's told me so much about Hong Kong, I want to experience everything he's described for myself.'

'There might not be much of a future for westerners, Natasha. Have you considered that?'

'Oh,' she waved her hand dismissively, 'you mean the handover in nineteen-ninety-seven?' taking a sip of her wine, 'Nicholas says,' she began, and Clarissa inwardly groaned, bracing herself to hear more words of wisdom from this paragon who, apparently, had captivated her daughter, 'there is nothing to worry about,' Natasha continued, 'he's told me that everyone he knows out there is saying the same. *Things*,' she emphasised, 'will continue as they have always done.'

'I think it might be a good idea,' Clarissa said slowly and making one final attempt to sway her, or at least, make her stop and think of the radical step she was taking, 'if you spoke to your father, unless, of course, you have already.'

'I did think about phoning him,' Natasha replied, 'but then decided not to. He would only have said the same as you, so I thought I would just surprise him instead. *Fait accompli* and all that!'

'When are you planning to leave, Natasha?' Clarissa asked resignedly. It would be pointless to pursue the subject, knowing if she did she would only succeed in making her even more resolute.

'Quite soon, actually.'

'How soon?'

'Sunday.'

'So, everything's booked, then?'

'That's right; I collected my flight ticket at lunchtime.'

'What about your job, Natasha?'

'What about it?'

'Please, Natasha, you know what I mean. I don't know how long you've been thinking about all of this, but surely you would have had to hand in your notice?'

'Of course I did and they were really good about it actually. I think,' she added, 'most of them are envious of me; going out to the exotic Far East and making my fortune!'

'When you arrive in Hong Kong,' Clarissa asked, choosing to make no comment, 'where will you be staying? I don't like the idea of you booking into any third-rate hotel.

'Don't worry about me, Mum; I'll be living with Nicholas. He has an apartment in Causeway Bay and that,' she added, for the first time a flash of defiance on her face, 'is one of Hong Kong's most respectable areas!'

*

In a quiet street off from the Strand, close to the Victoria Embankment and overlooking the Thames, the offices of Bristow and Innis, Consultants, were closing up for the day. Joanne, their secretary, had cleared her desk in preparation for the following morning and switched off her computer and, as she always did, locked the front door behind her. The two partners had the building to themselves.

'Scotch, Hugh?' Edward Bristow asked him, walking over to the drinks cabinet.

'Please.'

'I've been thinking.' Edward said, pouring generous measures of "Grouse" into two glasses and passing one to him.

'Yes?'

'I haven't had a chance to tell you yet,' he went on, sitting down; not at his desk, but on one of the leather club chairs in the centre of the room, 'but now Nicholas is on his way back to Hong Kong it might be a good idea if we bring forward our plans.'

'Why exactly?'

'Well, I had a telephone call from Marion Godwin earlier today and she told me McLellands will be holding their AGM next Thursday. You know what this could mean, don't you?'

'I believe I do,' Hugh said thoughtfully, taking a sip of his whisky, 'the formula; they may have reached the final decision to patent it.'

'Quite.'

'It is possible, I suppose.'

'I think it's more than possible, Hugh. We know, thanks to Marion, the company have been making exhaustive tests on this new drug for some months now. Time is money, as you well know and, if I am right, I believe they will want it on the market as soon as possible.'

'What do you suggest, then, Eddie?'

'That you and Nicholas move in on the Monday. It means, of course, you'll have to fly out there within the next couple of days, but that shouldn't pose any problem, should it?'

'No, I can do a bit of re-shuffling of appointments. Knowing I would be away later in the week, I had actually made a start, so that won't be too much trouble.'

'Good. Quite honestly, Hugh, the sooner that formula is in our hands, the happier I will be; you fly back to London as soon as you can get a flight, together with the formula, and we can get it over to our contact in the States within a matter of hours and, as usual with deals like this, their payment to us will go straight into our accounts in Zurich.'

'And no questions asked.'

'Exactly, as you so adroitly put it, no questions asked. This, Hugh,' Edward went on, replenishing their drinks, 'will be one of our more lucrative transactions.'

'We wouldn't have got this far without Marion, though, would we?' Hugh reminded him, taking the glass from him.

'That's true.' Edward agreed, leaning back in the chair and feeling particularly pleased with the way events were turning out. He had met Marion Godwin fifteen years ago when she was a very young solicitor working in London, but right from the start he sensed someone who was as dishonest as he was. Even after she moved to Hong Kong and formed her own law firm out there, they had continued to keep in touch. It had been Marion who had mentioned McLellands, affecting a casualness which hadn't fooled him, saying how they were on the brink of developing a drug which, once on the open market, would revolutionise an effective cure for malaria, in particular, cerebral malaria. Apparently, she had handled their affairs since the company was formed and there wasn't much she didn't know about the structure of McLellands Medical Research Laboratories, including the name of their merchant bankers in Hong Kong and, the *piece de resistance* being they were holding this formula in one of their safe deposit boxes. She had been quick to come up with a plan which she assured him couldn't fail, telling him at the same time she knew just the man who would help them; Nicholas Eastman, one of the bank's executives. They had since met Nicholas a couple of times when he had been in London attending an advanced management course for his bank and both agreed that Marion may be right. Nicholas Eastman could well be the man they were looking for. Although only in his early thirties, he was not only streetwise, but he was Hong Kong streetwise; perhaps coming over as a trifle too smart, but Edward had no doubts that, with Hugh there with him, he would be able to pull this off.

'You wouldn't have been able to inform Nicholas before he left this morning?' Hugh asked him.

'No, but in any case, I wanted to pass it by you first, Hugh.'

'Fair enough,' Hugh nodded, 'so it's all systems go, then?'

'That's right,' Edward agreed, 'You shouldn't hit any snags. Nicholas has worked for the bank for a number of years; he's familiar with the set-up and, from what he was saying the other day, there will be no eyebrows raised when he takes you into one of their vaults, even although it will be after hours. You won't even have to give your name, Hugh.'

'I hope he's right.'

'It isn't all that unusual, apparently, for customers to want immediate access to their safe deposit boxes. There will be nothing furtive about your visit, Hugh; it isn't as if it will be in the middle of the night, only about an hour after their normal closing time.'

'It all sounds straightforward enough,' Hugh said, appearing more relaxed now, 'I guess we just have to trust him.'

'Well, Hugh,' Edward smiled grimly, 'if you think about it, when McLellands discover the formula is not in their safe deposit box, Nicholas will have to come up with a plausible explanation for escorting a non-existent McLellands' employee into their vaults.

'He came over as extremely confident.'

'I know he did,' Edward agreed, 'but let us hope for his sake his confidence is not a misguided one.'

Chapter Three
HONG KONG

For the second time that day Roddie was over in Kowloon, having taken the MTR instead of the Star Ferry. In his opinion, Hong Kong's state of the art, the Mass Transit Railway, put any other underground trains he had ever been on to shame. The shiny see-your-face-in stainless steel seats, so slippery there were many occasions when he had had to hold on to the edge to prevent sliding along the whole length of it! The structure, a feat of relatively modern engineering, resembled a long undulating tube; no boxed-in carriages creating, even to the most blasé of travellers, a feeling of claustrophobia. There was something reassuring to be able to see, on either side from where you were sitting, an impression of openness although he had to admit the notices instructing the passengers on how they should behave were a little off-putting, being subjected to the fact that no eating, drinking or hawking were permitted! Each time he used the MTR, Roddie was conversely reminded of the London underground where people avoided any eye contact, either spending the journey reading or staring into space, but, here, they sat stoically, their expressions totally inscrutable as they kept their eyes on you all the time; blank and unblinking. At first, when he had arrived in Hong Kong, he had found the experience unnerving, but eventually he got used to the steady lifeless scrutiny. Now, on his way to meet Juliet Warburton, it was no different than it had ever been but, as always, although the journey was a short one, he was glad to get off the train in Tsim Sha Tsui, the first stop on the other side of the water.

It was a warm evening; the air outside the station a breath-catching concoction of humidity mixed with petrol and diesel fumes from the steady stream of traffic screeching along Nathan Road. Nathan Road, cutting through Kowloon from the south which was the bustling Tsim Sha Tsui district, in a straight line north to finally ending at the approach to Prince Edward Road West, was four kilometres of shops, bars, nightclubs and restaurants and, above, the flashing neon signs, advertising everything from "Marlborough" cigarettes to "Kiwi" shoe polish. How anyone, Roddie marvelled, waiting to cross the road and looking at the man standing next to him, can possibly hear one single word on a mobile phone above this ear-shattering racket! He actually had two phones, managing by some miracle and balancing act to talk into them both simultaneously and without even raising his voice.

They had arranged to meet in "Aqua Spirit", an ultra-smart cocktail lounge on the top floor of the One Peking Road building with stunning views over to Hong Kong Island, especially at this time of the evening with the dazzling myriad of lights stretching along from the harbour and sweeping upwards towards the Peak.

Juliet was already there waiting for him and waved over as soon as he walked into the bar. Tonight, she was wearing a plain black dress, sleeveless with a neckline his mother would have approved of. There was nothing flashy or obvious about Juliet Warburton he decided; like the dress she had worn earlier, it was under-stated, almost demure, but at the same time managing to compliment her figure and her flawless peaches and cream complexion.

'You do realise "Annie's" will be all downhill from here?' he warned her, once the waitress had brought over his drink.

'From what you said this afternoon,' she smiled at him, 'I rather thought it might be. But, Roddie,' she added, leaning over towards him, 'I don't expect this meeting with Annie Steed to take all that long. I thought perhaps we could have a meal later, if that's alright with you?'

She certainly wasn't slow in coming forward he thought; not used to women taking such an obvious lead, especially when he had only just met them. He couldn't make up his mind about her; take a bit of getting used to, he decided and then wondering whether after tonight he would ever see her again.

They only had the one drink, Juliet insisting on paying, before walking the short distance to "Annie's" in Granville Street; quieter, but only fractionally, from Nathan Road, although the pavements were still congested with pedestrians wandering aimlessly along and stopping to read the menus outside the restaurants; not only Chinese, but many who could only be tourists, judging by the casual way they were dressed: the women, at least the majority of them, in short-sleeved dresses and the men in light-weight suits, most of them carrying their jackets. Roddie had been here long enough to have learned that as far as the Cantonese were concerned, they were extremely dress-conscious, not to mention being well versed in prominently displaying designer-labels. The men weren't a great deal different from the women, where Gucci, Dior, Giordano and Givenchy predominated.

"Annie's", half-way along the street and sandwiched unobtrusively between an Indian restaurant and a massage parlour, was on the top floor. The lift took them up the five flights, finally coming to an abrupt and juddering halt opposite a dark-green painted door with a printed notice telling them this was "Annie's" Nightclub and to please ring the bell.

'You still want to go ahead?' Roddie asked her, his finger poised over the bell, 'We can always turn back, if you would prefer.'

'Oh, no, Roddie,' she said quickly, 'it probably won't be so bad. Anyway, this is a business meeting.'

'That's what concerns me,' he said, 'not exactly prepossessing, is it?'

'Go on,' she laughed, 'press the bell!'

Having been there before, Roddie knew what to expect, and although it had probably been at least a couple of years since then, the place had hardly changed: a large room, dimly lit, a long bar at the left-hand side, most of the floor space being taken up by tables, chairs and two-seater sofas and in the far corner, across from the bar, a tiny, circular dance floor overlooked by a raised platform. Even the drummer and the two guitarists looked the same, although it would appear they had chosen that moment to have a break, watching as one of them slipped a CD into the player, turning the volume to its full capacity, the room immediately beginning to pulsate with Tom Jones singing his heart out.

'Well?' he smiled at her, 'What do you think?'

'It's okay, Roddie. Much better than I thought it would be.'

'I don't see Annie around, so would you like a drink?'

'No thanks, I don't think I should. I want to keep a clear head, but, please you go ahead; don't let me stop you. That could be her office over there,' she added, 'I'll go and find out.' pointing to a door along a narrow passageway to the left of the bar.

'Possibly,' Roddie said, 'but why not ask the barman.' he suggested, not wanting her to walk into something she may not be expecting. From the stories he had heard about Annie Steed, she could be up to anything in there.

As he finished speaking, the door opened and Annie Steed came out. She noticed them both instantly and walked briskly towards them.

'Hi there, Juliet! You've brought your boyfriend, I see.'

'Well –'

'– Say,' she interrupted, moving closer to Roddie, 'I've met you before, haven't I? It's Roddie, isn't it?'

'You've a good memory.' was all he could think of saying, inane although it was, but he should have been prepared. And he thought Juliet was forward! As before, the woman reminded him of Joan Rivers; tall, thin, a mane of yellow-blonde hair, but without the humour, at least, although he had known Annie to crack the odd risqué joke, they had never been to his taste. He was probably being a prude, but there was something about a female telling rude jokes which he had always found distasteful and definitely *not* sexy.

'I never forget a good-looking guy, Roddie. How are you, it's been a long time since I've seen you? You really should come in more often, but perhaps you will now you're with Juliet?' but not waiting for his answer, which was just as well; he hadn't a clue how he would have answered.

'Okay, Juliet,' she went on, swivelling on her kitten heels and looking at her, 'business first. Roddie can amuse himself for the next half hour, I guess.' she added, taking Juliet by the arm and leading her away.

The expression, "lamb to the slaughter", came instantly into his mind, but he dismissed it just as quickly. Juliet, he was sure, could well look after herself. He ordered a glass of wine, deciding to remain at the bar rather than sit at any of the tables. He knew from experience to have done so would only act as an open invitation to any one of the half dozen hostesses disguised, although somewhat ineptly, as bona fide customers.

Roddie took a couple of sips of his wine and asking himself what the hell he was doing here: a man of forty-four, old enough to have learned more sense, standing at the bar of a decidedly tacky nightclub which, from what he had heard, was little more than a cover-up for, not to put too fine a point on it, a brothel and not all that up-market either he thought, noticing that within the last few minutes the hostesses had almost doubled in number. It was still too early for the late night customers. There were only a few couples and a party of four women having a night out and beside the dance floor some poor sod who had made the unfortunate mistake of buying a drink for one of the hostesses. He'll learn, Roddie sighed, feeling far more than his forty-four years.

By this time, Tom Jones had faded into the far distance as the group re-positioned themselves on the platform and began the opening bars of "Pretty Woman". They weren't bad, Roddie grudgingly conceded, looking across at them. He noticed a girl standing close to them he remembered from the last time he had been in; she was from Taiwan, and seeing her there again could only mean they were in for a repeat performance of her stripping act, which had been so excruciatingly awful he had actually turned away in disgust!

'Hello,' a voice said next to him, 'my name is Primula.'

He hadn't noticed her walking over; a carbon-copy of most of the young women from the Philippines and working in Hong Kong, although she must be well on in her thirties he guessed, not all that young; no doubt supplementing her meagre wage as a maid by working at night for Annie Steed. Not that she would be over-generous Roddie thought, but every dollar counted with these girls and he had heard that most of their money was sent back to support their families in the Philippines. A tough life, but they knew what they were doing and, as far as he was aware, they had freely chosen to come to Hong Kong and must have known in advance what it would be like, but he was still reluctant to get into conversation with her. Again, experience had taught him that particular lesson.

'You're on your own?' she persisted, looking up at him; the dark brown almond-shaped eyes almost obscured by her fringe. She wasn't even pretty Roddie decided, although she had made an attempt to improve her wan and drawn appearance, but the bright pink lipstick and the blusher weren't helping much.

'I'm waiting for a friend.' he said to her at last, hoping she would take the hint.

'I'll keep you company until she arrives.' she said, pulling up one of the bar stools and sitting down. She didn't have a drink and he had no intention of buying her one, quelling the feeling of meanness and, once again, wishing he was anywhere but in this seedy place and wondering what Louisa would say if she saw him now. Thinking of her made him feel guilty; he should have rung her, but it had been a strange day. He would call her tomorrow he decided.

'Are you married?' the woman asked, nudging him lightly on the arm to attract his attention, the irony of being asked that twice within a matter of hours not going unnoticed.

'No, I'm not.' he answered, glancing at her briefly. He could have lied and said he was married, but it wouldn't have made any difference. To these women, although she had asked the question, marriage didn't mean a great deal, most of them already had husbands; men they had left behind in the Philippines, also their children. Roddie had visited the country once and he knew what sort of life the majority of the people led; not the rich cats in Manila, but the poor classes and especially outside the capital their situation was grim; their villages, although as clean as they could be, were no more than mini-shanty towns, the lanes and roads hard-packed mud and the one-roomed dwellings on stilts which offered little privacy or protection from the fierce heat during the day. He should feel sorry for her, but he couldn't afford to even think like that. If she gained the slightest inkling, instinctively she would take advantage. If there was anyone he should be feeling sorry for, Roddie thought, looking across at the man over by the dance floor, it should be him. By this time, his companion was almost sitting on his knee, with an arm draped possessively around his shoulders. He looked utterly miserable and, presumably, powerless to do anything about the situation he had fallen into.

'I'm very thirsty.' she said, pointedly looking at his glass which was now almost empty.

'Look,' Roddie said, moving further away from her, 'I'm sure you will think me rude, but, as I've said, I am waiting for someone and in the meantime I would prefer to be on my own.'

'Don't be like that,' she pouted, 'I was only trying to be friendly.'

'I'm sure you were,' he answered, 'but I would suggest you try and find someone else to talk to.'

Sulkily, she took the hint, climbed down from her stool and flounced off to the far end of the room to join the others. Fortunately, the place was beginning to fill up, and he was relieved to see he wasn't the only man on his own at the bar. He caught the barman's attention and ordered another wine.

He didn't have much longer to wait until Juliet came back, no more than fifteen minutes and she was on her own he was thankful to see, having fully expected to see the over-sexed Annie Steed with her.

'Alright?' he asked, moving along the now crowded bar to make room for her.

'Fine.' she smiled, 'Annie has confirmed she wants me to handle the accounts of the club, a fairly straightforward job really.'

'Will this mean you'll have to pay regular visits?'

'It will, yes,' she said, placing her bag on the bar and sitting on the stool recently vacated by the opportunist Primula, 'once a month to collect the receipts and invoices, although it does mean I'll be on call if she has anything further she wants me to deal with on her behalf; meetings with her bank, you know?'

'You're happy with that arrangement?' Roddie asked, genuinely wanting to know. She continued to fascinate him; not only as an extremely attractive woman, but as someone who had broken away from the mould of what he imagined the accountancy profession must be like and to immerse herself in a totally different environment. It wasn't only a shark-infested market, as he was sure it must be and one of which he knew nothing, but if her new client, Annie Steed, was anything to go by, Juliet must be pretty resilient, also shock-proof he concluded, noticing the young woman from Taiwan was now on the dance floor, having discarded the top layer of her flimsy garment, and fast approaching the first stages of her gyrating performance.

'I am, Roddie,' Juliet answered, glancing over towards the stripper, a small smile of amusement hovering on her lips, 'I'm doing a job I enjoy and to have no-one cracking the proverbial whip is marvellous. I've always been something of a rebel, I suppose.'

'It could be a bit risky, though.'

'In what way?'

'Well, and I probably don't need to even mention this to you, but there are a lot of very mean people out there.'

'You mean the Triads?'

'Not necessarily, although their presence shouldn't be discounted, but what I am saying is, you could, if you're not careful, be putting yourself in a vulnerable position. Some of these clients you have may not be exactly what they appear to be.'

'Listen, Roddie,' she said quietly, placing a hand on his arm, 'I do know what you mean, but I know what I'm doing. Also,' she went on, looking at him closely, 'I never taken people at face value.'

'Not even me?' he couldn't help asking.

'No, Roddie,' she laughed, 'not even you.'

'Well, thanks a lot!'

'Don't take offence,' she said quickly, the smile leaving her face for a second, 'I didn't mean it like that, but, believe me, I know exactly what it's like living here.'

'Okay, okay,' Roddie said, finishing off his wine, 'point taken. Shall we go and eat now?'

'I thought you'd never ask!' Juliet said, jumping down from the stool and picking up her bag, 'Have you anywhere in particular in mind?'

'Well,' he said, 'it depends on what sort of food you would like, but we could go to "Gaylord's"; it's not far from here.'

'The Indian restaurant?'

'Yes, you do like Indian food?'

'I love it,' she said, taking his arm, 'let's go!'

There were many Indian restaurants both in Kowloon and on Hong Kong Island and Roddie had visited a fair number of them, but he'd always rated "Gaylord's" as one of the best: authentic Indian-cooked food; excellent service which somehow, magically, created the illusion you weren't in the cosmopolitan and over-populated streets of Kowloon, but in an exclusive and luxurious restaurant in Mumbai. An abundance of starters would be brought to their table in blue and white glazed pottery bowls, all mouth-wateringly delicious: finely chopped red onions; mango chutney; Bombay mixes; hot spicy dips and poppadums and "Gaylord's" speciality, freshly baked bread from their tandoori oven. Definitely compulsive eating, hoping Juliet had a good appetite.

They had been deferentially shown to a table discreetly positioned in one of the high-backed alcoves when Juliet's mobile rang.

'Damn!' she muttered under her breath, switching it on, 'Hello ...... Oh, hello, Denny' .... another pause, longer this time, ... 'No, it's okay. It's just I didn't expect to hear from you again today .... tomorrow? .... Well, I'm not sure; I have a couple of appointments in the morning and another in the afternoon, but I suppose I could do a bit of juggling ....I tell you what,' she went on and he could see by the tiny frown which had appeared on her forehead she was anxious to bring the call to a close, 'I'll give you a ring in the morning; it's too late to phone either of them tonight. Okay?' she finished, pressing the off switch.

'Sorry about that.' she smiled apologetically, 'There are times when a mobile is more trouble than it's worth.'

'Useful though,' Roddie said, 'when it's to do with work.'

'True.' she smiled, putting the mobile back into her bag, 'Let's talk about you, Roddie, do you get much opportunity for any travelling in your job, or are you confined to your laboratory all the time?'

'Now and again I visit the States and an occasional trip to London. As a matter of fact, I'm booked to fly over there next Thursday; there's a seminar they want me to attend.'

'Really? That will make a change for you.' was all she said.

Why was it, he wondered, he was getting distinct vibes she was now making an attempt to change the subject, as though her mind was elsewhere. It could be she was thinking back to the call she'd had. Of course it was none of his business, so why should it matter who was phoning her at ten o'clock at night. It sounded as though it had something to do with her business, but on the other hand, perhaps not. So what? It was no concern of his, he reminded himself, and picking up one of the menus the waiter had placed in front of them.

*

McLellands Medical Research Laboratories, established for almost fifteen years; an offshoot from its parent company in California, was based in Des Voeux Road, the laboratories and suite of offices occupying the whole of the sixth floor and overlooking Victoria Harbour.

There was a yellow 'post-it' sticker on the centre of his computer screen, where he couldn't possibly miss it, when Roddie arrived for work the following morning: "Don't forget Jimmy's stag night! We're all starting off at "Dragon-1" at seven!" It was just as well one of his colleagues had reminded him, he thought, peeling it off the screen and switching on the computer, because he'd completely forgotten. It seemed as though Juliet had, from when he had first seen her yesterday, cast a spell over him and even this morning she was continuing to occupy his mind. They hadn't made any plans to see each other again, as much as he had been tempted to ask her, but intuitively, he had held back, anticipating and perhaps fearing rejection, at the same time admitting to himself he was behaving, not only out of character, but like a complete idiot. Meanwhile, he had a full day ahead of him, the most important part being the meeting with two of the company's directors to discuss the forthcoming AGM when the first item on the Agenda would be the final decision to patent the new anti-malaria drug he'd been involved in for the past twelve months. He would, he decided, go along to "Dragon-1" that evening and, as far as Juliet Warburton was concerned, he would try to distance himself from the thought of her, although realising he might find this impossible. He hadn't yet called Louisa; he should have done, knowing the longer he delayed getting in touch with her, the more awkward he was going to feel trying to think up some sort of credible excuse. You really are in an emotional turmoil, Roddie Mortimer, he told himself, keying in his password.

By late afternoon, the decision of when to phone Louisa was resolved for him when he received a call from her on his mobile.

'Hello, Roddie,' she said, 'I thought I would give you a call. You are alright, aren't you?'

'I'm fine,' he answered, 'busy, of course. You know how it is?' mentally wincing at his inadequate response.

'Sorry,' she said quickly, which only made him feel more guilty, 'have I called at a wrong moment?'

'No, Louisa, not at all; I was on the point of finishing for the day.'

'That's good, any chance of meeting up later?'

'I would have liked that, but I've promised to put in an appearance at Jimmy's stag night this evening. I really think I should go, Louisa.'

'Of course you should; you'll probably be late, so perhaps I'll see you tomorrow, Roddie, unless you've got something else planned.'

If he didn't know her better, and coming from any other woman he had ever known, he would have thought she was being sarcastic and on the verge of one big nagging session, but Louisa wasn't like that. She had never put any pressure on their relationship, had always taken what he had told her at face value and he had been grateful for that, but, on reflection, perhaps it may have been better if she had been more assertive, even remotely curious about, not only what he was doing, but what he was thinking. A bit of a paradox really, Roddie concluded, not liking himself very much at that moment. What the hell did he want, he wondered. Louisa was a lovely woman and she deserved something better. She certainly didn't deserve someone like him prevaricating the way he was doing.

'It's alright, you know, Roddie,' interrupting his thoughts, 'you don't have to explain. Like me, you have a job to do and I fully appreciate that. Let's leave it like this, shall we, when you're ready, just give me a call.' letting him off lightly. Part of him wanted to reassure her, tell her she had nothing to worry about, that he'd phone her later, but he couldn't. He couldn't even tell her he loved her; he'd never done that and now, he was all too sadly aware, he never would. When he finally brought the call to a close he felt oddly bereft. They'd had some good times together: a steady and undemanding relationship between two mature adults; no pack drill and not too many questions asked, no doubt, neither of them wanting to dig too deeply and resurrect painful pieces from the past.

He checked his emails for the last time that day; there were a few, but nothing that couldn't wait. He took one of the lifts down to the ground floor and, saying goodnight to the concierge on the desk, pushed his way through the swing doors and out on to De Voeux Road, the clamminess after the coolness of the air conditioning inside the building, instantly enveloping him. He was in no mood for socialising; all he wanted was to find a quiet bar somewhere and have a couple of beers before taking a taxi back to his apartment in Mid Levels, but he couldn't let the others down; they would be expecting him.

There was no need for him to go by Pedder Street to reach the "Dragon-1" bar; it would have been far quicker to go directly across Des Voeux Road to Queen's Road Central and then up into Wyndham Street, but he felt compelled to walk further along Des Voeux Road, exactly as he had done yesterday, and into Pedder Street. It wasn't as though he expected to see Juliet; he wasn't *that* stupid, but the shop where he'd bought his picture intrigued him and he wanted to have another look at the place, not go in or anything like that, but to merely re-trace his steps and try to reach some sort of sensible explanation, at least to himself, of why it should be positioned where it was and not down some side street in Mong Kok or somewhere similar, closer to the street markets, where pictures like the ones he had seen yesterday were in abundance.

He had thought he could remember exactly where the shop was: on the right-hand side past the herbalist, the antique shop and the cafe where he'd met Juliet, but he must have been mistaken. Puzzled, he walked a little further, although knowing he hadn't been as far up Pedder Street as this, deciding to turn back and have a closer look. Once again, he passed the now familiar cafe when he came to the conclusion the picture shop was no longer there. It had completely disappeared! Now, in its place, there was a shop with a newly painted frontage and selling, of all things, cake decorations. This is positively unreal he gasped, staring into the window.

Arranging the display must have taken hours: long glass shelves were filled with a mind-boggling range of everything imaginable for flavouring and decorating cakes and other tempting confectionary: slim packets of vanilla pods; jars of vanilla, orange, lemon and strawberry essences; plastic see-through tubs of angelica and glazed cherries; packets of flaked and powdered almonds, pistachios and coconut; 'hundreds and thousands', multi-flavoured and multi-coloured and more packets of raisins, currants and sultanas alongside tiny sugar roses, iced press-on anniversary and birthday messages, candles and cake frills, the latter in every colour of the rainbow. And not a picture in sight!

He simply had to go in and, as he had done before, turned the handle on the door which had been replaced by a brand new brass one. The interior had also had a rapid facelift; no dark and dusty corners; brightly lit with more shelving running the length of two of the walls. There were only a couple of similarities: the shop was empty and he wasn't mistaken about that today, also the stairs leading up to the floor above had not been altered. And, this time, Roddie didn't hesitate, he went immediately upstairs.

There was no-one in here either, although he saw that the door at the top of the stairs was slightly open and he walked over to it, pushing it wider until he was inside. The darkness which descended on him was instantaneous and without any warning. He didn't feel any pain, only the musty smell as something thick and sack-like was flung over his head and the only sound he was aware of was the soft thud as he fell to his knees on to the wooden floor.

Chapter Four
LONDON

'Does the name Francesca Cristofoli mean anything to you, Howard?'

'It certainly does. Don't tell me you've traced her after all this time?' Howard Westwood, a senior officer with Interpol, asked him, experiencing a familiar tingle of anticipation. There had been a time, well over ten years ago now, when the name was on all of their lips. The elusive Francesca Cristofoli: the woman who had succeeded in outwitting each and every one of them, and finally making a speedy and mysterious exit from the scene. Single-handedly, she had been responsible for carrying out a number of jewellery robberies on both sides of the English Channel. A Parisian by birth, she knew her way around the flesh pots of Europe, being invited to glittering embassy parties in numerous capitals, posing as the perfect guest, a witty conversationalist, a multi-linguist, with the ability to switch to the language of anyone she was talking to, and probably her main attribute, apart from being dexterously light-fingered, she was extremely attractive.

'I thought that would surprise you.' Robert Anderson, his superior, chuckled, leaning forward to top up their glasses. They were in Robert's penthouse apartment overlooking the Mall and enjoying an aperitif before walking round the corner to his club. Howard hadn't seen him for several months, having only that morning returned from Brussels where he had been based while conducting and successfully concluding a rather prolonged bribery and corruption case.

'Well, I have to admit it does,' Howard smiled, raising his glass, 'how did you manage it and where on earth has she been?'

'I can't take any credit, Howard,' he said, 'you could say it was due more to pure chance than anything else. She's been living in Columbia, still is, as far as I know. Also,' he added, taking a sip of the excellent sherry, 'she changed her name, but she was actually spotted recently while on a visit to Hong Kong.'

'She hadn't changed her appearance, then?'

'Apparently she had, but it wasn't any similarity to the way she used to look which alerted the lady who, incidentally, had been some years earlier relieved of an eighteen-carat gold bracelet which had been in her family for over a hundred years.'

'No?'

'The lady and her husband; he's in the diplomatic service, are now living in Hong Kong, but twelve years ago when they were still in London, she threw a party to celebrate his fortieth birthday and, as I'm sure you've already worked out, the notorious socialite, Francesca Cristofoli, had been among the guests. None of us, of course,' Robert went on, 'had ever heard her speak, far less meet her and, apart from a number of photographs which were circulating around that time, that was all we did have. Francesca Cristofoli has, I've now learned, a rather distinctive voice.'

'Ah.'

'Yes,' Robert nodded, 'it is rather high-pitched and particularly croaky and, although she could speak English fluently, her accent could, at times, be difficult to follow.'

'I see,' Howard said slowly, 'while you can change your appearance more or less completely, it's virtually impossible to alter your voice.'

'That's right.'

'I wonder what she was doing in Hong Kong.'

'I don't know. Perhaps her visit was only for a holiday, tired of remaining in her self-enforced exile, but equally, she could be up to her old tricks again. The interesting thing is, though, Immigration have confirmed she has been making a number of visits out there on a fairly regular basis over the last few years.'

'You could be right, Robert,' Howard said, 'she may never have stopped playing them.'

'I don't believe she has, you know. Francesca always struck me as a highly professional thief; ice-cold nerves and always covering her tracks well and as she did back then gauging exactly when to leave Europe, but except for knowing where she is living now and the name she's going under, that is about all we know about her, although all my instincts are telling me there is some significance in these visits she's been making. I wanted to discuss this with you before doing anything further; see if you can come up with any ideas.'

'The main criterion is not to alert her.' Howard said thoughtfully, trying to think what their best moves ought to be, 'She'd only do another vanishing act.'

'She'll get careless,' Robert warned, 'they invariably do.'

'True. The lady who told you she'd seen her, Robert; she is certain it was Francesca?'

'She was absolutely positive;' he said, 'I've known Virginia and Guy Bannister for years, ever since they were first married, in fact, which must now be at least eighteen or twenty years ago. Virginia is an intelligent woman,' he went on, 'very much down to earth and not given to fanciful ideas, no matter how much she would like Francesca Cristofoli brought to task. I was invited to Guy's party, actually,' a rueful smile appearing on his face, 'but I was working in Rome at the time and it was impossible to get away.'

'Fate certainly moves in a strange way sometimes, doesn't it?' Howard sympathised, 'If you had been there you would most likely have met Francesca.'

'I know. Anyway, I haven't mentioned this to you yet, but when Virginia saw her, which incidentally, was in the Clipper Lounge in the Mandarin Hotel; you've been there, haven't you?'

'I have, yes, a number of times; a peaceful oasis in the centre of the hustle and bustle of Hong Kong.'

'How right you are.' Robert agreed, 'Well, Virginia had been in the lounge for several minutes having tea with a friend of hers, when Francesca came up the stairs and, fortuitously, sat behind her and close enough for Virginia to hear her talking to her Chinese companion.'

'Interesting.'

'Very, and it gets more so, Howard. Virginia told me she recognised Francesca's voice immediately.'

'She was speaking in English?'

'Oh, yes, and referred to him as Denny. They were both obviously on first name terms as he called her Frances.'

'Not so different.' Howard commented, 'I take it, then, her surname wasn't mentioned?'

'Don't look so disappointed,' Robert smiled at him, 'I told you Virginia is an intelligent woman, didn't I, and when she heard him asking how her flight from Bogota had been that morning, she started putting two and two together.'

'- And?'

'And,' still smiling, 'hoping she was right in assuming Francesca would be staying at the Mandarin, she somehow – don't ask me exactly how – managed to find the information she was looking for from reception.'

'Good grief!'

'She not only discovered her full name, Frances Catania and that she had indeed booked into the hotel earlier that day, but her address in Bogota.'

'And she remembered it?'

'She most certainly did.'

'So, where do you suggest we go from here, Robert?'

'Well,' he began, 'if you're agreeable, I'd like you to fly out to Hong Kong; introduce yourself to Virginia. I've only spoken to her over the phone, it's always better face-to-face, I think, also she should be able to give you a description of the man who was with Francesca.'

'There's is a drawback, though.'

'Which is?'

'I can't help wondering how many Chinese there are in Hong Kong called Denny.'

'A great number, I would say. I realise it's going to be a bit like looking for the proverbial needle in a haystack, but we have to start somewhere.'

'Do you believe there could be a connection between Columbia and Hong Kong?'

'I believe there very well could be, but before we start thinking along those lines and possibly reaching the wrong conclusions, which may only make our task even more difficult than it is already, let's try and get as many facts together as we can.'

'That makes sense.'

'We'll send someone out to Bogota to find out what she's doing there; how she is living and even who she may be living with; her friends and what sort of people they are. Meanwhile,' he continued, 'if she should decide to make a return visit to Hong Kong, Immigration will let us know and we can take the enquiry on from there.'

'We'd have time possibly to put a contact on to her.'

'Especially, if someone like you, Howard was actually there, on the spot.'

*

Friday, early evening, and Natasha was clearing her workstation on the editorial floor of the newspaper company where she had worked for the past three years, when her mobile rang. Juggling a pile of research notes in one hand and the phone in the other, she pressed the on-button.

'Hi,' she said, slightly out of breath and feeling more than a little emotional having spent the last half hour saying a final farewell to her sub-editor and those colleagues she wouldn't be meeting up with later in "Annabel's".

'Natasha.'

'Nicholas!' she gasped, 'Are you okay?'

'Yes, I'm fine, although tired. I haven't been able to get to sleep yet.'

'Poor you. It must be very late with you, but I'm so glad you phoned; it's wonderful to hear your voice.'

'And yours too, darling. Listen, Natasha, I won't be at the airport to meet you on Monday evening.'

'Oh, no!'

'I'm sorry, I really am, but I have to work late, I'm afraid.'

'Nicholas!'

'Don't worry, Natasha,' and she could tell he was trying to calm her, 'you'll be arriving at six, right?'

'Yes.'

'Well, all you have to do is take a taxi from the rank outside Arrivals and ask the driver to take you to Causeway Bay. You've got the full address, haven't you?'

'Yes, it's in my wallet, but, Nicholas,' unable to stop herself, 'you won't *be* there!'

'I know, darling, and, believe me, I wish I could be, but I can't do anything about it. These things do tend to happen from time to time, you know.'

'Sorry, Nicholas, I'm just terribly disappointed, that's all.'

'I understand,' he said, 'and I want you to make yourself at home as soon as you're in the apartment. I've already told the concierge to expect you; he has a key and I don't expect I'll be all that late, Natasha.'

The disappointment she felt, once Nicholas had rung off with repeated reassurances that she wouldn't have any difficulties, was disproportionate. Where, she wondered, had all that new-found pioneering spirit gone. Perhaps her mother had been right and Nicholas was the main reason for her wanting to leave London and move to a country she had never been to before, but her mother had been wrong! She had told her that Nicholas was only part of it and she had meant it and still did, she silently insisted to herself. She realised she was in danger of allowing everything to get out of perspective, severing those ties with which she had been so familiar; her job and the friends she'd made and having no idea whether she would see or even hear from again and now, learning there would be no Nicholas waiting at the barrier to meet her, to hold her in his arms and to tell her he loved her.

It wasn't until later, when she was on her way to meet up with the others, the thought occurred to her that she could have phoned her father, but quickly calculating that the seven hour difference between here and Hong Kong meant it would by now be three in the morning there. She should have given him a call before; perhaps her idea of deciding to surprise him wasn't such a clever one after all. Natasha had seen little of him over the years, but this fact had never bothered her unduly. He had left England years ago and hardly ever made any return trips and Conrad had been a good father to her; she had no complaints and didn't feel deprived in the way some of her friends did, whose parents had divorced and then re-married. She could, she supposed, always give him a ring tomorrow morning and let him know what she was doing.

Natasha had told Nicholas about her father shortly after they had met, but as though sensing her reluctance to elaborate and talk about a father she hardly knew, he hadn't pressed her. Eventually, no doubt, she would introduce Nicholas to him, but later. She wanted first to find a job; at least then, she felt she would be able to prove to him, and to herself, that she was really making an effort to establish herself in Hong Kong.

She did try to phone Roddie the following morning, but there was no answer from the only number he had given her when he had first moved into his apartment. She knew where he worked; not that he would be there on a Saturday anyway, she concluded, replacing the receiver. She wouldn't be seeing her mother until Sunday evening; Conrad and she had offered to take her to Heathrow, not that she would mention trying to contact her father. There would be no point. From a very early age, Natasha had realised her mother was reluctant to mention his name and, understandably, if she ever did, it was never when Conrad was around.

*

Hugh Innis prided himself on being a good judge of character. He had, over the years, and many of them spent travelling, devised his own private game of tying metaphoric labels on to people; it helped to pass the time and what better place than the departure lounge at Heathrow airport? He was never able, naturally enough, to prove whether he was correct in these mental assumptions, but that didn't concern him. It was only a game after all and perfectly harmless, but as soon as he noticed the tall, broad-shouldered man in the light-weight suit and open-necked shirt, he had no doubts. In Hugh's opinion, the man sitting opposite and turning over the pages of a brand-new paperback, had policeman written all over him. He should know, he sighed, remembering with old traces of bitterness; he used to be one! When he had gone into partnership with Eddie, he had mentioned it to him, but only the once, briefly explaining how he had quickly decided that life in the force wasn't for him and Eddie hadn't appeared all that interested. They had far more important issues to discuss than his failed career in the police force. Take this current project for instance, Hugh thought, going over in his mind each step of their carefully laid out plan. Of course it was risky, everyone involved was well aware of that. From the moment he arrived at Kai Tak Airport until he was on his way back to London, he would be totally dependent on Nicholas Eastman. Hugh, having only been in his company a couple of times, although he was reasonably confident he wouldn't let them down this didn't prevent him from continuing to have certain reservations about the man. Also, it didn't follow he had to like him. Nicholas was a shade too slick for his liking. Both he and Eddie belonged to a different school where the "what if" principle played a crucial part and when a contingency plan was essential. Nicholas had repeatedly stressed to him that his position as one of the bank's top executives was respected and telling him he knew all the security staff, being familiar with their roster, including not only who would be on duty on Monday evening, but the exact time of the changeover to the night staff. Not once Nicholas had said, had anyone asked for the identity of any client he had escorted to the area in the vaults where the safe deposit boxes were stored and he was positive that this Monday would be no different. As this part of the set-up was out of Hugh's control he had no option but to rely on him, although at the same time aware that if they suspected he was an imposter and had no connection with McLellands, and the matter was reported to the authorities, the outcome would ultimately lead to the exposure of Bristow & Innis. This, of course, must not happen. As far as Hugh could see, this possibility was the only weakness in an otherwise foolproof plan. Eddie and he had discussed at length the strategy they should adopt which was that Nicholas was to know nothing of the existence of their firm, not even their real names. Hugh had to admit Nicholas also was taking a great deal on trust, which should mean both sides had to work closely together. There was only one person in Hong Kong who knew him and the reason behind this visit of his, but she would never say anything. Of all of them, Marion Godwin had the most to lose.

They had another fifteen minutes before they would be boarding Hugh saw, glancing up at the monitor. The man across from him appeared to have lost interest in his paperback and, like most of the other passengers, was staring around disinterestedly, although, if he was what Hugh suspected, he knew this wouldn't be the case. His training, as his own had been, would have taught him to make mental notes of, not only the obvious and memorable characteristics of complete strangers, but much more. He would have sussed out their nationality, also whether they were travelling alone. This would be no game; not something to while away the time and then quickly forgotten; each and every observation would be neatly categorised in his memory in the event he would, at some time in the future, need to retrieve them and form a credible identi-kit picture. How would he view him, Hugh wondered idly. A man in his early fifties, not so very different from many other men around the same age; clean shaven; medium height; medium build; dark hair, greying at the temples. Even the dark-framed spectacles Hugh was wearing were ordinary, also the brown cords and leather jacket. And, unless the man was a mind reader, not much else!

At that moment and reaching the end of his ramblings, he heard a mobile ringing which reminded him he hadn't yet switched his own off. The man he had been watching was now on his feet and starting to walk further away from the row of seats towards the window, at the same talking into his mobile. Cautious fellow, Hugh thought, which only proved to him he had been right. Reception would be no better where he was now standing, but there was nobody within ear-shot near him, so obviously Hugh smugly concluded, that was what he wanted.

*

'Ah, Howard,' Robert Anderson said, 'I'm glad I've caught you before you boarded.'

'Another five or six minutes yet, Robert.'

'Right, this won't take long, but I thought you should know as soon as possible.'

'Yes?'

'I've had a call from Immigration. A Miss Frances Catania is booked on the Cathay Pacific flight for Hong Kong, leaving Heathrow tomorrow night.'

'Not from Columbia, then?'

'No, apparently she flew in from there early this morning.'

'She does seem very sure she won't be recognised; London was her stomping ground after all.'

'Exactly. No doubt believing no-one will after all this time.'

'What time will she be arriving in Hong Kong?'

'Eighteen hundred hours on Tuesday.'

'Do you want me to be there?'

'Not necessarily, Howard; you don't have to keep a constant eye on her. I'll have someone else do that, with strict instructions not to make himself obvious. This will leave you free to move about as you think best.'

'Who do you plan to send?'

'Frank Mitchell. He's still in Bangkok, so he'll easily make it to Hong Kong in time.'

'Alright, Robert. I'll have to go now; they've just called our flight.'

'Fine. Have a safe journey, Howard. I'll wait for you to call me unless there are any further surprise developments at this end.'

Howard switched off his mobile, putting it back in the pocket of his jacket and joining the end of the queue to the boarding gate. It looks like being an extremely interesting few days he thought and wondering, as he showed his travel documents to the girl at the desk, whether Robert had been right about Francesca Cristofoli. Was she, in her super-confidence, becoming careless?

Chapter Five
HONG KONG

Sun streaming through the grime-smeared windows finally woke Roddie shortly after nine on the Saturday morning. After regaining full consciousness around midnight with, surprisingly, only a slight headache after being bundled and trussed up within the thick folds of an ancient army blanket and subjected to a blow on the back of his head, he had spent most of what remained of the night trying to find a comfortable position on the narrow camp bed where his captors had flung him.

He could recall very little from the moment he had entered what he believed had been an empty room above the shop in Pedder Street; they were only faint and sketchy pieces of memory. At some point, he had a vague recollection of being dragged up some steps and the sound of water slapping against what could have been the wooden hull of a boat, also harsh whisperings in Cantonese drifting above where he lay, presumably where they had dumped him, on to the deck. Later, and he couldn't be sure how much later it had been, but he thought he heard Juliet Warburton's voice, but even in his befuddled state he had dismissed this as hallucination and then, the only other thing he remembered, was opening his eyes to peer into the dense blackness of the room where they had brought him.

Now, pulling himself upright and shrugging off the blanket which smelled disgusting, he had to find out where he was. He wasn't a prisoner; apart from the total silence, not only inside the house, but outside also, the door was wide open and, from where he was lying, he could see a tangled mass of greenery stretching down towards a wooden fence and a dilapidated gate which had also been left open. He had no idea where he could be, but remembering the water he had heard, presumably not on Hong Kong island; perhaps in Kowloon, or possibly more likely, on one of the outlying islands. He had the impression the journey from Pedder Street hadn't been a long one, but there was only one way to find out he decided, climbing out of the bed.

He didn't waste any time in having a look round. The house was no more than a cottage with one main room where he was; a small narrow kitchen; a bathroom and, upstairs, two miniscule-sized bedrooms. A grey film of dust lay over the wooden floorboards and the few pieces of utility furniture: a couple of rattan chairs with frayed and faded cushions; a bookcase with, incongruously, a dozen or so paperbacks neatly aligned along the top shelf. A single light bulb hung from the low-beamed ceiling, although he soon discovered the supply had been cut off. Going into the kitchen, he turned on the tap, having to wait several seconds until the choking and gurgling in the pipes had subsided before a spluttering trickle of rusty water splashed into the sink. He would have liked to freshen up, but even if he waited until the water ran clear, there were no signs of any towels, either in the kitchen, or the bathroom. What a hole, he thought in disgust, taking off his crumpled jacket and glad to see his shirt had survived the ordeal, although his trousers hadn't faired so well, but there was nothing he could do about that. The main object was to get back without any further incidents he decided, checking through his jacket pockets.

'Damn!' he muttered. He might have known it! Both his mobile and keys had gone. His wallet was still intact, also his credit cards and the dollar bills, so that wasn't the reason why he had been attacked, by now beginning to reach a few conclusions. Obviously, he had stumbled into something decidedly shady here. That shop in Pedder Street wasn't there for the sole purpose of selling pictures, not to mention the dramatic switch to cake decorations. They, whoever *they* were, wanted to know why he was so interested and so much so to make a second visit. Was it as simple as that? Why not; whatever other explanation could there be? It wasn't as though they had injured him in any way; manhandled him, yes, but not enough to permanently remove him and, when he thought about it, they could have done. He had been caught unawares and within seconds had been powerless to do anything. Therefore, he concluded, the logical conclusion must be they wanted him out of the way long enough to give them time to check up on him. They had the keys to his apartment and they would have seen his company pass, so they would know where he worked and his full name. All they had to do was find out his address, which wouldn't have posed much of a problem, especially, as it happened, he was in the phone book. No doubt, by this time, they would have been into his apartment, had a damn good look through his things. He began to think of anything which could be of special interest to anyone and, mentally running through everything in the apartment, he remembered the file he had brought back from the office a couple of nights ago, intending to spend some time over the weekend in collating the various hand-written notes on his current project. The impact of these having been stolen had the immediate effect of bringing him to a standstill in the middle of the shabby room, but then logic and common sense kicked in. He was being paranoid; no-one, unless they were conversant with the technical language in his field of chemistry, also being able to decipher his pencilled scrawl, would have seen the potential of any of it. No, he decided, he was over-reacting; whoever had taken it into their heads to transport him to this island could not have known then he worked for the laboratories – could they? You are really behaving in a crazy way, Roddie, he told himself; you had the misfortune to walk into a shop which is not really what it claims to be. End of story.

As much as he wanted to reach a rational explanation for what had happened, leaving the cottage and stepping on to the overgrown narrow path leading away from it and hoping he would find some signs of habitation, he knew deep down he was kidding himself, but at the same time, stubbornly ignoring what the analytical part of his brain was trying to tell him.

As he quickly discovered, the cottage where he had spent the night had no neighbours, but, after walking downhill for about a mile, the ground flattened out and in front of him he saw the first house. This one, a stone-block, two-storey building with a high hedge separating it from the path, had been well maintained; window panes, ledges and the front door all painted white and sparkling in the bright sunlight. He could hear children laughing as he grew nearer and sounds of patio furniture being scraped across a concrete area and saw a man, possibly their father, erecting a metal barbecue. A small coffee-coloured terrier was yapping excitedly at his heels; an ordinary family on an ordinary Saturday morning, looking forward to enjoying a day in the garden and possibly entertaining their friends. There were moments like these when Roddie felt pangs of regret for never really experiencing a family life. Natasha had only been four when Clarissa left him, taking Natasha with her. A pity he thought, walking further along the path and now passing more houses, wondering just how much Natasha did remember of those early years. Probably nothing, he thought morosely. It wasn't often he wallowed in self-pity, having learned to blot out such negative thoughts from his mind before they had a chance to take hold. What he needed, walking more briskly now, apart from a shower and a change of clothes, was a long cool glass of beer.

He had now reached the village: a long narrow street with a line of shops on one side and then, opposite to a flower shop, the village pub and as soon as he saw it he remembered he'd been here before. He was on Lamma Island and, to immediately confirm this, a signpost telling anyone who didn't know already, that this was Yung Shue Wan.

Yung Shue Wan was Lamma's biggest village at the north-western end of the island, with, he recalled, a regular ferry service to Hong Kong. Relieved he was in relatively familiar territory, with ferries every half-hour, Roddie decided to have that beer while he fathomed out a solution to the obstacle he still had to overcome. He was minus the keys to his apartment and the only other set was with Louisa. He could quite easily phone her from the pub, that wouldn't be a problem, but he was reluctant to do this. He continued to have an over-riding feeling of guilt as far as she was concerned; all too aware he had treated her badly. Thoughts of Juliet continued to occupy his mind and the last he wanted was to give Louisa some cobbled-together explanation of why he couldn't get into his apartment, realising too well if he had never seen Juliet in the first place he wouldn't be in this situation. Also, he had no wish to lie to her, but what sort of reason could he possibly come up with anyway? Some unknown person had attacked him last night, transported him to Lamma Island and stolen his keys? It not only sounded bizarre to him, but how would it have come over to her. She would have been appalled and he was certain her immediate reaction would be to tell him to phone the police and that was something he had no intention of doing. He would have come over as a complete idiot: I was shopping in Pedder Street last evening, officer, and someone threw a blanket over my head and the next thing I knew I was in some derelict house on Lamma Island! And when, inevitably, they would ask if he had seen his assailant; what could he say? He would have to think of another way, which only meant he would need to find a locksmith. The lock would have to be changed in any case.

Steps led up to a shaded terrace outside the front of the pub and, once Roddie had bought his long-awaited beer and a packet of cheese and onion crisps to stave off the hunger pangs, he went back out there and sat down at one of the tables overlooking the street which was becoming busy as the local residents shopped for their weekend supplies. Having made up his mind not to call Louisa, he turned his thoughts once again to Juliet. He wanted to see her again, of that there was no doubt. And, despite the tiny shred of memory which kept niggling away at him, he opened his wallet and took out the card she had given him: "Juliet Warburton, Accountant" it read, "Sixth Floor, Wing Apartments, Begonia Road, Yau Yat Tsuen, Kowloon" and her telephone number: 3524 7626.

It was three o'clock in the afternoon before Roddie was back in the apartment and dialling Juliet's number. The delay was caused by having to wait for the locksmith to arrive. When he had finally tracked one down it was almost midday. By then, Roddie had resigned himself to the wait, however frustrating, and spent the time, after he had purchased a new mobile, by doing what most other people in Hong Kong were doing; having lunch. He chose a restaurant within easy walking distance to where he lived; not one of the smarter ones, he was far too aware of his scruffy state, but the small one on the corner of his street and, being ravenous, having not eaten for more than forty-eight hours, ate his way through dishes of sweet and sour pork, beef with black bean sauce, crispy prawn balls, Cantonese rice and, rounding it all off, with a bottle of San Miguel.

Today certainly wouldn't go down as one of his best, Roddie decided, after he had come off the phone. Fully expecting to hear Juliet's voice, he had been taken aback for a moment by the person who answered, who sounded remarkably like the pushy Primula in "Annie's" the other evening, but then, he concluded, many of the Filipinas sounded the same and, presumably, she was Juliet's maid.

'You say Miss Warburton is away for the week-end?' he had asked her, trying to play down his disappointment.

'Yes, that's right, sir,' the Primula sound-alike answered, 'she won't be back until Monday.'

'I would like to get in touch with her,' Roddie said, 'is she still in Hong Kong; perhaps you have a number for her?'

'Oh, no, sir,' she'd giggled; a sound he didn't like all that much; shrill and parrot-like and setting his nerves on edge, 'Miss Warburton is staying with friends on Lamma Island and I don't have any contact number for her.' she added, quickly ringing off.

*

'Sorry to disturb your weekend, Conrad,' Denny Yuan said, 'but there has been a slight change of plan.'

'Not another one?'

Denny could hear the deep sigh of exasperation at the other end of the line. That was the problem with Conrad; he could be quite inflexible at times. He always had been. It was alright for him, sitting there in his deluxe office suite in London with his team of minions on call, while he was here; at the sharp, and extremely vulnerable, end of the whole operation. Conrad didn't have to worry about liaising and sweet-talking the Bogota people; he didn't have to meet the woman who had acted as their courier since the beginning of their negotiations. And the most complex part of the proceedings, Conrad didn't physically have to take receipt of the emeralds and plan their onward journey to London. All Conrad had to do, once he received the package, was to arrange their distribution. Not too arduous a task and relatively risk-free and from then on, his work was over, with precious little fear of any comeback, but not his. He had to be continually on his guard. He was the one who had to be in constant contact with Bogota. These people knew who he was: knew his name, where he lived and, perhaps more importantly, because he had met them, knew what he looked like, while Conrad was a faceless and nameless cog in the whole business. And now, Denny thought bitterly, we have this bloody nosey parker who was definitely not, in his opinion, all he seemed. Not some innocent, albeit meddling, Englishman with far too much time on his hands, poking his nose into something which was none of his business.

'I'm afraid so, Conrad.' Denny answered him at last, 'I told you I would get back to you, didn't I?'

'Yes, you did.'

'Well, this Mortimer guy turned up again yesterday in the shop and I'm sorry to tell you but we had no choice but to take some rather drastic measures.'

'What? You don't mean –'

'– not *that* drastic,' he interrupted, 'but we had to put him out of action for a while, long enough to find out just who he is.'

'How the hell did you do that?'

'I don't think there is anything to be gained by giving you a detailed account of how this was accomplished,' Denny said, 'sufficient to say it succeeded. We were able, while he was temporarily incapacitated, not only to find out more about him, where he lived, etc., etc., but as my men had the presence of mind to extract his keys from him, I was able to have a very good look around his apartment. I might add,' he went on, 'we had already received a few snippets of extremely useful information which I now intend to use to our advantage.'

'You're talking in riddles, Denny.'

'I'm sorry about that, Conrad, but you should know me by now. And remember,' he paused for a fraction of a second, 'as so often, it is to your advantage you don't learn too much about the ins and outs of how I, personally, conduct this side of the business.'

'I suppose you're right, but I would appreciate it if you were a little less obtuse.'

'Alright, Conrad, alright. Point taken. You will remember our conversation on Thursday when I phoned you.'

'Of course.'

'Well, I've talked to our contact in Bogota and the goods will be here on Tuesday.'

'That's good news.'

'On the face of it, yes, but I'm still continuing to be concerned about this cache which would, if everything hadn't been thrown into chaos by this Mortimer guy, already have been with you. I'm acting on the side of caution here, Conrad, but I decided to off-load that particular package.'

'What the hell do you mean by 'offload'?'

'Bear with me, my friend. And trust me.' He added.

'Alright.'

'First of all,' Denny went on slowly, 'Mortimer is booked to fly out to London next Thursday night and when he lands at Heathrow he will have those emeralds securely stashed away in the lining of his travel bag.'

'What the hell!'

'Surprised?'

'Surprised, Denny! I'm bloody flabbergasted! You'd better explain and pretty damn quickly!'

'Oh, I will, if you'll give me a chance.'

'I'm listening. Go on.' another sigh, but this time it made Denny smile. His old friend, Conrad Bailey, true to form, never failed to finally react exactly as he expected him to. He would huff and puff, but then invariably he would capitulate, coming round to his point of view.

'I know this is the first time we have taken such an action,' Denny explained, 'but keeping those emeralds any longer on the premises has, quite frankly, become a liability. I had to act quickly on this, Conrad. I'm not entirely convinced he hasn't some connection with the authorities and you know what that could mean. If they get an inkling of what's going on, well —' hesitating for a second; the consequences were so dire he could scarcely bare to think about them, far less put into words, '- need I say anymore, Conrad?'

'Alright, Denny, I hear what you say. So,' he continued, 'what's the next step?'

'The next step, Conrad,' Denny said, 'will be up to you.'

'I had a rather nasty feeling it might be.'

'I don't mean you,' he told him, 'but you have someone you can trust, I presume. When Mortimer reaches Heathrow - you will, of course, have checked on the time of arrival - it may be possible to extract the bag, either from the carousel before he does, or from him. In the event this doesn't work, it will have to be from his hotel room. I should be in a position within the next couple of days to give you the name of the hotel and —' pausing once more, 'I'm going to leave it to your initiative, Conrad.'

'So, it's over to me.'

'Yes, my friend, it will be over to you. My part in that particular consignment will have been completed, and not, I may add, without considerable personal risk.'

'Okay, Denny. Now, what about this next delivery and as you said the other day, it's probably going to be the last one for some time. I hope this one isn't going to act as a precedent for all future transactions, because if it is, quite frankly, I don't think I could take the strain.'

'Don't worry, Conrad;' Denny laughed, 'the next consignment will be perfectly straightforward. The emeralds will be concealed in confectionary packages.'

'Confectionary packages!'

'Sorry, Conrad, 'It isn't my intention to sound facetious, and you weren't to know, but I no longer sell paintings in my shop in Pedder Street, but, instead, a rather prolific and attractive assortment of cake decorations, including a selection of glazed cherries and angelica; the latter which bear an uncanny resemblance to emeralds!'

*

It was nine o'clock on Monday morning and the passengers from the British Airways flight from Heathrow, having passed through Immigration and collected their baggage from the carousel, emerged through the swing doors into the Arrivals Hall at Kai Tak airport.

Howard, grateful to stretch his legs and to clear his lungs of the air which he had been absorbing for the last ten hours in the air-conditioned cabin of the aircraft, walked the few metres to the taxi rank and tagged on to the end of the queue. He had lost count of the times he had been in Hong Kong; always on business, never for pleasure, but each time he had to admit he enjoyed coming back and to embracing, not only a totally different way of life from what he was used to, even in London, but merging in with the different nationalities. Here, everyone appeared to have a purpose for where they were going. Nobody hesitated, nobody stopped abruptly on the pavement in front of him, all of them just kept moving, as though blinkered and intent only in reaching their destinations. One day, he promised himself, as he reached the beginning of the queue, he would come here on holiday, really find out about the culture, the history and the marvellous restaurants without having his mind pre-occupied with the task he had been given; namely, finding the villains!

The journey, through the Cross Harbour Tunnel from Kowloon and emerging into daylight on Hong Kong Island, passing the Royal Hong Kong Yacht Club before the approach to Gloucester Road, skirting Wanchai, and continuing into Harcourt Road, with the spectacular Exchange Square on the left with the three granite buildings, one of them being the Hong Kong Stock Exchange and in the foreground the three monolithic statues, and finally into Connaught Road Centre, took almost an hour. The traffic was heavy, delays at road junctions frequent and Howard was thankful when the taxi finally pulled in at the main entrance to The Mandarin Oriental Hotel and, stepping out on to the pavement, he paid off the driver.

A bell-boy, resplendent in his uniform of scarlet and gold, hurried down the steps of the hotel, immediately taking Howard's suit-carrier and bulky travel bag from him. The double glass doors swung open and he was deferentially ushered inside one of Hong Kong's oldest and most prestigious of hotels. Booking in was cordially and effortlessly dealt with, and by the time he had been silently and smoothly transported up to the seventh floor, his baggage had already been placed in his room and the curtains drawn back to reveal the panoramic view of Victoria Harbour: two of the green and white Star Ferries passing each other half-way across the expanse of water between Hong Kong Island and Kowloon and the flotilla of smaller vessels; fishing boats and junks with their tarpaulin canopies as protection from the fierceness of the sun or, at other times of the year, from the torrential wind and rain which would surge up relentlessly into the estuary from the open sea.

A shower was definitely first on his list Howard decided, undressing; his shirt with the immediate change in temperature as soon as he'd left the plane was clinging to his back and his trousers would have to go to the laundry before he could wear them again. Why was it, he wondered, turning on the shower to full power, that travelling, although relatively speedy, could reduce you to feeling and looking like someone who'd been sleeping rough for days.

By the time he had freshened up and unpacked the few clothes he'd brought with him it was midday. Time, he decided, for some light refreshment, and doing his best to forget that as far as his body-clock was concerned, it was still only two o'clock in the morning, but before going downstairs, he must call Virginia Banister.

Using the room telephone, he gave the receptionist the number of Robert's friend and within a matter of minutes he had been put through to her.

'Hello, Howard.' her immediate response, once he had introduced himself, 'I've been expecting you to call. Robert rang me yesterday to tell me you were on your way out here. How was your flight?'

'Reasonable.'

'Not suffering from jet-lag, I trust?'

'I always try not to think about that,' Howard said, 'mind over matter, you know?'

'How sensible. One simply cannot give in, can one?'

Howard couldn't help smiling; she sounded exactly as he thought she would. The wife of a diplomat, well used to small talk with no doubt a spontaneous repartee to fit each occasion, but he was sure there was a more serious side to her, remembering how Robert had described the lady and looking forward to meeting her.

'If you can spare the time, Mrs Banister, -' he began before she interrupted him.

'- please call me Virginia.'

'Virginia,' he said, 'I wonder whether it would be possible for us to meet; perhaps this afternoon?'

'Of course, Howard, I would be delighted. Where did you have in mind? I would ask you up to the house,' she continued, 'but the whole place is in the throes of preparing for a dinner party this evening for our new governor and his family.'

'I wouldn't dream of imposing,' he reassured her, 'I'm staying at the

Mandarin; we could have tea in the Clipper Lounge.'

'That would be perfect, except,' she halted, and he could detect a smile in her voice.

'Yes?'

'I have no idea what you look like.'

'Of course you don't, Virginia, but I tell you what, I'll get the hotel to page me as soon as you arrive.'

"The Captain's Bar", on the ground floor of the hotel, was like no other bar Howard had ever been in. The ambience, one of understated elegance and comfort; subdued lighting; a highly-polished bar on the left-hand side of the room with two white-jacketed stewards in attendance; low, soft upholstered chairs and sofas and, at the far end, the pianist playing melodies from another age. He had always liked it in here, right from the very first time he visited Hong Kong almost fifteen years ago: the impeccable service and atmosphere of quiet luxury never failed to give him that feel-good feeling, especially after a long flight. He ordered half a lager and took it with him to one of the tables at the far end of the bar and from where he could indulge in some people watching. It was too early in the day to phone Robert, but he could do that later, after he'd spoken to Virginia. He didn't hold out a great deal of hope he would be able to learn anymore than Robert had, but it was always possible Virginia may have remembered something which she had missed from the afternoon she had seen Francesca Cristofoli.

Howard had only been sitting there for five minutes or so, contentedly enjoying his beer as the bar began to fill up with lunchtime customers, when he had the uncomfortable feeling of being watched. There were a number of people standing at the bar, but none of them were looking his way; the young couple at the table next to him, being totally absorbed in each other, certainly weren't interested in him, neither was the woman on his left; faded blonde hair tied back in a ponytail, unflattering and reminiscent of the seventies and trying with some difficulty, judging by the way she was screwing up her eyes, to read a magazine in the inadequate lighting. Puzzled, he glanced around the room. He knew he wasn't mistaken. Too many years of observing, also of being observed, had fine-honed his senses and this built-in antenna had never so far let him down. There was someone in here who had more than a casual interest in him and, intrigued, he continued to sip his beer while continuing to look at each person in the room.

The pianist had stopped playing and was now standing up from the stool to re-fill his glass from a carafe of water which had been placed on top of the piano, when a man, sitting close by, shifted slightly in his seat and moved his head to one side as if to get a clearer view of the rest of the room. He had seen him before, Howard remembered. It had been yesterday afternoon in Departures and he had thought then he had seemed unusually interested in him, but had merely dismissed it at the time as meaning nothing. He was going now, he noticed, watching him get to his feet and walking away from the table over towards the door and it was precisely at the moment he turned his back Howard recognised him. It was not how he walked, but in the way he pushed his head slightly forward from his shoulders. Hugh Innis had been like that; the name coming to Howard instantly from his memory bank. This was before he joined Interpol and he was with the Metropolitan police force and, although never working with Hugh Innis, he had known who he was, but especially when he left the force rather suddenly. Rumours were literally flying around at the time; something to do with accepting bribes in exchange for withholding and distorting evidence. Howard never learned the details and shortly after that he was moved to Interpol. Why, he wondered, was Hugh Innis so interested in him. Could it be that he'd also recognised him? Perhaps, but if he had, what did it matter, Howard thought; a lot of water had surely passed under the bridge since then but nevertheless continuing to speculate. What was Hugh Innis doing now? Could be, his dismissal from the Force had taught him a salutary lesson, although Howard didn't think so. Back then, he had been playing a daring and dangerous game which, in Howard's view, proved the man had a strong nerve and was not averse to taking irrevocable risks. Had he changed? Being labelled as a 'bent copper' couldn't have been a comfortable mantle to live with, but unless Hugh Innis' presence here, in Hong Kong, impinged on the case Howard was currently working on, he would have to dismiss him, or at least put any thought about him to the back of his mind, but it still didn't stop him from being curious why, for the last ten minutes, he should have been subjected to such a close scrutiny, also the previous afternoon at Heathrow.

*

Virginia Bannister was a pretty woman; short dark brown hair framing a heart-shaped face and immediately he saw her, standing in the foyer at the bottom of one of the twin sweeping staircases leading up to the Clipper Lounge, Howard realised what Robert had meant; the way those intelligent grey eyes appraised him as he walked towards her said it all. He didn't think they would miss much.

'What is the general feeling in Hong Kong about the new governor and the crucial role he has to play in taking the colony up to the handover?' Howard asked her, once he'd ordered a pot of tea and, typically English for that time in the afternoon, a plate of scones with strawberry jam and fresh cream.

'Oh, Howard,' she smiled, 'I believe the general consensus of opinion is one of, quite frankly, suppressed excitement. We've known for so long and, especially in recent years ever since Margaret Thatcher's decisive meeting in Beijing, most of us have been talking ad infinitum about what it will be like after the handover, but,' she added, 'we will just have to wait and see. And, as for our new governor; I cannot think of anyone more suited to take us all up to nineteen-ninety-seven.'

'Had you met him before his arrival here?'

'I hadn't, no, but my husband has known Chris Patten for a number of years. He and his wife, Lavender, have three lovely daughters, you know, Howard and already, although they've only been here for a matter of days, the Chinese are making a great fuss of them, especially the young men. In fact, our two sons are no exception, I can tell you!'

She was interesting to talk to, also fun and it was a pity he would have to turn the conversation on to a more serious level, but he waited until their tea and scones had been brought to the table before mentioning Francesca Cristofoli's name.

'It was some time ago, of course,' Virginia explained, after he had asked her to describe the woman to him, 'but I remember quite clearly what she was like then. To many of the men who met her, I truly believe she came over as some exotic creature who had suddenly appeared in their midst and I have to say, they rather disgraced themselves. In other words, for some unfathomable reason they simply couldn't resist her and, I'm sorry to tell you, more than one marriage came to an abrupt and, in some cases, a somewhat dramatic end! Francesca gave the impression of being totally oblivious to the effect she was having, or uncaring perhaps, I don't know. We women, cats which we probably deserved to be called, didn't like her all that much, or to be more accurate, we didn't trust her.'

'A modern-day Mata Hari.' Howard commented, fascinated; not only by what she was saying, but the mental picture she was giving him.

'One could call her that.' Virginia gave a small rueful smile, 'I have been wondering since I discovered she was living in Columbia now, why she chose that particular country in South America. I would have thought she would have found a more lucrative and glamorous lifestyle in, say, Rio or Buenos Aires. I'm sorry, Howard, what *must* you be thinking of me. I'm not always so waspish, but talking about Francesca has reminded me of how she behaved towards people, many of them our friends, who had invited her into their homes. Quite dreadful.' she finished softly, slowly stirring her tea.

'It couldn't have been pleasant; I can appreciate that all too well, Virginia, and I'm sure Robert has already told you that we have you to thank for giving us a much-needed lead into where she'd gone. Meanwhile,' he continued, 'and I know this is rather like going over old ground, but when you saw her a few weeks ago, what sort of impression did you get of the relationship between her and this man, Denny, she was with?'

'Well,' she said thoughtfully, 'although they were on first name terms, there was nothing intimate, romantic, I mean, about the way they were talking to each other. It's difficult to put into words, Howard, but I was able to take a closer look at them both because I left before them and had to walk past their table –'

'– Yes?' he prompted, interested to hear what she was going to say next and whatever it was, he felt it would be useful to them.

'It was more her expression than anything else. She didn't like him.'

'Was it so obvious, then?'

'To anyone who didn't know her, I don't think it would have been, but,' she said, 'although I had never been a close friend of Francesca, had only exchanged sociable niceties, in fact, I had watched her often enough. I wasn't the only one; many of my women friends were the same. There was something snake-like about her; the way she used to sidle up to people, men, of course, and only those she was particularly attracted to. She would never take her eyes from them and the only time was when she became either bored or decided she didn't like them after all, and then she had this habit of looking past them and probably didn't realise it, but her eyes would narrow, making absolutely no attempt to disguise her boredom. Not an attractive trait at all.' Virginia finished.

'I see,' Howard nodded, understanding completely and learning even more about the characteristics of Francesca Cristofoli, 'you've been extremely descriptive; thank you, Virginia.'

'If I've been any help, I'm glad.'

'Oh, you have. She appears to have been travelling on her own, but it is always possible she has other friends in Hong Kong, apart from the man she was with in here.'

'It's strange you should say that, because it has just reminded me of something which had completely slipped my mind until now.'

'Yes?'

'As you know, I was already here before they came up the stairs, and she stopped to shake hands with a woman who was sitting further away from me.'

'I don't suppose you know who she was?' realising he was really expecting too much.

'I do, as it happens,' Virginia smiled, 'although I've never met her, but parts of Hong Kong are very much like a village to us expatriates.'

'I can well imagine.' Howard said.

'Her name is Louisa Lambeth and she's the editor of "Woman's World".

Chapter Six

The flight from London to Hong Kong arrived on time at Kai Tak Airport on Monday at six o'clock in the afternoon. As soon as she reached the baggage reclaim area, Natasha switched on her mobile to find a text message waiting from Nicholas: "Welcome to Hong Kong, sweetheart," she read, "I should be with you around eight this evening and we can go out and celebrate your safe arrival in Hong Kong."

Kai Tak Airport, she decided, a little disappointed, was like any other international airport she had ever been in. In her naivety, she had really believed this one would be different, but it wasn't. The same high ceilings; the line of trolleys linked together and the carousels, they were all identical, also she noticed with resignation, taking an inordinately length of time to come to life and for the first piece of luggage to appear through the rubber flaps. A good ten or fifteen minutes later, with both pieces of luggage piled on to a trolley, Natasha, following the instructions Nicholas had given her, took one of the taxis from the rank outside the building, giving the driver Nicholas' address in Causeway Bay. As he had said, the concierge behind the desk in the foyer knew who she was and immediately handed her the spare key to Nicholas' apartment on the ninth floor. The view from the lounge window was fantastic; in the foreground, Victoria Park and over towards the left, the enormous Times Square mall where he had told her she would quite literally be able to shop until she dropped! But, apart from what she had learned from him over the last few weeks, she had done her own homework and longed to get out there and experience for herself the various delights practically on the doorstep: the restaurants; the chic cafes and bars and the shops. Natasha was looking forward to browsing around the four Japanese departmental stores and to venturing into the stylish Southeast Asian Lane Crawford store, although knowing it was unlikely she would ever be able to afford to pay their prices. But then there was Jardine's Bazaar, one of Hong Kong's oldest street markets, right in the heart of Causeway

Bay where she could probably go on a spending spree. It would certainly take a bit of getting used to Natasha thought, reluctantly moving away from the window and deciding to occupy the time until Nicholas arrived by unpacking. Also, she wanted to freshen up, have a shower and find something cool to wear, wanting to look her best for him and wondering what kind of restaurant he would be taking her to. It did occur to her, but only briefly, to phone her father and let him know she was here, but decided not to. It wasn't as though he would criticise her for giving up her job with the newspaper; that wasn't Roddie's way, but at the same time she thought it might not be such a bad idea to wait until she was more settled, hopefully with something substantial, such as finding employment and wasn't totally reliant on her boyfriend, a man he had never met or, if it came to that, even heard of. Somehow, she didn't think he would approve. She had seen so little of her father over the years; if someone had asked her what he was like, really like, that is, she would, she knew, find it difficult to describe him. She had been too young when he'd left and while recognising this had created a void in her earlier years, it hadn't worried her unduly. It could have had something to do with how reluctant her mother had been to discuss him and then, once she had married Conrad, his name was seldom mentioned and instinctively, even as young as she had been, Natasha had sensed it would be more harmonious not to. Perhaps now she was here, living near him and away from England, she could get to know him, but she didn't know. It may be possible she sighed, going into the bathroom.

The telephone in the lounge was ringing as she stepped out from the shower. Grabbing one of Nicholas' large fluffy white towels from the rail, she wrapped it around her and, fully expecting to hear his voice, picked up the receiver.

'I'd like to speak to Nicholas, please.'

'Nicholas isn't here;' Natasha said, 'he's working late this evening.'

'He can't be.'

'Sorry?'

'I've already phoned the bank and they told me he'd finished for the day.' the woman said; her voice young with an accent Natasha couldn't place. 'Anyway,' she continued, making no attempt at any politeness, 'who are you, anyway?'

'My name is Natasha Bailey,' Natasha told her, very much wanting to bring the conversation to an end, 'and I'm Nicholas' girlfriend.'

'Girlfriend!'

'That's what I said.'

'Never!'

'Listen,' Natasha said sharply, 'I don't know who you are, but I can't help you. Either you call back later when Nicholas is here or you give me your name and I'll tell him you called.'

The only reply Natasha got was the disengaged tone. She had been cut off. Replacing the receiver and trying to dismiss the unpleasantness of the call, she walked over to the window, at that moment, the first time since leaving England, feeling very much on her own. She'd mention the call to Nicholas she decided and hear what he had to say. The woman could have been an ex-girlfriend. Natasha wasn't so naive to think he had never had any, but, he had made it abundantly clear he was in love with her and had wanted her to come out to Hong Kong and be with him and she had believed him and still did.

At the same time as Natasha was staring unseeingly across towards the shores of Kowloon, Hugh Innis was outside the bank building shaking hands with Nicholas and thanking him for a satisfactory conclusion.

'That went well, Nicholas;' he said to him, 'far smoother than I expected, in fact.'

'I never doubted we wouldn't pull it off, you know. As I said to you and your partner, I've worked for the bank for a number of years and they have considerable respect for me. There won't be any problems.'

'I hope not.'

'Of course not. I understand the way things work out here and, besides, by the time they notice the formula is no longer in their safe deposit box, you will, I expect, be winging your way back to London.'

'That's true.'

*

It had been Juliet's suggestion they meet for a drink in 'The Captain's Bar' at seven that evening after surprising him by her phone call earlier in the day. Roddie hadn't tried to contact her again, deciding to wait a couple of days and hoping in the interim he could, if possible, dilute the strength of his attraction for her. He knew also he would shortly have to do something about Louisa, continuing to suffer pangs of guilt, tinged with self-disgust by his behaviour, and had made up his mind to phone her when he finished work, but hearing Juliet's voice again immediately prevented him. It was as though she had cast a spell over him although the rapidly diminishing common sense part of his brain was warning him to hold back on furthering a relationship which, if he could only have the sense to realise it he could be entering a kind of no-man's land. By the end of the weekend, he had almost convinced himself he had heard Juliet's voice on Friday evening, but that was as far as he had allowed himself to work out whether he was right or not. But now, this evening, seeing her again standing in the foyer of the hotel waiting for him, any good intentions he may have had, vanished. She was wearing a white linen two-piece and had tied her hair back loosely, the myriad of lights from the chandeliers picking up the copper highlights.

'Hi.' she smiled up at him.

'Hi. Sorry I'm a bit late; got caught up at the last moment. I hope you haven't been waiting too long.'

'No, it's okay; I've only just arrived. Shall we go in?' she suggested, linking her arm with his.

Trying not to show his surprise, although she had done exactly the same on Thursday, but feeling ridiculously pleased with himself and trying not to place too much importance on what to her could very well be quite a natural gesture. 'The Captain's Bar' was busy as it always was at that time of the evening, being a favourite rendezvous for office workers in Central and hotel guests having a pre-dinner drink. There weren't many free tables; only one or two at the far end of the bar, and they made their way over there. Roddie spotted a few familiar faces, including Nicholas Eastman from the bank. He was in deep conversation with someone although he did look up as they passed their table.

'Roddie.' Nicholas smiled, standing up to shake hands with him. 'How are you?'

'I'm fine, thanks.' he answered, 'I'd like to introduce you to Juliet, a friend of mine.' he added and not missing the way Nicholas looked at her. No doubt she was accustomed to such open admiration from the opposite sex; she was decidedly good to look at.

'Juliet.' Nicholas Eastman said, taking her hand, 'A pretty name for a pretty lady.'

'Thank you.' Juliet said, pulling her hand away from his firm grasp.

'Perhaps the next time I see you, Roddie, I'll be able to introduce you to another pretty lady.'

'Oh, yes,' Roddie smiled; the man was so incredibly transparent, 'A new girlfriend, Nicholas?'

'Yes, Roddie. A new girlfriend and she is *the* one! She has actually given up her job in London to come out here to live with me.' he added.

The man he was with was showing no interest, also Nicholas had made no move to introduce him, but it wasn't until they were sitting down a few tables away from them, he began to wonder why. Roddie had known Nicholas Eastman for some years; only through the bank, never socially, and he had always labelled him as a gregarious sort of guy. Super-confident, in fact, therefore it seemed a little out of character he hadn't made any attempt to draw his companion into the introductions, but then mentally shrugging off why this was, Roddie turned his attentions to Juliet.

'I tried to phone you on Saturday,' he said to her, 'but was told you were away for the weekend.'

'I know you did, Roddie; at least,' she continued, 'I assumed it was you, but my maid told me you hadn't given her your name.'

'Anyway,' he said, 'I'm glad you phoned, Juliet. I enjoyed Thursday evening; at least after we had left "Annie's"!'

'Some place, eh?'

'I should say so, but surprisingly popular, or some might say, not so surprisingly!'

'Quite.' she laughed.

'What sort of day have you had?'

'Busy, but fairly productive. I'm trying to remember where I've seen him before, Roddie.'

'Who, Nicholas Eastman?'

'No, not him; the man with him. They're just leaving.' she added, looking over his shoulder to where they were sitting, 'But, I'm sure I've seen him somewhere; a couple of weeks ago it would have been, but I can't think where.'

'It'll come to you .'

'Probably. And, what about you, Roddie; have you had a busy day in your laboratory?'

'Not particularly,' he smiled at her, 'but I don't spend all that much time in the laboratory, mostly in the office in front of a computer screen.'

'All high tech stuff, then?'

'These days, yes.'

'You said on Thursday you were off to London this week.'

'That's right, but only for a few days. As I mentioned to you, I have to attend a seminar and on the last day I'll be lecturing in Oxford, then flying back next Tuesday.'

'Where do you stay when you're in London?' she asked, 'At a hotel or with friends?'

'A hotel, usually the 'Hotel Russell' in Bloomsbury; regrettably, I've lost touch with the friends I used to have there.'

'That's a pity,' she sympathised, 'and no family even?'

'I have a daughter; she's called Natasha and she's working in London.'

'Have you really? How old is she?'

'Twenty-two.' he told her, by now, becoming accustomed to her directness.

'A big girl.' was the only comment she made, looking at him closely under lowered lashes, making it impossible for him to fathom out what she was thinking.

'I'm forty-four years of age, Juliet;' he said quietly, 'quite old.'

'Forty-four is not old, Roddie.' she smiled, touching him lightly on the arm.

'A lot older than you and,' he added, 'before you say anything, I'm not going to ask a lady how old she is.'

'Thank you, kind sir,' she was still smiling, 'but it's no secret; I'm thirty-five, or I will be next Wednesday.'

'Happy birthday.' he grinned. Nine years wasn't such a big gap, he thought.

*

Howard waited until early evening, almost seven Hong Kong-time, before phoning London and was put through to Robert Anderson immediately.

'Hello, Howard,' Robert said, 'glad to hear you arrived safely; I've been waiting for your call. I expect you're tired?'

'Not too bad, Robert,' he said, 'but I'm looking forward to getting my head down tonight.'

'Travelling doesn't get any easier, does it?' Robert sympathised and not for the first time over the years Howard had worked for him, he felt grateful for the depth of understanding of his superior. Robert Anderson, as far as Howard was concerned, never had to crack the proverbial whip; merely by his personality, coupled with his fairness and without making too much of an issue of whatever case they were working on, had the ability to bring out the best in his officers.

'No, you're right,' Howard agreed, 'I met your friend, Virginia Bannister, this afternoon.'

'Good. And did you learn anything new?'

'I believe I did, as a matter of fact.'

'I thought you would. She's a very switched-on lady, don't you agree?'

'Very much so.'

'So, Howard,' he asked him, 'what did you glean?'

'The most important,' Howard began, 'was the excellent picture she portrayed of Francesca; 'in fact he went on, a photograph of that particular lady would have been almost superfluous.'

'Go on,' Robert chuckled, 'this, I want to hear.'

'It wasn't so much as Francesca's appearance – we already had a good idea of what she looked like even although she had made an attempt to change it – it was her mannerisms. Virginia was able to give me a very clear insight to the woman's personality, in particular, how she behaved when she was with someone; a man naturally.'

'That figures.' was all Robert said.

'Yes, well,' Howard went on, 'Virginia got the distinct impression Francesca didn't like this man, Denny.'

'It was no romantic liaison, then?'

'Far from it, from what she said. You see, Francesca upset a number of Virginia's women friends before she made her quick exit from the London scene. Not only in stealing their jewellery, but their husbands also!'

'Well, well, let's hope her days for that kind of behaviour are coming to an end. It's too early to have heard from Bogota, but as soon as I do, I'll give you a call. Did Virginia remember anything else?'

'She did, yes. It only occurred to her this afternoon when I was with her, but Francesca appeared to be relatively, and I use the word loosely, Robert, friendly with a woman called Louisa Lambeth. She had been in the Clipper Lounge at the same time.'

'Louisa Lambeth? Now, that rings a bell.'

'She's the editor of a woman's magazine here.'

'Of course she is. I remember now.'

'Did you ever meet her?'

'I did once,' he said, 'it was some years ago; I'm trying to remember the circumstances. I think it was at a book fair on Kowloon side and Virginia and her husband introduced me to her. I can't really say I took to her; a bit too self-assertive for my liking. A good-looking woman, but not terribly approachable, if you know what I mean?'

'I think so.' Howard said hesitatingly.

'Let me put it to you this way,' Robert explained, 'if it had been seventy-nine years ago she would have been a good candidate for the Pankhurst lot!'

'Oh, dear.'

'I'm probably being unkind; my caustic tongue runs away with me at times, Howard, but I do like my women friends to be feminine!'

'I agree; we men don't like the feeling of being emasculated, do we?'

'No, we do not!' and Howard could tell by his voice he was smiling, 'What do you plan to do next, Howard?'

'As much as I'd like to approach Louisa Lambeth, I think it would be best to stand back, bearing in mind Francesca will be here tomorrow. I don't know how friendly the two women are, but I don't want to run the risk of her alerting Francesca of our interest.'

'I think you're right. Incidentally, Frank Mitchell should have arrived in Hong Kong by now, so you can expect a call from him some time tomorrow.'

'Where is he staying?'

'He's booked into the 'Excelsior' in Causeway Bay; considered it wiser, in case she will be at the 'Mandarin' as before and on the off chance she may have spotted him at Kai Tak, but at least she won't realise who you are, Howard.'

'And, if she is booked in here,' Howard said, 'I will then be able to take over from him.'

'Yes, that's exactly what I mean. I am aware, you know, Howard, we are very much groping around in the dark with this case. We haven't a great deal to go on yet, but I firmly believe, given time, we will. Meanwhile, I know I needn't say this to you, but watch your back. I don't like the sound of this Denny chap; he could be bad news and remember he's on his own territory and will know the Island inside out.'

*

Marion Godwin, partner with Godwin, Cheung & Fong, Lawyers, had invited Hugh for dinner, arranging to meet him in the restaurant, 'Jimmy's Kitchen', in Wyndham Street.

After leaving Nicholas, knowing it was extremely unlikely he would ever see him again, and not particularly wanting to, he had returned to the Mandarin Hotel, taking the lift up to his room on the seventh floor. Ever since leaving the bank with the formula in the inside pocket of his jacket, he had felt uncomfortably vulnerable; as though that single sheet of paper had become fluorescent. He was far too conscious of walking around with it on his person, in particular with the incriminating piece of evidence printed on the laboratory's headed notepaper, and decided his briefcase would be a more secure place, but first, as an extra precaution in the event an over-zealous airport official taking an interest in it, he placed the formula in one of the hotel's envelopes, tucking it down the inside of the briefcase and re-setting the combination lock.

In his life Hugh Innis had been in some precarious situations, most of which he had always managed to extricate himself, emerging relatively unscathed, but that half hour when Nicholas Eastman had taken him into the bank's vault and along the underground passageway to the area where the safe deposit boxes were stored, had taken its toll. He had, during his long career of working on the wrong side of the law, always made sure he had been in complete control, but this evening, he'd had to relinquish that role to Nicholas and this had unnerved him. As Nicholas had told Eddie and him, a security guard had been on duty in the hallway. He had been outside the door to the vaults; a copy of the evening's newspaper open on the desk in front of him and had, as Nicholas had predicted, shown little interest when they walked in. And, again, after Nicholas, bringing down the McLellands' safe deposit box from the top shelf and extracting the formula for which he had travelled all the way from England, and walked out of the vault, the guard hadn't even looked up from his paper. Even although, Hugh had still felt nervous and it hadn't been until he had reached the relative safety of his hotel room, he began to relax. He wasn't looking forward to spending the rest of the evening with Marion Godwin. He hardly knew the woman; she was Eddie's friend, but he thought to himself as he made his way downstairs, he didn't have a great deal of choice.

Marion was already in the restaurant by the time he arrived, walking the short distance from the hotel to Wyndham Street. 'Jimmy's Kitchen', in the basement of the South China Building, was one of Hong Kong's longest established restaurants, going as far back as the 1920s. Split level, dark wood flooring and wall panelling gave it a comfortable and colonial feeling and, as he walked up to where she was sitting, Hugh thought perhaps the evening might not turn out to be so bad after all. He had been there a couple of times before and remembered how much he had enjoyed their house speciality of beef stroganoff, suddenly realising he was hungry.

'Hello, Hugh.' she greeted him, 'Good to see you again. Everything alright?'

'So far, Marion,' he said, leaning forward to kiss her on both cheeks, 'at least, I'm here and there are no bells ringing!'

'That's a relief,' she laughed; 'so, do I take it this means we can relax and enjoy our meal?'

'I hope so.' Hugh said, pulling out the chair in front of her and sitting down.

'Shall we have an aperitif?' she asked him, 'I've waited until you arrived before ordering anything.'

'I'll have a campari; what about you?'

'A kir royale, please.'

They were half-way through their drinks before she made any further reference to the reason why he was in Hong Kong.

'When do you plan returning to London, Hugh?' she asked, looking across the table at him; the dark brown eyes serious now.

'Early Wednesday morning. Why?'

'I think it might be a good idea for you to leave the Island as soon as possible.'

'You're alarming me.'

'I don't intend to,' she said, 'but earlier this evening I had a call from McLellands' managing director and he's instructed me to go ahead with the patenting of the formula.'

'Yes? And what does this mean exactly.'

'It means, Hugh,' she said, lifting the glass to her lips, 'they will be sending someone to my office tomorrow morning, after collecting it from the bank, and as soon as they discover the formula isn't where it's supposed to be, well –' hesitating for a fraction of a second, her eyes not leaving his face, '- need I say anymore?'

'But,' he said quickly, 'surely it was only a matter of time before that was going to happen?'

'I don't think you understand, Hugh,' she stressed, leaning forward slightly in her chair, 'I'm not only concerned about your cover, also, quite frankly, I am thinking about my own personal position in this business.'

'I'm sorry if I'm being obtuse, but I really don't know what you mean.'

'I'll put it differently, then, shall I? Before eleven tomorrow morning I'm going to get a call from the laboratory to tell me the formula isn't in the bank and, depending on how they want to take the matter on from there, they are bound to report this to the manager and questions will undoubtedly be asked. Nicholas Eastman, not to put too fine a point on it, is a loose cannon; he'll do or say anything to save his skin. That's the way he is and the further away you are, the better in my opinion. As for myself,' she added, a twisted smile marring her features for a second and reminding him that here was a woman who was well used to a fight, 'I can deal with the likes of Nicholas Eastman, but the bottom line is,' she emphasised, 'nobody should know about my connection with Bristow & Innis!'

'Nicholas Eastman doesn't know our names, Marion.'

'Yes, Eddie had already told me that, but that doesn't mean Nicholas won't be able to find out. He's too clever by half, Hugh,' she went on, 'also, I'm all too aware of his background; in a nutshell, he is not exactly squeaky-clean!'

'I didn't think he was; otherwise he wouldn't have agreed to help us.'

'Yes, but I don't think you fully realise what he is like. He's only thirty-three; he's learned how to survive in his self-made jungle. Oh, he hasn't a police record or anything like that, but from what I've been hearing, he has, over the last ten years or so, been very close to it, where honesty gets tangled up with dishonesty, if you know what I mean. So far, he's been lucky and that cannot last forever.'

'You say you can deal with him,' Hugh reminded her, 'in what way?'

'Best not to ask, Hugh. Nicholas is smart, but he isn't that smart and I've been around for considerably more years than he has. Also,' she added, 'I, too, know how to save my skin and I play a very dirty game in the survival stakes!'

Chapter Seven

Roddie had gone personally to the bank the following morning to collect the formula and take it to the lawyers' office; a couple of blocks away, in Queen's Road Central. It wasn't Nicholas Eastman who escorted him to the vaults, but one of his colleagues, who told him Nicholas was taking a day's leave to spend time with his girlfriend who had recently arrived from England.

He had often heard the expression of when one's blood ran cold, but he had never really understood what it meant, but on that Tuesday morning, as he stared in disbelief at the remaining contents of the safe deposit box, the realisation hit him with the same force he was sure as having a bucket of icy water thrown over him. The formula, for what they had hoped would revolutionise a cure for malaria and ultimately eradicate the life-threatening disease, had gone! The lease and supporting documents for the company's premises in Des Voeux Road were in there, but nothing else.

'Is there something wrong, Mr Mortimer?'

'I'm afraid there is,' Roddie said, dragging his eyes away from the box and looking at the concern on the young man's face, 'the document I came for isn't here.'

'Could someone else from your company have collected it?' he suggested.

'No; no-one else would have been given the authority.'

It was obvious to Roddie the man was completely out of his depth, no doubt never having been in such a situation before and he almost felt sorry for him, watching as he locked the safe deposit box and placed it back on the shelf. Now he would have to report the matter to his superior, probably realising in advance there would be a full enquiry among the executive staff at the bank, which would be bound to cause unease and suspicion because it was clear to Roddie that whoever took the formula must have had a member of the staff with him; there had been no break-in after all. He would, of course, accompany him to the manager's office and after that, it would be his turn to face his directors at McLellands. Roddie had spent the last six months working on perfecting the formula, being solely responsible for collating the satisfactory feed-back from the various tests which had been carried out over this period. Apart from his opposite number in California, with whom he had been collaborating on the project, no-one else knew the exact constituents of the drug and, although they had taken the normal steps to maintain secrecy, very much aware of the fierce competition in the field, there were a number of people who had had to be informed, namely the directors of the company, both here, in Hong Kong, and in the States, including their lawyers, Godwin, Cheung & Fong, in order for them to prepare the necessary paperwork for the time when they would be instructed to apply for patenting rights. In essence, Roddie concluded, it was no secret; also, the thought suddenly occurring, someone had known where to find the formula.

Roddie spent less than half an hour with the bank manager before returning to Des Voeux Road. The man had been as shocked as he was when he heard and immediately did all he could to try and establish when and how this could have happened. There were, he explained, six of the bank's employees, including himself, who had the authority to take any of their customers to where the safe deposit boxes were stored, and after asking them if they had accompanied anyone in there since Roddie had placed the formula in the box fourteen days ago, only two executives said they had, but it had been quickly verified neither of the customers were from the laboratories, which left only Nicholas Eastman to be questioned. The manager did try to phone Nicholas, but without any success and promising to try again later; for the time being Roddie had no alternative but to curb his impatience.

Andrew Howe, or Andy as he was more affectionately known, the managing director of McLellands; a Scotsman from Aberdeen, fast approaching sixty, had spent his whole career in Hong Kong. In all the years Roddie had worked for the company he had always found him to be a reasonable, down-to-earth man. Andy Howe had never forgotten his roots and had brought with him from Scotland a strong measure of stoicism and dry humour, although, as Roddie faced him now, he couldn't help feeling nervous; not knowing how he would react when he heard the news.

'This is not good, Roddie.' he said at last.

'I know, sir. We never expected anything like this to happen.'

'It does make you wonder though, doesn't it? Can't help seeing the irony. We could have put the formula in our own company safe, but in our infinite wisdom, we decided it would be more secure in the bank's vaults!'

'It looks as though someone managed to convince one of their executives to gain access to the safe deposit box and as I've already mentioned,' Roddie continued, 'the manager still has to speak to Nicholas Eastman, so I expect once he has, he'll get back to us.'

'Yes, Roddie,' Andy Howe said, 'in the meantime, we are minus the formula.'

'The original, yes,' Roddie answered, 'although I still have it on my computer. It's in code, of course, but it wouldn't take me all that long to put together again. The final result would be identical, sir.'

'That is certainly one option we have,' Andy Howe said slowly, 'but we are in a bit of a cleft stick here in not knowing when the formula was taken, which automatically leads to the question of where exactly it is at this moment.'

'You mean whoever has the formula may have already patented it?'

'Yes, and if that was the case and we decided to go ahead with a replacement, by the time it was eventually patented, the drug may actually be on the market, or worse, the media would have heard about it and the news would be plastered over the pages of the newspapers!'

'And, then we would be in breach of the patenting regulations.'

'Yes, Roddie; for trying to launch our own invention!'

'Ironic.'

'Indeed it is. By all means, Roddie, go ahead and make out the replacement formula, but I think we should wait until the bank manager has a talk with Nicholas Eastman. That's the best advice I can come up with, unless you have another suggestion.'

'I wish I had,' Roddie said, 'but I agree with you entirely. If it's possible, we have to find out more.'

'Right. And now I need to speak to the Board.'

'Perhaps we should let the lawyers know, sir. They would have been expecting the formula to be with them by this time.'

'I'll take care of that, Roddie; I expect you have enough to do and I'll let you know as soon as I hear from the bank.'

*

'I apologise for disturbing you, Nicholas, on your day's leave, but I would appreciate it if you could come into the bank.'

'That's alright,' Nicholas said, glancing across to Natasha and giving her an apologetic smile, 'I can be there in ten minutes or so. Is there a problem?' realising as soon as the words left his mouth it had been a pointless question. This was the first time his manager had ever phoned him at home and he didn't need two guesses to know why. Sooner than he'd expected, certainly, but he was prepared.

'Rather a serious one, Nicholas, but I'll wait until you get here.'

Replacing the receiver, he joined Natasha at the open window.

'I take it that was your boss, Nicholas?'

'Afraid so, sweetheart,' he said, kissing her lightly on the cheek, 'but hopefully, I won't be there long. Why don't you come with me; there's a cafe next door to the bank, you can wait for me there and then we can find somewhere for lunch.'

'Of course I will. I'd like to buy a newspaper when we're out; I want to start job-hunting as soon as I can.'

'There's no rush, you know,' he said, kissing her again, 'but if it will make you feel happier we'll get one. The 'South China Morning Post' is the paper you need and we'll be able to get a copy at the MTR station.

Nicholas had meant what he had said; he wanted Natasha to take her time in finding a job, not just to take anything for the sole reason of earning a salary. He had wanted her to come out to Hong Kong and realised she was giving up, not only her career in London, but severing her ties with what had become part of her life. He was eleven years older than Natasha and from the very first moment when he'd seen her in the wine bar in Kensington, he'd fallen in love with her. At thirty-three, he had been in love before, but what he had felt for Natasha was different. All those previous affairs had instantly faded into insignificance and now she was here, living with him, her presence was giving him a rare feeling of wellbeing; his life now had a purpose and he hoped Natasha would settle into what was a totally different lifestyle and, most importantly, she must never learn of that other side of his nature, the one that thrived on the thrill of taking risks, albeit always calculated ones. Nicholas Eastman had no illusions about this flaw in his character, but was confident he could continue playing the two roles and ensuring they were kept well apart. Natasha was intelligent; her training in journalism would have added that extra dimension to her perception. She would be quick to suss out anything untoward or out of the ordinary in his manner. She had told him about Marcia phoning yesterday; also how rude she'd been, going as far as putting the phone down on her. That had been unfortunate and he'd had to think rapidly, deciding on being honest; namely, that Marcia was a woman he used to know and although he had finished with her some time ago, she still continued to pester him. Natasha had been understanding; she didn't ask questions and all she said was that Marcia would give up eventually and he hoped she was right.

Leaving Natasha in the cafe, the bulky edition of the newspaper tucked under her arm, he made his way directly to the bank manager's office.

'Ah, Nicholas,' his manager said and beckoning towards the chair in front of his desk, 'thank you for coming in. I could, of course, have asked you this question on the phone, but due to the serious nature of the problem which will need to be discussed, thought it best you were here.'

'Yes, sir?' Nicholas said, sitting down.

'First of all, Nicholas, have you escorted any of our customers to their safe deposit boxes during the last couple of weeks?'

'Only two, sir. One last week, Wednesday it was; I'd need to check my diary for the exact time and then last evening.'

'And they were?'

'Mr Cheung from the Golden Dragon restaurant in Nathan Road on the Wednesday and Mr Thomas from McLellands Laboratories was here yesterday.'

'I don't think we need to concern ourselves with Mr Cheung's visit, but it is becoming a little clearer, so let me put you in the picture, Nicholas. Earlier this morning Mr Mortimer came to the bank to collect a document from his company's safe deposit box, only to find it was missing.'

'Missing, sir? You mean it has been stolen?'

'It looks very much as though it has been. Now, this Mr Thomas; had you met him before?'

'No, I hadn't. You see, I received a call from him in the afternoon, quite late it was,' he added, 'and we made the arrangement for him to be here at seven-thirty.'

'And as you didn't know him,' the manager asked, 'presumably you would have asked to see his company pass.'

'Oh, yes, I did, sir. He was from the laboratories' parent company in California; he'd already told me that on the phone.'

'I see, so you saw the company pass?'

'Yes.'

'Tell me, Nicholas, have you seen any of McLellands' passes?'

'No, I haven't, now you come to mention it. There's never been any need, sir. Only their MD, Mr Howe, and Mr Mortimer, also their accountant, ever came to the bank and I've known them for a number of years, so there was never any need to check their identity.'

'I understand.'

'I'm sorry, sir; it looks as if all of this is my fault; that is, if Mr Thomas wasn't a bona fide employee of the company.'

'No, Nicholas, I'm not blaming you, but it does look as though he was an imposter. Obviously he was standing next to you as you were opening the safe deposit box?'

'Yes, he was.'

'So you would have noticed whether he took anything out of the box?'

'He did, but naturally I had no idea what it was, sir; a single sheet of A4 which he immediately put in his jacket pocket.'

*

It was late afternoon when Howard received a call from Robert Anderson, shortly after talking to Frank Mitchell who would by now be on his way to the airport to await the arrival of Francesca Cristofoli.

'The report from Bogota has just come in, Howard.' were his first words sounding exactly as though he was picking up from where he'd left off the previous day.

'Anything interesting?' Howard asked him, although knowing Robert as well as he did, he could tell by the slight quickening in the normal soft timbre of his voice, he thought there could be and waited for him to elaborate.

'It is possible, but I'll give you the gist of the report and you can decide for yourself. Our contact out there did a thorough job and in a relatively short time. Apparently, Francesca Cristofoli; incidentally, I suggest we continue to refer to her in her real name, as Virginia has said, she's living in the capital, although not in an apartment, but she occupies a suite on the top floor of 'The Imperial Hotel' in the centre of Bogota which is, given what we know of her character, not so surprising, paid for by Senor Antonio Gomez, a senior member of the government. In other words, and I make no apologies for my rather archaic description, Howard, she's his mistress.'

'You mean, of course, he's married?' hearing the familiar chuckle at the other end of the line.

'Very much so; he has five children! Quite grown up, but he continues, in a superficial way, to give all outward appearances of being a respectable member of Bogota's more affluent society including holding a high position in the control of the country's economic and financial affairs.'

'When are they able to meet, I wonder.' Howard said, 'I know Bogota is a vast city, but surely, in time, it would be inevitable for someone to spot them together.'

'By making frequent trips into neighbouring Brazil. A much-travelled lady, Francesca Cristofoli.'

'Quite. No wonder we've never been able to find her.'

'I know;' he agreed, 'included in the report was a fairly precise profile on Senor Gomez, but the most interesting piece of information was that he is a joint owner of an emerald mine.'

'Well, well,' Howard said, 'I wonder if that has any significance or not.'

'As to that, we don't know, but at least we can keep this knowledge to the forefront of our minds during the investigation of this case.'

'We will indeed. It would make sense, though, wouldn't it, Robert? If emeralds were being brought in by her, it could explain her regular visits and short ones at that.'

'I don't discount that for a moment. Let's hope that between you and Frank working together out there will succeed in opening up this case.'

'Hopefully that will start as soon as she steps on to the tarmac at Kai Tak. I've spoken to Frank and he'll be keeping me informed from then until she arrives at the Mandarin.'

'You know for sure she'll be staying there?'

'Yes, I was able to make a discreet enquiry.'

'Good. Before I ring off, Howard, I've had some feedback on Hugh

Innes.'

'Right; I have seen him in the hotel today, so he's still here.'

'Not for much longer though; he's booked out on a flight back to Heathrow tomorrow morning.'

'Ah, so whatever business he was doing in Hong Kong is now complete.'

'Again, another imponderable, I'm afraid. However, it would seem he is in partnership with a man called Edward Bristow with offices in Savoy Street, off from The Strand, the description of their business the somewhat ambiguous one of Consultants.'

'Which could cover a multitude of things.'

'You're right. They appear to be genuine, by that I mean we couldn't find anything to the contrary. There is one thing though,' he went on; 'this visit is his second within the last few weeks.'

'Is it, now?'

'When you've seen him, Howard, has he always been on his own?'

'He has, yes. Wouldn't you have thought if he was here on business he would have given the impression of conducting business, at least be noticed as meeting up with the people he may have travelled out especially to see.'

'I would, yes.' Robert agreed, 'All I can say is, apart from us being aware of his past, there's absolutely nothing to go on. Afraid, we're a bit stymied there. We can keep an eye on him, also his partner, and if any more trips are made, not only to Hong Kong, but to anywhere else, we can arrange to have a tail put on either of them. That's the best I can come up with.'

*

Roddie had spent the afternoon putting together the duplicate formula and had almost finished when Andy Howe came into his office.

'I've had a call from the bank, Roddie;' he said, waiting until Roddie had switched off his computer, 'it looks as though we were right this morning. According to Nicholas Eastman, he escorted a man, purporting to be from our Californian offices, to where the safe deposit boxes are stored, also taking a sheet of paper out of the box.'

'And when was this, sir?'

'Last evening, around seven-thirty. According to Nicholas, he had taken a call from him earlier in the day, asking to make the appointment.

'And presumably Nicholas had never seen the man before?'

'That's right, he said he hadn't.'

'Didn't he ask to see any means of identity?'

'Oh, yes, and this is the ironic part of the whole incident, if one could call it that, but the man, calling himself Thomas by the way, did show him a card with our name printed on it, but as he had never seen any of our company cards before, I'm sorry to say, he assumed it was in order.'

'There's something bothering me, sir.' Roddie said, not really knowing where his thoughts were leading and the last he wanted to do was jump to conclusions which could make the matter worse than it was already.

'Yes, what is it?' Andy Howe asked, his expression serious as he looked at him and sitting down in front of the desk. 'I can see something is bothering you.'

'Well,' Robbie began tentatively, choosing his words carefully, 'you've told me this man arrived at the bank around seven-thirty –'

'- Yes?' prompting him.

'I saw Nicholas Eastman in 'The Captain's Bar' last evening about seven.'

'Go on.' Andy urged.

'He was with someone; I'd never seen the man before, not that that means anything, of course, but I've known Nicholas Eastman for some time and he didn't introduce him. Later, I thought it to be a little out of character.'

'Did you notice when he left the bar?'

'About ten or fifteen minutes later, I think, and they left together.'

'The manager did tell me the arrangement had been for this Mr

Thomas to meet him at the bank.'

'I dislike throwing aspersions at anyone, sir, but I can't help wondering, that's all.'

'Oh, I don't blame you and it doesn't stop us considering alternatives though, does it?'

'I suppose not. Will we be making a report to the authorities, sir?'

'I have to say, although it's my opinion we should, I don't have full agreement from the other directors, but what do you think, Roddie?'

'Like you, I believe we should. This is a serious matter and we don't know how often the same man has carried out similar thefts and if he was to be traced and found guilty, it would put a halt to them, at least for a while.'

*

Frank Mitchell positioned himself slightly further back from the crowd, waiting for the passengers to filter through to Arrivals, but close enough to where he would easily be able to follow Francesca Cristofoli when she finally appeared. This was the tricky part he thought; making sure he kept as close to her without making it obvious. Unless there was anyone here to meet her, she would be bound to make her way towards the taxi rank immediately outside the main doors and, although both he and Howard thought it likely she would go directly to the Mandarin Hotel, there was always the possibility she may call somewhere else first and he wanted to be able to hear what she said to the driver. Frank had been in the police force since leaving police college twenty-five years ago and for the last five of those he had been with the International Police. Working with Interpol suited him; he found the work more interesting, although at times a little bit too exciting, especially his last case in Singapore. But that was now successfully tied up and he was looking forward to becoming involved in this long unsolved one of bringing Francesca Cristofoli to task and with her final arrest to hand over the whole business to the courts to decide on her fate. Without a doubt

Frank concluded, keeping his eye on the passengers filtering through, more of them now, and each of them with that travel-weary look of people grateful to be on terra firma, Francesca had had a damn good run for her money.

He had no difficulty in recognising her. He hadn't had much to go on, but watching the frizzy blonde-haired woman pulling the scarlet travel bag behind her down the ramp, he knew this was Francesca Cristofoli. She was like an exotic bird he thought; tiny quick steps in those ridiculously high heels, the short tight silky skirt restricting every movement; the pointed features and the vivid red lipstick. It simply had to be her. None of them knew her age, and immediately, his mother's voice came to him. She would have said, without any hesitation, "Frank, she's mutton dressed as lamb." His mother had always had a caustic tongue, although he had to admit, there had been times when she hadn't been far away from the truth. Whatever age Francesca Cristofoli was didn't come into the equation: the woman was a crook and had, for years, somehow managed to evade the law and as he continued to watch her, as she confidently reached the end of the walkway to where everyone was standing, it was his brief to expose her. And he would!

He had to move quickly to slip in front of a couple, but he managed it, until he was immediately behind her in the taxi rank. The queue moved along steadily, as it usually did; as one taxi pulled away, another one rapidly replaced it. He waited until Francesca Cristofoli's taxi came to a halt beside her before stepping up closer until he could almost have touched her. She leaned towards the open window and in the voice he had already been told about; shrill and croaky and not in the least attractive, asked the driver to take her to number twenty-four Pedder Street. That was all he needed to know. Memorising the number of her taxi,' he took the next one and asked to be taken to number twenty and as they drew away from the kerb he took out his mobile and dialled Howard's number.

'She's arrived, Howard.'

'Good. Where are you at the moment?'

'About to approach the tunnel, so reception will deteriorate, but just to let you know she's on her way to twenty-four Pedder Street. I'm going there now and I'll give you a ring later. It will probably be difficult to follow her from there, so let's hope she'll go straight to the hotel.'

'Okay, Frank, thanks a lot. I'll be waiting here.'

The crackling on the line made it impossible to continue and they brought the call to a close. Frank knew Hong Kong well. He knew exactly where Pedder Street was, the road leading directly up from Des Voeux Road and, having a good memory, he also knew many of the cafes and shops on both sides of the street, including the antique shop at number twenty. Some minutes later they had emerged from the tunnel linking Kowloon with Hong Kong Island and driving speedily along Gloucester Road towards Central. Turning into Pedder Street he saw her taxi parked outside number twenty-four. Walking the short distance to the cafe next door, he went in, choosing one of the tables by the window and from where he would have a clear view of not only Francesca Cristofoli, but of anyone else who should emerge from the shop, which, after only a cursory glance, appeared to have changed hands. They had sold pictures before, he remembered, and not very good ones at that. He would take a closer look after she had gone, trusting he'd been right and she would be going straight to the hotel.

Frank was half-way through his espresso when she emerged; there was no-one with her, but still he would wait another five minutes or so before going into the shop. He wasn't disappointed; no sooner had Francesca's taxi moved away and was out of sight, the door of the shop opened again. The man who stood there for a second in the open doorway was Chinese: slim, in his early forties, not much more; the dark hair cut ultra-short; a lightweight grey suit and a pink and grey striped tie. In fact, Frank concluded, continuing to watch him, a typical Hong Kong businessman, although this one was slightly different. It wasn't only the confident set of the shoulders or the obvious affluence in the designer clothes; apart from the unmistakable Chinese features, he could almost pass as a westerner. Frank wasn't biased or prejudiced in any way, but he had seen enough ex-public school boys to recognise one when he saw one. The man had now moved away from the shop and was walking past the cafe window. He didn't look in, but straight ahead, all the while talking into his mobile. Could he have been the person Francesca had called in to see? She must have seen someone in there; she would hardly have asked to be brought to Pedder Street to go shopping!

Once again outside, Frank took the few steps to twenty-four and, looking in the window, tried to make out by the rather unusual display what it was the shop did sell. A freshly painted sign above the lintel didn't tell him much: "Dolly Mixtures". Dolly Mixtures were sweets; at least they were when he'd been a young lad, remembering back to each Saturday morning when his mother would give him his weekly pocket money and the first thing he used to do was buy a packet of sweets and very often, because he had discovered they went further than the others, he would buy four ounces of dolly mixtures. But, this window display, as far as he could see, didn't stock anything like that. It would seem they dealt mainly in cake decorations for various occasions; birthdays, weddings, Christmas and Easter and, puzzling over the incongruousness of it all, he turned the door handle and went inside where another surprise awaited him. Apart from the transformation of the interior, he fully expected to see there had been a change of staff, but this wasn't the case. The same Chinese man was in there but not sitting, as he had been the last time he came in, at a small table with a tin acting as his cash box, but in front of what looked like a brand new desk, complete with cash register and positioned in the centre of the shop.

'Good evening, sir.' he greeted, putting into place the ingratiating smile Frank remembered, although then he had thought it had been because he hadn't bought any of his pictures, but perhaps not; it could be a permanent part of his features.

'Good evening,' matching the man's politeness, 'I see you no longer sell pictures.'

'Already, sir, there are too many picture shops in Hong Kong.'

'You could be right.' This is like a game of chess Frank thought, each of them trying to fathom out the other's next move.

'And is there much call for – for cake decorations?'

'You would be surprised, sir. We, Cantonese, are becoming very interested in, as you say in Great Britain, doing our own thing.'

Tempted to use the word 'touché', Frank deliberately brought the banal conversation to an end and, making the excuse he had merely been interested to know what the inside of the shop looked like, made his exit, followed all the way back to the door, he was quite certain, by the Cheshire cat's smile.

Chapter Eight

'This is a quick call, Conrad,' Denny Yuan said, 'to let you know our courier has made her delivery.'

'No problems, then?' Conrad Bailey asked, his voice crackling with static.

'Not so far. However,' Denny went on, 'with regard to your end of the business, is everything on track?'

'As you so succinctly put it,' Conrad said, 'yes, everything is on track. This guy Mortimer arrives on Thursday at midnight and we'll take it from there. Trust me.'

'Oh, I do, my old friend. He'll be staying at the Hotel Russell incidentally; that may help you, in case things go awry at Heathrow.'

'I can assure you, Denny, they won't.'

'You sound confident.'

'And why shouldn't I? I've put considerable planning into this, you know and, I might add, it hasn't been easy; having to arrange everything virtually at the last minute.'

'Come on, Conrad, not so very much last minute! You've had three days to make your arrangements.'

'Alright, I get your point, Denny. I haven't had quite as much experience as you with all this strategy stuff!'

'Well, all I can say, my friend, as one very famous statesman once said: "I don't care how you do it; just do it!" '

'If I didn't know you better, Denny, I would think you were taking the proverbial Mickey!'

'Enough of all this, Conrad; as I've said, we now have this cache to dispose of and as speedily as possible. I'm making arrangements for the package to be sent out tomorrow night by DHL direct to your office.'

'I would much prefer to pick it up at Heathrow.'

'Sorry, but that won't be possible. Using the carriers is the best way, Conrad; believe me, I know what I'm doing.'

'I'm sure you do; I suppose I will just have to put up with it.'

'Too right you will. The situation, I would like to point out, is not too great here and I'm having to tread warily. Also,' he went on, 'we still don't know about this Mortimer guy. What I mean by that is, we don't know what he's up to.'

'That is, if he's up to anything.' Conrad reminded him.

'True, but as I said to you the other day, we really don't have any choice. The man was definitely snooping around and, hopefully, he's decided by this time, everything is above board in our little shop in Pedder Street.'

'Still selling pictures?'

'Don't ask, Conrad.' Denny warned him, 'Don't ask.'

Denny had reached the end of Pedder Street and was halfway along Des Voeux Road, keeping a look out for the first taxi which came along, when his mobile rang.

'Denny; it's me, Freddie.'

'Freddie. What's wrong?'

'I'm not sure, but I think there could be a problem.'

'Another one?' stifling a sigh of exasperation, well used to Freddie's recent paranoia about practically anyone who entered the shop.

'Yes, I think so.'

'Explain.'

'He's been in before, Denny; a few months ago and,' he added, petulance creeping into his voice, 'he didn't buy anything then.'

'So, why the panic?'

'I am not panicking, but I think there is something fishy about him.'

'Fishy?'

'You know what I mean. Fishy.'

'There are times, Freddie, when I wish you would remember you are a Chinaman and not some hick Englishman who doesn't know how to talk properly. But,' Denny went on, 'I know what you mean. For some reason you didn't like this man; perhaps you're going to tell me why?'

'I saw him arrive by taxi,' Freddie started to explain; 'it was just after your – your guest came in.'

'I trust we aren't going to conduct this conversation in some sort of code, Freddie.'

'No, I don't mean to, but someone may be listening.'

'Unlikely, but go on.'

'He got out of his taxi at the antique shop and then he went into the cafe next door and waited until you had left before coming along here. He tried to tell me the only reason he came in was because he wanted to see what sort of changes we had made to the shop.'

'It could have been true. You say he'd been in before; perhaps he was surprised to see the place as it is now.'

'That is possible,' Freddie grudgingly admitted, 'but I do not think so. He had a purpose alright; I'm certain about that. Perhaps he's police.'

'Come on, Freddie; don't be so melodramatic. We thought that about Mortimer and we were wrong there, weren't we?'

'I know,' he said, 'but perhaps we're right this time, Denny.'

What Freddie had told him was disturbing, although he had tried to make light of it to him. Freddie had worked for him for a long time and he had learned over the years to trust his judgement, although Denny had to admit, flagging down a taxi, Freddie had misjudged the intentions of Roddie Mortimer. There had been nothing incriminating in his apartment which he'd gone through thoroughly on Friday night. He appeared to be what he claimed to be and what he had told Juliet: an industrial chemist working for an American company here and had been for some time. Nothing sinister in that surely, but then, Denny had to admit, that was no proof he didn't have some connection with the authorities. Juliet Warburton was vain and had been convinced Roddie Mortimer had followed her up from the Star Ferries because, in her own words, he had fancied her! Perhaps he had, but in Denny's chauvinistic world, that was extreme behaviour. Alright, Juliet was a good-looking woman, but there were many like her out there and, although having had a number of English girlfriends in the past, he didn't think they were all that special, besides, he always made it a rule never to mix business with pleasure.

Juliet had been working for him almost from the time she went freelance. Right from the beginning he had realised her appearance was deceptive; behind her natural beauty lay a streak of ruthless determination equally matching his own. Juliet Warburton was an extremely ambitious young woman. She had a quick analytical brain and had, on more than one occasion, impressed him in the way she could juggle and manipulate figures to present an acceptable and credible balance sheet. On the strength of this ability he had made the decision to tell her about the emerald smuggling side of his enterprise, judging his knowledge of the way she worked, would act as her Achilles heel if she should take it into her head to become too smart!

Denny had one more call to make before he could call it a day, one he had put off doing for a few days and, dialling the number he knew off by heart, he waited to be put through to Marion Godwin.

'This is a surprise, Denny.' the dulcet tones of the woman he had once been passionately in love with, reached him, making him for a fraction of a second, regret the end of their relationship. He had first met Marion at London University when she had been striving to reach her goal of becoming a lawyer and while he, much to the disappointment of his father, had spent the time playing around. He hadn't wanted to go to university in the first place and at each opportunity he had done his utmost to prove this to him, but to no avail. He'd had no option but to see the course he was on right through to the end, emerging finally with an Honour's Degree in Languages and Business Economics. Even now, years later and looking back, he didn't know who had been more surprised. Certainly, he had been and, as a reward, his father had set him up in business with a plush office suite in Central; in the hub of Hong Kong's business centre and from where he was in a prime position to further his career as a professional opportunist. They had been good years and, apart from making the mistake of marrying Stella, the spoilt daughter of one of Hong Kong's oldest families, he had managed to conduct his life pretty successfully. Meeting Senor Antonio Gomez at a Government House reception eight years ago had added the icing to his particular cake. From then on, his lifestyle had improved dramatically and, ironically, as his bank balance grew, so did his status in Hong Kong. He never forgot he was a Chinaman, not for one minute, but at the same time he was very much aware of the other half of his heritage, namely his English mother and with the additive of being educated in Britain contributing towards his occasional attraction to the western woman. Stella, being the exception. Like himself, her family were from Beijing and when he met her at his cousin's wedding, young misguided fool he had been, he thought it was a good idea to marry her, also, as always, wanting to please his father.

'Hello, Marion;' he said, 'I've been meaning to get in touch, but you know how it is?'

'Do I, Denny?' the same caustic note in her voice which used to irritate him, 'Tell me about it.'

'Can we meet; this evening?'

'Why should we; I thought you and I had said everything we needed to, Denny.'

'I have another proposition to put to you which may be of interest.' he added quickly before she had a chance to interrupt.

'What sort of a proposition?'

'I'd rather discuss this with you face to face, Marion. Easier.'

'Alright, then, Denny.' she said, 'Where shall we meet?'

'How about the 'Yung Kee' in Wellington Street; it's practically on your doorstep.' he added, knowing how much she liked Cantonese food, and in his opinion, the 'Yung Kee' was among the best Chinese restaurants in Hong Kong with several awards to prove it.

'That will suit me fine, Denny.' she said and he knew she was smiling, that enigmatic cat-like smile which once he had known and even loved, although never quite understanding what lay behind it.'

*

Natasha had an interview at the offices of 'Woman's World' at eleven the following morning. She had been surprised how quickly they had responded to her emailed application, but Nicholas had told her this is what it was like in Hong Kong. "They don't hang about, sweetheart;' he'd said to her as he was about to leave for work earlier, "if they want something to happen, they make it happen. Don't worry," he'd added, "you'll get the job."

She wished she could share his confidence Natasha thought wryly, looking critically at her reflection in the dressing-table mirror for the hundredth time that morning and wondering whether she should have tied her hair back, but Nicholas had assured her it was perfect the way it was; falling in a straight line to her shoulders. After considerable deliberation she had decided to wear a pale lemon sleeveless dress; relatively smart, hoping the way she was going to present herself would convince them that although lacking in years of experience in the journalistic world, she was seriously committed and would be able to tackle whatever task they gave her. Always assuming, that is, she did get the job. As she'd said to her mother before she left England she was only a club reporter. Anyway, she thought, taking a deep breath, and picking up her bag from the bed, here goes, Natasha. It might not be such an ordeal after all.

She took a tram from Causeway Bay to Central, having already, thanks to Nicholas' tuition, learned what had appeared the first time to be a complicated procedure was really quite easy. 'Woman's World' offices were in Pottinger Street; one of the many roads leading from Queen's Road Central and she had no trouble finding them. The concierge directed her to a waiting room; a large spacious room overlooking Central and over towards Victoria Harbour. If she hadn't felt so nervous, Natasha would have enjoyed the view and one, she felt, she would never grow tired of, but instead, deliberately chose one of the chairs away from the window and where she wouldn't be distracted. She wanted to spend these few minutes preparing in her mind everything she thought her interviewer would ask her. It was like going to the dentist she thought, although hopefully not as painful!

'Miss Lambeth will see you now, Miss Bailey.' the girl said, standing in the open doorway; she was about her own age and as she waited giving what Natasha immediately interpreted as an encouraging smile. 'She's okay, really;' she whispered, 'she won't bite you.'

Miss Lambeth's office was on the second floor at the end of a carpeted corridor; the sign on the door telling her immediately that the lady she was about to see was the editor of the magazine.

The tall woman came round to the front of her desk to shake hands with Natasha; a firm handshake, the dark brown eyes appraising her. 'We'll sit here, shall we,' leading Natasha to the round table in the centre of the room, 'less formal than talking to each other across a desk?'

Placing her bag on the floor beside her feet Natasha sat down. The girl who had brought her upstairs had gone as quietly as she'd arrived in the waiting room. Natasha's first impression was the smooth efficiency pervading the place, not at all what she had been used to in London. The beginning of yet another learning curve she decided, taking a closer look at the woman who was about to interview her.

'You mentioned in your email, Miss Bailey,' she said, 'you had only recently arrived in Hong Kong?'

'That's right; on Monday evening.'

'And,' she continued, 'are you on your own here?'

'No, I'm living with my boyfriend; he's worked in Hong Kong for many years.'

'That's good. He'll be able to make this settling-in period considerably easier for you. Hong Kong can be a little intimidating at first, but you'll find it's worth the pain.'

'I hope so.' Natasha returned her smile. She was obviously making an attempt to put her at ease Natasha decided and was grateful.

'Well,' she continued, 'let me tell you a bit about us. I don't expect you will have had time to see a copy of our magazine?'

'Not yet, although I did try to find one on the newspaper stand earlier this morning.'

'No, you wouldn't have; it won't be out until tomorrow. 'Woman's World' is a bimonthly magazine. It has an extremely tight schedule; we cover a number of topical issues and as I'm sure you already appreciate, this means that each and every one of us is controlled by deadlines. I'll give you a copy before you go and you can see for yourself the type of content. We employ a number of freelance writers for the regular columns and everyone else works in-house and are full-time members of staff.

Miss Lambeth continued for another ten or fifteen minutes, interspersing what she had to say about the general structure of the magazine, with questions as to what she had been involved in, how much responsibility she had been given and not once did she mention the title of 'club reporter' and for the second time during the interview Natasha was grateful. Half-way through, she began to drop the Miss Bailey and was calling her Natasha, which immediately had the effect of making her feel more relaxed, sufficiently to ask a few questions.

'I'm going to offer you a position with us, Natasha; that is, of course, if you would like to be part of the team. As I've already mentioned, apart from features and articles on beauty and fashion, we do cover more serious, more topical issues. We have no political bias and we do make every attempt to remain entirely impartial. We've found over these last few years our readers have developed a fast-growing thirst for knowledge; not always on their own home ground, here in Hong Kong, but further afield. They want to learn about what is happening, changes, attitudes, not only on a domestic level, but in the workplace generally. Our readership, Natasha,' she went on, 'we have found, is made up of at least seventy-five per cent of professional working women and the majority of those are in China, with strong ties to the colony and the countdown to nineteen ninety-seven is uppermost in their minds. I believe, having newly arrived here and the fact you've been working for a number of years for one of England's largest newspapers, you will be able to bring a fresh approach to us at 'Woman's World'.'

'I sincerely hope I can, Miss Lambeth,' Natasha said, hardly believing her luck. She had been given the job! 'I do realise as far as Hong Kong is concerned I have a lot to learn, but I'm sure I will, because I want to very much. I feel I need to be stretched and from what you've been saying, perhaps working for 'Woman's World', I'll get that opportunity.'

'You will, Natasha. Now,' she said, standing up, 'I have a lunch appointment, however, I'll get Mandy, she's the young lady you've already met, to show you round the offices and,' she added, walking over to a bookcase, 'here's a copy of our magazine. I can't give you the latest one because it doesn't come off the press until late tonight.' handing the glossy magazine to her.

'Thank you.' Natasha said, taking it from her.

'And we look forward to seeing you next Monday morning.'

*

Juliet was in the middle of telling him where she had seen the man who'd been with Nicholas Eastman on Monday evening, when, looking across the crowded restaurant, Roddie saw Louisa being shown to a table. They had come again to "Gaylord's" in Kowloon and he had been looking forward to a pleasant meal with her on the eve of his trip to England, but now, seeing Louisa had noticed him, even giving him a small wave of recognition, he wasn't so sure. This could be awkward, he thought, taking a deep breath and trying to concentrate on what Juliet was saying, but it was no use. He had to go over and have a word with Louisa. He couldn't just sit there with another woman while the one whom he'd had an ongoing and steady relationship for a number of years would be wondering what he was up to. Surely he wasn't such an insensitive cad, but deep down, old-fashioned expression though it was, that was precisely what he did feel. An unmitigated cad!

'Are you alright, Roddie?' Juliet asked him, 'I don't believe you've heard a word of what I've been saying.'

'I'm sorry, Juliet, but there's someone over there I feel I must have a word with. I won't be long.' and putting the menu he hadn't even looked at yet back on the table, he stood up and not giving her a chance to say anything, walked across to where Louisa was sitting, all the time aware of the quizzical expression on Juliet's face.

'Hello, Louisa.' he said, reaching her table.

'Hello, Roddie,' she smiled up at him, 'who is your friend?'

'Her name is Juliet Warburton,' trying to find the right words and ones which wouldn't be hurtful, 'and she is only a friend.'

'Look, Roddie,' she said quietly, 'it's quite obvious to me you're feeling extremely awkward about this, but we always knew there was unlikely to be any real solid future to our relationship.'

'I had hoped.'

'Be honest,' she said, continuing to keep her voice low, 'and admit the affair, if we could describe it as such, had run its course. I knew when we spoke on the phone last week, or I should say, I sensed, you had met someone else.'

'Was it so obvious?'

'To me, yes.'

'What can I say? You always were a lot more perceptive than me, Louisa. I should have been more upfront with you and I apologise for that; I really do. But, as I've said, we are only friends, you know.'

'At the moment, perhaps you are, Roddie and even if you and Juliet don't take the friendship any further, the fact remains you would not have been attracted to another woman if you had been entirely satisfied with what we had.'

There wasn't much more he could say and she was absolutely right of course, Roddie thought sadly, walking back to join Juliet. She didn't say anything when he sat down, only leaned over and handed him his menu.

'Thanks,' he said, taking it from her, 'also, for not walking out of the restaurant.'

'I'm not like that, Roddie. You told me you had to speak to her and I accepted that; it doesn't matter.'

'I've known Louisa Lambeth for a while and yes, as you've no doubt guessed, we did have a close relationship, but it's over now.'

'Okay, that's fine.' she said lightly. 'I've had lovers as well, Roddie.'

'What about now, Juliet.'

'No-one.' she smiled at him; 'in fact,' she continued, 'you are the only man I'm seeing at the moment.'

'Good.' and for the first time since he had spotted Louisa was able to return her smile. He knew he could, at times, be too serious. Clarissa had told him often enough. "Lighten up, Roddie," she used to say, "you really are extremely heavy-going." Shrugging off old memories which should have been buried years ago, he returned thankfully to the present. 'You were saying,' he said to Juliet, 'you'd remembered where you'd seen Nicholas Eastman's friend before?'

'Yes, I was,' she said, glancing up from her menu, 'it was about two weeks ago. He was coming out of the lawyer's office in Wellington Street; you may know them, Roddie, Godwin, Cheung & Fong they're called.'

'I do, at least I know Marion Godwin, but not all that well.'

'I've never met her as I only deal with Simon Cheung, but I know what she looks like and she was with this man. Don't ask me how I recognised him; he wasn't exactly all that memorable, was he, but I expect it was the glasses; a bit like those Michael Caine wears.'

'They were, now you come to mention it.' wondering why that hadn't occurred to him.

'Do you have any particular reason for wanting to know who he was, Roddie?'

'Not really,' he said quickly, not wanting to say anything further. He could have had something to do with the missing formula and be the same man who went with Nicholas that evening into the vault. Until Andy Howe advised him how they intended to proceed, the theft of the formula remained definitely under wraps. Roddie had a meeting with him in the morning and should know then what had been agreed with the other directors. He didn't have to be at Kai Tak until the afternoon which would give him enough time, if Andy Howe gave him the go-ahead, to take the replica formula along to the lawyer's office. The timing was extremely tight in succeeding to have it patented, but Roddie reckoned if Marion Godwin moved quickly they might be able to make it, although tomorrow morning, at the very latest, would have to be their deadline.

'I see someone has joined your friend now.' Juliet commented, breaking into his thoughts, reminding him he wasn't much company this evening; too much on his mind and meeting up with Louisa again hadn't helped, looking across in her direction.

'Fancy.'

'I suppose that's one way to describe the lady.' Juliet giggled, quickly putting a hand up to cover her mouth. 'Sorry, I'm being bitchy.'

'Well, shall we say, somewhat exotic, even for Hong Kong? How does that sound?'

'Not much better!'

The woman sitting across the table from Louisa and appearing to be doing all the talking, with a great deal of arm flapping, wasn't young; in her early fifties at least, he guessed. She had a mass of yellow-blonde curls, heavy dark eyeliner which, even from where they were, seemed somewhat over the top. She was wearing a pink lacy concoction; a low neckline and tight-fitting. Not Louisa's type of woman friend was his first reaction, but perhaps their dinner was a business meeting he decided, looking away.

'It takes all sorts.' he grinned at Juliet.

'It certainly does, Roddie.' unable to keep the smile from her face.

'Are you looking forward to your trip?' she asked him, changing the subject, as though she had lost interest in what had caused her so much amusement.

'Yes and no.' he replied.

'Why yes?'

'Because, as it will only be a short visit I know I will enjoy being back in London and revisiting all my old haunts at the end of each day.'

'And no?' she prompted, the sapphire blue eyes sparkling as she waited for his answer and no doubt guessing what it would be.

'Because I won't be able to see you.' There, he had said it and with every word probably committing himself.

'That's nice of you, Roddie.' she smiled; not one of her short, spontaneous smiles, but lingering and taking several seconds to look away from him.

'Roddie,' she said softly, placing a hand on his arm, 'I would very much like to come back to your apartment with you tonight, but I have an eight o'clock appointment tomorrow morning in Kowloon and I need to get home to collect all my papers. Perhaps when you return from London?' she suggested, not moving her hand away.

For a moment he was speechless. How was he meant to handle this? It wasn't the first time she had come directly to the point in a way he'd never experienced before, but this time, well! Perhaps since her teens she had always been precocious, just as a young woman might be, especially if she had never experienced rejection. Juliet, he felt, had recognised early on how she appeared to the opposite sex and had learned how to discourage any unwanted advances, recalling her haughty expression on the Star Ferry, and at the same time, because of her incredible self-confidence, she considered it perfectly normal to make the first move, exactly as she had done that day right from the moment when she had walked over to him in the cafe in Pedder Street.

'Have I shocked you?' she asked him, her expression, for once serious.

'No, of course you haven't;' trying to reassure her, 'what you've said was unexpected, that's all. I guess I'm flattered.'

'That's alright then.' she said, 'You go on your London trip and I'll be waiting for you when you return. In fact, if you give me your flight details I'll be at the airport to meet you.'

*

Roddie bought a newspaper on his way to work. The article, only two columns, was at the bottom of the front page; the headline, in bold print, caught his attention immediately:

"IS THIS THE END OF MALARIA?

The 'Grand Hyatt' in Singapore was the venue yesterday afternoon for a press conference, following the announcement by one of Singapore's leading Research Laboratories of a new drug which it is claimed will cure and, possibly eradicate, the tropical disease of malaria, in particular, that of the life-threatening cerebral malaria. The anti-malaria drug, shortly to be distributed worldwide, will be available on prescription. Anthony Chui, head of the research and development of the new drug was quoted yesterday as saying: 'After months of research and exhaustive tests, we are confident this product is a breakthrough in medical science, especially in the field of combating tropical diseases which have for centuries been endemic in third world countries."

Singapore! Not so far from Hong Kong; no wonder it hadn't taken them long to get the drug on the market! Roddie read through the article for the second time in dismay, before folding the newspaper and continuing down towards Des Voeux Road. In the six or eight minutes it took him to reach his office, he knew each word of the article by heart, but as he opened the double swing doors and walked into the foyer, he realised something wasn't right. Something didn't quite gel somehow. The formula was taken from the safe deposit box at seven-thirty on Monday evening; presumably it was flown the relatively short distance to Singapore where it was patented and by Wednesday afternoon, if the article was correct, the drug was in the process of being distributed, not only in Singapore, but throughout the world. This was not possible! There was no way, Roddie was positive, could the whole process have been completed in such a short space of time.

Andy Howe was already there, waiting for him, in his office and staring out of the window with his back to the room. As soon as he heard the door opening, he turned round, a grim expression replacing his normal one of good nature.

'You've heard, then, Roddie?' he asked, looking pointedly at the newspaper he was still carrying.

'Yes, I have, sir. It's what we feared, isn't it?'

'You're right. It looks very much as though we've lost this one,' Andy Howe said slowly, deliberately, and moving into the centre of the room, 'a great deal of hard work literally gone down the drain, not to mention the cost of our research. I can well imagine how you must be feeling this morning, Roddie. You've put in many hours on this project.'

'I have, it's true,' Roddie agreed, 'but I've been thinking about the timing of all this; something doesn't ring true.'

'In what way?'

'Well,' Roddie started to explain, 'how were they able to, not only prepare the drug, but to be in a position to make the announcement that it was ready to be put on the market. Quite frankly,' he continued, 'it doesn't add up.'

'Do you know, Roddie, that hadn't occurred to me. And, of course, you are quite right. Given that Singapore is considerably closer than, say America, or Britain, it just isn't feasible.'

'Unless the formula was stolen before Monday.'

'What are you saying?'

'I'm not exactly sure, sir, but I put that formula into the safe deposit box two weeks ago; if it had been stolen nearer to that time, it could possibly have been patented and reached the stage of distribution which, presumably, it is at the moment.'

'This is more serious than we thought.'

'I know, but it could have happened.'

'Indeed, Roddie, but why this farce of someone, namely the man calling himself Thomas, turning up at the bank on Monday?'

'I haven't had much time to think this through yet, but perhaps it wasn't a farce; perhaps he didn't know –' faltering.

'- that it had been switched.' Andy Howe finished for him.

'Yes, that was what I was thinking.'

'We mustn't jump to conclusions here.' he warned, beginning to walk up and down the office and Roddie waited patiently, all the time his own brain working overtime, 'What I meant was, it does seem to point a finger at Nicholas Eastman, but then he could, in fact, be perfectly innocent. As he told his manager, although he hadn't met this Thomas man before, he did ask to see some proof of identity and you know all the rest, Roddie. He could have genuinely believed the man was from our company in the States and as you've suggested, the formula could have been replaced two weeks ago by someone else.'

'So the one Thomas took away with him may have been a forgery?'

'Exactly.'

'Bad.'

'Very.' Andy agreed, 'Incidentally, I had a word with the bank manager yesterday after you'd given me a description of the man you'd seen with Nicholas, although I avoided any mention of that; I merely asked if Nicholas could give us some idea of what the man looked like.'

'Did you hear back from him?'

'Quite quickly, as a matter of fact, and his description tallied pretty well with yours, Roddie. I know it's no proof, but it is interesting all the same.'

'I didn't mention this to you at the time, sir,' Roddie began, not wishing to bring Juliet into this business, but he now felt he should, 'but the lady I was with in the "Captain's Bar" told me at the time she recognised him, but she couldn't remember where.'

'Yes?'

'Well, last evening she said, although she had never met him, she had remembered where she'd seen him;' pausing to take a deep breath and grateful Andy didn't put any pressure on him to come to the point, 'he was coming out of the lawyer's office and Marion Godwin was with him.'

'Interesting. Was she sure it was the same person?'

'Oh, yes.'

'I don't know what to say, Roddie, but what I do know is I believe it's time we had another talk with the manager, also to call a board meeting as soon as possible.'

'I think you're right.'

'I'm afraid this is going to mean having to ask you to change your travel plans, Roddie, but I think it's crucial you come with me to the bank, also I'd like you to be present at the meeting.'

'I understand, sir. Do you want me to cancel my trip altogether?'

'Goodness, no,' he smiled for the first time, 'I don't think that will be necessary. We can, I'm sure, get all of this done by the end of today. I'll get my secretary to try and book you a flight to London tomorrow, if that suits you.'

'That would be fine; I shouldn't miss any of the seminar and even if I did, sir, this business is considerably more important.'

'Thank you, Roddie; I knew I could rely on you.'

Chapter Nine
LONDON

It was almost midday by the time Hugh's taxi drew up outside the offices of Bristow & Innis in Savoy Street. He'd taken the Express Train from Hounslow West and picked up a taxi from there. Eddie was expecting him, Hugh having given him a call on his mobile as soon as he reached the terminal at Heathrow. He couldn't remember when he had felt so thankful to be back on familiar territory. Although used to city life he'd come to the conclusion that Hong Kong didn't suit him. He had found the place too claustrophobic and likened it to living in a goldfish bowl; the ever present blank-eyed stares of the Chinese disconcerting. Realising, although they gave the impression of looking directly at him, this meant nothing, made no difference; he had still felt uncomfortable.

Joanne was in the outer office and looked up from her computer screen when he went in, dropping his travel bag on the floor by the door.

'Hello,' she welcomed him, 'How are you, Hugh?'

'Shattered!'

'Would you like some coffee?' she asked him. Joanne was an excellent secretary, with the added ability of dexterously and without any fuss being able to juggle the work she did for them both and Hugh couldn't recall in the three years she had been with them of her making any preference, managing to treat both partners equally, also she never complained when asked to work overtime, nor did she, like so many secretaries Hugh had known in the past, expect to have time off to make up for those extra hours she'd put int. In fact, he thought, looking at her now; as always neatly dressed in a tailored navy two-piece, a single string of pearls her only jewellery, she was invaluable to the business.

'There is nothing I'd like better, Joanne.' he smiled at her and walked towards Eddie's office, tapping lightly on the door before going in.

'Ah,' Eddie stood up to shake hands with him, 'you're back, Hugh. You look knackered!'

'I feel knackered!'

'Sit down and have some coffee; that will help.'

'Joanne's bringing me some. Am I glad to be back! Hong Kong is something else; it really is. It never sleeps!'

'Tell me about it,' Eddie said, 'it's been some years since I've been there, must be ten at least, but I don't expect it's changed all that much.'

'It hasn't, I can assure you. No doubt will be a lot worse in five years' time.'

'What; with the new regime, you mean?'

'Yes, that's right. That's all people seem to be talking about, especially since the arrival of the new governor. Anyway, Eddie,' Hugh went on, unlocking his briefcase, 'here's the much-travelled formula.' pulling out the envelope and passing it over to him.

'Thanks, Hugh.' he said, taking the sheet of paper, scanning quickly down the print before holding it up to the light.'

Immediately he did so, Hugh felt a quick stab of guilt; he hadn't thought to do that. It just hadn't occurred to him and it should have done. As soon as the formula had been in his hands he had naively and foolishly taken a watermark for granted.

'Hugh,' Eddie said quietly, putting the paper on his desk, 'this is a forgery. You and I have been well and truly duped!'

'Oh, no! I'm sorry, Eddie; I really am. I had no idea and I must confess, I didn't check for the watermark. I'm sorry.' he repeated, standing up and walking over to the window, for a moment unable to trust his voice. He felt gutted. How could he have been so remiss?

'Look, Hugh,' Eddie said, walking over to him, 'don't be so hard on yourself. It's not your fault.'

'But I should have checked for the watermark.'

'Even if you had, it wouldn't have made any difference, would it? What could you have done?'

'Nothing, I suppose.'

'Exactly. Okay, it's a blow and the exercise has cost us a fair bit which we have no choice but to write off.'

'It must have been Nicholas Eastman who switched the formula.' Hugh said.

'Well,' Eddie said deliberately, 'not necessarily.'

Hugh was interrupted in asking him what he meant, by Joanne coming in with his coffee.

'Thanks, Joanne.'

'Would you like some, Eddie?' she asked him, placing Hugh's cup on the desk.

'No thanks, Joanne; I'll be going for lunch soon.'

Hugh waited until she had gone before saying anything further.

'Drink your coffee, Hugh;' Eddie advised, anticipating him and going back to his desk, 'it will revive you.'

'I hope so.' Hugh said, taking a sip and instantly feeling the aromatic warmth of the coffee begin to take effect, 'Joanne makes a good cup of coffee, doesn't she?'

'She certainly does.'

'Eddie,' Hugh said, 'if it hadn't been Nicholas, who else could it have been? Another member of the bank staff?'

'I don't think so.'

'Who, then?'

'You've no ideas?'

'You don't mean Marion, do you?'

'Why not? Apart from the bank manager and Nicholas Eastman she was the only other person who knew that formula had been placed in the safe deposit box.'

'Who the hell can we trust, Eddie?'

'No-one.'

'Whoever took it must have known how they could profit.' Hugh said thoughtfully, by now beginning to think more clearly, also to rationalise. 'They must have had the right contacts as well, ones who would be able to manufacture the drug. Would Nicholas Eastman have been able to do that?'

'Possibly, I suppose,' he shrugged, 'but we had already paid him extremely well for his part in all of this and, unless he was extraordinarily greedy – and stupid – I can't see him taking the risk. No, Hugh, the more I think about it, the more I believe it could have been Marion. Mind you,' he went on, 'she would still have needed someone from the bank to hand the formula over to her and it's stretching credibility a mite too far to think it would have been anyone else but Nicholas.'

'True. Also, she would have had the know-how, wouldn't she; to put together a fairly good replica, complete with McLellands' name and logo.'

'I'm sure she would, Hugh. I have no doubt about that.'

'I wonder whether McLellands will report this to the authorities. Marion told me when I had dinner with her on Monday evening; they would be picking up the formula the following morning.'

'It's debatable, Hugh, whether McLellands will take this any further and not one which should worry us unduly. However,' he went on, 'I've been thinking, and I believe it would be best if I went out there.'

'Why?'

'Because I need to talk to Marion Godwin. Don't worry; about our position I mean. She has far too much to lose in mentioning our names. Besides, what could she say?'

'Nothing,' Hugh agreed, 'and if she did say anything that would only implicate her further.'

'Exactly. I'm going to try and get a flight out as soon as possible and have a few words with the lady.'

*

Robert took a call from Howard as he was about to go for lunch. It would be eight at night in Hong Kong he calculated as his secretary put the call through to him.

'Good afternoon, Howard,' he said, 'or should I say evening?'

'Confusing isn't it, sir?'

'Very. Have you and Frank made any progress yet?' Robert asked him, but not expecting much. As he'd already said to Howard he fully appreciated how difficult it was going to be; they had so little to go on.

'Some, I believe.' Howard answered, 'Francesca arrived here as planned last evening and Frank was there, at Kai Tak, and managed to follow her alright, but not as far as 'The Mandarin' because she'd instructed the driver to take her to a shop in Pedder Street.'

'A shop? Sounds intriguing.'

'It probably is, Robert,' Howard said, 'that is, if we knew why she went there, but as to that we can only make guesses and of course that's no good. However,' he went on, 'she could only have been inside the shop for about ten minutes. Frank turned up there shortly after her and went into the cafe next door to wait and see what would happen, if anything.'

'And did it?'

'Well, yes;' Howard answered, 'she'd kept her taxi waiting and rather than make an attempt to follow her which would have been pretty impossible, Pedder Street not being the best place to find a taxi, but in any case he waited to see whether anyone else emerged from the shop and he wasn't disappointed because someone did, only minutes after Francesca left.'

'So,' Robert prompted and Howard recognised the suppressed excitement in his voice, 'it would seem she went in there for the sole purpose of meeting someone, perhaps this person Frank saw?'

'Frank and I think it was very possible. He was Chinese and, as you can imagine, the description could fit thousands. Anyway, after he'd gone, Frank decided to have a look at the shop and this is where it does become somewhat mysterious.'

'Yes?'

'You see, Frank had been in the shop before; when they had sold pictures, most of them unframed. I'm sure you've seen many shops like that when you've been here, Robert?'

'I have indeed. They are in great abundance!'

'This one, though, no longer sells pictures, but cake decorations. That, in itself, didn't strike Frank as all that unusual, at least not in Hong Kong, but he went inside to have a look round only to find the same man he'd seen in there a couple of months ago was still there. He'd thought with a complete change of product, the place would have changed hands completely, but this apparently hadn't been the case. That did strike him as odd for Hong Kong because, as you know, they are a great race for changing jobs, especially when there's new management and very often they don't get the chance to stay on, even if they wanted to.'

'Food for thought, eh?'

'We think so. Without assuming, it could be that Francesca called in, not only to see the man who left, but to deliver something.'

'And we all know what that something could have been?'

'Yes. From this little exercise one important and interesting fact has emerged. The shop in Pedder Street, which, incidentally, has the rather unlikely name of "Dolly Mixtures" –'

'– I thought you said they sold cake decorations, Howard?' he interrupted, 'Dolly Mixtures were sweets we used to have when we were children.'

'I know,' Howard laughed, 'you're right. I remember them well. However, the place is owned by a Mr Denny Yuan.'

'The same Denny, do you think?'

'It would be reasonable to assume so. The shop, according to Company Records is not his only business; he's listed as being Chairman of "Yuan Enterprises Hong Kong" with offices in D'Aguillar Street.'

'In other words, he's a businessman?'

'Yes, with as far as we've been able to establish, an unblemished record, not even a parking fine.'

'Too good to be true, eh?'

'Could be. However, I took the liberty this afternoon of giving Virginia Banister a ring.'

'And how is the lady?'

'Very well, although much involved with a number of welcoming receptions for the new governor, whose arrival here is still very much the main talking point.'

'I can well imagine;' Robert said, 'all wondering, I expect, what's going to happen in nineteen ninety-seven.'

'That's right. Anyway, she didn't mind me phoning, even when I asked whether she would be prepared to attend an identity parade, if and when, we decided to pull Francesca Cristofoli in for questioning.'

'Good thinking, and did she agree?'

'She didn't hesitate; said she would be only too pleased if it meant she was able to help bring Francesca to justice.'

'No doubt by now you've realised Virginia is one very spunky lady. It wouldn't be too difficult to bring part of this case to a satisfactory close, Howard, namely, if we have sufficient proof that the woman purporting to be Frances Catania is one and the same. We could then obtain an International Arrest Warrant and bring her back to England to face trial, but –' he paused.

'- but you have reservations?'

'I do, yes; unwittingly, her presence in Hong Kong could assist us in a far more serious crime on, possibly, a worldwide scale. If we are thinking along the right lines and emeralds are being imported into Hong Kong from Columbia, this could turn out to be of astronomical proportions.'

'I think you could be right,' Howard agreed quickly, 'and, if they are being brought into Hong Kong, what we need to find out is where they go from here.'

'Exactly and that's why, for the present, I'd like you and Frank to stay on for a few more days. By all means keep your eye on what she's up to, if you can, but perhaps more importantly, to try and delve deeper into the activities of our entrepreneur.'

'Denny Yuan?'

'Yes, Denny Yuan. The name of his company sounds a little ambiguous to me. Why add Hong Kong? It could mean he has subsidiary companies elsewhere.'

'That's a good point,' Howard said, 'I hadn't thought of that.'

'Also,' Robert continued, 'don't concern yourselves too much if Francesca should slip through your fingers; let's face it, she's done that often enough in the past. The reason I'm saying this is because Immigration and Reservations, both here and in Hong Kong, are in constant touch with us and as soon as she books her flight out of Hong Kong we'll be notified and have time to arrange for someone to follow her, in the event she gets wind that we're on to her and does another disappearing act. This time, hopefully, we'll be ready for such an eventuality. We do know,' he added, 'she is still in Hong Kong.'

'I know,' Howard said, 'she seems to be in no hurry to leave, for some unfathomable reason.'

'And,' Robert suggested, 'perhaps there is something significant in that.'

No sooner had Robert replaced the receiver when the report on Hugh Innis came in, or more interestingly, on his partner, Edward Bristow. The report was short and concise with one point which could be important: shortly after midday, Reservations at Heathrow Airport had received a telephone booking from Bristow & Innis' travel agents in Oxford Street, for a flight out to Hong Kong tomorrow night, in the name of Mr Edward Bristow.

Why the rush, was Robert's immediate reaction. He read through the report once more, verifying that his partner, Hugh Innis, had arrived at his office in Savoy Street at eleven forty-two precisely. Had it been a sudden decision to make the reservation so soon after Hugh's return, Robert wondered, and the only logical and feasible conclusion he could come up with was that it must have been. The fact he had gone directly to the office, presumably to report on his trip must mean something. Perhaps whatever he'd brought back with him, whether information or of a more solid nature, could have promulgated the decision. Howard's instincts about Hugh Innis could have been right, Robert thought, pressing the buzzer for his secretary.

Before he spoke to Howard again he needed to know in which hotel Edward Bristow would be staying; there was a good chance it would be the "Mandarin", but he wanted to make sure; it would make Howard's job considerably easier to keep an eye on the man. While Robert didn't necessarily believe there was anything seriously amiss about the activities of Bristow & Innis, at the same time, it didn't stop his professional antennae going on full alert. It had taken him many years to perfect this skill and he had learned not to ignore indications, no matter how unlikely, that there was something wrong. There could be a link here, also there appeared to be a sudden interest in Hong Kong, which could very well mean nothing whatsoever, although it was almost as if in some bizarre and inexplicable way, Francesca Cristofoli's appearance was acting as a catalyst, ridiculous as that may sound. These thoughts, for now, Robert intended to keep to himself and to let events take their course, which inevitably meant relying on both Frank and Howard's findings and he knew from experience he wouldn't be disappointed.

*

Roddie slept for a good part of the flight to England which was unusual for him, but put it down to being utterly exhausted. He'd had a restless night on Thursday; most of it spent tossing and turning until around four in the morning he had given up any attempt to get off to sleep and decided to get up and make himself a pot of coffee, although fully realising after drinking it he would never be able to sleep for the few hours until he needed to get up and make his way to the airport.

His brain just would not let up; events of that inordinately long day running at high speed; from the meeting in the morning with his MD, followed by the talk they had both had with the bank manager, who, although giving every indication he was as keen as they were to find out who was responsible, was unable to be much help and had had nothing to add to what he'd already told them, except he agreed, reluctantly, when

Andy told him there was a strong possibility if it was finally decided to call in the police, there would undoubtedly be questions they would need to ask him. And, then, later in the day, being present in the conference room while Andy patiently spelt out the whole business to his fellow directors and eventually, after a great deal of resistance, gaining a unanimous decision to report the theft of the formula.

Roddie could have phoned Juliet after the board meeting to tell her the change in his travel plans, perhaps taken her out for a meal, but he didn't; the main reason being, remembering what lousy company he had been the evening before, there would be no point. He would be back in Hong Kong on Wednesday, remembering she had told him this would be her birthday, and hoping, if she had nothing else planned, they could have a special celebration, just the two of them. And, now, as they were approaching the runway, he made a supreme effort to mentally switch off from what had been happening and concentrate exclusively on the next few days.

The "Hotel Russell" on the corner of the square and overlooking Russell Square Gardens, was one of London's oldest hotels, built during the time of Queen Victoria's reign; the dark sombre stonework a reminder of much of the architecture around that period, and the high wood-framed windows making it impossible to see inside from the pavement; the whole edifice exuding an air of aloof seclusion from what was going on outside in the street below. Roddie always stayed there when he came to London and each time he entered the ornate wood-panelled reception area he immediately felt cocooned from the rest of his world, not an unpleasant feeling, and today was no exception. It was still light, and would be for several hours yet, but in here, the lighting was discreetly subdued, with only the steady flickering of the computer screen at the desk to remind him the hotel had moved forward into the technological age from those earlier days when Roddie had first stayed there.

The receptionist handed Roddie the key to his room, together with a buff-coloured envelope with the distinctive logo of the college in the left-hand corner. He waited until he was in his room before opening it.

"Dear Mr Mortimer," he read, "We are looking forward to your talk on Monday and would cordially invite you to be one of our guests at dinner that evening. The occasion is to celebrate fifty years since the college's inauguration; a significant date in our collegiate calendar. Also, we would like to extend our hospitality by offering you accommodation for the night within the college campus. Yours sincerely, M.L. Standish, B.sc."

Curbing his disappointment, Roddie replaced the somewhat pompous and formal letter into the envelope. He had hoped that, after returning from Oxford on Monday afternoon, he could have spent his last evening having a few drinks and winding up, perhaps, with a meal in one of his favourite restaurants in The Strand. It would appear, he thought, this trip of his was destined to be disrupted. A pity, but it couldn't be helped. He had to accept the invitation and, as so often in his career, realising he really didn't have a great deal of choice. At least he still had this evening and Saturday and Sunday after the seminar, he concluded philosophically.

The "London Pub", only a short walk from the hotel, and one in which he had spent many happy hours when he'd been a student and, pushing open the double swing doors, he saw with pleasure it had hardly changed since those days: the same wood flooring which creaked slightly as he walked over towards the bar. Taking his lager to one of the seats on the raised platform alongside the windows, he sat down, and for the first time since he'd arrived, began to unwind. He hadn't realised just how tense he'd been; a build-up he reckoned since the morning when he'd discovered the formula had been stolen, but he should make an attempt during the following few days to put to the back of his mind what was probably going on there now that the police would have commenced their investigation, but it wasn't easy. Also, there was Juliet. She persisted in making her presence known, which he supposed wasn't a bad thing, but in spite of what he felt for her, he continued to have nagging doubts. Nothing he could actually pinpoint, but instinctively he felt something wasn't right. It was possible he needed this time to separate his troubled thoughts and metaphorically pull away from her, although he knew only too well, that once he was back in Hong Kong he wouldn't feel or act any differently than he had up to now. I truly am a hopeless case, he concluded, taking a long grateful sip of his beer.

He remembered there used to be a small Chinese restaurant further along the road; one, again as students, they had often frequented, mainly because it had been cheap, but the food had been consistently excellent. Sure enough, it was still there and as always reminded him of someone's front room: the one and only window, the view of the street partially obscured by an oblong fish tank; half a dozen tables and in the centre, the two traditional round tables. He had learned early not to go into a Chinese restaurant unless it was hot and steamy and the "Lucky House" tonight fitted this description exactly!

Roddie waited until the morning to try and get in touch with Natasha and, being a Saturday, he guessed she would be at home. Although he would be spending the following two days at the seminar, he would have each evening free and he'd had the idea they could have a meal together. It had been at least six months since he'd seen her; not since he had last been in London; not an entirely happy situation which meant they never had sufficient time to get to know each other properly. He let the phone ring a number of times and was on the point of giving up, when a voice, slightly out of breath and one he'd never heard before, answered.

'Hi.'

'Hi,' Roddie said, 'is Natasha there?'

'Natasha?'

'Yes, my daughter,' he told her, 'I'm only in London for a few days and I was hoping to meet up with her.'

'Oh, Natasha,' she drawled, 'I know who you mean now, but she doesn't live here anymore.'

'I hadn't realised,' Roddie said, looking at his watch; he would have to leave within the next ten minutes, but first, he must find out where she'd gone. 'I don't suppose you know where she's moved to,' he asked the girl, 'I mean, do you happen to have her phone number?'

'Sorry,' she said, 'I'd like to help you, but I only moved in here yesterday, so I've no idea.'

He rang off and once again, since arriving the day before, experiencing disappointment. There was nothing unusual in the fact that Natasha had decided to move and he couldn't understand this strong feeling of exclusion from her life, when he reasoned he only had himself to blame. The father-daughter relationship had always been a flimsy one, so why should he be feeling like this now? He could phone her office, but as he didn't have a note of the number, he would have to ask reception and that would take time; the quickest thing to do, therefore, was to get in touch with Clarissa. She would be bound to know although it was with reluctance he rang her number.

This time, he didn't have to wait as almost immediately Clarissa's voice reached him: 'She obviously hasn't been in touch with you, then.' Her first words after he'd explained why he was phoning.

'No,' Roddie admitted, 'not that I expected her to, but as I'm in London I thought we could meet.'

'Natasha is in Hong Kong.'

'What!'

'You heard, Roddie. Natasha took it into her head a couple of weeks ago to give up her job with the newspaper and to join her boyfriend out in Hong Kong.'

'Didn't you try to stop her?' unwarranted indignation and something to which he had no entitlement.

'I did make an attempt to *dissuade* her,' she emphasised, 'but you know, Natasha. She always did have a mind of her own, besides,' Clarissa went on quickly and he could tell by the impatience in her voice she was anxious to get off the line, 'she is twenty-two, no longer a child; in case you had forgotten.'

'Would you give me a contact number for her, please, Clarissa?' he asked, ignoring the heavy sarcasm.

'No problem,' and he recognised the relief; she was finding this call as distasteful as he was, 'I have it here.' and read out the telephone number of Natasha's boyfriend, but it wasn't until after he had replaced the receiver and was halfway down the stairs to reception when he remembered he hadn't asked Clarissa for his name.

Roddie took the tube to Trafalgar Square and walked to where the seminar was being held in Cockspur Street, by which time, the previous disappointment at not being able to get hold of Natasha had been replaced by an intense feeling of hurt. The unpalatable fact that his daughter was now living in Hong Kong and had made no attempt to get in touch with him was hard to take. Didn't she want him to know she was there? Had she been too busy? Too busy even to dial his number? This wasn't like the Natasha he thought he knew. She wasn't like that. But, by the time he was walking up the flight of steps to the conference hall, he had forced himself to be realistic. The bottom line was he didn't know Natasha at all.

*

'Who was that on the phone, Clarissa?' Conrad asked her, when she returned to the kitchen, sitting down at the table and taking a sip of her coffee, which surely must have become cold by now.

'Roddie.'

'Roddie?'

'Yes, darling,' she looked across at him, 'my ex.' a look of exasperation on her face.

'Oh.' In all the years they had been married he never remembered her ex-husband phoning her before. She must have mentioned his Christian name when they had first met, but he couldn't remember. She and Natasha had been living on their own for a while by then, so perhaps she never had; there never had been any need. Although when he had signed the adoption papers for Natasha, he must have known.

'I expect you're wondering why he phoned.'

'Well, I suppose I am.'

'It's quite simple, darling,' Clarissa said, 'he's in London and wanted to get in touch with Natasha, but of course, she isn't here.'

'I'm surprised she didn't phone him when she reached Hong Kong.' and as soon as he uttered the words, each one of them penetrating his brain like coins falling neatly into a slot machine, he felt a shiver of apprehension. Why on earth had he not made the connection earlier? It had taken him exactly one week since Denny had told him about the man who, in Denny's words, had been snooping around the shop. A Mr R Mortimer he'd said, presumably the R stood for Roddie, and also he'd been no tourist as he had paid with a Hong Kong credit card. How many more clues did he need Conrad thought, irritably, to jog his sluggish memory. Mortimer was not such a common name and it couldn't be a coincidence that he also was in London this weekend. It wasn't as if he hadn't been aware, for God's Sake, that he was living in Hong Kong! How obtuse can one be? Conrad was still mentally reeling from the flak he'd had to take from Denny when he'd told him Mortimer hadn't been on the Hong Kong flight on Thursday and when he'd protested by asking him whether he expected his men to hang about Arrivals until he eventually turned up, Denny's response had been characteristically unsympathetic, remembering exactly what he'd said. "Conrad, my friend, you were so very confident the other day; all I can say is, it was indeed fortuitous I was able to give you the name of Roddie Mortimer's hotel. You will now have to think again how you can get hold of his bag. It shouldn't prove too difficult a task." had been his parting remark before bringing the call to a close. Denny Yuan, the man he had worked with for so long had, apparently, left this side of the transaction entirely in his hands.

'Conrad, you're not listening to me.' Clarissa said, her voice sharp with barely suppressed impatience. He had been miles away, trying to decide what he should do now, whether to give Denny another ring or not, not forgetting the problem of concocting another way to retrieve those emeralds which, quite frankly, had become a pain in the proverbial!

'Sorry,' he apologised, forcing a smile, 'what did you say?'

'I was saying,' Clarissa said slowly, enunciating each syllable separately which was a sure sign she was on the verge of losing her temper with him, 'Roddie should have realised Natasha would want to get settled before she got in touch with him. The last thing she would want would be a lecture.'

'You're probably right, darling, and only understandable.'

Was this the real reason Conrad wondered but knowing how fiercely independent his step-daughter could be, he was inclined to agree with Clarissa. But, overriding this perfectly reasonable explanation, he still continued to fret over why her ex-husband should have taken such an unprecedented step to telephone her. Had Roddie Mortimer been so concerned about a daughter he hardly knew and made little effort over the years to keep in regular contact? Perhaps not. Perhaps there had been another reason, and one he couldn't even begin to fathom out. No doubt Denny would be quick to come up with a likely explanation; all the more reason Conrad decided he should give him a call. This whole protracted business was giving him a headache. Not only had he to organize the distribution of the emeralds which had arrived on Thursday morning, something he had delayed until he'd had confirmation that Roddie Mortimer had been relieved of his travel bag at Heathrow, but he had to rapidly make further plans to somehow gain access to his hotel room and, so far, he hadn't been able to come up with a foolproof solution.

Chapter Ten

Five o'clock was chiming somewhere in the distance when Roddie, along with the twenty or so others who had attended the lectures on the first day of the seminar, filed out of the conference hall, spilling on to the pavement in Cockspur Street. He had enjoyed the day, finding the concentration good for focusing his brain, but by this time in the afternoon he'd had enough and, although a couple of guys who had been seated next to him, asked if he would like to join them for a drink he had declined. It wasn't only because they had been considerably younger and judging by their intense absorption during the hours they'd been in there, which had decided him, but he felt far more strongly than he had before, that he had been out of England for too long. Unlike them, he didn't work in industry in England, where time was keenly measured and productivity was at an absolute premium. He had been fortunate; his work with McLellands being, he was fairly certain, from what he had picked up from snippets of conversation throughout the day, conducted along more laid back lines. Perhaps it was because he worked for an American company, whose working methods differed so much; he didn't know, but for whatever reason, he knew he had set himself apart from these eager and ambitious young men and women and had to admit he didn't even talk the same language anymore.

As he would have expected on an early Saturday evening, "The Lord Moon of the Mall" pub was packed, with a noisy mixture of late-afternoon shoppers and those customers in the preliminary stages of having a good night out. Roddie didn't fit into either category, but it didn't matter; he liked the atmosphere, also he liked "The Moon", another of his old haunts and, for a fleeting moment, wished he wasn't on his own, but the only person he could think of as he walked into the smoky atmosphere, was Juliet, automatically calculating it would be just after midnight there, making Hong Kong seem even further away.

Roddie was two-thirds of the way through his beer when he noticed him: the man who had been with Nicholas Eastman only five days ago. This is positively surreal! Here he was, in Whitehall, and the first person he recognises is this guy whom he'd last seen in Hong Kong! The man was standing further along the bar from him and as he lifted his glass, Roddie caught sight of the gold signet ring. The man with Nicholas had, he recalled now, been left-handed, also he'd worn a ring on his third finger. At that moment, the couple who had been between them, moved away from the bar and, whether he felt Roddie's eyes on him or not, turned round to look at him.

'Busy pub.' Roddie commented, not understanding quite why he had chosen to speak to him. He wasn't the gregarious type, preferring his own company rather than run the risk of ending up talking to someone who would ultimately bore him to tears, sufficiently so, to force him to drink up and leave, but the urge to communicate with him had been too strong. While admitting he was no detective, the bare-faced audacity of the theft of the formula which had cost months of hard work and dedication, still rankled.

'It usually, is,' he answered, 'especially on a Saturday.'

'Hmmph.' there was still time to pull back and say nothing further, but he didn't: 'I believe I saw you earlier this week.'

'Really?' no hint of surprise in his voice.

'Yes, you were with a friend of mine; Nicholas Eastman.'

'Nicholas Eastman?' he repeated, 'I don't know anyone called Nicholas Eastman.'

'You were in Hong Kong though, weren't you?' Roddie insisted, 'It was on Monday evening; in the "Mandarin" hotel.'

'I'm afraid you're mistaken.' the eyes behind the heavy-rimmed spectacles unblinking and devoid of any expression.

'Well,' Roddie said, 'all I can say is, you must have a double.'

'Everyone has, I'm told.' he said quickly, turning his head away and taking a further sip of his beer.

So much for that, Roddie thought, and not convinced for one minute.

The man was lying, which only proved, as far as Roddie was concerned, he was guilty. He *had* gone to the bank with Nicholas Eastman, calling himself Mr Thomas and purporting to be from the company's parent company in the States. There was no doubt in Roddie's mind and he wondered what his reaction had been when he'd discovered the formula had been switched.

No doubt somewhat miffed; not that that was any consolation. The original had been stolen, whether by this Thomas guy or someone else, was neither here nor there. It had gone and the drug would very soon be on the market.

Roddie was reading through the extensive menu, having made up his mind to have a meal in "The Moon" rather than move on elsewhere, when one of the barmen called over to the man who had, by this time, moved further down the bar: 'Your taxi is here, Mr Innis.'

'Thanks, John.' he said, draining his glass and, without looking in Roddie's direction, walked quickly to the door.

Well, Roddie thought, at least I've found out his name; not that it is a great deal of help. In any case, it would have to wait until he was back in Hong Kong and he could pass it by Andy and see what he had to suggest.

The remainder of the weekend passed uneventfully enough. The second and final day of the seminar wound up at the same time, shortly before five and this time, Roddie took a bus directly back to Bloomsbury, getting off at the stop outside the "London Pub". He spent a pleasant evening there and later had a meal in the hotel restaurant.

He didn't need to be at the college in Oxford until two on Monday afternoon, but had decided he would take an earlier train and spend the morning re-exploring the town. Apart from packing his travel bag, all he had to do before he was ready to leave, was settle the hotel bill, having already told reception he would be cutting short his stay. Pulling the bag down from the top shelf of the wardrobe, and not looking at what he was doing, his mind thinking ahead on how he would pan out those hours before, once more, becoming absorbed into an academic environment, he didn't notice when one of the straps became caught round the handle of the wardrobe door. Tugging it free, but too hard, forcing the bag to swing out towards him until it landed on the floor at his feet. Picking up the bag and about to place it on the bed, he heard, rather than felt, a soft muffled movement and, thinking he must have left something inside when he'd unpacked on Friday, he unzipped it, but there was nothing in there. Puzzled, Roddie shook the bag and, sure enough, he could hear the same sound. Whatever it was, he thought, must be under the lining; perhaps a piece of the leather had broken away, running his fingers lightly along the bottom seam. There *was* something; a small round pouch which fitted snugly into the palm of his hand through the lining. What the hell is it? he muttered. And why hadn't he noticed it before? Had the sudden movement when he'd dropped the bag caused it to become dislodged he wondered and, impatiently, and none too gently, he ripped open the lining, just large enough for him to be able to put his hand inside.

He had been right. It was a pouch; made of some silky material, a thin narrow ribbon acting as a drawstring which, his movements quickening and feeling the clamminess of the sweat breaking out on his brow, he untied it, emptying the contents on to the bed. Roddie was no precious stones expert, but he was fairly positive what he was staring at were emeralds, spreading them out. There were thirty altogether; the dark green a startling contrast to the pale cream of the quilt.

His hands were shaking as he scooped them up and put them back into the pouch. All the time, his mind was on overdrive. Questions, one after the other, each vying for position, tumbled into his brain; the main one being, why had he been chosen to bring them into England. He knew when they'd been put in his bag. He didn't need to make any guesses; whoever it was, would have had ample time when he was lying in a semi-conscious state on Lamma Island, but, again, *why*? When had they planned to retrieve them, for goodness sake? Also, how did they know he was coming to London? But, he knew the answer to that and the realisation sickened him.

Juliet. She had known. And, he admitted to himself now, it *had* been her voice he'd heard that night. He hadn't been mistaken and, being such a love-sick idiot, he had elected to ignore what he had known deep down to be the truth. Indeed, who else? He had told her on the first evening they'd met he was planning this trip, and then later, even the hotel where he'd be staying. She also knew when he would be returning to Hong Kong. Roddie tried to put himself into the role of an emerald smuggler, realising how utterly bizarre that sounded, but he persisted in working out how they could have planned to intercept his bag and the only possible time he came up with was when he reached Heathrow; perhaps while he was at the carousal waiting, along with a good hundred other passengers, for the baggage to come through. Yes, he decided, that would have been the easiest way; but of course, he hadn't been on the Thursday night flight! And when he remembered he had very nearly given Juliet a ring on Thursday to tell her he would be coming out here a day later, he stifled an involuntary shudder at what may have happened if he had. Not only would he have been minus a travel bag containing his clothes, but also a heap of lecture notes, also, if the way he had been manhandled the last time was anything to go by, he may not have emerged entirely unscathed. Well, they didn't, but that didn't mean *they*, whoever they were, won't make an attempt while he was still in London, but before he made any further changes to this trip, he had to get in touch with the police. This had to be reported and the sooner the better. Roddie had no intention of carrying them around with him for any longer than he had to. It never occurred to him to act any other way or to spend time wondering what most men would do in similar circumstances. He was a law-abiding sort of guy; that was the way he was and he didn't think there was anything particularly noble about that.

*

Robert Anderson phoned Howard only minutes after he'd finished talking to one of the senior officers at New Scotland Yard. It would be seven in the evening in Hong Kong; not too late, although once he'd conveyed to him the latest turn of events in what they had named, "The Cristofoli Case", Robert was certain Howard wouldn't mind what time he called.

'There's been a rather unexpected development here;' Robert said to him when the usual preliminaries had been exchanged, 'an industrial chemist working for McLellands Medical Research Laboratories in Hong Kong walked into New Scotland Yard a short time ago,' he explained, 'as, apparently, he'd found a cache of emeralds hidden in the lining of his travel bag.'

'My goodness! This is incredible!'

'It is, isn't?' Robert chuckled, having already anticipated what Howard's reaction would be. Poor Howard; there he was in Hong Kong, Frank as well; the pair of them working diligently away trying to get to the root of what they suspected could be the smuggling of emeralds and some of them turn up in London.

'Has he any idea of how they got there?'

'Not exactly,' Robert said, 'although what he did have to say to the officer was indeed a strange tale.'

'Yes?'

'I'll only give you the bare bones over the phone, Howard,' Robert went on, 'and I'll follow it up in more detail by email later today, but, suffice to say, the shop in Pedder Street has reared its head once more.'

'And why am I not surprised?'

'My reaction as well.' Robert agreed, 'However, it would seem he had rather an unpleasant experience just over a week ago during a visit he had made there.'

'Yes?'

'For some reason, which I can't quite fathom out, he'd already been there the day before and had a compulsion to go back again, finding incidentally they were no longer selling pictures and for his interest, if that was all it was, he was duly rewarded by a bump on the head, resulting in him being carted off to Lamma Island for the night!'

'Very dramatic.'

'Very.'

'Presumably,' Howard suggested, 'somebody wanted him out of action for a while?'

'I would say so; long enough for them to find their way to where he lives and to deposit the emeralds into his bag.'

'They must have known he was planning to fly to London, though, Robert.'

'This is where the officer came up against a bit of a stumbling block.'

'In what way?'

'Our man then became somewhat reticent and said he had no idea how they could have known.'

'You don't believe him?'

'No, Howard, although I still have to meet him, I don't.'

'Did he say when he intends to get back to Hong Kong?'

'He has a flight booked for tomorrow night, but he mentioned to the officer he might well stay on for a couple of days.'

'And gave no reason, I suppose?'

'You suppose right.'

'Where do you suggest we go from here?'

'Well,' Robert took a deep breath, rearranging his thoughts in order of priority; never easy long distance over the phone, 'anything to do with the smuggling of precious stones is obviously an international matter, but I think it's now time for you to make yourself known to the head of police in Hong Kong, because,' he added, 'it looks as though we'll all have to work closely on this case, especially from the Hong Kong end.'

'I'll introduce myself to him first thing tomorrow morning.' Howard immediately suggested.

'That will be fine, Howard. Meanwhile I'll get this email off to you and as soon as we get word of when this chap is leaving, I'll give you a ring. He's called Roderick Mortimer, by the way.'

'English?'

'Oh, yes, he's been working for the laboratories for the last ten years, divorced, but all this will be in my report.'

'You'd like me to get in touch with him when he arrives, Robert?'

'I would, yes. I'll try and have a word with him myself, but it will have to be tomorrow sometime; he's in Oxford for the rest of today, giving talks at one of the colleges there, and won't be coming back to London until the morning. Meanwhile, Howard,' he continued, 'and only briefly, it's getting late there with you, but have you anything further to report?'

'Not a great deal. Francesca Cristofoli is still here, but then you'll know that already. She spends a considerable amount of time in the hotel, mainly in the Clipper Lounge.'

'On her own?'

'Mostly, yes, although on Friday afternoon she was with the editor of 'Woman's World'.

'Louisa Lambeth?'

'That's right, and then,' he went on, 'a slight deviation to her normal routine.'

'Ah.'

'She came into "The Captain's Bar" last night, but not going to one of the tables which I expected her to do, she stayed up at the bar.'

'Meeting someone?'

'I don't know,' Howard said slowly, 'although within a matter of minutes I saw her talking to Eddie Bristow.'

'Well, well. What do you think, Howard? A chance encounter or not?'

'Hard to tell,' Howard admitted, 'but if her body language was anything to go by, remembering what Virginia had told me, I would say they already knew each other, yet –'

'Go on, Howard; this is what I want to hear,' amused in spite of the seriousness of what they were discussing, sure that Howard had no idea how splendidly graphic he could be sometimes without over-elaborating in any way. Robert could imagine only too well the picture he was trying to portray: Francesca Cristofoli, notorious jewel thief, fugitive from justice, collector of the male species and, maybe Francesca Cristofoli, the vamp. He couldn't explain to himself why that particular and archaic expression came to mind, but he didn't think he was far wrong.

'Well,' Howard hesitated for a second, and to Robert's sensitive ear, was making an effort to express his thoughts and ones he had no doubt been puzzling over since he first saw the woman, 'she appeared to be making quite a play for him, if you know what I mean? She really is an incongruous sight, you know, Robert; her actions are of a woman less than half her age, but even so, nothing remotely resembling the way young women behave in these enlightened and broad-minded times.'

'I know what you mean, Howard. Coquettish, I suppose could be an apt description.'

'Yes, that's pretty much the way I saw her, although there was something deliberately scheming about the way she was behaving, not quite natural in fact. I did wonder if she may have been – er, trying – '

'- trying to pick him up?' helping him out.

'Could have been.' Howard's turn to laugh now as it was apparent to Robert at the other end of the line he was mulling the idea over in his imagination.

'But, we don't really know, do we? It could have been a rather smart ploy on her behalf. Also, we don't even know whether she realises she's under surveillance.'

'If she does,' Howard put in, 'don't you think she would have left Hong Kong by this time?'

'That's a good point;' Robert agreed, 'but I think what we have to remember is, the lady is a past master at deception; the way you saw her behaving the other evening could have been a rather clever double bluff.'

'What, leading us up the garden path, you mean, and then at the last minute doing another of her disappearing acts?'

'Yes, that's exactly what I was thinking, Howard.'

'Incidentally, you'll be interested to hear you were right in suggesting Yuan Enterprises may have subsidiary companies elsewhere.'

'Really?'

'Yes, we heard back from Companies House this afternoon and apparently his business extends to Singapore, Sydney and Johannesburg, although what they actually do is not clear. Enterprises can cover a multitude of things and in this particular instance, perhaps is on international proportions.'

'How right you are, Howard. But, Johannesburg; rather like taking coals to Newcastle, wouldn't you say?'

'In a way, yes,' Howard was quick to agree, 'that is if he is in fact extending his involvement in the distribution of emeralds, whether legally or otherwise.'

'They could, on the surface, be perfectly legitimate, as I'm certain if we made further checks, they would be. However,' he went on thoughtfully, 'as far as I'm aware, Howard, emeralds are mainly mined in the South American countries.'

'Like Columbia, for instance?'

'Exactly, and if you consider where he is geographically placed, namely in Hong Kong, what better position for him.'

'Tricky to get to the bottom of all this,' Howard said and Robert could hear the frustration in his voice, 'but it has occurred to me, we may be wasting our time here; kicking our heels, so to speak, and not really getting anywhere.'

'I wouldn't say that, you know,' Robert put in quickly, 'although I do understand how you and Frank must be feeling, but nevertheless, Howard, I wouldn't concern yourself about that unduly; I believe there may soon be further developments out there and then I rather think, you'll be more than fully occupied.'

'In the wake of the waiting game?'

'I couldn't have phrased it better myself, Howard.'

*

Conrad remained undecided whether to get in touch with Denny or not and tell him what he'd discovered about Roddie Mortimer; the main reason, apart from this, he had nothing else to report, at least nothing which would have satisfied him. He had made no attempt to gain access to Roddie Mortimer's hotel room, realising there would have been little chance of succeeding anyway. A hotel of the high standard of "The Russell" would have heavy security installed, making what Denny expected him to achieve virtually impossible. Once again, Conrad had set up exactly the same procedure as he had done for Thursday, although this time, the plan was for Roddie Mortimer's bag to be taken from him during the time he would be in the queue to check in for his late night flight to Hong Kong. This time, Conrad was equally as confident it would work; they wouldn't fail and within a matter of less than a couple of hours the first cache of emeralds would be with him. After all, he reasoned, it hadn't been his fault Mortimer had decided to change his flight; indeed, how was he to know? And, come to that, Denny hadn't known either. So much for the reliability of whoever was keeping him informed.

Conrad's men, two of them, were in position in Departures at eight-thirty on the Tuesday night, more than two hours before checking in: one of them at the automatic doors leading from outside where the taxis drew up and the second, a man who had worked for him for a number of years and had never let him down, at the barrier for the Cathay Pacific flight. They both had full descriptions of the man they had to look out for, also of his travel bag: dark blue leather with a broad band of lighter blue along one length of it.

When there was no sign of Roddie Mortimer and, after waiting until the last straggling passengers for Hong Kong had booked in, even until the final call had been announced for the flight, they came to the inevitable conclusion he wasn't going to turn up. Once again, within a matter of a few days, their plans had been thwarted and neither of them looked forward to passing this on to Conrad Bailey. Not to put too fine a point on it, they remarked to each other as they made their way back to their car, he would not be pleased.

This was a complete understatement; Conrad was furious and at first, before he had managed to calm down, he accused them of missing Mortimer; of not recognising the man; of not arriving in Departures early enough; in fact, plucking randomly, anything to stop him thinking of what must have happened, namely Mortimer was on to them. He had known what was going to happen; he'd discovered the emeralds and, either he had left earlier or he was still in London, how the hell was he to find out, but far more than this was how he was going to explain this latest debacle to Denny who, naturally enough, would blame him!

Conrad waited until after breakfast the following morning to phone him, being reluctant to break the news to him and having to undergo Denny's inevitable verbal onslaught. By the time he had explained and was bracing himself for the characteristic tirade of criticism, Roddie had been back in Hong Kong for more than ten hours.

He waited until he reached Kai Tak before sending Juliet a text on the mobile number she had given him the previous week, keeping it short, but sufficient to let her know he wouldn't be arriving at the time she expected him and adding he would be in touch. Roddie made no excuses for what she would immediately recognise as a deliberate vagueness on his part. A romance to end all romances, he thought cynically, unlocking the front door of his apartment, and although by now, there was no doubt in his mind about her duplicity, he couldn't help wishing, foolish though it was, that the situation had been different, unable to get rid of the indisputable fact he had been used. How could such loveliness act as a foil for something so dishonest, he wondered, switching on the air-conditioning. It was stifling in the apartment although he had only been away for less than a week and his maid would have completely aired the place when she had been in, as usual, on Monday morning.

It was still early, not yet seven o'clock, but he had no intention of making the mistake of trying to catch up on some lost sleep, knowing from experience, if he did, he would never be able to sleep at night. Instead, he would have a shower which should help, followed by some coffee and toast at one of the early-morning cafes on the way down to Des Veoux Road. Work, he decided, was the best remedy for discarding what were rapidly becoming negative and useless thoughts, although, as she had been in the habit of doing, Juliet continued to be on the periphery of his mind and he guessed it would take more than a day spent in the office to finally dispel.

Roddie had come to the conclusion he had recently been spending too many hours on his own, concentrating too much on trying to analyse practically every moment since the other Thursday when he'd met her, especially those memories, hazy and so far incomprehensible, when he had been drifting in and out of consciousness, but now, for the first time, he was starting to recall snippets of disjointed whisperings, but they still didn't make much sense. No doubt because most of what was said had been in Cantonese, with only the odd English word, but he had been right in the first instance; Juliet *had* been there. He could hear her voice again, quite clearly this time: "I hope you haven't hit him too hard, Denny." That was what she had said, wondering why it had taken him so long to remember. And the name, Denny; why hadn't he made the connection earlier? That first evening when they'd had dinner together, she had taken a call from a man she had called Denny.

Combing his hair, still damp from the shower, and looking at his reflection in the bathroom mirror, Roddie pulled a face. You probably knew all the time, but refused to admit it to yourself, he muttered under his breath. Juliet Warburton, from the very first moment he'd seen her, had it would appear, not only captured his heart, but had taken over his brain!

Chapter Eleven
HONG KONG

Eddie spent the first forty-eight hours, after he had arrived in Hong Kong on Friday and had booked into the "Sheraton Hotel" in Kowloon, planning exactly how he would achieve what at first, even before he had finished talking to Hugh on Wednesday, had only been a germ of an idea and one which he realised could go either way, but there was one thing for sure, Marion Godwin had gone too far. Nobody, not one single person in Eddie Bristow's world, messed with him and that was precisely what she had done. Realising she would not have been the only person involved was not paramount to him.

As for Hugh; he had meant what he had said, he didn't blame him for not noticing the formula had been a forgery and as he had pointed out, he could have done nothing about it anyway; the damage had already been done. The pair of them, both old and experienced enough to have known better, had been well and truly set up. They had been used and that, to Eddie, was an extremely bitter pill, and one he was totally incapable of swallowing.

It was true they had lost a considerable amount of money, in particular the advance payments to Marion and that young smart-arse, Nicholas Eastman, but it was more than that, important though it was and would make a significant hole in their budget for some months to come, but not one they wouldn't be able to overcome; the main unpalatable fact remained, at least as far as he was concerned, Marion had to be sorted for once and for all!

He had given Hugh no hint of the way his mind was working; indeed, it was doubtful whether he would have understood the exact extent of the wrath he felt towards a woman they had both trusted. He had long acknowledged Hugh was not exactly in his league. Of course he knew about his shady past; Eddie had made it his business back in the early days before they went into partnership to find out all he could, which, in the final analysis, wasn't all that much, although apparently sufficient to convince Hugh he was a hardened criminal, albeit he was found out before he could do too much damage. Accepting bribes and suppressing evidence didn't rate too highly in Eddie's scale of illegal activities. Also, Hugh was a chronic worrier and, perhaps more importantly, lacked the ability to think and plan ahead and consider, even reject each move well in advance and this was what Eddie had been doing since he left London on Thursday night.

Hugh had only been in touch with him once since he had arrived; the reason for the call still rankled and reminded him, not that he really needed any reminding, that, quite frankly at times, Hugh did not have it. He had totally mishandled the situation the other evening in "The Moon" and by his thoughtless reaction could very well have made this guy who had recognised him in Hong Kong even more interested than he was already. But, why on earth had Hugh denied he'd been there? That had been really dumb! Why couldn't he have been a little more innovative? What he should have said was, Eddie, somewhat belatedly writing the script for him, "yes, I was in Hong Kong earlier in the week and, yes, I do remember seeing you." That was all he needed to have said. It would have been enough. But, instead, Hugh had immediately gone on the defensive, saying, apart from not knowing anyone called Nicholas Eastman, he hadn't been there. Who was this man anyway? Hugh didn't even know his name; only that he had known Nicholas. Fat lot of good that was, Eddie decided, shoving what could or could not be of any importance to the back of his mind where it belonged; he had far too much to think about.

His partner was an out and out alarmist, Eddie reminded himself, walking down the steps of "The Sheraton" and along the pavement towards the Star Ferry terminal, weaving in and out of the early Sunday evening strollers; a noisy mixture of tourists and local Cantonese making the most of their weekend. At last, the sizzling temperatures were lessening; a cool and refreshing breeze blowing up from the estuary as the ferry approached Hong Kong Island. Every stage of his plan was now in place and by this time tomorrow he should be on his way back to Kai Tak, his mission hopefully concluded. Eddie wasn't fooling himself; he was far too realistic to go down that road, also he had no illusions of what he was about to carry out or why. His pride, always a rather sensitive part of his make-up, had been hurt and he was dealing with the aftermath in the only way he knew how.

First things first, though, he decided; a couple of drinks, followed by something to eat. Italian, perhaps? Or, Spanish? It didn't really matter; provided the restaurant was small and relatively quiet, if that was possible. It would be several hours before he could take a taxi up to Mid Levels and he needed to pace himself for what promised to be a long night.

He had taken one step inside "The Captain's Bar" when he saw her. He could have changed his mind; she hadn't seen him and later he was to question why he hadn't followed his first instincts. Frances Catania was the very last person he expected to see here, and even as he walked across to where she was sitting, perched on one of the bar stools and showing plenty of deeply tanned thigh, he knew why. As she had always done, right from the very first moment he had met her in Bogota almost ten years ago, she absolutely fascinated him. Eddie had been around and freely sampled what, especially in his earlier days, always seemed to be in plentiful supply, but he had never known a woman like her. She simply exuded her special brand of sexuality; she wasn't beautiful, far from it, at least not in the traditional sense, and probably never had been, but for some inexplicable and tantalising reason Frances Catania made it abundantly clear she didn't need to depend on anything so commonplace.

'Hello, Frances.'

'Hello, Eddie.' swivelling round on her stool, those remarkable cat-like eyes looking up at him without the slightest trace of surprise and then he realised she had already seen him; the mirror on the wall behind the bar was facing her and he would have been in her line of vision even before he entered the bar.

'It's been a long time.' Eddie said inadequately, pulling out the stool next to her.

'Ten years is not so long, Eddie.' she smiled, a brief quirky smile which immediately transformed her features, making her appear years younger, not that he had any idea of how old she was and even if he had been bold, or rude, enough to ask, knew she would never have told him. Not that he could blame her for that. He, also, had more than a streak of vanity and all too conscious of his looming sixtieth birthday. 'So,' she went on slowly, her eyes narrowing as she took in every aspect of his appearance, 'what are you doing these days; still in finance?'

'Mostly, yes. I started up my own consultancy business in London some years ago.'

'A consultancy business;' she repeated, his words sounding oddly foreign coming from her, but then he reasoned, why shouldn't they? She was half-French after all; at least that is what she'd always told him and he'd had no reason to disbelieve her. 'the same old Eddie, sparing with the details.'

'Less of the old, if you don't mind.'

'Oh, dear,' she chuckled softly, 'I've hit a nerve, have I?'

'Not really, Frances, but what about yourself? Are you still living in Columbia?'

'For the time being,' she answered, 'although I believe the time has come for me to move on. I'm finding life over there a trifle -' hesitating for a second, although she didn't fool him. Frances Catania knew exactly what she was going to say, also how much she was prepared to tell him. She, too, could be sparing with her explanations, '- how should I describe it to you, I wonder,' she continued, 'too insular for me, perhaps, even boring at times. I'm not sure, but I'm beginning to think I've been there too long.'

'No man in your life, then?' he asked, although fairly sure there would be.

'What do you think, Eddie?' the return of the smile, her head on one side exactly as he remembered.

'Well, is there?'

'Of course there is! But since when was that ever a hindrance to me, Eddie when I make up my mind to do something different? I've never found it all that difficult to say goodbye; one little word, that's all, and far less complicated than saying hello, with all the hidden connotations that can imply. But then, I don't need to tell you this. You had no such problem as far as I can remember when you decided to pack up and leave Bogota.'

'I told you at the time, Frances; I had no choice. My contract was at an end. You could always have come with me, you know. I did ask you.'

'I know you did,' her expression serious for a moment, 'but London held no appeal for me, Eddie.'

'A pity.' and meaning it; in spite of the many reservations he had about her and aware of her promiscuous behaviour from time to time, he had hoped once he had taken her away from so much availability in and around Bogota, their relationship could have developed.

'Perhaps,' she smiled, echoing his thoughts, 'but that's something we'll never know, although, seriously Eddie, I don't really think it would have worked out.'

'No, you're probably right.' he agreed and she *was* right. Their affair, although intensely passionate, had been relatively short-lived and in those days she had been moving in some wealthy and high-powered circles where there could never be any place for him, not that he ever wanted to; Eddie was entirely non-political, neutral to the core of his being, and he remembered her mentioning the names of a number of government ministers in the capital and he had already worked out she was on intimate terms with at least one of them, although, at this moment, sitting next to her in the convivial atmosphere of one of Hong Kong's most prestigious hotel bars, he was finding it difficult to remember back in much detail to those days.

'Are you here on business?' she asked him; as always going directly to what she wanted to know, no skirting tactfully around the edges with Frances, that wasn't her way. And it was here his internal alarm system began to kick in. She never asked an idle question, therefore, he concluded, for some reason, she did want to know. Eddie had been in her company too many times in the past not to recognise her tactics. There was a side, a secretive one, to her which he didn't think anyone had been able to penetrate. He had never questioned her about her flamboyant lifestyle. Once again, it wouldn't have achieved anything; he would never have got the true answer, if he got one at all, but suffice to say she never seemed to be short of money, also she didn't appear to work. He'd always assumed, knowing she had been married before – she'd actually told him that much – that she'd been left sufficiently well provided for, whether through being widowed or from a lucrative divorce settlement. Frances Catania was a woman with a past; there was no doubt about that, also it would seem she was a woman without any visible means of support. And, now, here she was, waiting for him to tell her why he was in Hong Kong.

'Well, Eddie,' she prompted, 'why so quiet?'

'No reason,' he said, 'I was thinking, that's all; about our time together. Seeing you this evening has brought it all back, I suppose. Sorry, you were saying?'

'I was asking whether you were in Hong Kong on business.'

'I am, yes,' he answered, affecting a casualness he was far from feeling, 'but only for a few more days and then it's back to London.'

'Mmmph,' pursing her scarlet lips, which said she didn't believe one word he'd said, 'you know what they say, Eddie,' she smiled again, 'all work and no play?'

'You could be right,' parrying now and playing her at her own game and this was territory he was quite familiar with, 'and you, Frances, are you on holiday?'

'No, not exactly,' she answered, 'I'm house-hunting as a matter of fact.'

'Really?'

'You sound surprised?'

'I am, yes, and you consider it would be a good time for such an investment?'

'Oh,' she waved a hand in the air dismissively, 'I suppose you mean this handover business?'

'You don't seem concerned.'

'I'm not, not in the least;' she repeated, 'on the contrary, in spite of what the pessimists are muttering, I think this is a good time to buy. Property will always be in demand, Eddie and eventually, when I begin to tire of living here and want to sell up I could very well make a healthy profit.'

'And have you seen anything you like?'

'Plenty, actually,' she said, 'but one in particular appeals to me. It's an apartment in Princes' Terrace and from what my lawyer has told me, the area is earmarked for improvement: cafes, restaurants and boutiques which should make it more desirable; close enough to Central, but self-sufficient for the various amenities.'

'Well,' Eddie said, 'you certainly seem to have done your homework. I hope you're successful.'

'Oh, I will be; Marion knows what she's talking about; she's even bought one of the apartments herself. She is a very shrewd lawyer, completely switched on, in fact.'

'Is she Cantonese?' he asked her, but knowing instinctively she must be talking about Marion Godwin. There couldn't be two lawyers in Hong Kong called Marion; that would be stretching coincidence too far!'

'No, she's as English as you are, Eddie. In fact,' she put in, 'I have a meeting with her tomorrow morning to sign up on my offer.'

*

It was approaching dusk when Eddie reached Princes' Terrace and, having paid off his taxi in Caine Road, he walked down the short, but steep, incline to the first apartment block. Princes' Terrace; a quiet part, a ten-minute walk to Central and the steady drone from the traffic surging along Caine Road the only sounds to break the stillness. He had been here the day before and even then, although it had been during the day, there had been few people about and tonight, apart from a man with a small dog on a lead a hundred yards in front of him, the entire length of the terrace was deserted. Eddie held back until the man had let himself in through the main door before continuing slowly along the pavement. He already knew there would be a concierge on duty in the front lobby, also that the building was equipped with security cameras. He had done his homework since he'd arrived in Hong Kong and, as he was doing now, he'd walked past the front entrance until he'd reached the rear of the building and running the first risk of being noticed, climbed the steps of the fire-escape until he'd reached the glass door leading on to a narrow balcony of where Marion Godwin lived on the fourth floor. He had familiarised himself with the geography of the place, gratified to learn that each apartment occupied a whole floor which meant he would have no difficulty in finding the one he was looking for.

Keeping close to the edge of the fire-escape and crouching below the cameras positioned on each floor, he finally reached her apartment. She hadn't closed the curtains and there were no lights on inside. She was either in bed, which he dismissed as unlikely, or she was out. Either way, he wasn't unduly concerned. He had plenty of time; the remainder of the night if necessary. The lock, as he had found out yesterday, was a simple one and he managed silently and without any difficulty to manoeuvre the mechanism until he heard the soft click as the device responded. Turning the handle and pulling the door open towards him, he stepped into Marion's lounge

Breaking in was easier than he expected and, as he had thought, the apartment was empty. He took the precaution of closing the curtains before switching on the desk lamp next to her computer in the corner of the lounge; an area she obviously used as a study and not in the least surprised. Marion Godwin, he knew from experience, was an extremely methodical woman, also with a keen sense of self-preservation. She would never leave any record of anything unconnected with her legal business in her office, where someone sufficiently inquisitive and with the necessary expertise, would be able to access. She was far too shrewd for that. This, Eddie decided, could be interesting, sitting down at her desk and switching on the computer.

Entering the system was no problem to him, having spent a good part of his career being involved with more than the basic computer skills; something else in which Hugh lagged sadly behind, he thought, scrolling down the screen. He had no preconceived idea what he would find, incriminating or otherwise, therefore he wasn't too disappointed to see the documents file was empty and then wondering whether she had made a list of contacts, although if she had, they could all very well be stored separately. If he had time before she returned, he would make a search of the apartment; there must be floppy disks somewhere, or other means of storing what she would consider to be sensitive material, and highlighting the icon he double-clicked on 'Contacts'.

There weren't many; no more than a dozen names, some with addresses, but, intriguingly, she had included underneath a couple of them, the name of a sub-file she labelled 'Diary'. Moving quickly now; he had already been here for nearly an hour, he returned to the main menu until he found what he was looking for and, sure enough, there it was; an abbreviated day-to-day diary, luncheon and dinner appointments, nothing of any great significance, at least not to him, but he spotted two names from the list of contacts; one, he immediately recognised, that of Nicholas Eastman with whom she'd apparently had lunch two weeks ago, but it was the other name, Denny Yuan, which interested him and going back once more to 'Contacts', he scrolled down until he found it: "Yuan Enterprises HK (Denny)", no address, although there was a telephone number.

Fifteen minutes later he heard the whine of the lift as it came to a halt outside the front door of the apartment. Eddie, by this time, had turned off the desk lamp, pulled back the curtains and, apart from the pale light from the moon, the room was in semi-darkness.

'Eddie! How the hell did you get in here?' Marion gasped, her slight figure framed in the open doorway from the light she had switched on in the hall.

'Good evening, Marion,' he said smoothly, not standing up and remaining where he was on the sofa, having by this time moved away from her desk. 'I don't think you really expect me to answer that.'

'You have a damn nerve! I can get you thrown out, you know, right this minute! Alternatively, I can phone the police!'

'Both of us know you won't do that, Marion, don't we?'

'Don't be so sure!'

'Why don't you sit down,' he suggested calmly in the same low tone he'd used since she had come in, 'you and I have a lot to talk about, Marion.'

*

Francesca was not merely annoyed; she was far more than that. Her appointment with Marion Godwin had been for eleven o'clock and she fully expected her to be there. Francesca Cristofoli was not accustomed to being kept waiting, far less to be given no acceptable reason why she should be. The ingratiating words of apology from one of the partners, at least that was how it had sounded to her, meant absolutely nothing. Also, the man's excuses were totally inadequate. What was it he had said, and that was after he'd offered her a cup of luke-warm coffee which she had found undrinkable? It was now eleven forty-five and she had a luncheon appointment in fifteen minutes and all he could offer in the way of an attempt to pacify her was that he would be only too pleased in the event of Miss Godwin being unavoidably detained to handle the signing of the purchase offer for her. This makeshift suggestion she found quite unacceptable and had insisted he tried again to contact the lawyer. When there continued to be no reply from the number he had been ringing she had very nearly lost her temper in that claustrophobic atmosphere of what was intended to be a reception area, but, instead, with a cool dismissive nod to the doe-eyed girl behind the desk, she turned her back on them and walked out of the office.

She inwardly seethed as she walked along the pavement towards Queen's Road Central over the off-hand manner to which she had been treated. She hadn't travelled this far, and she didn't mean the journey from Columbia to Hong Kong, but the far longer one she seemed to have been on for as far back as she could remember, to be insulted in this way. Francesca didn't suffer fools gladly and that little man with the fake deferential expression on his face had without any doubt been one! Unfortunately, she didn't have a number for Miss Godwin and had had to depend on the ineptness of one of the other partners and she was not at all impressed. Also, and more importantly, she wanted to secure the purchase on the apartment she had viewed in Princes' Terrace and when she set her mind on anything, invariably and without exception that was exactly what she achieved.

It was now Monday and Francesca had been in Hong Kong for almost a week and already Antonio was becoming impatient. He had telephoned her twice in the last couple of days asking her whether she had booked her flight back to Bogota and each time she had prevaricated, although realising the somewhat lame excuse of needing a change of scenery for a few extra days wasn't what he wanted to hear. It made no difference that Antonio was married with a demanding family and an equally demanding position in the government; he was, above all, a hot-blooded South American and incredibly jealous. When she had first known him, she had found his possessiveness exciting, even flattering, but over the years, and more especially recently, this had begun to pall. Francesca wanted her freedom; the freedom to be herself and one of which she had almost lost trace. Those years in Europe seemed to her such a long time ago and if she ever thought about them, one aspect predominated, which was she had always conducted her life exactly as she wanted. The men, and there had been several, were on the periphery and had never been aware of what she'd been doing and that was the way she had wanted it, but ever since she met Antonio he had, right from the very first day, taken control and now, as she walked through the swing doors of The Mandarin Hotel and up the curving staircase to the Clipper Lounge, she made a promise to herself that as she had apparently reached a crossroads in her life, she would sever all her ties with him and that meant anyone else she knew in Bogota, before it was too late. She *would* move to Hong Kong. Of that she was absolutely certain. Perhaps, on reflection, she had been too hasty in her refusal to allow one of the other partners to deal with her business, but she had been angry; also, she hadn't liked the look of him all that much. At least she had the choice, Francesca reasoned; however much she had set her mind on buying the apartment in Princes' Terrace, there were other properties on the market, equally as attractive. Not for one moment did she consider Marion Godwin, whom she had only met once, could have been taken ill. That possibility simply didn't occur to her. To Francesca, everything was, as it had always been, either black or white: the lawyer wasn't in her office waiting to meet her at eleven and there had been no message to say she had been delayed, therefore, she had let her down.

Denny Yuan was already there, waiting for her in The Clipper Lounge. At least he was punctual, she grudgingly admitted to herself, walking briskly towards him.

'Hello, Frances,' he said, getting to his feet to shake hands, 'you look a trifle annoyed.'

'That's perceptive of you, Denny,' she said, sitting down across the table from him, 'although that's very much an understatement. I am, in fact, extremely annoyed. I had an appointment to meet someone this morning and she didn't turn up.'

'Any idea why?'

'None. Unfortunately I don't have her home number, but her office tried a couple of times without any success.'

'I'm sure you'll find there's a perfectly simple explanation.' and she could tell he was doing his best to calm her down, but he need not have bothered. There was nothing Denny or anyone else, it if came to that, could say to make her feel any differently.

'No doubt there is.' she said sharply, 'Anyway, Denny, how are you?'

'Not that great as a matter of fact,' he answered, 'like you, I'm pretty angry as well.'

'Oh?'

'Yes, my contact in London has made an absolute cock-up; sorry about the language, Frances; it's all to do with the package you brought over a few of weeks ago. I don't want to bore you with the ins and outs of it all, but it would appear, although the goods did manage to make their way to London, somewhat circuitously it's true, they are now on their way back here!'

As she listened to him giving her a brief outline of what had happened, her mind was moving away. She wasn't interested in the whereabouts of those emeralds once she had handed them over to him; that was entirely out of her hands. Soon, Bogota would have to find another courier and all of this would be history.

'Anyway, Frances,' he said at last, at the same time waving over to attract the attention of one of the waitresses, 'when do you plan to return to Columbia?'

'I haven't made up my mind yet.' she said slowly, having no intention of mentioning her plans. The last she wanted was for Denny to let Antonio know and she had no doubt that was exactly what he would do. That would be disastrous. She must be the first person to tell him. There was no saying how Antonio would react, but one thing was certain, it would not be pleasant. No, she would bide her time and do her best to convey to him why she would soon be leaving Bogota. 'Actually, I've got quite a full week, including a cocktail party at the Hilton on Wednesday night;' she added, hoping this would distract him, 'rather a splendid affair

I expect being held especially for a group of foreign dignitaries.'

'I'm surprised Antonio isn't putting on any pressure for you to get back.'

'Not that much,' she lied, 'but I just felt, Denny, I needed these days on my own; recharge my batteries, you know.'

'I see,' he answered, 'well, I was speaking to him earlier this morning and without alarming him, I've mentioned we should curtail these deliveries for some weeks. There have been a number of problems recently and I want everything to cool down a bit.'

'Watching your back, Denny?'

'How clever you are, Frances,' he smiled across at her, 'and so succinctly put. But, you're right, of course. Always consider number one first; that's my policy and don't tell me you are any different?'

'No comment.' she smiled back at him.

Chapter Twelve

Natasha's first day on Monday at 'Woman's World' passed uneventfully; most of the time she spent familiarising herself with the style and content of the magazine, interspersed by being taken around the offices by Mandy, the girl she'd seen on Wednesday, and being introduced to her new colleagues: an even mix of male and female with an average age of around twenty-six she guessed, which, after skimming through a number of back copies of 'Woman's World' magazine, proved to her the theme, in the main, was young, modern and, as Louisa Lambeth had already told her, a fair portion of the material was of a topical, even controversial, nature. Natasha had been surprised, and pleasantly so, to discover there appeared to be no limit to the range of topics being covered and she looked forward with an eagerness she had not experienced so far in her career to becoming part of such a vibrant team and wondering what her first assignment would be. She had given some thought to what had been said to her at the interview and sensed, in advance, that whatever it was, it would be a challenging one.

She didn't have long to wait. Towards the end of the afternoon she was called in to the editor's office and, this time, being asked to sit down opposite to her at the desk.

'Well, Natasha,' Louisa Lambeth said, leaning forward in her swivel chair, both hands clasped firmly in front of her, 'what are your first impressions?' Direct and very much to the point, but already in so short a time Natasha didn't expect anything less. She was accustomed to being talked to in this way; those years, few though they had been, had taught her that much. A magazine was probably no different from a newspaper; both had deadlines, a specific day on which they had to be out and there simply wasn't any time for prevaricating; in other words, the honeymoon was now over. From here on, she had to be seen to produce.

'I've read through a number of the magazines,' Natasha said, not sure whether she was going to come up with the right answers or not, but she had started and really had no choice but to finish what she wanted to say, 'and I believe I've been able to get the gist of what the general policy is and I like what I've been reading. I've tried to put myself into the minds of the readers you have already described to me, Miss Lambeth, and I am sure, in essence, the magazine must have considerable appeal. Also,' Natasha continued, 'I rather think they will look forward to the next issue.'

Louisa Lambeth was silent for two or three seconds; only a short space of time, but sufficient to make Natasha feel she may not have said enough to prove she'd been accurate in her précis of the magazine, or worse, she had sounded over-zealous.

'Of course, Natasha,' she said at last, 'those are exactly the words I wanted to hear, but I do believe you are quite sincere in what you're saying and, hopefully, those hours spent today will have given you a grounding, or perhaps I should say, a preparation for what we're looking for from our editorial staff. However,' she went on; the intelligent grey eyes never leaving Natasha's face, 'no doubt you are wondering what is going to come next?'

'I was, yes.' unable to keep from smiling. She was beginning to understand this woman and noticing how effortlessly she moved from one point to another. Not only was her work going to be challenging, equally, her new editor was going to take a lot of adapting to.

'I intend to run a series of articles, profiles, in fact, on a selection of women living in Hong Kong, who have chosen demanding, even unconventional careers and lifestyles; the essence of these profiles being informative as well as thought-provoking. For instance, Natasha, at what time in their lives did they make the decision to take that particular path to arrive where they are today? Had they always, as far back as they can remember, always had the pioneering and ambitious spirit, the inherent desire to be different, or had they experienced some event, traumatic or otherwise, which had made the decision for them? In other words, I believe what our readers will want to know is what makes these women tick.'

'How selective will you be, Miss Lambeth,' Natasha asked her, 'with your choice of subject, I mean?'

'As selective as I can be.' she answered, 'I've compiled an initial list made up of women I've known personally for some years and those I've heard about and I've approached each of them and, gratifyingly, they all reacted positively.'

'Perhaps they've never been asked to talk about themselves before.' Natasha suggested, relieved to learn she wouldn't be expected to act as a talent scout.

'Probably not,' Louisa agreed, 'you see, Natasha,' she went on quickly, obviously warming to what sounded like a brand new approach for the magazine to capture an even wider readership, 'so far, I've discovered they all have one trait in common, which is pragmatism. Although,' she added, 'you may not agree with me after you've conducted your first interview.'

'Why?'

'Don't look so alarmed,' she smiled, 'I'm not testing you, Natasha, although I suppose I'm warning you, that's all.'

'Yes?'

'The word pragmatism,' she began, 'may conjure up someone who is down-to-earth, practical and modest and although Anne Steed certainly has most of those qualities, I would not describe her as modest.'

'She sounds interesting.' was all she could think of saying, but at the same time, in spite of a slight nervousness, intrigued to hear more about her first subject, her first project with the magazine. Suddenly, London, the familiarity with which she was accustomed and had taken for granted, seemed a very long way off.

'I think so.'

'When would you like me to see her, Miss Lambeth?'

'I've arranged a meeting for tomorrow morning at ten o'clock, I'll give you the address in a moment, but I'll briefly outline a few essentials; Anne

Steed is the owner of a nightclub in Kowloon, called "Annie's" and has been for the last ten years. She's an American; in her mid-forties, but I'm afraid you won't get anything more precise than that. Like most women of 'a certain age' you'll find she is reluctant to tell you exactly how old she is. However, Natasha, I know I haven't given you much of a background, but I think that's probably best.'

'What sort of length should I be thinking about for the article?'

'Between eight hundred and a thousand words; the main thing is to get her talking. Start off the piece from when you first meet her; use your initial impressions as the basis for your questioning. I think you'll find one answer will take you on naturally to the next one. Don't spend more than an hour with her, Natasha; also you'll have one of our in-house photographers with you. I'd like your initial draft by four tomorrow afternoon, if possible. Also, while you're there, you can arrange with Miss Steed a suitable time to call back with your draft copy. Make sure she's happy with what you've written, Natasha, that's paramount; we don't want any libel problems. So,' she asked, 'what do you think?'

'A bit nervous, actually,' she admitted.

'That's understandable, but I'm sure within minutes of talking to Anne Steed, you'll feel better. In spite of her extrovert personality, she happens to be a very nice woman. You may feel by this time tomorrow,' she continued, 'you've been literally thrown in at the deep end, but I must be entirely honest with you, Natasha, because that is the way it is in Hong Kong.'

*

By five o'clock in the afternoon Simon Cheung, one of the partners in Godwin, Cheung & Fong, decided enough was enough. He had spent a good part of the day answering calls for Marion and pacifying irate clients who had turned up for their appointments. Not only was he frustrated at not being able to get on with his own heavy workload, but he was becoming increasingly concerned when there had been no word from her. He had lost count of the times he had tried to call her; both at her apartment and on her mobile, but each time nothing. He had to do something. Marion could have been taken ill, but even so, he reckoned, surely she would have been able to get in touch with the office. The three of them had been in partnership for a number of years and, as far as he could remember, this was the first time she had failed to make any appearance in the office.

Simon buzzed through to his partner's office to say he was finishing for the day, but first he intended to take a taxi up to where Marion lived and see what he could find out. He'd been there once before, not long after she had moved into her new apartment in Princes' Terrace, and remembered seeing a concierge on duty in the lobby. It was possible he may be able to help. Apart from that, he had no idea what else he should be doing. The last he wanted was to overact and call the police. That, to Simon's legally cautious mind was tantamount to panicking, but even although, as he left the building in Wellington Street and looking out for a passing taxi, which were invariably scarce at that time in the afternoon, he had to admit to himself he was worried.

Fifteen minutes later, he was pushing open the glass doors of the apartment block and crossing the highly polished tiled floor to the desk and introducing himself to the uniformed concierge who told him he had been on duty the previous night, also that he remembered Miss Godwin coming home around eleven and taking the lift up to her apartment on the fourth floor. And, perhaps more importantly and significantly, he hadn't finished his shift until nine that morning and Miss Godwin, as far as he was aware, had still been in her apartment. And, no he insisted, there had been no visitors, either last night or this morning.

From then on, everything happened in kaleidoscopic rapidity, at least so it seemed to Simon. Although well versed with police procedure, having attended numerous court cases over the years, what was happening during the next sixty minutes was to him positively bizarre.

After the concierge pressed the intercom to Marion's apartment and there was no response, with Simon's agreement, he telephoned police headquarters. Within minutes, an un-marked car had pulled up outside the building and two police officers were striding into the lobby. Again, Simon explained who he was and why he was so concerned. They hadn't hesitated, but made straight towards the lift and, with Simon following closely behind them, one of them pressed the button for the fourth floor. With the pass key the concierge had given them, they opened the front door of Marion's apartment and the three of them walked along the hall to the open door of what Simon knew was the lounge.

At first he found it difficult to readjust his eyes to the dimness of the room; the curtains were drawn and even from an overhead light which had been left on in the hall behind them most of the furniture was a shady outline, but not so much he was unable to make out the slumped figure of Marion on one of the chairs; her head thrown back at an awkward angle and both hands clenched against her throat. It was not the first dead body Simon had seen and he recognised rigor mortis when he saw it. Marion had been dead; he was sure, for a number of hours. He must have stood there for several seconds, transfixed, only partly aware of the activity around him and, once more, everything was happening at an unbelievable speed. The forensic team; photographers, more officers and what was once Marion Godwin, now covered by a blanket and placed on a stretcher and taken away, the sound of the lift staying with him long after it had reached the ground floor.

*

The following morning, shortly before ten, and Howard was pushing open the heavy double doors of the main police station. As he had promised Robert the evening before he would make a point of touching base with them first thing. He had phoned them earlier and had to admit the way the desk sergeant immediately stood to attention as soon as he reached the desk and introduced himself was impressive. Within minutes, he was being escorted along the white-tiled corridor to Inspector

Clarke's office.

'Good morning, Mr Westwood.' he said, standing up and coming round the front of his desk to shake hands with him; a tall, gaunt figure of a man with a shock of grey hair which reminded Howard of an ageing badger. 'It's a pleasure to meet you and, quite frankly, we're grateful for your presence here, in Hong Kong, given the recent rather puzzling events and we look forward to working with you. However,' he continued, almost in the same breath before Howard was able to respond, 'first things first, don't you agree? Coffee. I'll get my secretary to rustle up some and then we can get down to business.'

'Sounds fine by me, Inspector.' Howard said, doing his best to hide his amusement: Inspector William Clarke was so incredibly colonial; his every mannerism, his tone of voice, all epitomised another era when the colony had known different times. Looking at him, it was hard to believe in a matter of five years, that is if he hadn't retired before then, he would probably no longer be in the same position; in the hierarchy of police headquarters where it was possible the shadow of the impending handover had not yet made any real impression to remind them of the inevitable changes it would bring.

'Francesca Cristofoli,' he began, after the pretty Chinese girl had brought their coffee, deferentially pouring it out for them both and, Howard noticed, adding two generous teaspoonfuls of sugar to the Inspector's, 'the name of the lady you have, I understand, been trying to locate for some years and now, according to what Mr Anderson has told me, you believe she is in Hong Kong.'

'That's right,' Howard said, 'she has certainly given us a good run for our money. It shouldn't have taken us this long, but after she left Europe, in particular London which had apparently always been her base, she cleverly covered her tracks by hiding herself away in Columbia, plus going so far as to change her name; all of which hasn't helped us at all.'

'To Frances Catania?'

'Quite; also her appearance to a certain extent, but I don't know whether Mr Anderson told you, she was actually recognised by her voice.'

'Yes, he did and, of course, that is something practically impossible to disguise, to anyone with a keen ear. And, Mr Westwood, your people feel there could be considerably more to her activities, if I can describe them as such, in that she is involved in something far more widespread?'

'We do, Inspector. We might be mistaken, but if not, and she is bringing in regular supplies of emeralds from Columbia for distribution elsewhere, it is possible the set-up is on an international scale. Up to now, we haven't got a great deal to go on, little more than conjecture.'

'But, Mr Westwood,' he asked, taking another sip of his coffee, 'you feel this latest development of emeralds turning up in someone's luggage in London has some connection with her?'

'We believe it could be,' Howard answered, 'but, coincidences aside, and as I'm sure you will agree, they are usually in plentiful supply in any enquiry, the fact remains the man who supports her in Bogota is part-owner of an emerald mine out there and she has been making regular visits to Hong Kong for the past six years or so, but, perhaps more importantly, the first place she visited last week as soon as she had arrived at Kai Tak, was the shop in Pedder Street and this was from where Roderick Mortimer was abducted.'

'Yes, Mr Anderson mentioned that somewhat strange occurrence, but,' pausing, his cup half-raised to his lips, 'just a moment, Mr Westwood;' he went on quickly, 'you mentioned the name Roderick Mortimer?'

'Yes?'

'I do believe I've been a little slow here, you know,' he admitted, 'but a week ago one of my officers filed a report from McLellands Medical Research Laboratories. Apparently, they'd had an unpatented formula stolen from their bank deposit box and the industrial chemist involved in the research and development of this formula is called Roderick Mortimer.'

'That is no coincidence, Inspector!'

'How right you are.'

'I have yet to meet him.' Howard said, 'We are not altogether happy about what he told New Scotland Yard; there are a number of gaps which need to be filled in. However,' he went on, 'I've heard he's booked on the midday flight from Heathrow and I'll be getting in touch with him tomorrow.'

'A great deal seems to be happening here at the moment,' Inspector Clarke said quietly, 'and much of it I can't help but feel is connected in some convoluted way.'

'You mean between the theft of the formula and the latest development in pinning Francesca Cristofoli down?'

'Well,' Inspector Clarke said, 'a trifle more than that, actually. You may not have heard, but last evening we were called out to the home of one of Hong Kong's prominent lawyers, namely, Marion Godwin. Her partners in the law firm had become increasingly concerned during the day when she hadn't arrived for work and they hadn't heard from her, so much so, in fact, one of them decided to find out what was wrong. It was he who called us and indeed he had been quite right to be worried. She had been dead for several hours when two of my officers entered her apartment; since late on Sunday night in fact.' he added.

'How had she died?'

'We believe she had been poisoned, but we're still waiting for the pathologist's report to officially confirm this.'

'You mentioned a possible connection, Inspector?' Howard prompted him.

'Sorry, I'm coming to that; in a roundabout fashion I admit, but Marion Godwin acted for McLellands and had been their lawyer since the company was first formed in Hong Kong. When the managing director of the laboratories reported the theft of the formula last Friday he also mentioned that arrangements had been made, once Roderick Mortimer collected the formula from the bank, for him to take it personally to Marion Godwin in order for her to finalise on the patenting of the drug.'

'As you say,' Howard said, trying to assimilate everything he had been told, 'if these various factors are connected in some way it is certainly convoluted; it won't be easy to untangle.'

'That is what has been worrying me, Mr Westwood. Perhaps once you have the opportunity of meeting up with Roderick Mortimer, the picture may become clearer. Meanwhile,' he added, 'before you go, I'll give you a copy of the report regarding the theft of the formula and, as soon as we receive the one from the pathologist, this will be delivered to you at your hotel. Meanwhile, I'll make arrangements for an office to be made available for you while you're in Hong Kong.'

'Thank you,' Howard said, 'I would appreciate that.'

*

'You're Natasha, aren't you?' the young woman asked, standing in the open doorway of Anne Steed's office; every line of her body rigid with undisguised animosity, 'Nicholas' *girlfriend?* she emphasised, her dark, almost black eyes narrowing as she glared at Natasha.

As soon as she'd uttered the first spite-filled words, Natasha knew she was the same person who'd phoned Nicholas' apartment the week before. Glad she was on her own in the office, Anne Steed having been called to deal with what she had described as a minor crisis in another part of the building, although Natasha didn't know how long she would be away and, somehow, she had to get rid of this woman before she came back. So far, the interview had gone well and already Natasha had half-filled a tape with what she hoped would turn out to be an interesting article.

Anne Steed had certainly led an eventful life and, after the first couple of minutes, needed little prompting; it was as though she wanted the outside world to know how she had arrived at where she was now; the sole owner of what she had insisted to Natasha was a successful and lucrative business. Without checking back on the tape, Natasha could remember her words quite well: "It's like this, Miss Bailey," she had said, "when I arrived in Hong Kong twenty years ago with my husband, who, incidentally, I am no longer married to, I simply had no idea how I was going to earn my own living. In fact," she had continued, crossing and re-crossing her long legs dramatically, reminding Natasha of the comedian, Kenny Everett, at his most outrageous, "believe it or not, where I came from; a one-street apology for a town right in the heart of Texas, I knew nothing about the entertainment or the hospitality business. I had never been in a nightclub, so I guess you could say that Hong Kong changed not only me, but my life as I once knew it and there has been no looking back. No way!"

'Well?' she was still there, leaning insolently against the wall, her body language demanding a response from her, 'Just how long to do you intend to stay in Hong Kong?'

'I'm sorry,' Natasha said, keeping her voice low, 'I really don't think that is any of your business. I told you on the phone I was Nicholas' girlfriend and, as you can see, I'm trying to do my job and I would be grateful if you would allow me to get on with it.'

'If you know what's good for you, Natasha Bailey,' spitting out each syllable of her name, 'you will pack your bags and go back to England! Nicholas belongs to me and until you came along and spoiled everything we were going to get married!'

'Look,' Natasha said, expecting Anne Steed to return at any moment, 'I don't wish to continue this conversation; I suggest you talk to Nicholas.'

'You don't get it, do you!' she hissed, 'You just don't get it! You have no idea what it is to be poor, *really* poor, but where I come from in the Philippines, we are familiar with poverty and marrying Nicholas would have pulled me out of that – forever!'

'All I can say,' Natasha replied, continuing to keep her voice down, 'none of this concerns me.'

'That's where you're wrong, lady,' she snapped, 'it *is* your concern because you are standing in my way. Oh, I know your sort –'

'Marcia!' Anne Steed called out from the passageway, preventing

Natasha learning what her sort was meant to be, 'Have you no work to do?'

'Yes, Miss Steed,' she meekly replied, swivelling round on her heels, 'I was just going.'

'Off you go, then; I don't pay you for moping around here all day. I'm sorry about that, Miss Bailey.' she said, once they had the office to themselves, 'Staff! Always a problem, I'm afraid.'

'I won't keep you much longer, Miss Steed,' Natasha said, 'it's obvious you're busy.'

The confrontation with the woman she had called Marcia had unsettled her, making it difficult to concentrate, but relieved she already had sufficient material which should run to the length Louisa Lambeth had suggested.

'That's true,' she sighed, 'but I must admit I've enjoyed this morning. Vanity, I suppose, but it was a luxury to talk about myself.'

'Before I wind up,' Natasha said, 'there's only one question I'd like to ask.'

'Fire away!'

'It's about the future; have you made any plans? For instance, will you remain in Hong Kong?'

'I guess you're referring to nineteen ninety-seven?'

'Not exactly, although obviously it must be at the back of your mind; whether, after the handover there may even be an opportunity for expansion or, alternatively, laws governing businesses in the entertainment field may become more stringent?'

'You're right, of course,' Anne Steed said, her expression thoughtful for a second, 'not one person in Hong Kong knows what life will be like here after the handover, but I have no intention of leaving, although I have started making plans to open a nightclub in Vietnam; having visited the country a number of times recently I believe there could be room for development there. It would be a good investment, but I won't move there; I'll employ a manager to run the business for me.'

'A contingency plan, perhaps?'

'Yes, exactly,' she smiled, 'I'm a gambler, Miss Bailey and I've learned that to succeed you must be prepared to take risks, but having said that,' she went on, 'they are always calculated ones.'

'And you always win?'

'My answer to that, Miss Bailey is,' she chuckled loudly, 'I win some and I lose some!'

*

Denny received a call from Inspector Clarke at three-thirty in the afternoon and up to then he had no idea what had happened to Marion. Although, as he normally did each morning on the way to the office, he had bought a copy of "The South China Morning Post", apart from the headlines, he hadn't had time to read anything else and later, once he had found the piece, sadly relegated to a short single column at the bottom of the third page, he had started to come to terms with what the inspector had told him: Marion was dead, the woman he had known for a number of years, once intimately, and with whom he had spent Sunday evening, neither of them realising that later that night her life would come to an abrupt end.

The news had been so shocking; to hear about her in that cool, upper-class English voice, he hadn't thought at first to ask why he should be phoning him. It simply had not occurred to him and then the inspector, pre-empting him, had told him about the message he'd left on Marion's answering machine the day before. From that moment, the first trickle of, not exactly fear, but certainly closely bordering it, made its appearance, remembering word for word the message he had left for her: "Marion," he'd said, "we need to talk again; it's become crucial we must move forward as early as possible." This is what the police had heard and what sort of connotation they'd put on that, he wondered. Not that Inspector Clarke had actually mentioned the contents of what he'd left on her machine, but that didn't mean a thing. They had heard alright and now they were asking him to call into the station in order, the inspector had said in his mealy-mouthed way, they could clarify a few points. I bet, Denny thought bitterly; they were going to stitch him up. He knew what they were up to. A murder enquiry and he knew practically nothing about any of the details, of an English woman living in Hong Kong. Okay, a lawyer and a pretty high profile one at that, and they would want to tie up the case rapido. And to do that, naturally they would need to pull in a culprit – or a fall guy; the unpleasant thought creeping insidiously into his mind. Well, Denny concluded, replacing the receiver which felt unpleasantly moist in his hand, they weren't going to win this one. He had managed so far to avoid the law and he had every intention of continuing. He was a whole heap smarter than the inspector, who, judging by his voice, must be tottering on the edge of retirement and, if it came to that, anyone else at police headquarters. Watch my tracer he muttered under his breath. Just watch my tracer!

Before leaving for his meeting with the inspector, Denny read through again what had been reported in the paper: "The body of Miss Marion Godwin, one of Hong Kong's leading lawyers, was discovered late yesterday afternoon in her apartment. Mr Simon Cheung, a partner in the same law firm as Miss Godwin, had become concerned when she had not turned up for work and had contacted the police. There had been no sign of any break-in and, according to the concierge who had been on duty on Sunday night, she hadn't received any visitors. The cause of death has yet to be established, but Miss Godwin's death is being treated as suspicious." .....being treated as suspicious, Denny muttered under his breath, recalling the reluctance of Inspector Clarke to elaborate on how she had died, except to convey to him without actually saying as much, that they were conducting a murder enquiry.

Police Headquarters were within easy walking distance from his office and during the time it took him to reach the building, memories of Marion encroached, making it difficult for him to concentrate on the forthcoming interview. It was similar to watching a film in reverse; right back to when they first met at university. They had both been attending the same lecture and she was seated next to him. He was struck by her deep concentration and the speed with which she could write down her notes and, when she had acknowledged his presence with a small enigmatic smile he had been immediately captivated. Their time together had been limited; Marion, from the beginning, making it very clear to him that her studies were absolutely paramount, her goal being to succeed and become a top lawyer, which she had and some years later, after they had lost touch, he had been surprised and not displeased to learn she had moved to Hong Kong. They had never resumed their relationship, not that being married to Stella, as he was by then, would have hindered him, but they remained friends, meeting occasionally for a meal. Often their conversation would be about work: her cases and a few schemes with which he had been involved, and it hadn't taken him long to realise that deep down they were indeed kindred spirits; both of them possessing calculated streaks of dishonesty. Denny had the knack of honing into that particular trait, exactly as he'd done with Juliet Warburton, although he would put her in more of a spy capacity, just as she was doing for him at the moment with this Roddie Mortimer guy, but Marion's particular brand of expertise had been exclusively unique: her ability to weigh up and assess a problem and literally get down to the bare bones had been exceptional, including her forgery skills which had been in the master class. He had to admit he would not have been able to get hold of that formula in such a way without her help. It had been Marion who had set the whole thing up and all he'd had to do was pass it on to his contact in Singapore. He hadn't asked her too many questions on how she accomplished it, although he had known about how she'd used those two consultants from London as scapegoats to collect the replica formula and, no doubt, was paid well from them also; this thought instantly having the effect to fast-forward to the present and to speculate on the person who had been responsible for her death.

Whoever it had been must have gained access to her apartment somehow, either while she was out earlier in the evening with him, or later that night. Denny had visited Marion a number of times and he knew there was always a concierge on duty at the desk in the front lobby, also that there was a security system. It was ironic to remember what Marion had once told him, this had been shortly after the system had been installed, of how protected she felt, having no fear of any intruder breaking into her apartment without being on camera in the lobby.

These troubled thoughts continued to occupy his mind as he walked into Police Headquarters and even to when he was sitting down and facing Inspector Clarke. He had been right. The man did look on the verge of retiring: not only did he appear years older than he probably was, but he looked tired, as though he hadn't been sleeping well. Job too much for him, Denny reckoned.

'Thank you for coming into the Station,' he said, 'and as I said on the phone, there are a few points we would like to clear up; only a few,' he added, 'so we shouldn't have to take up too much of your time.'

'That's alright, Inspector,' Denny answered, recognising the soft approach and wondering how long that would last, 'if there is anything I can do to help, I'll be only too pleased. I had known Miss Godwin for many years; she was a good friend.'

'And was your friendship a business relationship, Mr Yuan?'

'We weren't lovers, if that's what you mean,' Denny said, 'but we met occasionally for a meal; we enjoyed each other's company, having similar interests in common, although, from time to time, she did act for me on a number of my overseas transactions.'

'I understand,' he nodded, 'and the message you left for her; was this concerning business?'

'It was, yes,' Denny answered, 'you see, one of my subsidiary companies is based in Singapore and I'm hoping to buy another property there and Miss Godwin was going to draw up a formal offer for me.'

'And why was this, as you said on the phone, 'so crucial?'

'Because I'd learned someone else was seriously considering the same property and I wanted to get my offer in first.'

'I see.' the inspector said, 'Business tactics, I presume?'

'I've always found, Inspector, there is no other way, otherwise we would all become stagnant, we wouldn't be going anywhere.'

'When did you last see Miss Godwin?' a slight shift in his own tactics now, Denny noticed.

'We had dinner together on Sunday evening; at "Gaylord's"; in Kowloon.' he added.

'I am familiar with the restaurant, Mr Yuan. And afterwards?'

'We came back on the MTR and Miss Godwin took a taxi back to her apartment and I took one to where I live.'

'You didn't share a taxi, then?'

'No, there would have been no point. As you know, Miss Godwin lived in Mid Levels, while my apartment is in the opposite direction, Causeway Bay.'

'And that was the last time you saw her?'

'Yes, it was. Inspector,' Denny leaned forward in his chair, 'how did she die? You haven't told me, neither was it mentioned in "The South China Morning Post".'

'We are still waiting for the pathologist's report,' he answered, 'but there's every indication she was poisoned.'

'How?' feeling the bile rising at the back of his throat and wishing now he hadn't asked. Marion, as he had remembered her, coming immediately to the forefront of his mind, only to be replaced by another picture. They'd had a good evening; the food, as it always was at "Gaylord's", had been excellent. Most of the time they had talked about people they both knew, the latest gossip and, predictably enough, the handover. It hadn't been until they'd finished their meal they discussed the completion of the latest transaction; another satisfactory conclusion of the proposition he had put to her less than a week ago and this one could prove, once he received the final payment from Singapore, even more lucrative than the other one. It had been a stroke of luck finding those notes in Roddie

Mortimer's apartment and he had recognised straight away, especially as the laboratory's name was stamped clearly on each sheet, they could be important. He didn't have the expertise to sift through them and do the necessary collating, but Marion had; listing and regrouping until she had ended up with a formula in exactly the same format as the previous one.

'Are you alright, Mr Yuan; you look a trifle pale?' Inspector Clarke asked, looking at him closely above the rim of his spectacles.

'I will be, Inspector,' Denny said, taking a deep breath, 'I suppose it's the shock; imagining, you know.'

'Not pleasant,' he agreed, 'and as I've said, we don't have the official results.'

'But you suspect foul play; she couldn't have taken whatever it was, by accident?'

'Before I answer you,' he said, 'how would you describe Miss Godwin's manner on Sunday? Did she appear depressed?'

'Not in the least; quite the reverse, in fact. Miss Godwin was an extremely down-to-earth woman, Inspector. She didn't let people or events get her down and, incidentally, she was not the suicidal type.'

'I actually met the lady once,' the inspector said, 'and that was the way she appeared to me. And your suggestion about her death being an accident; I would consider that highly unlikely. Whatever the substance was, it looks as though it had been mixed with whisky. A half-empty glass was found beside her.' he added.

'Whisky?'

'You sound surprised?'

'I am surprised. Miss Godwin did enjoy the occasional whisky, but she wouldn't have had any in her apartment; she was quite adamant about that. Also, Inspector,' Denny went on, 'she never drank alone.'

'A lady of very strong beliefs?'

'Exactly. Someone *must* have been in the apartment with her.'

'Well, Mr Yuan,' Inspector Clarke said, standing up, 'that will be our task to find out.'

Chapter Thirteen

Half-way through Wednesday morning, having dealt with the back-log of emails which had accumulated while he'd been in London, Roddie received a call from Howard Westwood. The timing wasn't right. While the call wasn't totally unexpected; he realised he hadn't heard the last about those emeralds, but he had wanted to speak to Andy Howe first. He had planned to do this as soon as he'd arrived in the office, but hearing about Marion Godwin and seeing how visibly shaken Andy was, had decided instead to wait until later on in the day. And now, here was this man from Interpol wanting to see him, suggesting they meet at midday. At least, Roddie thought, replacing the receiver, he wouldn't have to make any excuses for leaving the office during working hours and fabricating some sort of explanation which probably anyone who knew him wouldn't believe in any case. This whole business: the implications surrounding the stolen formula; the emeralds and the lengths someone had gone to ensure they were put into his bag; the lies he had been told by the man called Innis and now the murder of Marion Godwin. It was all too much. He was in alien territory here and, of course, there was Juliet. Always Juliet; a woman he hardly knew, but couldn't ignore. Where on earth was it all going to end, he wondered, closing down his computer and walking along the corridor towards the lift, hoping he wouldn't meet any of his colleagues. Roddie was in no mood for socialising. At that moment, as he waited for the lift to arrive, all he wanted was to get this meeting with Howard Westwood over and done with and then, hopefully, he would be able to settle down and try to make some sense out of the situation he had fallen into.

Howard Westwood had suggested they meet in "The Clipper Lounge", telling him he was staying at "The Mandarin", and then going on to say, apart from some routine questions he wanted to ask him, the meeting would be an informal one.

'I would first like to say, Mr Mortimer,' he said, after Roddie had been told by reception where he would find him and they had shaken hands, 'it is our opinion, as far as those emeralds are concerned, you have been used as a scapegoat, or a victim of circumstances; whichever way you choose to look at it.'

'I think I have been.' Roddie agreed, having accepted his offer of a beer which he reckoned could signify that indeed what they were going to discuss was going to be conducted along informal lines, but, being a realist, he was certain every word he uttered would be recorded; perhaps not on tape, but in Howard Westwood's memory. Roddie didn't need to remind himself that the man sitting opposite to him on the low settle in the plush ambience of "The Clipper Lounge" hadn't asked him to come along for any social chit-chat. He was a high profile police officer and well versed in moving a conversation in any direction he wished.

'We are conducting a rather complex and unusual enquiry here, Mr Mortimer,' he said, once their beers had arrived, 'part of which started a number of years ago in Europe; a fairly mediocre one in comparison to what we believe has now developed into something of worldwide proportions.'

'Before you go any further, Mr Westwood, I would like to say I am completely out of my depth in all of this. Totally.'

'I am sure you are,' he smiled across at Roddie, automatically raising his glass to him, 'but bear with me, please, and I'll try to explain and perhaps you will have a better grasp of what we are up against.'

'Alright.' Roddie nodded, taking a sip from his glass.

'Let us go back to more than ten years ago when there was a spate of extremely clever jewellery robberies, starting in London; that is as far as we are aware, and spreading throughout the more affluent European countries: France, Italy, Spain, Sweden, and so on. I don't need to spell them out to you. The person responsible for these, carried out single-handedly, I might add, was a woman; your classic female cat burglar, in fact. She always mixed socially with the rich and famous and deftly relieved them of their jewellery, much of it family heirlooms and priceless. She left the European scene ten years ago and, regrettably, we lost trace of her and it is only very recently she has re-surfaced, although once again, it has taken us some time to locate her, because it would seem she may be operating as a courier between the country where she made her home and Hong Kong. This, Mr Mortimer,' he added, 'could very well be on a grand scale.'

'And the emeralds,' Roddie asked, 'they are part of all – all this smuggling?'

'We believe they could be.'

'And you know this woman's name?' the breath catching painfully in his throat. Surely he didn't mean Juliet. Surely not!

'We do know her name; she had changed it, of course, but it's the same person alright.'

'And,' Roddie asked quietly, dreading the answer, 'does she live in Hong Kong?'

'No, she doesn't.'

The relief Roddie felt when he heard those words was indescribable. Whatever conclusions he had formed about Juliet, he didn't want to learn she was involved in anything of such criminal magnitude.

'I'm going to go off at a slight tangent here, Mr Mortimer.' Howard Westwood said and Roddie could tell by his expression he hadn't missed his reaction.

'Yes?' bracing himself.

'When you reported finding the cache of emeralds to New Scotland Yard you told them how they must have found their way into your luggage.'

'Yes.'

'We can't help but feel there is something missing here.'

'Sorry?'

'Well,' he continued, 'you said you had no idea of who your assailants were that night, only that the incident occurred when you returned to the shop in Pedder Street.'

'That's right, I didn't. Also, Mr Westwood,' Roddie insisted, 'I didn't see them. The first thing I knew when I regained full consciousness was finding myself in the house on Lamma and from there I made my way back to Hong Kong Island.'

'Right,' Howard Westwood said, 'you say full consciousness; does that mean perhaps you were aware of hearing voices?'

'I was, yes,' Roddie admitted slowly and recognising this was the point of no return; he either told them what he had heard or remain silent, 'but most of them were speaking in Cantonese.'

'But not all of them.' It wasn't a question. And he knew he couldn't wriggle out of what he had to say.

'No.' taking a deep breath as he waited for the inevitable response.

'It's alright, Mr Mortimer,' he said, 'I do understand you are under considerable stress. Also, I get the impression you need to get this whole business off your chest, so to speak.'

'You're very perceptive.'

'I'm trained to be.' he said simply.

'There was a woman with them,' Roddie said, his voice sounding strange to him, 'I knew who she was.'

'Yes?'

'She's English and has lived in Hong Kong since she was a child. I met her the day before all of this happened. She had been in the shop in Pedder Street although that wasn't where I first spoke to her; this was in the cafe next door. I'd bought one of their pictures and had gone into the cafe in the hope I would see her leave the shop. I wanted to get to know her. Pretty adolescent, I know. It must sound that way to you, Mr Westwood.'

'Not at all,' he smiled again, 'many of us men have, at some time, been instantly captivated by a woman.'

'I suppose so,' he managed to return his smile, 'well,' Roddie continued, 'we met later that evening for a meal –'

'– and you told her you were going to London?'

'How did you know?'

'I didn't,' he chuckled, 'but in this game, Mr Mortimer, you learn to read a pattern into certain people's behaviour.'

'At first,' Roddie tried to explain, 'when I found myself on Lamma, and for a few days afterwards, I refused to believe I had heard her that night, but she was there alright.'

'And can you remember what she said?'

Here it comes, Roddie thought, his heart sinking: 'All too well; she said, "I hope you haven't hit him too hard, Denny." That was all.'

'It's enough, Mr Mortimer. Thank you. And now,' he went on, 'would you be so kind as to give me the lady's name?'

'Juliet Warburton.' Two words which meant the end of an affair that wasn't an affair and, in retrospect, was never likely to be, taking Juliet's card from his wallet and handing it to him.

'Once again, thank you.' he said, taking it from him.

'I hate doing this, you know.'

'I'm sure you do and we will be discreet as we progress; you can rest assured of that.'

'I have no intention of seeing her again.'

'As much as you would like to, I expect.'

'True, but Mr Westwood,' Roddie explained, 'I am a quiet man and, quite honestly, I don't need all this. I dislike very much the fact that I have been set up in this way. It leaves a very unpleasant taste.'

'I'm sure it does.' he sympathised, draining his glass, 'Would you like another one?'

'No thank you; I must put in a few more hours at work this afternoon and then I' going to have an early meal and get my head down. I only arrived back this morning and to be honest I'm shattered.'

'Perhaps you'll have a good night's sleep?'

'I hope so.'

'Before we finish, Mr Mortimer, I would like to talk about the theft of the formula from your company. I only heard about this yesterday from

Inspector William Clarke.'

'Yes,' Roddie said, 'my managing director would have put in a full report last Friday; I was on my way to England by then.'

'I know that; however, and I do appreciate you've been away, but have you formed any ideas about how this could have been orchestrated. I would add,' he said, 'anything you do say will be treated in confidence by us; I mean the Hong Kong police and ourselves, Interpol, and we would welcome any feedback.'

'Well,' Roddie began slowly, wondering how much he should say about both Andy Howe's and his own suspicions, 'I'm sure the report would have covered all the salient points.'

'I think it probably did,' he agreed, 'so, I'll recap, shall I? I've read a copy of the report and from what I understand, and I'm speaking for Inspector Clarke also, is that it is your considered and professional opinion the drug could not possibly have been patented within a matter of days; it would have needed at the very least a week?'

'Yes,' Roddie said, 'and according to Nicholas Eastman he escorted the man calling himself Mr Thomas to the vaults last Monday and that he had seen him extract what he believed to be the formula from the safe deposit box . My director and I couldn't help but reach the conclusion it must have been stolen before the Monday and substituted by a forged copy.'

'Quite; and then, naturally enough, this led you to suspect only a handful of people?'

'Less than a handful.' Roddie said, lowering his voice, reluctant to mention the name of the person they had thought it could have been, if not solely responsible, but involved in the plan.

'Let's leave that aside for the moment,' Howard Westwood suggested, as though sensing his discomfort. We'll return for a moment to the Monday evening shortly before Nicholas Eastman took Mr Thomas to collect the formula. I understand you saw Nicholas Eastman in "The Captain's Bar" having a drink with someone you hadn't seen before, also you were surprised when Nicholas Eastman didn't introduce him to you.'

'I was, yes,' Roddie agreed, 'it struck me as out of character somehow.'

'How would you describe his manner to you that evening? Did he seem nervous, perhaps reluctant to talk to you?'

'Not in the slightest; in fact he went on to tell me about his girlfriend who had recently arrived in Hong Kong and going on to say how she'd given up her job in London to be with him. Quite chatty, actually.'

'Well,' Howard said, 'I can understand why you would have expected him to make an introduction, even to include his companion in the conversation. However,' Howard continued, 'your description of him tallies very closely to the one given by Nicholas Eastman when he was interviewed by the police shortly after they'd received the report from your company. Also,' he added quickly, giving Roddie no chance to think, far less respond, 'I understand the lady you were with thought she recognised him.'

'That's right,' Roddie said, 'and since then, when we were having a meal shortly before I left for London, she told me she remembered when it had been.'

'Yes?'

'It was two weeks ago; she saw him coming out of Miss Godwin's office and the lawyer had been with him.'

'Interesting.'

'There's a bit more I can add, Mr Westwood.' Roddie said, 'During the time I was in London; last Saturday night, in fact, I saw him again.'

'You're sure it was the same person?'

'Quite sure. I was having a drink in the "Lord Moon of the Mall" in Whitehall; perhaps you're familiar with the pub?'

'I certainly am; excellent food.'

'That's true. Well, he was standing next to me.'

'So you would have been able to get a good look at him?'

'Yes and that only made me more certain I was right. I actually spoke to him, mentioning I'd seen him in Hong Kong the week before with

Nicholas Eastman.'

'And what was his response?' a look of expectancy on his face.

'He immediately denied either knowing anyone called Nicholas Eastman or having been in Hong Kong.'

'If you had been mistaken, Mr Mortimer and I'm not disbelieving your judgement for one minute, it is likely he would respond in that way, but on the other hand, if you are right, no doubt you could expect an identical answer.'

'I had thought of that, but you see, that evening in "The Moon" was the second time I'd seen him and each time I was as close to him as I am to you at this moment. Also,' he continued, 'I'm able to give you his name.'

'Can you indeed! Now, that is something positive for us, Mr Mortimer.'

'He's called Innis; I don't know his Christian name, but he'd ordered a taxi and I overheard one of the barmen call out to him.'

'Once again, we have to thank you. I believe I've assimilated the gist of, not only what you've told me, but with the information we already have and, given a number of loose ends, there does seem to be a common denominator; by that I mean between your stolen formula and the emerald smuggling.'

'Really?'

'Of course I can't say a great deal more at this stage,' he said, 'but suffice to say you may have helped us even more than you realise.'

'I don't see how?' puzzled and wondering where he was coming from.

'Well,' he explained, 'you have given me the name of that common denominator.'

'Not Juliet?'

'No, not Juliet Warburton, but the man called Denny.'

*

'Sweetheart,' he said, 'please don't give me a hard time.'

'That is the last thing I want to do, Nicholas,' she said, those large expressive eyes looking reproachfully across at him, 'but her behaviour was really awful, also, it could have been embarrassing.'

'But it wasn't.' he said, beginning to lose patience with her. He couldn't stand possessive women and Natasha was fast becoming one!

'No, but that isn't the point.'

'Listen, Natasha,' he answered sharply, 'let's drop it, shall we? Marcia isn't worth all this fuss and if she knew how upset she'd made you that is probably what she set out to do.'

'To make trouble between us, you mean?'

'Exactly.' hoping he'd heard the last of it. Marcia Rodrigo was the least of his problems at the moment. His head was reeling from what he'd been told that afternoon and he was still finding it difficult to believe what Inspector Clarke had said to him in that precise and archaic manner of his. He had practically accused him of murder; his words continuing to run through his brain: "The main reason," he'd said, "I've asked you into the Station, Mr Eastman is, because during the initial stages of our investigation into Miss Marion Godwin's murder, it transpires on checking any messages she may have received on her mobile up to the time of her death, there was one from you, made on Sunday at nine pm."

It had taken Nicholas several seconds to say anything, not even to protest and deny sending any text messages to Marion. When the inspector had phoned him shortly after lunch he fully expected to have to answer more questions about the stolen formula and hearing Marion's name mentioned had completely thrown him off balance.

"I'll jog your memory for you, Mr Eastman, if I may," he had gone on pedantically, "the message was brief; only a few words, telling her to expect you later."

"This is preposterous! Inspector Clarke, I made no such message!"

'Didn't you?"

"No, I did not!" indignation by that time beginning to get through to him, "Whoever sent that; it certainly wasn't me!" he had protested.

"Incidentally," he had put in, "how could you possibly prove it was me? I had my mobile with me all the time that evening and I neither made nor received any calls or texts either, if it comes to that. Was the sender's number recorded?" he had asked him, deciding it was time he started asking some questions for a change.

"As it so happens, no; the number had been withheld.'

"There you are, then, Inspector." he had said, although there was little satisfaction in his minor triumph. The unsavoury fact remained: someone *had* sent it and, whoever it had been, wanted to pass the dirt on to him for some reason.

The inspector had then continued with his questioning of whether he had known Marion, what had he been doing on the Sunday, at the end of which Nicholas had mentally labelled as an interrogation, he was once again asked to sign a statement confirming everything which had been said and, just as he thought the meeting was over, the inspector had referred back to the last time he'd seen him; shortly after the theft of the formula had been reported: "Mr Eastman," he had said, "I would like you to consider the contents of the first statement you signed; when you told us you had made arrangements to meet Mr Thomas at the bank. Before you say anything, I have to tell you a witness has come forward to say you were seen less than half an hour before that agreed time in the company of a man who bore a remarkable likeness to the description you gave us of Mr Thomas."

'I was with a friend of mine, Inspector, from England and we were having a quick drink in "The Mandarin" before my meeting with Mr Thomas and he may have looked similar, but I can assure you he wasn't the same person."

Surprisingly, the inspector hadn't pursued the point and rapidly brought the meeting to a close, which in many respects had been unsatisfactory. Nicholas had been left feeling suspended and, even now, several hours later, he didn't feel much better. He had phoned Natasha suggesting they meet here, in "The Dickens Bar" in the "Excelsior Hotel" before going back to the apartment, in the hope a few drinks and some light-hearted conversation would help and all they had talked about so far was what Marcia had said to her.

'Another drink, sweetheart?' he asked, leaning across the table and kissing her.

'Please.'

'Have you been in touch with your father yet?' he asked, 'You've not said.'

'I've tried a couple of times, actually,' she said, 'but each time there's been no answer.'

'A pity you don't have a mobile number for him.'

'I know; perhaps I'll drop him a line. Mind you, Nicholas,' she added, 'he could be away.'

'It's possible, I suppose, but there must be a quicker way than that to find out, surely. You know where he works, don't you?' he asked. She had told him so little about her father, apart from the fact she had hardly seen him over the years and that for the last ten of those he had been living in Hong Kong and that was about all.'

'Oh yes, of course, but I haven't liked to phone him there. He's going to be surprised enough when he hears I'm here, especially if any of his colleagues should be around at the time. Also,' she went on, 'if he's in the laboratory, it could be inconvenient.'

'Laboratory?' he repeated.

'Yes,' she said, 'he's an industrial chemist, Nicholas, and he's worked for his company for a long time now, ever since he arrived in Hong Kong.'

'What company is this, sweetheart?' he asked, but he already knew the answer, instantly appalled at the coincidence.

'McLellands Medical Research Laboratories;' came the inevitable response, 'they're actually an American company.' she added unnecessarily. 'Have you heard of them, Nicholas?'

'Yes, I've heard of them.' he replied, doing his best to keep the flatness from his voice. This was not good, he thought. Natasha, the girl he'd fallen in love with and persuaded to come out to join him had a father who worked for the company he had recently been largely instrumental in stealing from and not only that, inwardly cringing at the thought of her ever finding out, was the fact he had been paid double for his efforts.

'I believe they're more commonly known as just McLellands.' she told him. As if he didn't know!

'Your surname, Natasha;' he asked her; sure he hadn't heard of anyone called Bailey working for the laboratories, 'is it the same as your father's?'

'No,' she smiled at him, no doubt amused by his expression and misinterpreting it as one of mild curiosity, 'when my mother remarried I took on step-father's name.'

'I just wondered, that's all,' trying to explain and realising he was doing it badly, 'you see, not only do McLellands bank with us, but also many of the employees, and over the years I've met quite a number of them. I may even know your father.' he finished lamely.

'He's called Roderick Mortimer, but all his friends call him Roddie. *Do* you know him, Nicholas?' she asked.

'I've spoken to him a few times,' he said, wishing he hadn't started this conversation and remembering the last time he'd seen Roddie. Could he be the witness who had, to quote the inspector, come forward to say he'd seen him with someone who looked remarkably like Mr Thomas? But, just a minute! There was something odd here. The inspector had gone on to say this likeness was similar to the one he had given them, but why had Roddie been so certain? He had only seen Thomas once, as far as Nicholas knew, and that had been in "The Captain's Bar" and he hadn't introduced Thomas to him. It wasn't as though Roddie had seen them actually going into the bank together. It just did not make sense, but then, trying to reason it all out, who else could it have been? It must have been Roddie Mortimer.

'Shall we go and eat now, Natasha?' he asked her, hoping they could talk about something else. He needed to give his brain a rest.

'Okay; where shall we go?'

'You choose, sweetheart.' Her enthusiasm was contagious and as he watched her sipping the last of her wine, he hoped he wouldn't be the one responsible for disillusioning her should she ever find out what he was really like. Often, he was reminded of how young she was, although there had been times, especially since she'd arrived in Hong Kong, when she would surprise him with a quick flash of maturity as she had shown the first time she mentioned Marcia to him; in the way she had given him the impression of fully understanding he would have had other girlfriends and he hoped that after what Marcia had said to her wouldn't sow any seeds of suspicion in her mind. Nicholas realised he had been a fool to have had anything to do with the woman, his main mistake being to prolong a relationship which had become cloyingly claustrophobic. They were all the same, these women who came to Hong Kong with the sole purpose of finding a husband sufficiently well off to take them away from a country which had nothing to offer them, especially if, like Marcia, they'd had little or no education and no means to drag themselves out of the squalid and ramshackle villages in the heart of the Philippines where they lived and miles away from the fleshpots of the capital. All too often, prostitution was their only solution and, at least Marcia hadn't succumbed to that, but he'd already discovered there was an unpleasant side to her nature which he had explained away to himself she was reacting in the only way she knew, but it was primitive and calculating and he would have to try and see her soon and make her understand he was with Natasha now.

'I'd like a Chinese meal, I think, Nicholas.' Natasha said, interrupting his unpleasant thoughts.

'That suits me fine. Come on then; I don't know about you, but I'm hungry.'

'Nicholas?'

'Yes?'

'I've been meaning to ask you, but last week when you took me to that

Chinese restaurant in Central.'

'The "Yung Kee"?'

'That's right; I can't quite get my tongue round these Cantonese names yet.' she admitted, 'but I will. Anyway,' she continued, 'why is it that at the end of the meal they put an orange in front of all the customers? Does this mean something?'

'Yes,' he couldn't help smiling; he'd been in Hong Kong so long now, he had become blasé, 'it's one of their old customs; their polite way of telling you it is time to leave.'

'Really? I like that and as you say it is polite. Do you know,' she said, 'a few years ago I was at a party and the husband's wife brought out her vacuum cleaner!'

'Never!' he laughed out loud, 'Now, that is definitely not polite!'

*

Howard waited until the evening to phone Robert Anderson, reckoning he should have finished lunch and be back in the office. He'd already spoken to Inspector Clarke shortly after his meeting with Roddie and passing on to him what Roddie had been able to tell him; the most relevant point perhaps, being the name of the man who had been posing as Thomas, also it would appear Denny Yuan was once again to the fore of their investigations.

'I'm glad you've phoned, Howard,' Robert said, as soon as his secretary had put Howard through to him, 'as by all accounts you have your hands full out there.'

'You've heard about Marion Godwin, Robert?'

'Yes, this morning in "The Telegraph". Bad business. How far have the police got so far?'

'Not much progress, I'm afraid. The problem is there are far too many loose ends. Although,' Howard continued, 'it has transpired the lady was not what she appeared to be.'

'Ah.'

'I had a meeting with Roddie Mortimer earlier today and he made it quite plain to me that both he and his managing director were able to whittle down the number of people who actually knew the formula had been placed in the bank's safe deposit box, Marion Godwin being one of them and the more I think about what he said, the more I'm inclined to agree with him.'

'Inspector Clarke faxed through a copy of the report from the laboratory company and she was certainly a key figure in the secrecy of keeping news of the formula under wraps until it had been patented, so you could be right, Howard.'

'As a matter of interest, Denny Yuan was a friend of hers; they had dinner together the night she was murdered.'

'That is interesting.'

'Also, she acted for him professionally, mainly in respect to his overseas businesses. I'll ask the inspector to send you through a copy of Denny Yuan's statement.'

'If you would, Howard; that would be helpful. It's all a bit of a mess, isn't it?'

'You could say that. Have you thought anymore of how soon we should be moving forward on dealing with Francesca Cristofoli?'

'I have, as a matter of fact,' Robert said, 'I've been waiting to hear where she applied for her current passport; we've got the earlier one, but it's not much good to us without a copy of the one she's using now. I'll chase that up and get back to you, Howard, but to answer your question, yes, I think it's time we stepped up the pressure in regard to her. In case there's any further delay over the passport, I suggest you go ahead and get in touch with Virginia and arrange an identity parade which, of course, will have to be held at Police Headquarters, and this means formally detaining Francesca Cristofoli for the statutory twenty-four hour period. We are relying a great deal on Virginia here, but, given what else we've learned recently about Francesca, including the Columbian connection, I still have every confidence we're on the right track.'

'We'd be most frustrated if we lost her again, I know. She could decide to move out of Hong Kong at any time and not just by air either.'

'Yes, Howard and that's what is starting to concern me also, especially if she gets wind we're on to her. No, I believe we're doing the right thing.'

'If the outcome of the i.d. is positive we can move fairly swiftly with obtaining the International Arrest Warrant. Then, at least, we'll have her back in London.'

'That's right,' Robert agreed, 'with Francesca off the scene it should give Frank and you a chance to concentrate on the other aspects of the case. Do you think there's a connection between the smuggling and the business of the formula, Howard?'

'I think there is,' Howard answered, 'and now, the murder. I wasn't expecting that.'

'No,' Robert said, 'how could you, but it looks as though whoever killed her had an extremely valid reason for doing so, at least to him. Have you any ideas?'

'I do, sir. I might be speaking out too soon, but I can't help wondering about those two consultants.'

'Bristow & Innis?'

'Yes. It now seems, according to what Roddie Mortimer was saying that the bogus Mr Thomas could be Hugh Innis.'

'How certain is he?'

'He was quite positive. Roddie says he saw him in "The Moon" last Saturday and that's when he learned he was called Innis.'

'And,' Robert put in, 'if he is correct he was with Nicholas Eastman when they went to the bank to collect the formula.'

'He struck me as a reliable witness, Robert; a straight down-the-middle sort of guy.'

'That's good. Where would we be in our profession, Howard, without people of that calibre to rely on?'

'I don't know.'

'Returning to the murder for a moment,' Robert said, 'obviously it wasn't Hugh Innis as he was back in London by then, but Eddie Bristow wasn't.'

'Yes, that's right and it could explain why he took a flight out here so soon after Hugh Innis returned to London. It's possible when he found out they had both been tricked it acted as a sufficiently strong enough motive to come out and deal with her.'

'Murders have been carried out for far less reasons.'

'That's true. There must have been a considerable amount of money involved if you consider the pair of them haven't been exactly sparing in their outlay; more than one return flight out here and staying at one of our most expensive hotels.'

'That's true,' Robert said, 'and then, presumably, the payment to whoever assisted them.'

'I'm surprised Eddie Bristow is still here; I saw him earlier when I came back to the hotel this afternoon.'

'I was thinking that also, Howard. He must have his reasons for remaining, the alternative being, he had nothing to do with the lawyer's death. I've had an idea,' he said before he rang off, 'I'll give Passports Records office in Swansea a call this afternoon and ask them to look out Eddie Bristow's details, in particular his photograph. Hopefully, it will be a good enough likeness.'

'At least then it will give the police here something positive on which to work and it is just possible someone may have seen him last Sunday night outside Marion Godwin's apartment.'

'That's right, Howard. Anyway, it's worth a try, so once I have the photograph from Swansea I'll send it through as a scanned attachment direct to Police Headquarters.'

'Fine, Robert; I'll tell Inspector Clarke to expect it.'

Howard was in "The Captain's Bar" and had taken his first sip of red wine, a pleasant change from his usual lager, when his mobile rang. Expecting to hear Frank's voice, it took him a couple of seconds to recognise Virginia Bannister.

'I'm frightfully sorry to disturb your evening, Howard, but,' she went on breathlessly before he had a chance to reassure her, 'I simply *had* to phone you -' pausing slightly, '- sorry, I'm not normally like this, but I rather think Francesca Cristofoli is up to her old tricks again.'

'Where are you phoning from, Virginia?' he asked, hearing voices in the background; the chink of glasses and the distinctive popping of champagne corks.

'Oh dear,' she said, 'can't you hear me properly? I'm at the Hilton,' she explained, 'but give me a moment and I'll go out into the hall. Is that better?' she asked, following a brief pause.

'That's fine.'

'Good. Well,' and he could hear her taking a deep breath, 'I'll try and explain. As I've said, I'm at the Hilton with Guy; it's a semi-formal occasion, a cocktail party to greet a number of overseas dignitaries and their entourage. About fifteen minutes ago, a good friend of mine, who is also here, told me she'd just had a rather valuable sapphire ring stolen.'

'How did this happen?' he asked, puzzled, 'A bracelet, a necklace and practically any other kind of jewellery I could understand, but not a ring. Presumably she *was* wearing it?'

'She had been, Howard, but she had taken it off to wash her hands in the cloakroom and had put the ring down at the side of the hand-basin.'

'Can I just stop you there?' Howard interrupted, trying to formulate some kind of picture in his mind.

'Of course you can.'

'Was there anyone else there at the time?'

'No, there wasn't, except for the attendant, of course. You see, Howard, Leticia had moved towards the woman to accept a hand-towel from her and when she turned back again, the ring had gone.'

'How odd. What about the attendant; could she have taken it?'

'That would have been impossible. Absolutely impossible. She was standing on the other side of the hand-basin and my friend would have seen her. Besides, it would have been more than the woman's job was worth to do anything like that. Many of these attendants have been with the major hotels in Hong Kong for years, probably most of their working lives, in fact. No, I'm convinced it was Francesca. Also,' Virginia added quickly, 'it's an exact replica of what happened to another of my friends in London!'

'I see.' Howard said, although he didn't see at all.

'She must have either come into the cloakroom and, being the opportunist she is, somehow managed to pick up the ring and leave, or,' she continued, 'she could have been in one of the cubicles, I suppose.'

'That's possible. But, Virginia, we first need to establish, if we can, where Francesca was at the time.'

'I can answer that for you, Howard.'

'You can?' this friend of Robert's was certainly full of surprises.

'You've seen her, then?'

'I've seen her alright; she's here, at the reception.'

'How long do you think this function will last, Virginia; have you any idea?' he asked, looking at his watch.

'At least for another hour, maybe even longer.'

'Right, it's eight-thirty now. I've got one phone call to make and I should be there in less than thirty minutes. Hopefully, Francesca doesn't decide to leave early.'

'She won't.'

'How do you know?'

'Because I'll make sure she doesn't, that's why, Howard.'

'You don't think she will remember you?'

'No, she doesn't. I've already had the dubious pleasure of talking to her earlier this evening and there was absolutely no sign of any recognition, but then,' Virginia went on, 'I wasn't too surprised, although we have met a couple of times in the past, but then Francesca prefers the company of men, don't forget.'

The antique wall clock Roddie had bought years ago and brought with him to Hong Kong, was chiming nine when the concierge buzzed through on the intercom to say a Miss Juliet Warburton was in the lobby. And what could he do? Of course he had to see her; not to do so, would be pointless, also spineless. So much for an early night he thought, opening the front door of his apartment and waiting for the lift to arrive at his floor, at the same time apprehensive about how he would feel when he saw her again.

'Hello, Roddie,' she said; a magnum of champagne in her hand as she stepped out of the lift, 'I hope I haven't turned up at an inconvenient moment?'

'No, not at all, Juliet.' opening the door wider and gesturing her into the apartment.

For the second time during the short time they had known each other he could feel his resolve melting; the spell she had cast over him was still working and as he stood there he was powerless to say anything. She was the most enticing woman he had ever known and more than anything at that precise moment he didn't want to lose her.

'Say something!' she laughed up at him; those remarkable eyes sparkling. He realised she was teasing him, but he didn't care. She was here, with him, and nothing else mattered.

'Sorry, Juliet.' he managed an apologetic kind of smile, 'I guess I'm surprised to see you, that's all.'

'Well,' continuing to look at him, her head tilted as she had done before, 'I thought one of us should make a move and after I got your text message I put two and two together -'

'- and did you make four?' he asked; it was his turn now, doing his utmost to snap out of the intensity of his emotions. Try and live for the moment, Roddie, he told himself.

'I think you know the answer to that, Roddie.' she said, 'Anyway, on a lighter note, aren't you going to open this bottle?'

She followed him into the kitchen while he took a couple of glasses from the cupboard and watched as he levered out the cork, laughing in delight when it responded with a resounding pop, and holding out the glasses to catch the pale amber liquid.

'Welcome back, Roddie!' she smiled, raising her glass. 'I've missed you.'

'Have you?'

'Of course. Why do you ask and why are you looking at me like that? You're so terribly serious at times, you know.'

'Perhaps,' he answered slowly, not sure whether to say anything to her or not. Howard Westwood hadn't said he couldn't, but somehow he didn't think it would be a good idea, 'I have every reason to be serious, Juliet.'

'You've lost me,' she said, 'why should you be? Didn't your trip to London turn out all that well?'

'Juliet,' he said, placing his glass down on the kitchen table, 'let's stop playing games, shall we?'

'I don't know what you mean.'

'I think you do; I think you know very well.'

'Can we not just have a pleasant evening and enjoy this delicious champagne, Roddie?' she said, moving up closer to him and kissing him lightly on the lips, 'Don't you think you're becoming a little bit too heavy?' she added, picking up the bottle from the table and replenishing their glasses.

'Perhaps I am,' he admitted, feeling uncomfortable the way the conversation was going, also unpleasantly aware, whether she realised or not, that he was being manipulated, 'but something has been bugging me for several days.'

'Yes?'

'I don't want to go into all the details, only to say that a week past Friday, I was taken forcibly to a house on Lamma Island. I didn't see any of my assailants, Juliet, but I distinctly heard your voice.'

'What?' a look of astonishment on her face. Either she was a very good liar or he was way off beam, 'For goodness sake, Roddie,' she said at last, 'and you honestly thought I was there?'

'I did, yes. At first, I refused to believe it, but I'm pretty sure you were.'

'Well, I wasn't.'

'If that is right, Juliet, I will be the first to apologise.'

'Why didn't you mention this when we met the next time?'

'As I've said, I didn't want to believe it.'

'What made you change your mind?'

'Most of that Friday night I was in a semi-conscious state and the voices I heard weren't clear; it was only later when I was able to sift the various snippets of what was going on around me.' a half-truth, but he had decided he'd said enough, although having mentioned the incident had done little to reassure him. Juliet continued to remain a mystery and there was so much he wanted to ask her, but he doubted whether in his confused emotional state, he would be able to assimilate properly, or even whether she would tell him the truth.

'It sounds to me as though you were hallucinating, Roddie. Did you consider that?'

'I did.'

'So,' she gave him a tiny smile, 'where do you and I go from here?'

'I'm not sure,' he answered, 'perhaps as you've already pointed out, I am being too intense.'

'It's in your nature, I suppose,' she said, 'but after all of this happened and you were back home why didn't you report it to the police?'

'Because I didn't think they would believe me, that's why.'

'That makes sense.'

'Shall we drop the subject, Juliet? And,' he added, 'you're right, this champagne is truly delicious and far too good to be drunk standing up in the kitchen. Let's go into the lounge and enjoy it.'

She never failed to amaze him; she must surely be the most incurious woman he had ever met in his life. Whether this was by design or not didn't make any different. If she had been there that night wouldn't she have wanted to know what else he may have remembered? In fact, the only question she'd asked was why he hadn't gone to the police. He must stop all these meandering and useless conjectures; they were getting him nowhere, only succeeding in throwing his mind into an even bigger turmoil.

'Tell me about London, Roddie. It's been so long since I was there.'

He had started to describe the places he'd visited, trying to make it as light-hearted as he could, when the telephone rang.

'Mr Mortimer?' a voice he didn't recognise at first, mentally running through in his mind who he could be.

'Roddie Mortimer, yes?'

'It's Nicholas Eastman here, Mr Mortimer. From the bank.' he added.

Having no idea why Nicholas Eastman should be calling him and hoping it had nothing to do with the business over the formula and all too aware of Juliet sitting next to him, he waited for him to explain.

'I'm sorry to bother you, but I thought you should know –'

'– is there something wrong, Nicholas?' Roddie interrupted him, for the first time noticing how distressed he sounded.

'It's Natasha –'

'Natasha!' for a fraction of a second his brain stopped functioning. What had Nicholas Eastman to do with Natasha?

'She's in hospital.' Nicholas went on; each syllable, each word hitting him with an unbelievable force.

'What happened? Has there been an accident?'

'No, nothing like that,' Nicholas said, 'but a short time ago she collapsed; we were in a restaurant, we'd just finished our meal, and –'

'– what's wrong with her, Nicholas?'

'The hospital are still doing tests,' he explained, 'but the doctor in casualty said it could be a virus, mainly because of the suddenness, but I don't know.'

'Where are you, Nicholas; at the hospital?'

'I am, yes. Mr Mortimer?'

'Yes?' curbing the rising panic.

'She's in intensive care.'

'Is – is she unconscious?' dreading the answer.

'Yes.'

'Alright, Nicholas, give me the name of the hospital and I'll be on my way.'

Chapter Fourteen

Howard and Inspector Clarke arrived at "The Hilton" at the same time and immediately made their way across the marble foyer to the main desk. The inspector had already phoned ahead to let them know to expect them. Both men had agreed they wanted to conduct these proceedings as discreetly as possible; to minimise any embarrassment among the guests or disturb the smooth-running of the hotel.

The manager escorted them personally up to the floor where the reception was being held; in one of the hotel's largest function rooms: high-ceilinged, ornately carved; crystal chandeliers; thick dark-red carpeting and sumptuously decorated. Virginia Bannister had already spotted Howard, but remained where she was; standing next to a short blonde-haired woman wearing a figure-hugging black dress and, instinctively, Howard realised he was looking at Francesca Cristofoli for the first time. So, this was the woman they had been trying to pin down for more than a decade he thought wryly, remembering the details of the case vividly and not fooled for a minute by her appearance of fragility. Now, although well on in her fifties, Francesca Cristofoli had contrived to retain an outward appearance of youthfulness, but even from where he was standing, a few yard away, he could see the signs of ageing deeply etched on her face. Obviously not into plastic surgery; the cynical thought occurred to him, but then perhaps allowing the passing years to show had been deliberate. What better disguise when people who knew her all those years ago would only remember how she looked back then. Clever, but then there had never been any disputing Francesca's skilfulness and ingenuity; she was an expert in the art of deception.

'Inspector, Mr Woodward,' the manager was saying to them, 'if you would care to follow me over here for a moment and I'll introduce you to the lady who has experienced this unfortunate -' appearing to have considerable difficulty in bringing himself to mention the word 'theft' in relation to the impeccable reputation of his hotel, '- er,' he went on, ' –

this unfortunate incident.'

Virginia's friend, Leticia Hammond, came out of the same mould as Virginia: understated elegance from the top of her shiny bobbed hair to the black patent low-heeled shoes, but Howard guessed the worried frown on her face was not normal for her; she was obviously upset by what had happened.

'I don't want to make a fuss, Inspector Clarke,' were her first words, 'I really don't, but Virginia thought I should say something.'

'Don't worry, Mrs Hammond,' we understand how you must be feeling; a most distressing thing to occur.'

'We realise,' Howard put in, trying like the inspector, to put her at her ease, 'you didn't see the person who stole your ring, but –'

' – no, I didn't;' looking at him directly, 'there was no-one else in the cloakroom.'

'Except for the attendant, of course.'

'Oh, yes, but she was facing me.'

'Mrs Hammond,' Inspector Clarke said, keeping his voice lowered, although there was so much noise in the room, it was doubtful whether they could be overheard, 'your ring was stolen during the short space of time you had your back turned away from where you had placed it, on the side of the hand-basin?'

'Yes, that's right.'

'Somebody,' he continued, 'either came into the room behind you or from one of the cubicles.'

'Ye - es.'

'So,' he concluded, 'the attendant, if as you say was facing you, must have seen this person.'

'Good Grief! I never thought of that, Inspector Clarke.'

'Did you mention the theft to her, Mrs Hammond?' Howard asked.

'No, I didn't.'

'But she must have noticed your distress when you found it had gone?'

'I honestly don't know. She may have done. You must think me extremely stupid, Mr Westwood, but I knew you see, that she couldn't have taken it and I suppose I was just too upset. Also, I was reluctant to involve her, besides, she doesn't speak any English.'

'This is where you could perhaps help us, sir.' Inspector Clarke said, turning to the manager.

'You would like me to talk to her?'

'Please, if you would. We won't accompany you; she might find our presence inhibiting.'

'It's too much to hope you'll ever find my ring, isn't it? It is frightfully special to me actually,' Leticia Hammond explained, 'it has been in my family for years and my great-aunt gave it to me on my twenty-first birthday. Her name was Leticia also.' she added, sadly.

'I wouldn't despair, Mrs Hammond.' Howard made an attempt to reassure her, 'but there's a chance the culprit will still be here; a lot depends on what the cloakroom attendant has to say.'

'It must be a woman, mustn't it?'

'More than likely.'

'Oh, dear. That seems worse somehow.'

'We'll do our best, Mrs Hammond.' the inspector put in, 'but now, if you'll excuse us; we don't want to keep you from the rest of your party for any longer.'

The manager was only away for minutes and looking at his expression as he walked towards them, Howard found it impossible to read his expression. It's true what people say, he thought; the Chinese are inscrutable.

'The woman,' the manager said to them both, 'was exceedingly reluctant to say anything.'

'But what did she say?' Inspector Clarke prompted.

'Well,' he began slowly, 'you were quite right, she did see someone come into the washroom, but she stressed to me she didn't see her pick up Mrs Hammond's ring. From the way she spoke I don't believe she had even realised Mrs Hammond had taken off her ring.'

'Was she able to give you a description of this person?'

'Only a very vague one, Inspector; more of a fleeting impression I would say.'

'In what way?'

'Apart from noticing the woman had white hair; that's how she described it, but I would suggest her hair was blonde, not white. To many of our people, Inspector Clarke, as I'm sure you are aware, hair is either black or white; there is no in-between.'

'I know what you mean; of course I do,' Inspector Clarke said, 'but was she able to add anything else? Something which could give us some sort of an idea of the appearance of the woman we should be looking for?'

'Not really.' the inscrutable expression firmly in place, 'Except,' he added, 'the dress she was wearing.'

'Yes?'

This was very much like trying to extract blood from a stone Howard thought, inwardly groaning and only too aware of how quickly the time was passing. Soon, the party would be finishing and they were in danger of losing the chance of taking advantage of this opportunity; within minutes Francesca Cristofoli could have left the hotel.

'The dress,' the manager supplied, 'was black and extremely tight-fitting.'

'So,' Inspector Clarke said and Howard recognised the barely concealed exasperation in his voice, 'let me go over what you've told us, sir. The attendant did see someone enter the cloakroom and, as we suspected, it was a woman, also she was blonde-haired and wore a tight black dress. But, what about her features? Was she able to tell you what she looked like?'

'I regret no, Inspector.' he said and it was impossible to tell whether the man was sorry or not. It was starting to become obvious to Howard, and no doubt to the inspector, that the manager did not want to know. The last he wanted was any stigma attached to the hotel; it would be detrimental to his position if that should happen.

'Why?' Inspector Clarke asked; by now it was clear he was finding it extremely difficult to hide his irritation with the man.

'Because, Inspector,' the manager replied, 'she didn't see the woman's face. From what she said to me, it sounds as though she wasn't actually in her line of vision, her sole attention being focused on supplying Mrs Hammond with the hand-towel.'

'Alright,' the inspector sighed, 'I hear what you say, so there is no possibility of the attendant either identifying the woman or being able to supply us with an identi-kit image?'

'No, Inspector; that would not be possible.'

'Well, Mr Westwood,' Inspector Clarke said, once the manager had gone, 'how do you suggest we move on from here?'

'We still have little to go on in respect to this theft of Mrs Hammond's ring, an extremely sketchy description, in fact. How many blonde-haired women are here tonight wearing black dresses? Merely by taking a quick look round, I would say quite a few. However,' Howard went on, although not entirely disheartened by what the manager had been able to tell them. They were at a kind of crossroads at this point: they could leave the hotel and do nothing further, or they could follow on with what he knew Robert Anderson was in favour of, namely, pulling in Francesca, 'I suggest we take the lady back with us to the Station and if she hasn't that sapphire ring in her possession, I'll exercise the second option, all of which we've already discussed.'

'Ascertain whether she is Francesca Cristofoli and not Frances Catania and charge her with her past demeanours.'

'More or less.' Howard agreed, again amused by the slightly archaic and stereotyped phraseology, reminiscent of the sixties, 'If it becomes necessary, we'll set up the identity parade for tomorrow, Inspector, and once that's out of the way we can start to put on the pressure. She may, it is always possible, start to talk.'

'Alright, Mr Woodward; I'm with you. Do I take it that the woman over there with Mrs Bannister is our objective?'

'Yes, she's our objective,' Howard answered, looking across at Virginia and wondering how much longer she could keep Francesca in conversation. Even with Virginia's skill at small-talk the time which had elapsed since she'd phoned him, now over an hour, must be stretched to the absolute maximum.

'She *is* blonde,' Inspector Clarke pointed out as if he hadn't already realised the fact, 'also,' he went on doggedly and Howard couldn't make out whether the sparkle in his eyes was due to the strength of the overhead lights or whether he was finding this present situation amusing, 'she *is* wearing a black dress.'

'Yes, Inspector,' Howard replied, this time unable to conceal his amusement. Inspector William Clarke belonged to another era; one entirely at odds to what he had been used to, but he couldn't dislike the man. From the moment he had first met him he had respected his intelligence, 'those facts had not escaped my notice.'

'I'm sure they hadn't, Mr Westwood.' he replied. 'Shall we go over and approach the lady?'

'Yes,' Howard nodded, 'I'd like you to take the lead at this stage, working on the premise we are investigating the theft of a sapphire ring. We'll see how she responds to that before I bring in what is really the main issue here.'

'This emerald business?' the inspector supplied.

'Exactly.'

*

Natasha was out of danger. By midnight, she had regained consciousness and had been transferred to a small private ward. Roddie waited until then before leaving the hospital, but Nicholas stayed on; sitting on a chair at the side of the narrow bed, unable to take his eyes away from her; his mind, for the first time in his life, in a state of bewildered turmoil. He had known her for so short a time, but the intensity of his feelings far exceeded any he had felt for any other woman. He knew, without being told, he had been close to losing her and, even now, after she had pulled through from wherever she had been, her temperature returning to normal and she was sleeping naturally without any medical aid, he could feel cold sweat breaking out all over his body. He spent the remainder of that long night reflecting; reflecting on his life and how he had conducted it so far and by the time the first rays of the morning sun filtered through the slatted blinds and bathing the room in a pale light, he had reached a decision. From now on he was going to earn his living honestly. It wasn't going to be easy; he was well aware of that, but if Natasha and he were to have a future together, he wanted to be honest with her. Hopefully, cringing at the thought, this wouldn't mean he would have to tell her any of his past, realising she would find it not only difficult, but impossible to come to terms with, which could very well result in her viewing him in a totally different way.

Meeting Natasha had changed him. He couldn't explain to himself exactly why or how this had come about, but all he did know was, he had, over the last few days, ever since she had arrived in Hong Kong, begun to dislike what he had become. He tried to remember when this transformation had occurred, but he couldn't. All he knew was, when Marion Godwin had approached him, some weeks ago, at the time she had been setting up the transfer of the formula, he'd had no qualms whatsoever. He had been all for it, in fact. Even now, he had to admit her plan had been a brilliant one and it had worked: he had passed the original to her and within a matter of hours he had replaced it with a replica for which he had received a one-off payment. And then, the next stage of it all had been when, once again thanks to her ingenuity, he had made the deal with the consultants from London and all he'd had to do was escort one of them to the bank vaults, and had been paid in advance. Of course, he realised, there must have been someone behind the whole scam and whether he was actually known to them, he had no idea. For Nicholas' peace of mind, he had to believe Marion Godwin had been the only one who had been aware of his involvement and, now, with her no longer here, he should be in the clear. At least that was the way he reckoned. He just could not afford to think any differently. He wasn't worried about any suspicions the bank, or the police either if it came to that, may have about him, but, and here was the niggling and worrying part: finding out last night that Roddie Mortimer was Natasha's father. That had been a bit of a blow. And, it was this indisputable fact which was tugging at his conscience: by assisting in stealing property from the company who employed Roddie Mortimer, it felt like stealing from Natasha herself. He remembered how distraught her father had been the night before, but there had been nothing else in Nicholas' mind but Natasha; no space to wonder whether Roddie Mortimer suspected him of being involved, but now? This, he concluded, was the risk he must take. He would do anything to keep Natasha. His resolve remained strong; he would go straight from now on, no matter how hard it was.

'Nicholas?'

'Sweetheart,' he said, turning round to face her, 'how are you feeling?'

'I feel fine,' she said, propping herself up against the pillow, 'but, Nicholas, what happened? I passed out, didn't I; in the restaurant?'

'Yes, you did.' he said, going over to her and kissing her lightly on the brow, relieved to find her skin felt cool; the fever of last night had gone. 'They think you may have picked up a virus.'

'Not something I ate, then?'

'I don't think so,' he said, 'it could have been,' he added, 'but we both had the same, if you remember?'

'Strangely,' she smiled up at him, 'after being out for the count for most of the night, I do remember. We had bayonet *crevettes* and sweet and sour pork with Cantonese rice.'

'You're looking a lot better, Miss Bailey.' the doctor who had been in attendance spoke from the open doorway.

'I am, doctor,' Natasha said, 'will I be able to go home soon?'

'I should say so,' he nodded, 'but first I'll take your blood pressure, that sort of thing, but I don't see any reason why not. I would advise you to take it easy though for the next couple of days.'

'Was it a virus?' Nicholas asked him.

'That's a difficult question to answer, Mr Eastman,' he started to explain, 'viruses come in many guises, but from the tests we made last night, whatever it was, virus or not, the reaction was acute. You've already told me what you both had to eat last evening, so it is unlikely to be connected with any of the food, but what I would ask you, Miss Bailey, is what else did you have to eat or drink yesterday.'

Not much more, actually;' Natasha answered, 'in the morning, before I left for work, I had a cereal, and so did Nicholas, and at lunchtime one of my colleagues and I went out for a ham salad. We both had the same.' she added.

'And to drink?' he prompted.

'A coffee at breakfast-time, another one in the middle of the morning and a mineral water with our salads.'

'I see,' he said, 'and during the afternoon?'

'Nothing to eat, doctor; I only had a cappuccino to drink.'

'In a cafe or at work?'

'No, I had to go to Kowloon, around four it would have been,' Natasha said, 'my magazine is running a series of articles on women in business in Hong Kong and I needed to get approval for the one I had written. I had a few moments to wait and someone brought me the cappuccino while I was waiting.'

'It tasted alright?'

'Oh, yes; a little on the bitter side, but then perhaps the girl hadn't sprinkled enough chocolate on the top.'

'You could be right, Miss Bailey.' he said, and Nicholas hoped he hadn't noticed his reaction. Natasha had been back to "Annie's". And, there he refused to think any further. Later. He would think about it later, when he was on his own.

'It is possible,' the doctor continued, 'there may have been an ingredient in the cappuccino which had an adverse effect on you, delayed reaction of course, which only came into effect after you'd eaten in the evening. However, in the event this wasn't the case and there was something defective with the equipment they were using, we need to know where you were given the drink. It's all part of health and safety regulations, you understand, and will have to be entered against your admission into Casualty.'

'I had better stay off cappuccinos, then.' Natasha said lightly after giving the doctor the name of Anne Steed's nightclub and Nicholas could tell she had suspected nothing. As disturbed as she had been by Marcia's behaviour, it was clear to him it hadn't occurred to her what may have happened; that Marcia Rodrigo had attempted to remove her permanently. This, Nicholas promised himself, was something which he would have to deal with and the only way, knowing what these people dreaded more than anything, was the fear of losing their work permit. It would be a simple matter of confronting her with the threat of reporting her to the authorities; it wouldn't take her long to figure out it would then be a simple procedure for her visa to be revoked permanently along with a one-way ticket back to the Philippines.

*

Denny's first appointment on Thursday morning was with Juliet Warburton at ten-thirty, but he was in his office early, having spent a restless night. It had been several days now since he'd heard from his contact in Singapore and this concerned him, especially as he had expected the payment for the last transaction to have reached him by now.

He had asked Shirley to put the call through to Singapore when she pre-empted this by telling him there was a Mr Charles Bridges in reception asking to see him. Denny had never heard of anyone called Charles Bridges and, normally, his first reaction would have been to tell Shirley he would have to make an appointment once she had established the purpose of his visit, but this morning, his senses were on full alert and he didn't want any surprises. In Denny's experience, surprises were invariably unpleasant; a prelude of more to come. His life, these last few weeks, had resembled a roller-coaster. It wasn't knowing when to get off which worried him, but how he had managed to get on in the first place! Marion's death had gone a long way to make him feel this way; while not exactly unnerving him, it had made him even more alert than usual. He had heard nothing from the police, which didn't necessarily mean they were either satisfied or dissatisfied with what he'd told them. In fact, it meant nothing. There had been no further mention of her murder in the press which again could be ambiguous: either they were no further forward in their investigations or they were holding back on what they had been able to find out. How was he to know, or even guess? And, now, there was this guy, Charles Bridges. Obviously he knew who he was and the only way Denny would be able to find out was to agree to see him. It was at moments like these, he thought, rearranging his features into their polite mould, when he was grateful he bore more of a resemblance to the Chinese side of his family, having learned from during his time in England that a bland, expressionless Englishman was a rarity.

'Mr Yuan?' supplying Denny with the first clue; Charles Bridges had never seen him before.

'Yes?' he answered, 'I'm Denny Yuan.' and not making it easy for him, trying to weigh the man up and place him into some sort of category. He was English, from the southern counties, with a faint trace of a London accent; in his fifties, with a much-lined and lived-in kind of face; tall, about six-foot, Denny reckoned; in fact, a pretty mediocre type of guy, except for his eyes; a pale, penetrating blue, ice-blue, which acted as a silent signal: here was someone he should treat with caution. Charles Bridges, if that was his real name, had been around and, together with the air of confidence he exuded, Denny got the distinct impression that for whatever reason he was here, in his office, he meant business.

'Mr Yuan,' he said, sitting down on one of the chairs in front of the desk, 'I have no wish to take up much of your time, but' coming directly to the point which, in itself, was surprising to Denny, being used to most people who came into his office literally going round in circles to arrive at what they wanted to say, 'I have in my possession something which may be of interest to you.'

'Before you go any further, Mr Bridges,' Denny said, deciding it was time he started to control this conversation, otherwise he was in danger of not only losing his accustomed role of being in charge, but in allowing this stranger, someone he had never seen before, take over, 'perhaps you would be so kind as to tell me where you are from and why you are here?'

'If you would allow me,' he said, 'I'm coming to that shortly.'

'I'm waiting, Mr Bridges.'

'I will be frank with you, Mr Yuan,' he began, which in Denny's book meant quite the opposite; here were a load of lies and fabrications about to make their appearance, 'but what I would like to say is I do not like losing money.'

'No-one does, Mr Bridges.'

'I'm sure you are right. However, when I have, unwittingly I might add, been well and truly duped -'

'- duped?'

'Yes, duped, Mr Yuan. Do I need to elaborate? I'm sure that won't be necessary, but our mutual *late*-friend, Marion Godwin, recently put a proposition to me which, to be honest, I couldn't refuse. Now, I don't know whether you were aware of my involvement or not, and frankly, Mr Yuan,' he continued, 'that doesn't greatly concern me. The fact remains; I laid out at my own expense the necessary funds to meet my side of the bargain.'

'I'm sorry, Mr Bridges, but I'm finding it difficult to understand what you're saying.'

'Mr Yuan,' he said, leaning back in the chair and stretching his legs out in front of him, 'I would suggest you don't take that line. You are an intelligent man and as I said at the beginning of this conversation I have an item – an item which could prove to be most incriminating if it was to reach the hands of the authorities and, make no mistake, I won't hesitate to do this if I consider it necessary.'

'Alright, Mr Bridges,' Denny said quietly, 'perhaps you would like to enlighten me?'

'What I have, Mr Yuan,' he began, 'is a computer disc which quite clearly outlines, in much detail I might add, the theft of two formulas from McLellands Medical Research Laboratories, together with pretty damning evidence that you and Marion Godwin were working together.'

'And how did you get hold of this – this material?'

'First of all,' he said, 'you have to understand; that is, if you weren't aware already, but Marion Godwin was a woman with a passion for acquisition; in other words, she had an insatiable appetite for gain and she didn't care how many people she pushed aside to achieve her goal. I realise now, when it's too late, of course, that she couldn't be trusted and I had know her for fifteen years or more; ever since she was at law school, in fact, but she was deeply flawed, Mr Yuan. Not only did she fool me, but you also.'

'What do you mean?'

'Because,' he said, taking the disc from his inside pocket and placing it squarely on the desk between them, 'this,' he said, touching it lightly with his fore finger, 'came into my hands shortly after her death. There are a number of connotations one could work out from that, but one of them being, perhaps, it had been her intention to one day, when it suited her of course, to expose the name of the person who had been behind the thefts, in particular of the first formula; that is the only one I know about.'

'And how did you come by this disc, Mr Bridges?' Denny asked him, but already he had worked out the answer. The man sitting in front of him had been in Marion's apartment that night; therefore the logical conclusion must be that he murdered her. He wasn't sure as he looked at him what he felt about all of this. As far as Denny had been aware he had never met a murderer before and had no idea how he should be reacting. Shocked? Afraid? Certainly not that, but, yes, he was shocked. The man; Bridges was never his real name, was taking an inordinate risk in coming here this morning. Denny only had to report what he'd told him to the police, but he knew his own sense of personal survival would not permit that. He had to hear him out.

'This is all very interesting, Mr Bridges,' Denny said quietly, receiving no answer from him 'but what do you intend to do now? In other words, why are you here?'

'I am here, Mr Yuan, to sell you this information, otherwise - '

' – otherwise?'

'Otherwise, I make sure it reaches the right person at police headquarters.'

'Obviously you wouldn't go there personally?'

'Obviously.'

'How do I know you haven't made a copy?'

'You don't, of course, but I haven't. Once I receive payment that will be the end of the matter. I realise you only have my word for this, but quite frankly, it isn't something I am particularly comfortable about holding on to. I have no need of any mementos, Mr Yuan.'

The man calling himself Bridges didn't stay much longer. Denny had already made up his mind he had no alternative; the man had well and truly stitched him up and Denny knew when he was beaten. The amount he was asking for his silence was considerable, but, like all hush money, it had to be worth it. Denny had far too much to lose; it wasn't only because of those formulas, but the far larger part of his enterprises; the distribution of emeralds which, once all this business had died down, he would be able to re-continue, without the police breathing down the back of his neck.

By the time he had the office to himself again, he was once again delayed phoning Singapore by the arrival of Juliet. It would have to be after lunch now, he sighed, knowing that this meeting with her would last a while.

'Good morning, Juliet,' he greeted her, 'and, Shirley,' he added to his secretary, 'some coffee, please.'

'Good morning, Denny.' affording him one of her smiles which he always mentally labelled as her business, no-nonsense ones.

'I hope you have something positive to tell me.'

'I'm going to disappoint you, I'm afraid;' she said, 'the emeralds weren't in Roddie Mortimer's bag.'

'I can't say I'm all that surprised. So, Juliet, what do you think? He must have discovered them in there, but the question is what did he do? Hand them over to the police or keep them for himself?'

'I think he would have taken them to the police, Denny.' she said without the slightest hesitation.

'You sound very sure;' he said, 'he could have decided to say nothing and hold on to them instead.'

'You obviously don't know his character.'

'And you do?'

'Well enough to realise he's not like that, Denny.'

'It's human nature, Juliet. Faced with an opportunity like that, finding a cache of emeralds stashed away in the lining of your travel bag; wouldn't you, under similar circumstances?'

'I probably would,' she admitted, 'but then I'm not one hundred per cent honest.'

'And he is?'

'I would say so, yes.'

'You did check his bag thoroughly, didn't you?'

'I can assure you there was nothing in there.'

'And, what do you think,' he persisted, determined to find out as much as he could about this Mortimer guy who had turned up when he had, 'does he suspect anything about us, for instance? I take it you would have been able to detect any noticeable change in his manner towards you?'

'I don't honestly believe he has any idea of what's going on. I know it isn't much of an answer, but it's the best I can come up with, although, I have to say he has his suspicions.'

'Such as?'

'He told me last evening he had now remembered hearing my voice that night.'

'And that was the first time he'd mentioned this to you?'

'Yes; he said that after it happened he couldn't believe I would have been there.'

'And,' Denny frowned, trying to make sense of what she was trying to say. Either Mortimer heard her or he hadn't. To Denny, there were no grey areas. 'what finally decided him?'

'Well,' giving him one of her secretive smiles, 'it could have been because of the way he feels about me.'

'Explain, Juliet. Please.' he sighed. She could, at times, be the most infuriating of women.

'Denny,' she said, 'you're embarrassing me. Roddie is a man of few words and considering his age, incredibly naive when it comes to developing a relationship with a woman he is much attracted to; the way he is towards me. Okay,' she shrugged, 'the man's an academic, Denny, but that doesn't mean he isn't a normal male with normal appetites. Perhaps part of his brain was telling him what he really wanted to hear. What I mean is, he refused to believe I was there when we took him over to Lamma.'

'Juliet, Juliet.' he repeated. She was so conceited and he realised there was nothing he could say which would make her believe any differently. To her, Mortimer was besotted by the impact she had made on him: her beauty, her vivacious personality and her intelligence; take your pick he thought cynically, it didn't matter all that much. Juliet had obviously convinced herself she was so utterly desirable to this gullible Englishman and that was it.

'What do you mean, Denny?' she laughed, 'And you don't have to go on repeating my name like that!'

'Listen to me for a moment, Juliet, if you will,' he said, 'I don't think you've thought this through properly, but you should.'

'Alright,' she said, 'I'm listening.'

'What you're saying is, that Roddie Mortimer has waited several days before telling you he'd heard you that night; in fact, this was after he'd returned from London. If he's as clever as you make out, wouldn't you think once he found those emeralds he would immediately have come to the rather obvious conclusion that someone had passed on the information when he was planning on going to London and that it could only have been you? In spite of your undeniably alluring charms, don't you think that would have been too much for him to handle? He had discovered that you had been initially responsible for him being used as a carrier. I would suggest he must have felt more than a little used.'

'Put like that, Denny, you could be right, but he didn't mention finding the emeralds.'

'Well, he wouldn't, would he?' Denny insisted, surprised by her attitude. For an intelligent and switched-on modern woman, Juliet could not only be extremely stubborn as she was now, but missing the point entirely.

'I just thought he wouldn't have, that's all.' she said mildly, not like her at all and forcing him to look at her more closely, but he could tell nothing from the wide-eyed and deceptively innocent expression, hoping she hadn't gone so far as falling for the guy. If she had, she would no longer be a great deal of use to him; the possibility of 'pillow-talk' being the main reason, but for the present, there were more pressing issues he had to consider; his own personal situation for a start.

'Juliet,' he asked, 'you said that he heard your voice; did he mention what you were saying?'

'No, he didn't.'

'And, you didn't think to ask him?'

'Sorry, Denny; it didn't occur to me, but in any case, it couldn't have been all that much.'

'I'm not so sure.' he answered, thinking back to that evening, right from the moment Mortimer came upstairs in the shop to when they'd left him in the cottage. What few words which were spoken had been in Cantonese, being the only language the other two knew which had meant he had talked to them in their mother tongue. It had only been when he had said anything to Juliet it would have been in English. Perhaps, as she had suggested, it couldn't have meant a great deal; no more than half a dozen words at the most, although wishing he could remember. Fortunately he had never been in Mortimer's company, meaning there was no possible chance of being recognised as Juliet had been, all of which suggested to him Mortimer wouldn't have made any connection between them. But, this reassuring thought was short-lived. Denny's memory suddenly performed a rapid back-tracking to the evening before, to the Thursday when he'd called her on her mobile. She had mentioned his name! Twice! With the utmost clarity and total recall he now remembered what she had said: ".....hello, Denny," and then towards the end of the conversation, after he had said he wanted to see her, she had mentioned it again: ...... "I suppose I could do a bit of juggling .... I tell you what, Denny ....". As though this fragment of memory had triggered off what she had said to him later, he remembered those words also. They had been on the boat, after struggling to get Mortimer on board, when she had spoken for the first time since leaving Pedder Street. ".... I hope you didn't hit him too hard, Denny." That was all, but it was enough. She hadn't spoken again, not even when they reached the shores of Lamma Island. She hadn't gone with them up to the cottage, but stayed on the boat until they came back. Even if Mortimer hadn't heard everything, he would have cottoned on to his name being mentioned again and this would, Denny was certain, have registered with him.

'Why the worried look, Denny?'

'We have to be prepared, Juliet,' he answered, 'for possible repercussions.'

'You mean if the police should start asking questions?'

'There's no *if* about it,' he emphasised, 'they will, providing you are right and Mortimer did report discovering the emeralds. They are bound to ask him whether he has any ideas of how they found their way into his bag and they won't just leave off there, you know. They'll want to know who had known he was planning to visit London. I realise you're the accountant here, Juliet, but a child of six can add two and two together and make four!'

Chapter Fifteen

Roddie phoned the hospital before leaving for work on Thursday morning to learn that Natasha had made a full recovery with no ill effects and would be discharged later in the morning. They couldn't enlighten him about whether she'd had a virus or not, and although not satisfactory, at least she was alright and that was all that mattered to him. He couldn't forget the way she had looked when he had walked into Intensive Care; so terribly forlorn and looking much younger than her twenty-two years. Where had those years gone he wondered; these troubled and self-blaming thoughts staying with him during those hours when he had tried, without any success, to sleep. Where had Clarissa and he gone wrong? Their marriage had been such a short one; no more than a matter of a few years, but together they had produced a daughter. He hadn't been much of a support to Natasha during her younger life and it made no difference that Conrad, a man he hadn't even met, had taken his place as a father and, according to Clarissa, had made a very good job of it. But, now, Roddie hoped, he may be given a second chance. Nicholas had told him while they had been waiting like two expectant fathers in the corridor outside the ward, that she had started working for 'Woman's World', the irony of that not escaping his notice. Of all the people in Hong Kong, his daughter, after a matter of a couple of days here, had landed a job working for Louisa. What a village Hong Kong is, he sighed heavily, feeling considerably older than forty-four and, going into the bathroom switched on the shower to full power, hoping it would do considerably more than prepare him for the day ahead.

He still hadn't had a chance to speak to Andy Howe, realising the longer he put off telling him about those emeralds and the subsequent talk he'd had with Howard Westwood, the more difficult it was going to be. Andy, being a typically forthright Scotsman, would want to know why he had delayed telling him something of such importance. The fact they had nothing to do with McLellands would make no difference to him. Roddie knew the rules, also if he expected any support from him, this would be freely and generously given, but he had to play fair and that meant telling him everything which had to include how he believed the emeralds had ended up in his travel bag; this sobering thought bringing him once again full circle back to Juliet. He hadn't been all that clever the evening before when he'd tried to tackle her and, Juliet, being the type of woman she was, had instantly taken advantage of his awkwardness by adroitly changing the subject. Having to leave for the hospital as suddenly as he had, not only cut short their evening together, but, this morning, he wasn't sure whether he would have said anything more to her.

Andy was already in his office when Roddie arrived shortly before nine and having placed the file he'd brought back to work with him on the desk, he walked along the corridor and tapped lightly on his managing director's door.

'Good morning, Roddie,' he said, looking up from the diary in front of him; a daily ritual of his and one from which as far as Roddie was aware never deviated. Before the start of work each morning and before he made any phone calls, Andy always checked through how he intended to spend that day. 'My word,' he added quickly in his soft Scottish brogue, 'what's wrong; you don't look too great?'

'Just tired, sir,' Roddie said, not realising the way he was feeling was so obvious, 'I had a rather harrowing evening.'

'Sit down, Roddie. Sit down.' he repeated, pointing to the chair immediately in front of him. 'And tell me; what happened?'

'My daughter was taken ill suddenly; they believe it could have been a virus. However,' Roddie continued wearily, 'to cut a long story short, although she was unconscious for some time, she pulled through, but not until midnight.'

'She's in Hong Kong?'

'Yes, she is. Mind you, I only learned this when I was in London. Apparently she moved here over a week ago.'

'And she didn't tell you?'

'No, although according to her boyfriend, she had been trying to phone me, but without any success.'

'I see. And how is she now?'

'I phoned the hospital before I left this morning,' Roddie told him, 'and apparently she's fine now, although I must say, it did give us a scare.'

'I am sure it did. These viruses can be the very devil,' he sympathised, 'and the nasty thing is they can attack a person at any time. But then, your daughter is young; that would have been in her favour.'

'Probably,' Roddie agreed, 'the hospital hasn't yet been able to pinpoint the real cause, but to be honest, sir, all I'm concerned about is that she's alright.'

'Of course. Of course. I understand. Do you want to take some time off, Roddie; to be with her, I mean?'

'No, but thank you all the same,' he answered, 'I'll go and see her after work today. Meanwhile, she has a very attentive boyfriend to look after her, although, knowing Natasha she'll want to get back to work as soon as possible.'

'Just as you wish, Roddie.'

'Sir,' Roddie said and while grateful for Andy Howe's ready sympathy, wanted to get on with the main reason why he'd called into his office, 'there is something I have to tell you. I would have done yesterday, but I felt you had enough with which to concern yourself over the death of Marion Godwin; I didn't like to bother you.'

'It's true what you say, Roddie. I was upset. It wasn't as though we knew her all that well, at least not socially, but what happened to her is still a tremendous shock, but go on.

Andy listened to what he had to say without interrupting until he reached the part where he had been manhandled across to Lamma Island.

'This is outrageous, Roddie!' he gasped, his expression one of indignation, 'You poor man; what a dreadful thing to happen to you. And you didn't report this once you got back home?'

'Not then, no; only when I called into New Scotland Yard. They wanted to know if I had any idea of how the emeralds could have been put in my bag.'

'Of course. Well,' shaking his head, 'what on earth can I say? There is one thing, though.'

'Yes?'

'It looks very much as if there is a connection between everything which has been going on recently and then, of course, there is Marion Godwin's murder. Well, Roddie, the only advice I can give you, it might be best if you try to put all of this out of your mind and let the authorities tackle it.'

'Sound advice,' Roddie agreed, 'not so easy, though, but I do agree with you. Nothing will be gained, I know, by going over and over the various incidents and still reaching no comprehensible conclusion.'

'I am glad you told me, however. You were right to do so. Apart from, hopefully, helping you to share the burden, it should go without saying that you can rely on my full support.'

'Thank you, sir.' and Andy was right, wise man that he was; he did feel relieved after sharing the knowledge of this nightmare with him. 'I'll get back to my office, if that's alright with you?' Roddie said, making to stand up.

'Of course. Incidentally,' he asked, 'how are you progressing with the formula you've been working on? I appreciate you've had little time yet to catch up on your various other projects, but if you need any further assistance in the developing of this new drug, you only have to say.'

'I had intended to write up a full report for you this morning.' Roddie explained, 'I didn't receive the results of the tests until yesterday afternoon and, regrettably, it appears we're short of one important component.'

'That sounds serious.'

'It could have been, but once I had those results I was able to check through everything we'd worked on so far. It's disappointing, I know, having to go back to the beginning of our research, although sometimes this does happen.'

'Don't I know it! And that is why we have to be as thorough as we are. How do you intend to progress now?'

'I'll improve on the formula and arrange another series of tests. I hope to have made some headway on this by the end of the day, sir, and once I reach that stage, I'm going to scrap my original notes. Bearing in mind what has occurred recently with our anti-malaria formula it has made me ultra-cautious; I wouldn't like those papers to fall into the wrong hands.'

'Quite. And this time, Roddie, when we're satisfied with the final results, I suggest we move quicker than we usually do in patenting the drug.'

'I think that would be a good idea and perhaps then we wouldn't need to use our safe deposit box for such a sensitive document.'

'Yes, Roddie, also,' Andy continued, 'without sounding callous, we need to find another lawyer. I will have to pass it by the Board of course, although I feel we should continue to use the same firm. I've spoken to one of the other partners a number of times; Simon Cheung, and he always struck me as a very sound fellow. What's your opinion of him?'

'I've met him a couple of times also, and, yes, I'm inclined to agree with you. It's like banks, isn't it,' Roddie commented, 'it's never all that advisable to keep chopping and changing.'

'Better the devil you know, eh?' Andy Howe said, smiling for the first time since Roddie had come into his office.

*

Francesca Cristofoli had been detained overnight at police head-quarters and by midday on Thursday she was boarding a Cathay Pacific flight to London, travelling Club Class and accompanied by Frank Mitchell.

There had been three pieces of jewellery in her handbag: a gold chain necklace, a diamond-studded bracelet and a sapphire ring. She had been reluctant to hand over the bag to Inspector Clarke, but even she knew when she was cornered although, throughout the interrogation which followed, her cool confidence didn't waver.

'Are you in the habit of carrying your jewellery around with you, madam?' he had asked her, turning the ring round in the palm of his hand.

'When I'm travelling, yes,' she'd answered with an arrogant shrug of her shoulders, giving every impression to Howard, who had been watching her closely, that she considered such a question as totally unnecessary, 'I always maintain it's much safer than leaving it in my hotel room.'

'I'm surprised you don't take advantage of the hotel's safe.' the inspector commented dryly.

'I dislike the inconvenience of having to ask someone each time I want to take a piece out.'

'And this sapphire ring, madam,' he'd pressed her, 'does this belong to you?'

His tactics had changed by then; he was forcing her to slip up, to say something from which she would be unable to retract.

'Of course it does, Inspector.'

'You are lying, madam.'

'How dare you! How dare you accuse me of lying?'

'If this is your ring,' he'd said, slowly emphasising each word, 'why is the inscription in another woman's name, unless by some coincidence, you are also called Leticia?'

'If you *must* know,' she had said and Howard couldn't help but marvel at the speed with which she responded. It had been a stroke of luck that there had been the inscription inside the ring, and it was unlikely Francesca would have had the time or the opportunity to examine it properly. 'I bought this second-hand; in an antique shop in London.'

Remarkable. Even when she must have known she'd been caught and that whatever she added now would only exacerbate her situation, she continued to try and bluff her way through. From that moment onwards, Howard had taken over by first tackling the matter of her true identity and once again, she was completely boxed in, although he had to admit she certainly put up a good fight.

'Your name, madam,' Howard had begun, 'is, we understand, Francesca Cristofoli.'

'My name is Frances Catania.' she had answered sharply, her head held high and looking directly at Howard. 'I have my passport with me, in my bag, as no doubt you've already seen.' she'd added, throwing an indignant glare in Inspector Clarke's direction.

'We did notice it, of course.' Howard had replied, 'But, perhaps more importantly, I have here,' putting his hand into his jacket pocket, 'copies of two passports: one in the name of Francesca Cristofoli and the other in the name of Frances Catania and,' he'd warned, thinking how fortuitous that they should have arrived so shortly after he'd been talking to Robert, along with the photograph of Eddie Bristow, 'before you continue in your denial that you are not Francesca Cristofoli, I would mention we, and by that, I mean the International Police, have written confirmation from our hand-writing expert that the signature in both passports is identical.'

She hadn't had much to say about that, but then what could she have said? Howard had immediately taken advantage of her silence, which he was certain wouldn't last long, by moving on to the next stage of what had now developed into an interrogation; a fact which he didn't think would have been missed by her.

'Miss Cristofoli,' he had continued, 'I trust you have realised by now that you face being taken to court with a very strong possibility of receiving a prison sentence for a number of robberies carried out by you going back more than ten years; each and every one of them supportable by sufficient evidence to satisfy the courts that you are indeed guilty. At this stage, I have no intention of elaborating. However,' Howard had pressed on, a little surprised she hadn't tried to interrupt him, but instead had remained perfectly still; sitting perched on the edge of her chair immediately across the table from the inspector and himself, the expression of disdain firmly in place, with only a slight heightening of colour on her cheeks to indicate she was perhaps losing her grip on what presumably she had thought she would have been able to talk herself out of, 'I have a suggestion to make to you -' pausing for a second, giving her an opportunity to respond, but she said nothing, '- which you may find advantageous to your present situation.'

'My present situation?' she mimicked, her lips curling unattractively, 'All I'm aware is I'm being held here against my will and not once have you suggested I could call my lawyer.'

'You may of course,' Howard had said, 'I was coming to that. In fact,' he had added, gesturing towards the telephone on the table, 'feel free. I take it you do have a lawyer in Hong Kong?'

'I did have, but not any longer.'

'Are you by any chance referring to Miss Godwin?'

'How did you know?' apparently taken aback; she hadn't expected that he thought. Talking to the woman really was like a cat and mouse game: now you see me, now you don't and then, catch me if you can!

'I didn't Miss Cristofoli, let's say it was a calculated guess, but shall we continue? What I have to say may be of some interest to you.'

'What do you mean?'

'Perhaps you will hear me out first and then you can ask as many questions as you wish. I would like to talk about emeralds, Miss Cristofoli.'

'Emeralds?'

'That's what I said, but to be more precise, the smuggling of emeralds.'

'I don't know what you mean.'

'I believe you do. Allow me to elaborate.'

'If you must.'

'Right.' Howard had said, wondering how long she would be able to sustain her attitude of contrived disinterest, and recognising he was about to stick his neck out, but then he had to; Francesca Cristofoli could be their only chance to find out who was behind the smuggling. A few names, that was all he wanted, fairly sure that Denny Yuan's would be one of them. 'Your frequent visits to Hong Kong have been closely monitored for some time,' stretching the truth a fraction, 'also we know you've been living in Columbia for the past ten years and the name of the gentleman who has been supporting you for most of that time.'

'Antonio.' She had whispered his name, all the colour draining from her face, and from that moment, Howard knew he had her exactly where he wanted. She would talk now.

'Yes,' he had said quietly, 'Antonio Gomez; a key figure in the government, a much-respected citizen of Bogota, also part owner of emerald mines north of the city. We strongly suspect,' he had stressed, 'you have been acting as his courier by bringing caches of emeralds into Hong Kong and passing them on to your contact here and obviously you have been well reimbursed for your efforts. Have you anything to add?'

'No, nothing, except to say you are quite wrong.'

'You are talking to Interpol here, Miss Cristofoli,' he had reminded her, 'please don't take us for complete fools. What I have told you are plain hard facts; there is no way you can dispute them.'

'I have nothing to say.'

'Probably very wise. However,' he had persisted, 'we are sure if you were able to – to assist us, it could mean a lessening of the sentence which will undoubtedly be meted out to you for your part in the smuggling. Not –'

'– wait a minute!'

'No, I have no intention of waiting, Miss Cristofoli. I intend to finish what I set out to say to you which is, that not only will you face trial for the robberies you carried out in England and throughout Europe, you will also appear in court charged for being an accessory in an international emerald smuggling syndicate.'

'What do I have to do?' was all she had said; her words barely audible.

'We want to know the names of those involved.'

'I don't know much.'

'I would prefer it if you didn't prevaricate; you'll achieve nothing by that, you know. We will start at the source, shall we? Antonio Gomez. You're on his payroll, aren't you?'

'Yes.'

'Where does Denny Yuan fit in?' and as soon as he'd mentioned the name he thought for a moment she was going to pass out, but she didn't. Instead, she took a deep steadying breath before answering, her face if anything paler than ever.

'I take the emeralds to him.'

'At his shop in Pedder Street?'

'Yes.'

'And what happens to them after that?'

'I don't know.'

'Come on Miss Cristofoli, you can do better than that.'

'Nobody told me, neither Antonio nor Denny. That's the truth.'

'That may be technically correct, but you're not going to sit there and tell me that a woman of your intelligence and natural curiosity wouldn't have made it her business to find out.'

'They're transported from Hong Kong to London; after that, well, I think they must be distributed in Europe, but I don't know for certain.'

'Alright,' Howard had said, not displeased with what she had supplied him, 'do you know the name of Denny Yuan's contact in London?'

'He's called Conrad.'

'Doesn't he have a surname?'

'Bailey; Conrad Bailey. He has a jewellery business in London; in New Oxford Street.'

'Have you ever been there?'

'No, I haven't.'

'So how do you know?'

'Because he telephoned Denny once when I was in his office; that's how I learned his name.'

'And the rest?'

'I looked him up in the telephone directory.'

So simple. Just like that. She merely opened a London telephone directory and looked up the name of the person who was possibly the strongest link; without that they would have been stymied. At last, they had something tangible on which to work, both in Hong Kong and in England.

It would be three in the afternoon when Francesca Cristofoli would be arriving at Heathrow and as soon as Frank had handed his charge over to the authorities, he would be able to meet up with Robert to discuss the best way to move forward. Howard, also, needed to talk to Robert. It was too early to call him, although he had sent him a brief email last night which he should see before he left for his office around nine. Whatever they finally decided, he felt they should now move quickly, otherwise there was a grave possibility of this whole investigation, which had started at a snail's pace, running out of control. It was only a matter of time he reckoned before Francesca Cristofoli's sudden exit from Hong Kong would become significant to someone and he rather thought this might be Antonio Gomez in Columbia. She would have had no means of contacting him as her mobile had been taken from her, which would in effect have her left in limbo. There was also Denny Yuan to consider. News travelled fast in Hong Kong, Howard was well aware of that, and he didn't think it would be long before he heard she had been arrested. And then what? That was anyone's guess he thought cynically. They were up against a hardened gang here, also, with apparently no shortage of funds to either extricate themselves when they considered it necessary, or to pay for information. There would always be someone ready to talk, especially if the price was right, and probably by now it was common knowledge among the staff at the "Mandarin" that one of their guests had booked out of the hotel sooner than expected and this being done, not by the lady herself, but by a female police officer. Also, there was the manager of "The Hilton"; he shouldn't be dismissed. He had known, although he hadn't been present when they had approached Francesca Cristofoli, that there was something far more serious than the theft of a sapphire ring to justify the interest of a police officer from London. The fact no mention had been made of him being with Interpol didn't come into the equation. Howard had been to Hong Kong enough times during his career to understand these people. They talked. And they talked a great deal, thriving on anything remotely exciting and out of the ordinary and if the drama revolved around the expatriate community all the better, until in the end whatever they did hear would have been fabricated upon, but nonetheless, Howard didn't think it would be too long before Denny Yuan heard and that was something he didn't want to happen. There were occasions, he fretted, when the difference in the time zone between east and west could be a real hindrance. He couldn't realistically expect to hear from Robert until four in the afternoon at the earliest and he needed to confer with him before going any further.

Howard was halfway across the entrance hall at police headquarters when the desk sergeant called out to him: 'Excuse me, sir,' he said, 'but Inspector Clarke would like to see you.'

'Right, sergeant,' Howard smiled at him; a smooth-skinned Cantonese; still in his twenties and obviously eager to make a good impression, 'I'm on my way.'

'Good morning, Mr Westwood,' Inspector Clarke greeted him, exactly as he had each day, 'refreshed, I trust, after a rather dramatic outcome last night?'

'Surprisingly,' Howard answered, 'I do feel refreshed. No doubt that can be attributed to finally catching the lady. It's been a long time.'

'It certainly has,' the inspector agreed, 'and, if I may say so, I was much impressed by the way you questioned her. She didn't weaken though, did she? Perhaps a trifle less spunky after we'd brought her in here, but she's a fighter that one.'

'One could say she was a hard nut to crack!' Howard chuckled. 'I must admit it is a relief to know she will now be brought to task for those robberies and however long a sentence she is given it will mean she'll be out of action for a while, also, with the stigma of having a police record.'

'Do you think that will concern her unduly?'

'Probably not, but I know what will.'

'Yes?'

'Once the press get hold of the story they will undoubtedly make the most of it, together with her photograph appearing on the front pages, not only in England, but in those other places in Europe where she operated. Seeing that is going to stir up quite a few bitter memories; she'll discover what it's like to be ostracised from those social circles in which she used to mingle.'

'As notorious as that, was she?'

'Oh, yes, Inspector, we can be pretty certain her illustrious career will be at an end.'

'But then,' Inspector Clarke went on, 'there is her involvement in this other business. As you told her last night she will have to appear in court in respect to her part in that.'

'Yes, that's right, and whether the fact she gave us those two names will result in any reduction in her sentence remains to be seen.'

'*Que sera sera*, Mr Westwood.'

'Exactly.'

Howard was on the point of returning to his own office, having made up his mind he would spend the time before lunch working on his report for Robert, when they were interrupted by one of headquarters' police officers; a young man he'd seen a number of times and knew he had been assigned to the team investigating Marion Godwin's murder.

'I'm sorry to disturb you, sir,' he said, standing in the open doorway, 'but I wanted to speak to you as soon as possible and while Mr Westwood was still with you.'

'It's alright, sergeant;' the inspector was quick to reassure him, 'what have you got for us?'

'There's been a development in the Godwin case, sir.' he said, 'I've just returned from Princes' Terrace. As soon as I showed the photograph to the concierge he said he remembered seeing the man before. Also,' the sergeant continued, 'one of Miss Godwin's neighbours came into the lobby when I was there and told me he recognised him.'

'And this was on Sunday night?'

'Not exactly, sir; it was during Saturday morning. The concierge told me he'd seen him coming up the steps to the apartments; he didn't come in as he expected him to, but stood for a moment studying the plaque outside the door; this is the one listing all the names of the residents.' he added.

'And the neighbour?'

'He'd seen him around the same time, shortly after ten; he'd been walking along the pavement at the rear of the building.'

'I see.'

'Inspector Clarke,' Howard said to him, 'would you mind if I ask the sergeant a question?'

'Not at all, Mr Westwood.'

'Sergeant,' Howard turned to face him, 'what did you mean just now when the inspector asked you whether these two people had seen the man on the Sunday? You said "not exactly". Why was that?'

'Because, sir, the neighbour, he's called Major Stafford, said he did see him again on Sunday night.'

'But it would have been dark,' Howard pointed out, 'how could he be so certain it was the same person?'

'There are street lights along there and although the Major couldn't exactly make out his features, he was quite insistent he wasn't mistaken.'

'And whereabouts did he see him; did he say?'

'Yes, he did. He was returning to his apartment, it's in the same block as Miss Godwin lived in, after taking his dog for his evening walk and that's where he noticed him. He'd been walking behind him before that, but as soon as the major reached the first lamp-post, he happened to turn round to find he hadn't walked any further along the pavement, but was standing quite still, having moved further back into the shadows, as though he was waiting for someone.'

'Thank you, sergeant.' Howard said, glancing across towards the inspector to indicate he should continue. What the sergeant had said was interesting; there was no doubt about that, but how accurate both witnesses were would have to be examined more closely. If they were right and it had been Eddie Bristow outside Marion Godwin's apartment that would indeed be quite damning for him. He hoped, for Inspector Clarke's sake, Eddie Bristow was still in Hong Kong and hadn't returned to London, otherwise it would mean the murder enquiry would be prolonged. They would then have to pick up the threads for him in London, or alternatively, they could send Eddie Bristow back to Hong Kong, but either way, it would all take time. Meanwhile, he was certain the inspector would already be under pressure from his superior to make every effort to wrap up the case as speedily as possible.

'Alright, sergeant,' Inspector Clarke said, 'you've done a good job here and I suggest we arrange a meeting for later on this afternoon with you and the other officers on the case. By then, I hope to have some further directives for you all.'

'What are your views on all of that?' the inspector asked Howard after the sergeant had left the office, closing the door quietly behind him.

'Well,' Howard answered slowly, not wanting to suggest anything which may sway the man in an entirely wrong direction. This murder case was after all under his jurisdiction; it wasn't Interpol's right to intervene unless it turned out her murder was tied in with the smuggling, 'there's not a lot I can suggest, really, except to say we should get in touch with Eddie Bristow and the sooner the better.'

'Before he leaves Hong Kong, you mean?'

'Yes.'

'I can find out immediately if he's still at the "Mandarin". I know the manager personally and I can vouch for his discretion; I'll give him a ring now.'

Howard watched him while he rang the number of the hotel direct, without asking his secretary, and could tell by his grim expression the news wasn't good, waiting patiently until he had politely brought the call to a close to be enlightened.

He booked out earlier this morning.'

'Did they say what time?'

'Yes, shortly after ten; he'd ordered a taxi for the airport the evening before'

'Right,' Howard said quickly, 'if, Inspector, you would kindly phone reservations at Kai Tak and see whether in fact he was flying back to London, I can then call New Scotland Yard and have someone at Heathrow immediately he arrives.' wondering as he spoke whether he was on the same plane as Frank Mitchell. If that was the case, he couldn't blame Frank for not spotting him in Departures; he would have been fully occupied with keeping a close watch on Francesca Cristofoli. Even Frank couldn't do two things at once!

'He's on the same flight as Mr Mitchell and Francesca Cristofoli,' Inspector Clarke said, confirming his thoughts and replacing the receiver, 'estimated time of arrival at Heathrow fifteen hundred hours, British time. They would have been airborne twelve minutes ago.' he added.

'Too bad,' Howard sympathised, 'but all isn't lost, Inspector. We can conduct the initial questioning for you in London and get word back to you as quickly as we can. Perhaps, again to save time, you could arrange for any other sets of fingerprints taken from Miss Godwin's apartment sent through to New Scotland Yard. At least if Eddie Bristow's are among them it will prove he was in her apartment!'

Chapter Sixteen

'What the hell is going on, Denny?' Antonio Gomez's voice boomed in Denny's ear, so much so, he was forced to pull the receiver away.

'Alright, Antonio,' he said to him, 'why not calm down and tell me what you're talking about?'

'Oh, I will, Denny. I will, make no mistake. It's Frances; she's gone!'

'What do you mean she's gone? Left Hong Kong; is that what you're saying?'

'How the hell do I know! I've been trying to get in touch with her since last night and then again earlier today. Her mobile is absolutely dead.'

'Perhaps she's had it on charge,' Denny suggested, hoping by keeping his own voice lowered it would calm him down, but to no avail. 'Have you considered that?' he added.

'Of course I have! I've just called the "Mandarin", five minutes ago it was, and they told me she had already left the hotel.'

'Perhaps she's on her way back to Columbia.'

'Without letting me know? I don't think so, Denny. She would have told me.'

'Well,' Denny frowned, not knowing what to make of this, 'where is she, then?'

'You tell me!'

'I have no idea,' Denny answered, 'I had lunch with her on Monday and she didn't say anything about leaving, but I'll try and find out. She may have decided to move to another hotel.'

'That would be extremely unlikely; what reason would she have had? I can't think of one. There's something very wrong here, Denny and I mean *seriously* wrong!'

Antonio Gomez's concern, now approaching panic proportions, was getting to him, a dozen explanations surging through his brain, until he also was starting to see a sinister side to why Frances should have left the way she apparently had done.

'Listen, Antonio,' he said, affecting a calmness he didn't feel, 'as I've said, I will try to find out. In fact, I'll go along to the hotel right away. There could be a very simple reason why she had decided to book out when she did.'

'If you would, Denny and ring me back, won't you? I'm worried.' he added.

'About Frances?' Denny asked, although guessing Antonio's concern wouldn't revolve around her.

'No; I'm worried about myself! That should be obvious to you and if you have any sense of self-preservation, you should be worried about your own position. The hotel actually put me through to the manager, you know, which I thought to be a little strange, and he was extremely cagey. In fact,' he added, 'he told me no more than the clerk had done.'

'Which was?'

'I've already told you, Denny! Frances had already left the hotel.'

'Not that she had booked out; that's what they normally say.'

'I know that, but they didn't.'

'Okay, Antonio,' Denny said, stifling a sigh, he had enough to contend with at the moment without acting as a detective for Antonio Gomez, 'I'll try to get to the bottom of it and I'll get back to you.'

Denny had no sooner rung off when the long awaited call from his contact in Singapore came through and, once again, he picked up the receiver.

'Good morning, Bertrand.' Denny said.

'I don't think it will be a good morning for you, Denny,' Bertrand Tang said, 'once you hear what I have to say.'

'Allow me to be the judge of that, Bertrand,' he said, his heart sinking and expecting the worst, 'what's wrong?'

'In a nutshell,' Bertrand answered, 'after running tests on the formula it's been found to be no good.'

'What?'

'I'm no scientist, as you know,' he said, 'but the laboratories here conducted the tests and, quite frankly, they can't do anything with it. In other words, the formula as it stands is utterly useless.'

'I don't believe this.'

'I'm afraid you'll have to. I've been told if they decided to go ahead and produce the drug it could have an adverse affect, a quite serious one and they are not prepared to take the risk.'

'So,' Denny said, 'no deal?'

'No deal.'

'This is a real blow. The first formula was alright, wasn't it? There were no teething problems there?'

'That is already proving to be very successful, but this one, no-way and, Denny, calling it teething problems is an understatement. There appears to be a missing link somewhere and regrettably they are unable to locate it.'

'Missing link?'

'Yes,' he answered, 'there is something radically wrong with the formula; in other words I've been told it's incomplete. You may have been set up; that's always a possibility, but only you will be able to verify whether that is the case or not.'

'You've lost me, Bertrand,' Denny said quickly, 'I sent that formula on to you in all good faith. I believed the source was a sound one, but it would seem from what you've told me, there's been some sort of a blip here.'

'You can call it that if you like,' Bertrand said, 'but it's my credibility which is on the line and I don't like it one little bit.'

After he had replaced the receiver, Denny sat for a moment puzzling over what had happened. Perhaps, he now admitted, he had been too hasty in taking for granted those hand-written notes he'd found in Roddie Mortimer's apartment had been complete. He didn't agree with Bertrand's suggestion that he had been set up; that would have been impossible. Mortimer would have had no idea in advance they could have been stolen that night, or any other night, if it came to that. His arrival back at the shop had taken them all by surprise and the decision to render him unconscious and take him over to Lamma had been an instantaneous one, totally unpremeditated. Finding those notes the way he had in the apartment had, to Denny, been like a bonus. He inwardly cringed when he remembered the extra risk he'd taken in returning there a second time after going back to his office to have them copied; the sole reason being to make sure when Mortimer eventually came back the following day they would be exactly where he had left them. All of these reflections made him realise on this occasion he really had been too smart. A salutary lesson, he decided soberly, and one from which he should learn, otherwise the next time he might not be so fortunate as to emerge unscathed. Bertrand Tang, up to a point, was reliable. Denny had known him for years and they had worked closely together on a number of deals, each one of them being lucrative to the pair of them, but he knew instinctively Bertrand's loyalty only went so far. If, and thank goodness the laboratory in Singapore hadn't, but if they had decided to go ahead and produce an inferior drug, the first person they would blame would be Bertrand, especially if they found themselves with a law suit on their hands and it didn't take too many guesses for Denny to know who would ultimately be blamed. Bertrand would want some sort of appeasement and to Denny that meant only one thing: reimbursement and not a couple of thousand dollars, but considerably more. He was already smarting from having to pay off that creep who'd blackmailed him over the disc he'd found in Marion's apartment and the fact that it was more than likely he had murdered her made no difference. He had been cornered; a situation Denny had never experienced before and hoped never to again.

After walking along to the "Mandarin", which turned out to be a total waste of time; he had been unable to find out any more than Antonio, Denny returned to his office. Miss Frances Catania, the receptionist had informed him, after deftly checking on her computer screen, was no longer staying in the hotel and had, apparently, left the night before at ten-fifteen. It is possible, Denny thought, retracing his steps along Queen's Road Central, Frances had taken the late night flight out to Columbia and, if she had, she should have arrived there by now. Predictably enough, the girl didn't have anything further to add and he had been reluctant to pursue it. He had noticed the manager hovering in the doorway to his office and got the distinct impression he had been listening attentively to everything they were saying. Antonio had described his manner on the phone as cagey and he could well believe him. Albert Ho had worked for the "Mandarin" for years and Denny had spoken to him a number of times in the past and, no doubt, he would remember; not only that, he would know who he was. But, Denny shrugged, did it matter? Wherever Frances had decided to buzz off to was no concern of his, although every instinct was telling him he was wrong. Not only would she have told Antonio she was on her way there, but Denny would have expected her to give him a call to let him know she was leaving. Yes, as Antonio had said, something was wrong.

Even when, eight or ten minutes later, when he was in the front lobby and pressing the button for the lift which would take him up to the eighth floor to his suite of offices, Denny continued to mull over why Frances should have made such a speedy departure. Antonio's concern aside, whether warranted or not, at this point Denny refused to take all that seriously. Frances was an extremely independent woman. She was a survivor; being one himself he recognised the signs. He would have described her as someone who knew exactly what she was doing and where she was going, but not one to be impetuous. He was trying to recall exactly what she'd said to him over lunch when he'd asked when she planned to return to Bogota and as the lift bore him silently up to the eighth floor, her words came back to him: "I haven't made up my mind yet." she had said and he couldn't help noticing how she avoided looking at him directly as if her mind had been elsewhere, and then trying to regain her attention, he'd made the comment about being surprised

Antonio wasn't putting any pressure on her, feeling fairly certain Antonio wasn't the type of man to tolerate her being away indefinitely. She had been lying when she'd said: "Not that much, but I just felt, Denny, I needed these days on my own to recharge my batteries."

She had been planning something, but whether this had been how she was going to arrange her departure from Hong Kong in the way she had, there was no way of knowing. Even when the lift finally came to a standstill, he still couldn't come up with any feasible explanation or how he was going to find out. Antonio wouldn't be happy when he spoke to him again, but that was tough. If he was so concerned, let him do something positive for a change. Denny was becoming increasingly tired of being the 'front man'; the one who had to make all the major decisions and that inevitably involved taking the most risks. He hadn't liked the thinly veiled innuendos when Antonio had said he should be worried about his own position. Of course Denny had known exactly what he'd meant; intervention by the authorities and given the scale of the smuggling, Interpol would be brought it. He had always been conscious of that possibility if one of them should become careless. It was just as well he hadn't told Antonio the full reason for asking him to suspend deliveries for a time. He really would have been jumping up and down; meanwhile, perhaps this was the time to be putting one of his contingency plans into effect.

Denny walked briskly through the main office, nodding automatically in the direction of the receptionist, his mind racing ahead as he considered what he must do to ensure his continuing immunity, having now accepted the possibility that Frances may not have left voluntarily. Denny had made it his business to learn how the police operated in any sizable investigation and if they did have an inkling, no matter how tenuous, they wouldn't be content in pulling in only one of those suspects; they would want the whole gamut and would initially concentrate their efforts on the weakest link, gathering as much as they could from them any information which would take them further until they had finally wrapped up the case. Was Frances the missing link, he wondered. He realised he could be going off at a tangent here, but the risk of dismissing the possibility could not be ignored; it was one Denny couldn't afford to take.

Shirley had brought him coffee and he idly stirred in the sugar, all the while his brain working double-time. There was something he had forgotten, something he had heard which should have registered with him, but his brain was chock-a-block with so much garbage, it was difficult to sift his way through it all. He had finished his coffee before he remembered. It was what the receptionist at the "Mandarin" had said. Frances had left the hotel at ten-fifteen last night; that was what she'd told him, but Frances couldn't have left at that time; she would still have been at "The Hilton". For the second time that morning his memory went back to their lunch on Monday. It had been after he'd asked her when she planned to return to Bogota and she'd mentioned being invited to a function, a cocktail party was how she'd described it, given for a group of foreign dignitaries. She hadn't elaborated by explaining how she came to be included in the guest list and he had assumed she may have been there to represent Antonio as she had done a few times in the past.

Now he was able to do something positive, Denny thought, buzzing through to his secretary to say he was going for lunch. That promised call to Antonio would have to wait, he decided, leaving his office.

'It's good to see you again, Mr Yuan.' Donald Hsui said, smiling broadly, 'What would you like to drink?'

'A lager and lime, please, Donald. And yourself?'

'A mineral water would be fine, Mr Yuan.' he answered, exactly as Denny knew he would. Donald Hsui made it a rule never to drink anything stronger while he was on duty.

'How's trade these days?' Denny asked, watching as he measured out just the right amount of lime juice to suit his taste.

'Pretty good;' Donald said, placing the lager on the bar in front of him, 'take last night for instance; I don't know whether you heard or not, but there is a large group of foreign heads of state visiting Hong Kong this week; many of them staying in the hotel, I might add, and they were all here last night attending a welcoming function. This was in our Elizabethan suite; a very grand occasion.' he added proudly.

'I expect that kept you all busy?'

'It certainly did; we were run off our feet for most of the time,' he laughed, 'but we didn't mind. I always enjoy these functions although I must admit there was a little bit of extra excitement none of us bargained for.'

'Oh, yes?'

'Don't think I'm being indiscreet,' he put in quickly, 'but some of us couldn't help noticing what was going on, especially when the police arrived.'

'You'll have to tell me now, Donald,' Denny said, scarcely believing how easy it was proving to extract what he felt could be the information he was looking for, 'I'm beginning to imagine all kinds of things!'

'As well you might, Mr Yuan,' he nodded, 'but one of the guests, Mrs Hammond it was, she's married to George Hammond, he's high up in the British Embassy, well,' he went on, 'she had a very expensive ring stolen.'

'How on earth did that happen?'

'She'd taken the ring off to wash her hands in the cloakroom and when she turned round to where she'd left it, it wasn't there! Just like that, it had gone!'

'My goodness, Donald, that sort of thing isn't good for "The Hilton". Presumably she reported it to the manager?'

'She must have done I suppose, but here's the strange part,' Donald Hsui answered, halting for a second in his flow, a frown creasing his wide forehead, 'within minutes it seemed, the police had arrived.'

'What; more than one do you mean?'

'No, only one, Inspector Clarke from police headquarters. He did have another person with him, but no-one seems to know who he was; anyway,' there was no stopping him now and without any prompting carried on, 'they actually found the woman who'd stolen it!'

'A woman, you say?'

'Yes, that's right, Mr Yuan; she'd also been invited to the function.'

'How could they have been so certain it was her in such a short space of time?'

'That's what we've been wondering, but they took her away with them all the same.'

This had to be Frances. Who else? Could she have been foolish enough to do something like that where there was every likelihood of being found out, as indeed she had been, or, Denny wondered, had she been set up?'

'And who was she, Donald? Do you know?'

'Oh, yes; it was Miss Frances Catania; she used to stay here when she's been visiting Hong Kong, although more recently I understand she's been going to "The Mandarin". I've spoken to her many times.' he added conversationally.

He was interrupted by a sudden influx of customers, but Denny had heard all he needed to know. It was doubtful whether Donald would have been able to tell him anything further in any case. So, he thought, stifling a deep sigh of resignation, his forebodings had been justified. It looked very much as though Frances had had no choice, but he still had no proof she had left Hong Kong and to find out would be considerably more difficult than extracting information from Donald Tsui. There was one factor in all of what he had told him which he found disturbing, namely, the man who had been with the inspector. He couldn't be attached to the Hong Kong police force; if he was, Donald would have known. But, who was he? He must have been here in an official capacity and to Denny that could only mean one thing: Interpol. This more than reasonable explanation would mean Frances was no longer in Hong Kong; they would have taken her back to London. He was well aware that all of these speculations were no more than that; conjectures without one scrap of proof, but it didn't matter to him. He had no option, but to go ahead to ensure he was in the clear and had to move as rapidly as possible. There was much to be done and the importance of prioritising was crucial. First, although not necessarily at the top of the list, but at least it would prevent the man from harassing him, was to call Antonio and after that to get in touch with Conrad. He must be warned. It would only be five in the morning in England, but that was unavoidable. Conrad had to be told what might happen should Frances speak out; he didn't know whether she was even aware of Conrad's existence, but again, Denny couldn't take the risk. Conrad would have to make sure he had nothing which could link him with the re-distribution of the emeralds and, naturally, he would stress to him that must include his name and everything to do with his businesses were deleted permanently from his records.

The conversations with both Antonio and Conrad took much longer than he had expected, at the end of which, Denny felt emotionally and physically drained. Antonio, true to form, had reacted in his usual blustering and high-volume way, bombarding him with questions for which he must have realised he couldn't answer, while, Conrad, once Denny had managed to pacify him by explaining what they had to carry out were precautionary measures, did eventually come round to agreeing with him they were for the best, although when he finally rang off, Denny could recognise the suppressed panic in his voice. There was one last call to be made; to Freddie in Pedder Street, telling him to make certain there was nothing incriminating there. There was no reason why there should be, but he was taking no chances. The shop was in existence to act as a half-way house. Emeralds hadn't been the only illicit items filtering through over the years, but their procedure had always remained rigidly constant; once they were delivered they never remained there for more than twenty-four hours and that last cache Frances had brought over had left Hong Kong more than a week ago now.

It was well after three by the time he returned to the office, having stopped at one of the smaller Cantonese restaurants for a light lunch, just enough to fortify him for the remainder of the day and hoping he would be able to concentrate sufficiently on the paperwork which would by this time have piled up on his desk. He hadn't even had time to read through that morning's post or checked to see whether there were any emails. Shirley was a good secretary in most respects, but in the five years she had been working for him she had never quite learned the knack of making a précis and highlighting those salient points which should be drawn to his attention, meaning he always had to go through each piece of correspondence personally. Tedious though it was, especially at times like now, when he should be concentrating on what could be a crisis, but he didn't object too much. Denny knew he wasn't the easiest of employers and she appeared to understand him, otherwise like many of her counterparts in Hong Kong she would have left long ago.

'Coffee, Mr Yuan?' she asked him as soon as he reached his office.

'I'm drinking far too much caffeine, Shirley,' Denny commented, 'I'll have a lemon tea instead.' and sliding the pile of mail towards him.

Most of it routine stuff: an inordinate amount of bills, those he pushed to one side for Shirley to deal with; a long-winded communication from the Sydney office explaining what, in their considered opinion, was proving to be a major problem in the re-structuring of their office to accommodate the recent expansion of the business; another from Singapore, enclosing details of two more office suites for sale, in the event the current negotiations which Denny had made inroads into implementing, didn't materialize, gazumping not being unheard of in that part of the world. The rest was routine and could easily wait until the next day. The emails also were not of any great importance; replying to those could also wait until later.

With his desk more or less cleared, now enabled him to put the final stage of his contingency plan into place, and not overlooking the re-formatting of the disc he'd bought for an astronomical price from the guy with the unlikely name of Charles Bridges. That was paramount.

Denny had started to key in the code he used to access the file for

Antonio Gomez when the receptionist called through to say Mr Howard Westwood would like to see him. Don't tell me, Denny groaned, this was another 'Charles Bridges', and without asking her anything further, told her to show him in.

Howard Westwood, a tall, well-built man, about fifty, handed Denny a card which only took him seconds to read and realise what he was up against: "Howard Westwood Senior Officer – International Police", nothing else. So, Denny thought, this was it; the moment of confrontation, the moment also when he had to do some smart thinking.

'Mr Yuan.'

'Yes?' he, also, could play a mean game of chess, although realising this was no game; the man standing in front of him meant business and Denny waited to see what his next move would be and he didn't have long to wait.

'Mr Yuan,' he repeated, 'I have here,' he continued slowly, deliberately, 'a search warrant for your premises and it would be much appreciated if you would co-operate with us.'

'Am I permitted to ask why you consider this to be necessary?' play it cool, Denny told himself, which was far from what he was feeling at this precise moment. A search warrant was not what he had been expecting, at least not quite so soon.

'You are. I am in Hong Kong with the sole purpose of investigating the smuggling of emeralds and we have very strong reasons to believe you are involved.'

'This is ludicrous.'

'Ludicrous it may appear to you, Mr Yuan, but we are acting on strong evidence that a large number of caches of emeralds have been entering Hong Kong illegally from South America and passed on to a syndicate here –'

'- and you believe I'm part of this syndicate?'

'Your name, Mr Yuan, has been given to us. Now,' he went on, 'if you would kindly permit my officers to proceed with their search.'

'And if I refuse?' sticking his neck out, but on the spur of the moment Denny couldn't think of anything else to say. Above all, he needed to stall them.

'If you do,' he answered, 'and I would suggest this would not be wise, we'll have no alternative but to take you along to police headquarters for questioning and possibly detain you for the permitted twenty-four hours. Also,' he added, and Denny hated the smooth way he spoke; the super-confident manner, in fact everything about the man exuded smug impenetrable officialdom, 'we will still go ahead with our search.'

'I have no choice, then.'

'No, you don't.'

'I insist on calling my lawyer!'

'Please do; that is your prerogative, Mr Yuan.'

*

Juliet was in Anne Steed's office the following morning when the girl, after flinging open the door, stumbled into the room; her breathing ragged and uneven, her eyes wide and unfocused as she lurched towards her.

'Miss Steed!' she gasped, clenching and unclenching her hands in a way Juliet had never witnessed before. The girl was obviously right on the edge of hysteria and she tried to remember what she'd read about the best way to handle such a situation.

'Where is she?' her voice beginning to rise unsteadily.

'Miss Steed will be back shortly,' Juliet told her, keeping her own voice lowered, 'she had to go to the bank.'

'Oh, no! I have to see her ....!'

'Stop it!' Juliet said sharply, taking a step closer to her, not knowing whether she was using the right approach with her or not; she was totally out of her depth, wishing Anne Steed was here. She would know what to do.

'I can't! It's horrible! Horrible! Ooooh!' she screamed.

This time, Juliet didn't hesitate; she raised her hand and slapped her across the face; instantly deflated, she was silent, her eyes gradually beginning to focus properly.

'I'm sorry,' Juliet said, 'but I had to do that. You were hysterical.'

'I know I was, but I had such a terrible shock.' and then, as though memory was rushing back to her, she began to cry; quietly, almost apologetically, tears streaming down her cheeks, 'It's –' struggling to get her breath, '- Marcia.'

'Look,' Juliet said, leading her to one of the chairs in front of Anne Steed's desk, 'Shall I get you some tea? Remembering tea was good for shock, with plenty of sugar, 'By then, I'm sure Miss Steed will be back and you'll be able to tell her what's upset you.'

'No.' she gulped, wiping her cheeks, one of which was bright red from where Juliet's hand had been. 'Thank you; I don't want anything to drink.' but the tears continued, in spite of her continually brushing them away impatiently.

'What on earth's wrong, Maria?' Anne Steed said, running into the office, 'Was it you I could hear screaming as I came out of the lift?'

'I'm afraid it was, Miss Steed,' Juliet answered for the girl, 'also, I had to slap her; to stop the hysterics.' she added unnecessarily.

'You did the right thing, Juliet. I would have done exactly the same. Have you any idea what's happened?'

'I don't,' Juliet admitted, 'she hasn't been able to say much, but I think it's something to do with Marcia.'

'Alright.' she said and Juliet was grateful to hand over the responsibility of dealing with the girl, 'Listen to me, Maria. What I want you to do,' she continued slowly, as though talking to a child, but her words appeared to be getting through to her; already she appeared calmer and she'd stopped crying, 'is to try and tell me what's troubling you. Miss Warburton said you mentioned Marcia's name; is this something to do with her?'

'Yes, Miss Steed,' her voice much steadier now, 'she's dead.' Juliet was sure she had no idea of the impact those words had on both herself and Anne Steed as she carried on talking. It was as if that now she had started she didn't have the ability to stop. 'You asked me to go up to the apartment to find out why she hadn't arrived for work this morning; I think this must have been just before you left to go to the bank. Well, I did and the door to her bedroom was closed, just as it had been earlier, but I hadn't thought anything of it at the time, but –' hesitating for the first time, although not long enough for Anne Steed to say anything. Juliet looked at her; she had remained in exactly the same position as when she had come into the office, but her expression told her everything: Anne Steed looked absolutely stunned by what Maria was saying and probably at that moment had lost the power of speech. '- but,' the girl went on, 'I thought she may have slept in. She never used an alarm clock; she always said there was no need and it's true because she'd never been late for work before. Anyway, I knocked on the door and I called out to her; twice I did that, but when there was no answer, I –' and here she did falter, badly; her whole body began to shake and Juliet thought now she would never come to the end of what she was trying to tell them, but she did, making a valiant effort to pull herself together and after taking a deep breath, picked up from where she had left off, 'I opened the door and that's when I found her, Miss Steed. She was lying on top of the bed, she hadn't undressed or anything, and there was something round her neck; it was one of her scarves, I recognised it straight away. She'd only bought it last week; it was lovely, pale blue with lemon stripes –'

'Alright, Maria,' Anne Steed said, placing a hand on the girl's shoulder, 'that's enough. You've told us now so let it rest, dear; nothing can be gained by saying anything more.'

'She's dead, Miss Steed.' she said for the second time, 'She was my best friend and she's dead.'

'I know, I know. Juliet,' she said, turning round to face her, 'would you mind staying with Maria for a few moments. We'll have to phone the police of course, but first, well,' she paused and it was plain she was finding it difficult to express herself, 'well, first, I will have to go up to the apartment and see for myself. I'll be as quick as I can. There's a bottle of brandy in the cabinet over there,' she added, pointing to one of the built-in cupboards beneath the window; it might be a good idea to give Maria some, not much, of course, but it should help.'

Juliet did as she suggested, pouring out the smallest of measures, barely enough to cover the bottom of the glass and watched as Maria took a sip and as she swallowed, relieved to see some colour returning to her cheeks. Poor girl, she thought, it couldn't have been pleasant; the description she had given them had been graphic enough to imagine only too well what she had seen once she had opened the door to her friend's bedroom. No doubt a scene she would never forget Juliet thought, taking the empty glass from her and placing it down on Anne Steed's desk.

'Better?'

'Yes, much, thank you. You've been very kind.'

'Not at all, Maria. You've been through a lot. You do realise you will have to answer a few questions when the police arrive, don't you?'

'I know I will. She must have – have been like that all night,' she said, 'and I didn't know.' her eyes beginning to fill with tears.

'It's best not to dwell on it, Maria; it will only make you more upset.' Juliet advised, having no idea of what else she could say to her and realising how ill-equipped she was in a situation like this.

'I did hear her last night.' she said and Juliet wondered if she had heard a word she had said, 'I was already in bed, but Marcia came back to the apartment quite late and she wasn't on her own either.'

'Maria,' Juliet said, 'I think I should stop you there; this is something you should be telling the police when they arrive, not me.'

'But I have to tell someone, Miss Warburton,' she insisted, 'and I have to mention it now. It's been preying on my mind. I have to!'

'Okay,' Juliet sighed, 'carry on, I'm listening.

'It was about eleven o'clock. I had been asleep, but I heard the front door opening and then the voices. She took him into the bedroom; it's next to mine and they were talking quite loudly. Not so much I could hear what they were saying and they stopped. I think I must have fallen asleep then. I didn't even hear him leaving the apartment, but of course he must have done.' her voice a whisper.

Chapter Seventeen

'Roddie?'

'Juliet. It's good to hear your voice.'

'I'm sorry,' she said quickly, 'I shouldn't be phoning you at work, but –

'No, it's alright; it doesn't matter.' and she could tell by the spontaneous way he answered that he really didn't mind being interrupted. 'Is there something wrong;' he asked her, 'you sound different?'

'There's nothing wrong exactly,' she said, 'I have had rather a harrowing day, but that wasn't why I'm calling. I wanted to know how your daughter was, Roddie.   I wanted to phone yesterday, but I didn't like to intrude.'

'Natasha's okay now, I'm glad to say. It was pretty grim for a few hours, but she pulled through whatever had affected her so rapidly.'

'What was wrong,' she asked, 'had she picked up a virus?'

'We thought so at first, but after the hospital ran various tests they discounted a virus; instead they're saying that she could have suffered a severe allergy.'

'Something she'd eaten, do you mean?'

'Not that she'd eaten, no. She hadn't had anything different from what she's used to and the only suggestion they have come up with is that there may have been something wrong with the cappuccino she had during the afternoon. Apparently, Natasha mentioned to the doctor that she did find the taste a little bitter.'

'That doesn't sound good at all.' she said, 'What do you think the hospital are going to do? What I mean is, if Natasha had bought the cappuccino in a cafe or somewhere like that, they could be using faulty equipment. It's only an idea.'

'And a good one, Juliet, although the coffee didn't come from any cafe, or from her office either, but to answer your question, I don't know whether the hospital will be taking the matter any further, although I guess they may have to; hygiene rules and all that.'

'I suppose the important thing is that she's made a full recovery.'

'That's exactly what I thought. It was a relief I can tell you. Now,' he went on, 'what about you? You mentioned you'd had a harrowing day.'

'Roddie, can we meet? I don't feel all that comfortable telling you about it over the phone like this. Incidentally, I'm in Pedder Street.'

'In the same cafe?'

'Yes,' she smiled, imagining his expression and like her, he would be remembering the first time they had met and she had accused him of following her, 'the same.'

They arranged to meet for a drink after he finished work and, being a Friday, he told her they normally closed the office early. He'd asked her to choose where she wanted to go and she'd been quick to suggest "The Captain's Bar". Hearing what she had that morning had shaken her more than she had realised at the time. She couldn't help but admire Anne Steed's courage in going up to the girls' apartment to see, as she'd explained, for herself. Juliet knew she would never have been able to have done that, remembering the sickly pallor on Anne Steed's face when she came back into the office. And then, with the arrival of the police, having to stay on there with them while they questioned Maria, who by then, poor girl, had been in a dreadful state. There had been two officers; one of them female and Juliet couldn't fault them in the sympathetic way they spoke to her.

Maria hadn't been able to add much to what she had already said earlier, but it wasn't until she was asked about the man she'd said had been with Marcia the night before, that Juliet noticed a new alertness in both the officers.

'We realise you didn't see him, Maria,' the woman had said, 'you only heard his voice, but do you think you would recognise it again?'

'I don't know,' she had said, 'I might, I suppose.'

'Had you met any of Marcia's boyfriends?'

This question had obviously taken the girl by surprise; for a couple of seconds she looked almost vacant as she'd tried to comprehend what she had been asked.

'Not all of them.' she had said at last and Juliet had wondered whether they'd noticed how she had hesitated before answering, but it was more than likely they had. After all, she reasoned, that must be part of their training; to recognise the slightest change in a person's manner, not only in what they said or how they said it, but by their body language. And, then, looking at the withdrawn look flickering across the girl's face, Juliet sensed the reason for her reluctance. The girl was afraid. She knew who had been with Marcia.

'Did she have many boyfriends, Maria?' the officer had asked her and it was impossible to tell from her bland expression whether she had registered the girl's reticence in elaborating or not. If she had, she gave no indication. So far, her fellow officer had left all the questioning to her; perhaps thinking Maria would respond better to a woman. The last they would want would be to exacerbate another outburst of hysterics.

'A few, yes.'

'And did you ever meet any of them?'

'Not very often.'

Even from her viewpoint it was apparent to Juliet, at this rate the officer was getting absolutely nowhere; merely going round and round in ever-decreasing circles and, looking across at Anne Steed, came to the conclusion she was thinking the same, but there was nothing either of them could do. They were only onlookers and had no option but to remain silent.

'Maria,' the woman had said, all the time continuing to keep her voice on a low, soothing, level, 'we're not trying to put any pressure on you, but it is important we find the person responsible for what happened to your friend. You want that as well, don't you?'

'Yes.' so softly, Juliet had difficulty in hearing her.

'Last night, you've already told us, Marcia was late returning to the apartment.'

'She was, yes. I had gone to bed.'

'Did she tell you where she was going?'

'Not where she was going, no.'

'But, perhaps she told you who she was meeting?'

'I don't want to get anyone into trouble.' she whispered.

'Of course you don't, Maria, but if your friend had arranged to meet someone, it is important we are able to talk to him, only in that way if he has nothing to hide, then we will be able to eliminate him from our enquiry. Do you understand?'

'Yes, I do. He'd phoned her earlier in the evening to ask her to meet him.'

'One of her boyfriends?'

'Yes.'

'And do you know his name?'

'Only his first name,' she answered slowly and with the same reluctance in her voice, 'he's called Nicholas.'

'Nicholas?'

'Yes.'

'But you don't know his surname?'

'Marcia never told me.'

'Do you know anything else about him, Maria? Anything at all, in fact. Where he worked for instance; perhaps she mentioned that to you at some time?'

'He worked for one of the banks in Central.'

'And did you ever meet him?'

'Once or twice.'

'You've already said Marcia didn't tell you where they had arranged to meet, but have you any idea where this could have been?'

'It was in the bar at the "Shangri La Hotel"; I heard her mentioning this just before she came off the phone to him.' she added.

'You've been very helpful, Maria and I only have one more question I would like to ask you.'

'Yes?' and it had been at this point Maria had shown the first signs of literally falling apart; tears which she had managed to hold back since the officers had arrived had begun to trickle down her cheeks and, as previously, her hands were agitatedly clenching into fists.

'The voice you heard last night coming from your friend's bedroom; did it belong to Nicholas?'

'I don't know.'

They hadn't pursued their questioning for much longer after that and Juliet had been free to leave, but ever since, during lunch and going through the motions of attending a couple of meetings she had arranged a few days earlier but unable to cancel at such short notice, she couldn't get the image of what Maria, in her simple way, had conjured up in her mind; of how she had found Marcia Rodrigo. As the afternoon had slowly progressed Juliet had the overwhelming need to talk about it all and she could only think of one person whom she knew would be sympathetic and that was Roddie Mortimer.

Earlier, after she had finished her lunch, she had tried to phone Denny wanting to discuss a couple of points in connection with his accounts, but there had been no answer from his mobile and when she'd tried his office, the receptionist had sharply informed her that Mr Yuan was not available. She didn't really know why she had decided to walk along to Pedder Street; perhaps with the idea Denny may be at the shop, but when she did arrive there it was to find it closed and, although she rang the bell, thinking Freddie may still be on the premises, there was no response. By the time she phoned Roddie and arranged to meet him she hadn't placed all that much importance to any of this. Denny was a law unto himself. If he decided to make himself scarce for a while he would do so; she had known him long enough to realise that.

*

The reports from London started coming through to police headquarters between four and five in the afternoon, followed by a call for Howard on his mobile from Robert Anderson shortly after six. Howard was still at headquarters, having spent most of the afternoon with Inspector Clarke; the inspector's day having been interrupted when news had reached him of a second murder in less than a week. As he had remarked to Howard, this one; the strangulation of a young woman from the Philippines, gave no hint of having any connection with the death of the lawyer until he was given the transcript of the statement made by the girl who'd had the misfortune to find her. It could hardly be described as conclusive evidence of the man's guilt, but from what the girl had told the police officer she'd overheard her friend making arrangements to meet a man called Nicholas. Apparently, the two women shared an apartment belonging to their employer, Anne Steed, owner of "Annie's" nightclub in Kowloon and, although the girl had heard her friend returning late last night and accompanied by someone, she said she had been unable to recognise the man's voice. Hardly a reliable witness, if indeed one could call her that, Inspector Clarke had remarked caustically. There had been an additional report confirming that Nicholas Eastman had been seen in the front foyer of the "Shrangli-La" hotel around eight-thirty and had been joined by a young woman who fitted the photograph the officer had shown him. No doubt, Howard had thought, forensic will produce something more significant and wondering just how smart this Nicholas Eastman was, remembering how the inspector had described him as a bit of a Mr know-it-all.

Howard had just returned to his office when he took the call from Robert: 'Hello, Howard; it's Robert here. Have you had time to read everything we've sent through yet?'

'I certainly have,' Howard said, pulling the reports which had been addressed to him from the stack of papers on the desk, 'and it looks very much as though we're rounding up some of the villains at last.'

'Well,' Robert put in, 'at least Francesca Cristofoli, now she's been formally charged with those robberies, will be out of business for some considerable time to come.'

'Is the trial likely to be a lengthy one?'

'I would say the final verdict won't take all that long to reach and the general consensus of opinion, a fairly predictable one, is she'll receive a prison sentence alright, but because of the sheer volume of the various witness reports, all of which will have to be read through in court, means the trial period will stretch out. Also,' he continued, 'the robberies weren't all carried out in London and the Home Counties, but, as you know, a fair amount were scattered among many of the European capitals.'

'And, of course,' Howard said, 'the emerald case is considerably more complicated, 'it will probably be months before that eventually comes to court.'

'Yes,' he agreed, 'but at least you have the man who masterminded it all. Incidentally, Howard, it was a good thing you did, deciding to move in there yesterday. I'll be most interested to hear if you found anything of special note on his premises.'

'They are still accessing the computer files, but we did discover something as a matter of fact.' Howard said, 'Unfortunately, nothing to do with the smuggling business though.' proceeding to tell him about the disc the officers had found among Denny Yuan's papers and how it tied him in with the formula theft.

'Well, well,' he said, when Howard finally came to the end of the explanation, 'it looks very much as though he masterminded that as well.'

'I know; so Hugh Innis wasted his time in coming out here.'

'And money.' Robert reminded him.

'And his partner, Eddie Bristow? As we suspected, Robert, his fingerprints did tally with those found in Marion Godwin's apartment?'

'That's right.'

'That disc I was telling you about, Robert.'

'Yes?'

'Eddie Bristow's fingerprints were on that also.'

'My goodness! So, what do you make of that, Howard?'

'It's something Denny Yuan may be prepared to tell us.'

'You mean Eddie Bristow may have brought the disc from Marion Godwin's apartment on the night she was killed and was blackmailing him?'

'It's possible. I would say if that had been the case he would have been only too anxious to take it off him, even although it would have cost him.'

'He should have destroyed it immediately. That would have been the sensible thing to do, but then, he probably didn't expect you to come up with a search warrant as speedily as you did.'

'Probably not, but either way, Eddie Bristow has many questions to answer. It looks as though he'll be making a swift return here.'

'He will indeed, also his partner. Both the formula thefts and the murder of the lawyer are in their province after all, I'm glad to say. We have quite enough to contend with here.'

'That's true.'

'Returning for a moment to the emeralds, Howard,' Robert said, 'as I mentioned in my report, we weren't quick enough in respect to our search of Conrad Bailey's business premises. It was quite apparent he'd wiped everything from his hard disc, only a matter of hours before our officers turned up there and he kept no records at home; he didn't even have any computer there. A pity, but we'll see how he fares in the witness box; that is, if he survives until the trial!'

'Why, is he sick?'

'Not exactly sick, Howard. I would say Conrad Bailey is a very, very nervous man.'

'The opposite to Denny Yuan, then?'

'I would say. So, Howard, when can we expect the gentleman in London?'

'It's like the exchange of prisoners, or I should say the exchange of *potential* prisoners. But, seriously, Robert, we are making arrangements for Denny Yuan to leave here as soon as possible. He had requested bail, which was only what we expected him to do, but it's been refused. I get the strong impression Hong Kong want shot of him.'

'Too hot for them, eh? Anyway, Frank is on his way back to Singapore to see what he can discover out there and using Denny Yuan's company as a starting point. There might be some nervous people out there as well.'

'Have you decided what investigations you're going to conduct in Columbia?'

'Well,' Robert hesitated for a moment, 'we still have a man out there, but we shall have to tread with caution. We don't want to fall out with the Bogota government; that wouldn't do international relations a great deal of good.'

Before ringing off, Howard told him about Nicholas Eastman's name cropping up again.

'He certainly gets around, doesn't he?'

'You could say that, Robert. However,' he continued, 'the enquiry is only in its early stages yet; Inspector Clarke has still to see the forensic report, but he's going ahead and will be bringing Nicholas Eastman in for questioning today, but I'll keep you posted about that.'

'I wonder why the woman was murdered.'

'That's occurred to me also; a pretty vicious attack by all accounts.'

'A crime of passion, would you say?'

'It's possible, I suppose, but I've just had a thought.'

'Yes?'

'Nicholas Eastman already had a girlfriend. I learned about this from Roddie Mortimer on Wednesday when I spoke to him. Nicholas Eastman told him his girlfriend had recently arrived here from London; it makes me wonder why he should be meeting another woman, especially so soon after her arrival; unless of course he has problems in sustaining an honest relationship.'

'Perhaps,' Robert commented, 'he could have been two-timing her.'

'But why kill her?'

'She might have been in his way. Being a cynic, I would suggest this woman may have been surplus to requirements.'

'You could be right. All the same, I will mention this other girlfriend of his to the Inspector; although I have to admit I am a bit reluctant to intrude in what is his case.'

'I shouldn't worry too much about encroaching on what, technically, is his territory. I get the impression Inspector Clarke is grateful for your support at the moment and I'm sure he won't object to any suggestions you may have to make.'

*

'If I was a superstitious person, Natasha,' Louisa Lambert said to her, 'I would start thinking that this series we're doing has a jinx on it.'

'Why do you say that?' Natasha asked. She had almost finished clearing her desk and was about to leave when Louisa called through to say she would like to see her.

'Because,' she explained, 'two of the women who had agreed to be interviewed are no longer here.'

'Do you mean they've left Hong Kong?'

'Well,' she answered with an expression on her face Natasha hadn't seen before. There was a hesitancy about her which was at odds with how she usually appeared, even after knowing her for such a short time, 'I'd better explain,' she said, 'but first, no doubt you heard about the murder of the English lawyer?'

'I did, yes.' Natasha said, remembering how shocked she'd been when she read about the woman's death.

'I had arranged for Mandy to write up a piece on Miss Godwin, but regrettably, it wasn't to be.'

'And the second one?' Natasha asked by now believing the worse, wondering what had happened to her.

'Oh, she's different. By that I mean, unlike the other women in the series, as far as I'm aware, she's never had a career. She's English, although she did tell me she had a French grandmother, but the interesting part about her and would have made an excellent article, was where she's been living for the last ten years. It had actually taken me some weeks to persuade her to be interviewed, but eventually she agreed to discuss what her life is like living in South America. In fact, Natasha, I had planned for you to do the interview.'

'Has she changed her mind, then?'

'As to that, I don't know, but she appears to have vanished!'

'How?'

'You may well ask; she was at the "Mandarin" where, apparently, she always stays when she visits Hong Kong and all they've been able to tell me is that she is no longer there. All rather frustrating, but what I do know is that she had a boyfriend out there; the jealous type was how she described him, but the bottom line is, Natasha, I'll now have to scrabble around and find two replacements.'

'Perhaps she'll return to Hong Kong.' Natasha suggested.

'She might, but unfortunately I've no way of finding out. She never gave me her address, or even a telephone number. However, there is no point belabouring the point, is there? By the way,' she continued, 'I had a call from Anne Steed saying how pleased she was with the piece you had written about her.'

'I hoped she would be.'

'I would imagine she is not exactly an easy lady to please, quite demanding and now I expect you're wondering who your next subject will be?'

'I am, yes.'

'I've set up a meeting for you with our new governor's wife, Lavender Patten, for Monday morning at ten.'

'Is there any particular line of questioning you would like me to follow?' Natasha asked her, trying not to give the impression she was more than a little in awe at the prospect of interviewing someone with such a high profile, having noticed the amount of coverage the press was giving to her and her family.

'I'll leave the planning of that to you,' Louisa said, 'except, perhaps the main core of the article could be to get her to talk about the contrast from being the wife of a politician to that of a diplomat's wife and living in the luxurious environment of Government House. Also,' she went on, 'find out, if you can, what her feelings are about putting her own professional career 'on hold' for the next five years. Incidentally, I have met her; she's charming and I'm sure you will quickly discover she is first and foremost a wife and mother.'

Natasha, checking the time on her watch after leaving the editor's office, realised it was almost time for Nicholas to finish work and if she hurried she would be able to meet him when he left the bank.

She still had almost ten minutes to spare by the time she reached the bank building and decided she would have a cold drink in the cafe next door; the same one she had been in soon after she had arrived in Hong Kong. She could call Nicholas from there to let him know where he could find her, but in case he was with a customer thought it best to send him a text instead.

Natasha wasn't all that surprised when Nicholas didn't immediately respond expecting him to turn up at any moment. She had taken the first sip of her drink when the door of the cafe opened and one of his colleagues came in. Nicholas had introduced her to him a couple of nights ago when their choice of restaurants happened to coincide.

'Hi, Natasha!' Graham called out, walking over to her table.

'Hi, Graham,' she smiled up at him, 'how are you?'

'I'm fine, but more to the point, how are you? Nicholas has told me all about the other night; that must have been pretty frightening for you.'

'Not really.'

'Why do you say that?'

'Probably because I spent a good part of the time unconscious, that's why.'

'Poor you,' he sympathised, 'but you're okay now?'

'As good as new, Graham. I take it you've just finished work?' she asked him.

'Yes, that's right. Being a Friday, everybody likes to get away on time; even the customers stop coming in shortly after three-thirty.'

'I expect they're more interested in their weekend than doing any banking?' she suggested.

'You could be right.'

'I've just sent Nicholas a text message to tell him I'm here, but he hasn't answered it. He's not working late, is he?'

'Er, Natasha –'

'- yes, what is it?'

'Nicholas has already left the bank; it was about an hour ago.'

'A business appointment?'

'No –' hesitating again, a flush of what she immediately interpreted as embarrassment colouring his cheeks, '- you obviously don't know yet, but, er, there was a police officer with him.'

'I don't understand. Where were they going?'

'I'm sorry, Natasha, I didn't mean to alarm you.'

'Have you any idea what's going on, Graham? Any idea at all?'

'Actually, I don't,' he admitted, 'none of us do, in fact. The officer had come into the bank earlier and asked to be taken to the manager's office and then, shortly after that, we saw them both leave.'

'This does not make sense.' Natasha gasped, 'Why hasn't Nicholas told me?'

'Perhaps it's nothing to worry about,' doing his best to reassure her, 'they could just want to ask him some routine questions – or something.'

Natasha was about to speak when her mobile rang. She could tell by the tone that this was no call, but a text message, and pressed the 'on' switch. It was from Nicholas: "Sorry Natasha, but I've been called away and it looks as if I may be a bit late getting back tonight. Nicholas." Brief and to the point and with no endearments.

'What on earth is going on, Graham?' she asked, passing the mobile over to him to let him read the message, 'He's not telling me anything.'

'I can't answer that, Natasha,' Graham said quietly, 'I only wish I could. I think you'll just have to wait until he gets in touch with you again.'

*

He saw her as soon as he turned the corner into Connaught Street; she was about ten yards in front of him. He called out to her but, of course, she didn't hear him above the cacophony of the ever-present discordance in the streets of Hong Kong. Roddie quickened his pace and finally caught up with her at the bottom of the flight of steps leading up to the front doors of the "Mandarin" and called her name again. This time she did hear him and swung round to face him.

'Are you following me again, Mr Mortimer?' she laughed.

'This time,' Roddie grinned, 'I'll hold my hand up; yes, I was following you.' leaning over to kiss her on the cheek and together, with her arm linking with his, they walked up the steps and into the hotel.

Although not yet five, "The Captain's Bar" was beginning to fill up and, exactly as the last time they were in there, they didn't have a great deal of choice of where they could find a table. The resident pianist, a man who had been working for the hotel for as long as Roddie could remember, was playing a medley of tunes from one of Roy Orbison's albums; the opening chords of "Pretty Woman" reminding Roddie of the Monday evening when Nicholas Eastman, smooth character that he undoubtedly was, told him about his girlfriend who had recently arrived in Hong Kong and then, the other evening, learning the girlfriend was Natasha. He had yet to make up his mind what he felt about their relationship and each time he did try to think about it, the unsolved business about the formula kept intruding and fogging his mind. Both Andy and he were fairly sure that Nicholas had been involved, as certain as they were that Marion Godwin had been also, but there was nothing they could do about it. And now, he brooded; there was this other matter of the emerald smuggling.

'A penny for them.' Juliet said, leaning across the table and taking one of his hands in hers and raising it to her lips. 'You were miles away.'

'Sorry,' he apologised, 'it seems to have become a habit of mine lately.'

'You're not still worried about your daughter, are you?'

'No,' he admitted, 'I think concerned would be a more accurate description.'

'Why?'

'Oh, I suppose I'm acting like the proverbial protective father; it's her boyfriend -'

'You don't like him?'

'I wouldn't go as far as to say that, exactly. Anyway, you've met him.'

'Have I?' a look of surprise on her face.

'Yes, the other week, in here. It's Nicholas Eastman.'

'Nicholas Eastman.' she repeated, 'Do you know, Roddie, Hong Kong never ceases to amaze me. It is truly like living in a village here; eventually, we expats all know each other.'

'You're right,' he agreed, 'I've often thought that. Juliet,' he went on, 'you were going to tell me what was troubling you earlier.'

'It's not pleasant.'

'For goodness sake; just tell me.' wondering what it could possibly be. He had never seen her look as serious as she was at this moment.

'Well,' she began and taking a deep breath, 'I was in Anne Steed's office this morning, she had gone to the bank and I was sorting out a pile of invoices to bring back with me when a girl who works for her came bursting into the office in a terrible state -'

'- Go on.' he prompted.

'She was quite hysterical, Roddie; she even started screaming; in fact, I can still hear her, so I had to slap her.'

'So then what?' he asked, 'Was she able to tell you?'

'Oh, yes,' Juliet said slowly, her eyes never leaving his face, 'she'd just come from the apartment on the floor above the nightclub; she'd been up there to find out why her flatmate hadn't made an appearance for work, to find –' faltering, but this time he allowed her time to explain, '- to find,' she repeated, 'that her friend was dead.'

'What!'

'She'd been strangled, Roddie, with her own scarf!'

'So, what did you do next?'

'Anne Steed had returned by that time and she took over. She was marvellous with the girl; she even went up to the apartment to check for herself and then she phoned the police.'

'And could the girl help them?'

'I'm not sure. Anne Steed and I were there in the room with her all the time she was being questioned, but all she could tell them was that her friend had been out late the night before and had brought someone back to the flat with her.'

'Did she see him, then?'

'No, she said she was in bed, but she could hear his voice.'

'What a ghastly thing to happen. No wonder you were upset when you phoned me.'

'It's strange, but I felt alright while I was there,' she explained, 'it wasn't until later, after I'd left the club, when the impact of it all actually hit me.'

'Delayed reaction, I suppose.'

'I expect so, but there's something else, Roddie and I don't know how to tell you this, but when the girl was asked if she knew where her flatmate had gone that evening, she was able to tell her. Also,' once again hesitating, 'the name of the man she was meeting was called Nicholas.'

'Never!'

'That's what she told the police officer, Roddie. Apparently, she'd overheard her flatmate make the arrangements on the phone earlier in the evening.'

'The man's voice; did she recognise it?'

'She said she hadn't.'

'I suppose the question is,' Roddie said slowly, a sinking feeling at the pit of his stomach, 'had she ever seen Nicholas Eastman?'

'I can answer that for you,' Juliet said, 'she said she had met him a couple of times.'

'Wow!'

'I know what you must be thinking.'

'There is something rather strange here,' Roddie said, 'something doesn't add up, and quite frankly, Juliet, I don't know what to make of it all.'

'In what way?'

'I mentioned to you when I phoned about the cappuccino Natasha had had to drink and how bitter she found it.'

'Yes, I remember.'

'I went to see Natasha yesterday after work. I wanted to find out whether she really was okay and when I was there she mentioned the cappuccino to me and told me where she'd be given it.'

'In a cafe?'

'No, it was in Anne Steed's office. Natasha had recently interviewed her for a series of articles 'Woman's World' is running and she had called into her office to let her read through the copy for her approval and while she was waiting for Anne Steed to arrive, someone brought her the cappuccino.'

'You say 'someone', Roddie; did Natasha mention who it was?'

'No, she didn't. I assumed it would have been one of the staff; I think there's quite a few of them working there and, of course, Natasha would have had no reason to remember what he or she had looked like.'

'And you think it could have been important?'

'I do, actually,' he said thoughtfully, and for the first time since this whole business had begun, putting his thoughts into words, 'it's possible I might be reading too much into it, but the fact remains that if, for whatever reason, and one I haven't even started to work out yet, the coffee had been tampered with, it so happens from what you've just told me, one of Anne Steed's employees was murdered the following night.'

'It could have been nothing like that, you know, Roddie.'

'You mean, Natasha's cappuccino was perfectly alright, which still leaves a big question mark over what had caused such a violent reaction and the murder of this woman had been totally unconnected?'

'I suppose so. I don't know; it sounds so farfetched.'

'But, Juliet,' he persisted, 'there *is* a connection and a very strong one.'

'Nicholas Eastman?'

'Yes, that's exactly who I do mean. I realise we only have the girl's word for it that her flatmate was meeting him, but why should she lie?'

'I know, you're right, and I've just remembered something else which may go a long way to prove it is the same Nicholas Eastman.'

'Yes?'

'She told the officer that, although Marcia had never mentioned his surname, she did know where he worked.'

'Did she actually mention the bank?'

'Not the name of it, no; only that it was in Central.'

'I'm only guessing of course, but if it was Nicholas she'd arranged to meet and she had been his girlfriend and -'

'- and Natasha arrived on the scene!' she finished for him.

'It makes sense though, doesn't it?'

'It doesn't sound all that great for Nicholas.'

'No, he's in for a pretty rough ride, I would say, but somehow I can't see him as a murderer, Juliet. Not that I'm any judge.' he added, wondering how she would view Nicholas Eastman if she learned about the suspicions over his more than probable involvement in stealing the formula, but no matter what the final outcome of all this was, the unpalatable and disquieting fact remains; the man was basically dishonest.

'The police are bound to question him, Roddie.' she said, 'I've been thinking about your daughter; how will she cope when that happens?'

'I don't know. I guess it depends on the strength of her feelings for him. She's only known him for a few months, but obviously well enough to make the decision to come out here to join him.'

'Or, perhaps he painted a glamorous picture of life in Hong Kong and, being young and looking for something different, this persuaded her.'

'Yes,' he agreed slowly; Juliet was perceptive, he would never have come up with that possibility and she was quite right; Natasha was young and, again being reminded that he hardly knew his daughter and therefore had no idea how adept she was in looking after herself, 'I hadn't thought of that, but it's possible, I suppose.'

'We'll have to let events take their course,' she said, 'meanwhile, Roddie, shall we have another drink? All this talking has made me extremely thirsty.'

'Juliet,' he said to her once their drinks had arrived, 'there's something I've been meaning to ask you.'

'Yes?' she smiled, raising her glass to him.

'Who is Denny Yuan?' and wishing he hadn't had this overwhelming need to ask her; he didn't want to spoil the moment, but he knew if their relationship was to develop, he couldn't continue to have these doubts about her.

'Denny is one of my clients.' she answered, the expressive eyes looking directly at him. 'I handle his accounts, but to be more accurate, I handle the accounts of his company, Yuan Enterprises. Why do you ask? Do you know him?'

'No, I don't,' Roddie said, 'I'm just curious, that's all. His name has been cropping up a number of times recently and I remembered someone you referred to as Denny on the mobile the first night we had dinner together.'

'Oh, I see.' she said, taking a sip of her drink and continuing to look at him over the rim of her glass, 'No other reason?'

'No other reason, Juliet.' committing himself, but he meant what he had said; he had no wish to pursue the subject. He didn't want to ask her again if she'd been on Lamma that night. He had made up his mind. They were both adults; each with a past and he reasoned that sometimes it is best not to resurrect old ghosts.

'I won't be working for him anymore.' she said, putting her glass back on the table.

'Really? Is this is a sudden decision?'

'Not particularly,' she answered, 'let's say, I don't like him very much. One of the perks of being self-employed, Roddie; there's no need to hand in any notice. We didn't sign a contract; all I have to do is withdraw my services, which I intend to do tomorrow.

Chapter Eighteen

Nicholas still hadn't come home when Natasha left for work the following morning. She had finally been able to get off to sleep after spending several hours trying to fathom out what could have happened and all the time feeling desperately disappointed there had been no further calls from him. By the time the first light began to filter through into the bedroom she didn't know what to think anymore: about Nicholas, about her true feelings for him and about their relationship, but she knew one thing without any doubt; she needed to get away. Not from Hong Kong; she didn't mean that, but out of the apartment which by this time was having a claustrophobic affect on her. She felt suffocated and craving for somewhere she could be on her own, but realising that would be impossible in a place like Hong Kong. Here, she was in the centre of one of the busiest parts; Causeway Bay, where the traffic never stopped hurtling along Harcourt Road; even in the early hours of the morning when she had been lying staring into the darkness of the bedroom, she could hear the steady drone on the long stretch of road far below the apartment. She was at a complete loss to know what she should be doing. Should she phone the police, but her knowledge of Hong Kong was far too limited; she didn't even know which police station she should be contacting and imagining a multitude of complications in trying to get through to the right person.

By the time she had showered and dressed, choosing a bright red cotton shift hoping the extra colour would disguise the pallor of her complexion which, when she had glanced in the bathroom mirror, had shocked her. She mustn't fall to pieces. She mustn't. She was made of much stronger stuff than that. Wasn't she? Meanwhile, she had a job to go to and one she was thoroughly enjoying and already feeling at ease in her new environment. She liked and admired Louisa Lambert, recalling how sympathetic she had been yesterday morning when she had turned up for work having not been able to make it on the Thursday. She hadn't asked too many questions either which Natasha had appreciated. So far, she hadn't had the time to make many friends, although Mandy and she were building up a good rapport. She was good company; most days they'd had lunch together, but their friendship was too new, too fragile. She would have to sit this particular crisis out on her own and as Graham had suggested, wait until she heard from Nicholas, refusing to accept that he may decide not to get in touch.

This was her first Saturday working for "Woman's World"; another new experience. Natasha had never worked on a Saturday before, although it wouldn't be for the whole day, having been told their office would be closing at one.

Mandy was already at her desk when she arrived and looked up to give her a cheerful smile of welcome: 'Hi!' she called across to her, 'Alright?'

'I'm fine.'

'Natasha, you're lying! You're not alright! You look awful!'

'Thanks a bundle, Mandy.'

'Don't try and joke, Natasha. Something is wrong; I'm right, aren't I?'

'I don't want to lumber you with my problems, Mandy; that wouldn't be fair.'

'Okay, okay,' Mandy said, coming over and putting an arm round her shoulders and giving her a quick hug, 'we'll get through the morning and then we'll go for a drink and something to eat and if you want to tell me by that time, you can. How does that sound?'

'It sounds alright to me.' Natasha answered, scarcely trusting her voice.

The morning passed surprisingly quickly. Once Natasha had finished writing an article she had started on Wednesday, she spent the remainder of the morning reading up on the history of Government House and the governors who had been in Hong Kong, going back as far as the end of the Second World War. It was interesting stuff and she was sure, with the added knowledge, she would be better equipped when she came face to face with the governor's wife on Monday, hoping now she wouldn't come over as a complete ignoramus.

'Have you been to "Dan Ryan's" yet?' Mandy asked her shortly after one when they were in the lift on their way down to the ground floor.

'No, I haven't.' Natasha answered, trying to recall whether Nicholas had ever mentioned the name to her, 'Where is it?'

'On Kowloon side; in the Ocean Terminal, so if you're keen, we'll take the Star Ferry over; it's much quicker than having to walk from the MTR station in Tsim Sha Tsui. I think you'll like "Dan Ryan's", Natasha, it's a fun place and they make the best burgers you've probably ever tasted, but my advice is to leave room for their brownies; they are good!'

'It sounds American.'

'Clever girl!' she laughed, 'The real name is "Dan Ryan's Chicago Grill", but everyone knows it as "Dan Ryan's". Also,' she went on, pushing upon the double glass doors of their building, 'it's very, very popular, so much so, we may have to queue. You won't mind, will you?'

'Not in the least.'

They had emerged from the ferry terminal in Tsim Sha Tsui and were passing the newsvendor's stand at the entrance when Natasha came face to face with a larger-than-life picture of Marcia Rodrigo, although it was the words, in bold print, which brought her to a complete and shocked standstill:

"MAN HELD FOR QUESTIONING IN MURDER OF FILLIPINA MAID"

'Natasha!' Mandy's voice sounding unnaturally loud to her, 'What's the matter?' and grabbing her by the arm, 'Do you feel ill again?'

'No -' she answered shakily and struggling to catch her breath, glad Mandy was with her, 'it's the billboard. I know who that woman is!'

'Listen to me, Natasha;' she insisted, her usually cheerful face full of concern, 'I think it's time you told me what is causing you so much agro. You worry me; it's not doing you any good bottling all of this up, you know.'

'I know that,' Natasha agreed, 'you're right, but it wasn't only the picture of her which shocked me, but have you read the headline?'

'Yes, I have.' Mandy answered slowly, with no lessening of concern in her expression. 'Look, Natasha, we're not far from "Dan Ryan's"; once we have a seat and ordered a couple of drinks, you might feel more up to talking. Two heads are better than one.' she said, 'Didn't your mother ever tell you that?'

'She did, actually.' attempting a smile to show how much she appreciated her sympathy.

'Come on then,' she urged, 'but first of all, do you want to buy a copy of the newspaper?'

'Not now; perhaps I will when we're on our way back.' knowing she was behaving like a complete ostrich, but she really didn't think she was up to reading about the woman's death, although at the same time, fully aware of the real reason for her reticence; she didn't want to find out the man they were questioning was Nicholas. Even to allow his name to come to the forefront of her mind at that precise moment was too much for her.

"Dan Ryan's", as Mandy had predicted, was certainly a popular place: a spacious and airy bar and restaurant, with the added attraction of a miniature train running along the curving track above everyone's heads. They were fortunate in getting a table more or less straight away. Although there was a queue waiting, the customers in front of them were in groups of three or four which meant they were both soon shown to one of the restaurant's smaller tables at the far end of the room.

'You like?' Mandy asked, taking the seat opposite and picking up the menu.

'I like. It's different.'

'It is a bit noisy,' Mandy remarked, 'but I dare say by now you have already realised that?'

'I'm beginning to get used to the high decibels in Hong Kong, but I must admit there have been times when I've wanted some hush.'

'Fat chance here!' she smiled, 'Now, something to drink. What are you going to have, Natasha?'

'Oh, a wine, please.'

'Not a brandy, then?'

'What; to steady my nerves you mean?'

'Something like that, although I didn't really mean it. I don't see you as the brandy drinking type. Anyway,' she went on, 'you're looking a lot better than you did, which is a relief I can tell you. I thought back there you were going to pass out.'

They decided on half a carafe of white wine and once one of the waitresses had brought this to their table and taken their order, Natasha, taking her advice and choosing a burger with a side salad, Mandy asked if she was up to telling her what was wrong.'

'It's Nicholas.'

'Yes?'

'You don't seem surprised.'

'I must admit I am putting two and two together, but I couldn't think of any other reason.'

'Well,' Natasha made a start to explain which was difficult when she had no idea of what has, or was, happening herself, 'he didn't come home last night.'

'And I take it he hasn't been in touch.'

'You take it right! I sent him a text yesterday after I'd left the office, to tell him I would be waiting for him in the cafe next door to the bank and it wasn't until one of his colleagues came in there and told me Nicholas had already left the bank an hour before, I received a text from him, but all it said was he'd been called away and might be a bit late getting home.'

'And that was all?'

'That was all he'd put on the text, but there is more, Mandy,' she said taking her time and wondering how she would react to what she was about to say, 'Graham, that's the name of the colleague, told me that Nicholas had been accompanied by a police officer; apparently he'd come into the bank earlier asking to speak to the manager.'

'My God!' instinctively putting a hand up to her mouth, 'And I suppose when he didn't arrive you spent most of the night worrying yourself sick about what was going on?'

'Yes, I just reached the stage when I couldn't think anymore. My head was literally going round and round and then, a few moments ago -' but this time unable to go on. The last she wanted was to break down; that would solve nothing.

'- when you read those headlines,' Mandy said, helping her out, 'you naturally thought the worse?'

'I shouldn't have, of course.'

'Natasha.'

'Yes?'

'You said when you saw the picture of the woman you knew who she was?'

'Yes. I'd only seen her once and it wasn't a pleasant experience. It was on the morning I was interviewing Anne Steed and she had been called out of the office for a moment; some staff problem I think, and when she was away Marcia Rodrigo came in. I didn't know her name at that time, but she knew who I was alright and told me to get out of Hong Kong as Nicholas belonged to her, that he'd promised to marry her. She was particularly spiteful, but fortunately Anne Steed came back before she had time to say any more.'

'Good Grief, how unpleasant,' Mandy said quietly, 'and have you told Nicholas about this?'

'Yes, I did, but he made light of it, saying although he had taken her out a few times it hadn't meant all that much to him, but he knew how upset I was, Mandy. He told me I should forget it, that she was only jealous.'

'In a nasty and very extreme way.'

'Exactly.'

'Natasha?'

'Yes?'

'I don't want to put ideas into your head, especially if what I'm going to suggest is a load of rubbish, but I've been thinking. That cappuccino you drank; you said this was at Anne Steed's place?'

'Yes, that's right.'

'And the hospital was unable to actually pinpoint what had made you so ill, although they had whittled it down to the cappuccino.'

'That's about it, yes,' Natasha nodded, 'and I don't see what else it could have been.'

'The coffee could have been – dodgy.' Mandy suggested tentatively, 'Hasn't that occurred to you?'

'It hadn't, not until now, that is. Are you thinking it may have been tampered with, then?'

'It could have been, Natasha.'

'I've just remembered exactly what she said to me; this was just before Anne Steed came back. She said: "If you know what's good for you, you will leave Hong Kong".'

'Chilling words.'

'They were, but at the time I didn't take them all that seriously. I thought they were only idle threats, but -'

'- but now, you're not so sure?'

'What do you think I should do, Mandy?'

'A good question. I think you need to find out about Nicholas first; for your own peace of mind, I mean.'

'I will, of course, but meanwhile I feel I must move out of his apartment.'

'You feel as strongly as that?'

'I do, yes. I must have some space, Mandy, and that means being away from him, enough time to allow myself to breathe.'

'Do you think he has something to do with this woman's death?'

'Not really, but I'm looking at all of this from a different angle; you may think it's an odd one -'

'- no,' she interrupted quickly, 'I'm sure I won't, but try me.'

'I believe the bottom line is, as far as our relationship goes, and this is what's bugging me, he hasn't been in touch, apart from that pathetically short message yesterday afternoon. No matter what would have happened at the police station, because presumably that is where he would have been taken, surely they would have given him permission to phone me, or if not, someone else to do it for him. That's what is upsetting me and making me seriously wonder about the depth of his feelings towards me. He must have known I would have been worried last night when he didn't turn up and yet nothing; it's as if he doesn't really care all that much.'

'And where would you go, Natasha? Have you thought? I hope you won't decide to go back to England.' Mandy added.

'I'm not going to leave. In spite of what is happening, I like it here and feel I can make a new life for myself. I think you realise I like my work tremendously and Miss Lambert seems to be reasonably satisfied with what I've done so far. No,' Natasha went on, 'I'll try and find somewhere else to live, even if it is only temporary; it doesn't matter all that much, but the main thing is I can't go on like this. If I do, I'm going to end up a nervous wreck and I won't be much use to the magazine if that happens.'

'I believe I can solve one of your problems.' Mandy said, pouring them out another glass of wine.

'You can?'

'Yes, if you're agreeable, that is. I've already told you I share an apartment with another girl; Pamela she's called, she's a PA for a Dutch import and export company, but there is plenty of room for a third person. So,' she asked, 'what do you think?'

'You mean it?'

'Of course I do.'

'You don't think she would object to me living there?'

'I'm sure she wouldn't. Also,' Mandy added, 'there is method in my madness because I have a feeling she'll be making plans to leave fairly soon.'

'Why?'

'Because she's already made a couple of remarks recently about how her boyfriend wants her to move in with him. They've known each other for a couple of years now, so it's a pretty steady relationship.'

'Lucky girl.'

'Perhaps,' Mandy said, 'but she is twenty-seven so perhaps she thinks it's time to settle down.'

Their burgers were arriving and they spent the following thirty minutes doing full justice to them, but all the time Natasha was thinking over what they had been talking about. She would, she decided, take Mandy up on her offer; it would mean she would be able to leave the apartment in Causeway Bay quickly. As to whether she would be able to, or even want to, regain what she had believed Nicholas and she had once had, was something else. In retrospect, and remembering how sceptical her mother had been on the afternoon she'd told her about her plans, perhaps she had been too hasty in making such an important decision to come out here, but she had and for the time being she was stuck with it. There was no way she was going to pack her bags and take the next flight back to London. No way.

When Mandy had asked her whether she knew where she'd go next, it had never crossed Natasha's mind to get in touch with Roddie and pour out her woes to him. It was always an option, she knew, and Roddie would have been only too willing for her to stay with him until she got herself sorted out, but she was far too independent to take advantage of his good nature. It had been thoughtful of him to call in to see her the other evening and she recognised how worried he must have been, but it didn't make any difference. However well-meaning he would have been, she had an inkling she would have felt swamped by his protectiveness. Okay, she argued to herself, she was going through a rough patch, but she'd get out of it.

*

Howard called into police headquarters shortly after lunch. He was booked on the evening's flight back to London and had only a few points to clarify with Inspector Clarke before he left. There was nothing else for him to do in Hong Kong; most of the loose ends which they had been chasing for the last couple of weeks had been more or less tied up, apart from getting feedback from Frank in Singapore and their contact in Columbia. As he and Robert had agreed, the emerald case would take some time to be finally resolved; they all still had considerable work to get through before that could be achieved. Denny Yuan had left for London earlier in the day, escorted, for double security purposes, there always being the possibility of him making a dash for it at the last minute, by two members of the Hong Kong police force. Meanwhile, Eddie Bristow and Hugh Innis would soon be arriving at Kai Tak Airport; their presence adding significantly to the Inspector Clarke's workload. During the morning, Howard had spent a pleasant hour with Virginia Bannister over coffee in "The Clipper Lounge", when she had expressed her delight to learn that, as she described it in her eloquent way, Francesca Cristofoli was now "under lock and key".

'I must tell you, Howard; you have an admirer.' she'd said, smiling at him over the rim of her coffee cup.

'Have I?'

'Yes; my friend Leticia. She's told absolutely everyone how you managed effortlessly to retrieve her sapphire ring, which incidentally;' she had added, 'is a family heirloom. Alas, not so my bracelet. Goodness knows where that is now.'

'Either she has a cache of her spoils hidden away somewhere,' Howard had told her, 'or she found a buyer for them years ago. It's anyone's guess, I'm sorry to say.'

'Ah well,' Virginia had sighed prettily, raising her eyes to the ceiling, *'cela vie!'*

Inspector Clarke, no doubt pre-empting his arrival, had organised what Howard had by this time recognised as his afternoon ritual. Not coffee, but tea and, predictably, Earl Grey. Definitely a man from the old school.

'Ah, Mr Westwood,' he said, 'a most timely arrival. And,' he added, 'I have some news for you.'

'Good, I hope.'

'Like all turn of events, Mr Westwood, as I have discovered in this long career of mine, if the outcome happens to be favourable for one person, invariably it will not be so for someone else, as indeed it would seem in this case. Anyway, do sit down, and allow me to pour you a cup of this excellent English cuppa!'

The man was definitely on a high; his mood this afternoon positively buoyant and very much at odds from what it had been like the first morning when he met him, waiting now to be enlightened.

'A rather remarkable development, Mr Westwood,' the inspector said, having poured out the Earl Grey, even going as far as adding a slice of lemon from the small dish which presumably his secretary, a woman well used to his particular little foibles, must have brought in, 'and one which I believe you will find somewhat surprising.'

'I'm intrigued,' Howard said, taking a sip of his tea, which definitely lived up to expectations; it was deliciously refreshing.

'It happened this morning,' Inspector Clarke explained, 'practically at the eleventh hour, at least as far as Nicholas Eastman was concerned. We were almost on the point of taking the ultimate step of charging him for the murder of Marcia Rodrigo, when a call came in about a suicide and most fortuitously for Nicholas Eastman he had left a note telling us why he had taken such a drastic step.'

'Yes?' but having a fairly good idea what was coming next.

'The man, George Granger he was called, had been having an affair with Marcia Rodrigo, for a number of months apparently, but then he discovered he wasn't the only man in her life. He was having a drink in the "Shrangli-La" on Thursday evening when she had come in with Nicholas Eastman and when they left, he followed them back to her apartment. I think you can already imagine the rest, Mr Westwood.'

'Perhaps,' Howard said, 'but please go on.'

'Nicholas Eastman had left her outside the apartment and he followed the woman inside.'

'But, why did he commit suicide?' Howard asked, 'I can understand, perhaps, the rage of the man, sufficient to make him literally see red and strangle her, but why didn't he merely walk away and do nothing further?'

'The reason he decided to take his own life was relatively simple,' the inspector explained, 'guilt, plain unadulterated guilt. He didn't want someone else to be blamed for her murder.'

'He must have realised then that Nicholas Eastman would have been the prime suspect?'

'I think he did, although it couldn't have been from this morning's papers, perhaps that's something we'll never know. However, it certainly put Nicholas Eastman in the clear as far as her murder was concerned. Of course, we will still have to check through the authenticity of it all, but I believe this man, George Granger, did it all right. His wife has confirmed he had been having an affair with Marcia Rodrigo; apparently she had known about it right from the beginning, but like many wives in a similar situation had decided to ignore her husband's infidelities; if I could put it another way, Mr Westwood, she turned a "blind eye": what she didn't see, wasn't happening.'

'There's none as blind as those who cannot see.' Howard put in, finding himself falling into the out-moded way the inspector had of expressing himself.

'How right you are, Mr Westwood.' and not for the first time Howard wondered whether he was making fun of him, 'However, it couldn't have been too pleasant for her to find him the way she had; he'd taken an overdose, by the way.'

'Suicides are not usually too concerned about the feelings of those they leave behind; on the whole, a pretty selfish breed of person.' Howard said dryly, having lost count of the times he had seen evidence of this.

'Just couldn't face the consequences perhaps.' Inspector Clarke added, shaking his head and probably thinking the same.

'As a matter of interest,' Howard asked, 'did Nicholas Eastman explain why he'd met Marcia Rodrigo that evening?'

'He did, yes, and this is another intriguing twist. Apparently, the reason for this was to warn her off.'

'Why?'

'You may well ask,' he smiled, 'but it was because he had convinced himself Marcia Rodrigo had tried to poison his girlfriend.'

'Goodness!'

'Yes, she had recently arrived in Hong Kong to join him and Marcia had been consumed with jealousy. She had got it into her head that Nicholas Eastman was going to marry her.'

'Some story.'

'That's exactly what I thought when he came out with it, but it looks as if it may have been true. You see, the girlfriend, who is working for "Woman's World" as one of their journalists had been interviewing the proprietress of the nightclub earlier in the week, the same one where Marcia worked and the woman had confronted her, telling her to leave Hong Kong or else. And,' he continued, 'when the girl returned to the nightclub a couple of days later, although she didn't see Marcia again, that evening she became violently ill. I've received the medical report from the Hong Kong Central Hospital where she was admitted and after conducting the regulation tests discovered the cappuccino she had to drink while she had been there had been tampered with. Fortunately for her, she hadn't liked the taste of the coffee and had only taken a couple of sips.'

'Vicious.'

'Yes, very.

'And,' Howard suggested, piecing together in his mind what the inspector had told him and trying to make some sense out of it all, 'presumably, when Nicholas Eastman heard this, he had immediately suspected his old girlfriend, Marcia Rodrigo.'

'Not exactly, because the hospital didn't tell him about the poison which had been administered to the coffee, only that they had to conduct further checks and adding it could have been caused by defective equipment. They didn't want to set off any alarm bells, at least not until we had been notified, but all the same, as soon as Nicholas Eastman heard about the cappuccino and where she'd drunk it, that was sufficient to alert him and, in his own words, he had to do something about the woman.'

'But not to murder her?'

'No, apparently not, but he was lucky, otherwise it's my opinion he would have found it extremely difficult to prove his innocence.'

'So,' Howard said, 'that's one of your cases soon to be concluded.'

'Yes, but I don't think we are going to be as fortunate obtaining sufficient proof, irrefutable evidence, in fact, with the Marion Godwin case. It's all very well believing Eddie Bristow is guilty, but that's something which will finally have to be decided in court.'

'There's not a great deal I can add to what you're saying, Inspector, but I do agree with you. Our role is to dig up all the dirt and sieve through it painstakingly until we come up with a credible solution and that's all we can do. Frustrating at times, I admit, but I don't have to tell you that.'

'That's true.'

'I've been thinking of the disc your officers brought back from Denny Yuan's office.'

'Yes?'

'In particular, about the second formula which was mentioned; have you spoken to McLellands about it?'

'I phoned them this morning, although I wasn't able to speak to their managing director; he was attending a board meeting but his secretary put me through to Roderick Mortimer. At first, he didn't seem to understand what I was saying until he realised how it could have got into someone else's hands. You've already told me how he had been transported over to Lamma Island and how his assailants had extracted his apartment keys from him. Well, he was positive there had been nothing missing when he returned home the following day. He had been concerned though about some hand-written notes he'd left there, planning to work on them over that weekend. These notes concerned details of a project he had been involved in for a number of weeks.'

'But he'd said nothing had been taken from his apartment?'

'That's right; they were exactly where he'd left them.'

'And what sort of inference did he place on that?'

'There was only one he could come up with and I believe he must have been correct, which was, whoever gained access to his apartment must have taken the notes away that night, copied them and then brought them back.'

'Risky.'

'Quite, but then, if it had been Denny Yuan, I think you and I realise by now just how many risks he is prepared to take, Mr Westwood.'

*

Hearing what Inspector Clarke had to say not only alarmed Roddie, but it also presented him with the added problem of having to tell Andy Howe. Realising he couldn't be blamed for his notes being stolen made no difference to the way he was feeling after replacing the receiver. He was prepared to accept responsibility for leaving them where he had: in full view on the coffee table in his lounge where anyone sufficiently intelligent and dishonest enough would have been able to pick them up. The fact, whether this had been Denny Yuan or not, was neither here nor there, but whoever it had been must have taken them away to be copied, meaning they'd had the audacity to run the risk of going back to the apartment a second time.

The board meeting didn't finish until well after midday, but Roddie remained in the office, having made up his mind to catch Andy before he left the building. The inspector had not been all that forthcoming, although if he been able to speak to Andy, he may have been prepared to say more and Roddie, sensing his reticence, hadn't pressed him.

'I'm sorry, sir,' Roddie said, after he had finished explaining to him, 'I feel this is all my fault, but I had absolutely no idea.'

'No, no, Roddie,' Andy Howe said immediately, 'you're not to blame. So,' he continued, 'what you're saying is that the police have got hold of a disc with details of both our formulas?'

'Yes, that's right, although Inspector Clarke didn't explain how they acquired it.'

'Hmmph; no doubt they're keeping that information to themselves for the present, but it looks very much as though the same person was responsible for both of these thefts.'

'I would say so.'

'These notes of yours, Roddie,' he said, 'I take it they were hand-written?'

'Yes; they formed part of our initial research on the project.'

'And you'd jotted down the various constituents of the drug?'

'Yes, and my writing isn't the easiest in the world to read either; it would have needed a fair bit of deciphering.'

'You know who I'm thinking of, don't you?'

'Marion Godwin.'

'She would have been familiar with your hand-writing.' Andy said thoughtfully, 'Perhaps the disc came from her apartment. The police would have had to examine everything in there.'

'That's true; although I'm surprised she would have kept such incriminating material.'

'People do strange things, Roddie. Sometimes their actions are totally out of character, clever though she undoubtedly was. Did you mention when you spoke to the inspector that the formula for the second drug was incomplete?'

'No, I didn't, sir. I wanted to discuss that aspect with you first.'

'A wise decision.' he nodded, 'Well, as I see it, we have two choices here; either we say nothing and continue with the patenting of the formula as we've already discussed, or we mention it to the inspector. What's your opinion?'

'I don't actually see what would be achieved by telling him.' Roddie answered slowly, 'We've already lost out on the anti-malaria drug; to lose the second formula would be another financial blow. Also, we have no idea where that formula is, but I'm fairly sure if it is in the hands of any of our competitors, the laboratory in Singapore for instance, they would be bound to run their own set of tests and would therefore quickly discover it wasn't complete. I hope I'm making sense, sir.'

'You are, Roddie, and I'm inclined to agree with you. Let's go back to those notes for a minute, shall we? You mentioned they formed part of your initial research?'

'Yes.'

'Therefore you wouldn't have listed the possible side-effects, then? Presumably you would have done that later when you were satisfied with the results of the final tests?'

'That's right and I always key them into the computer; as you know, we have a standard template for the formatting of points of that nature.'

'Well,' Andy said, 'that would immediately stymie whoever had the formula, forcing them to conduct their own comprehensive tests and, as you've just said, they would discover the omission, all of which would take time. Meanwhile, your revised formula is in its final stages and, all being well, we can go ahead and organise the patenting.'

'I had already arranged an appointment with Simon Cheung for Monday morning, sir. Incidentally, he sounded quite pleased to hear from us.'

'No doubt he's been worried we would take our business away from them after what happened to Marion.'

'I expect so.'

'Alright, Roddie,' Andy smiled at him, 'it's the weekend, remember. Try and relax; you've had a stressful week.'

*

Natasha had finished packing her travel bag and had phoned for a taxi when she heard the lock turn in the front door of the apartment. She already knew Nicholas had been back earlier: the shirt he had been wearing the day before was lying crumpled on top of the linen basket in the bathroom and there were still beads of water on the shower screen, all of which only strengthened her resolve and convinced her she was doing the right thing. There was no excuse for him not getting in touch and she had given up trying to understand why he hadn't.

'Natasha!' Nicholas said, striding into the lounge, 'What are you doing?'

'I'm leaving.' deliberately keeping her voice down and forcing herself to remain calm.

'What? You're leaving Hong Kong?'

'No, Nicholas,' she answered, fastening the clasp on the bag, 'I'm leaving you.'

'You can't!'

'Please, Nicholas. I need to get away. Perhaps later, in a few days time, we can talk, but not now.'

'You're mad!'

'I don't think so; in fact, I've never felt more sane.'

'What's wrong?'

'I can't believe you've just asked me that.'

'I thought you loved me, Natasha.'

'I thought so, too, but it would seem I didn't love you enough. And perhaps you didn't either.' she added quietly.

'What do you mean?'

'If you did,' she tried to explain, 'you wouldn't have allowed me to spend the last twenty-four hours worrying and wondering what had happened to you. You could have phoned, Nicholas, but you didn't and I find that very hard to take.'

'You're over-dramatising. I'm here now, aren't I?' and with your breath smelling of whisky she wanted to say, but she didn't, tempting though it was.

'I've been remembering what you told me the other day about the last orange; well, I no longer feel welcome, I no longer feel I belong in your life, Nicholas. It is time I went.'

'Natasha,' pleading now, but she mustn't weaken, 'can't we talk and I'll try to explain?'

'No, Nicholas.'

The buzzing of the intercom prevented anything further being said, except to tell him that would be the taxi she had ordered and turning away from him she picked up her bag, opened the front door and left the apartment. Nicholas didn't follow her, but she didn't really expect him to do that and it wasn't until she was walking out the main door of the building she realised he hadn't even asked her where she was going.

Other titles by Margaret Alty:

Tangled Web – ISBN: 978 1 84549 422 3

Jenny – ISBN: 978 1 84549 442 1

Camouflage – ISBN: 978 1 84549 478 0

A Meadowbank Mystery

Murder in Meadowbank –ISBN: 978 1 84549 494 7

Double Act – ISBN: 978 1 84549 537 4

All published by arima Publishing.

www.ingramcontent.com/pod-product-compliance
Lightning Source LLC
Chambersburg PA
CBHW051531260626
47170CB00003B/884